Water
from
My Heart

Center Point
Large Print

Also by Charles Martin and available from
Center Point Large Print:

A Life Intercepted
Unwritten
Thunder and Rain

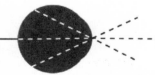

**This Large Print Book carries the
Seal of Approval of N.A.V.H.**

Water from My Heart

Charles Martin

CENTER POINT LARGE PRINT
THORNDIKE, MAINE

This Center Point Large Print edition is published in the year 2015 by arrangement with Center Street, a division of Hachette Book Group, Inc.

The text of this Large Print edition is unabridged. In other aspects, this book may vary from the original edition. Printed in the United States of America on permanent paper. Set in 16-point Times New Roman type.

ISBN: 978-1-62899-659-3

Library of Congress Cataloging-in-Publication Data

Martin, Charles, 1969–
Water from my heart / Charles Martin. —
    Center Point Large Print edition.
    pages cm
Summary: "When Charlie's choices produce devastating consequences, he sets out to right wrongs, traveling to Central America where he will meet those who have paid for his actions. Will their encounter present Charlie with a way to seek the redemption he thought was impossible—and free his heart to love one woman as he never knew he could?"
    —Provided by publisher.
ISBN 978-1-62899-659-3 (library binding : alk. paper)
1. Large type books. I. Title.
PS3613.A7778W38 2015b
813'.6—dc23
                                        2015015454

For Moises and Pauline Rick

Chapter One

I throttled down through Stiltsville, the reflection of the moon shimmering off Biscayne Bay. I loved this time of night. Behind me, a dark unlit boat slipped into my wake. I'd been watching her on radar. Been expecting them.

The key to having four supercharged Mercury Verado 350 engines—providing 1,400 horsepower and speeds reaching almost one hundred miles per hour—is knowing when and when not to use them. She hit her lights. Four spotlights up top lit up the center of my forty-four-foot Center Console Intrepid like noonday. The spinning blue lights above showered us. Agent Russ Spangler was ex–Special Forces and lived on full moon adrenaline nights like this. He was currently employing his shock-and-awe tactic of blinding me with a million-power handheld spotlight. We'd played this game before. His partner, Special Agent Melanie Beckwith, had a Napoleon complex and made up for what she lacked with anabolic steroids and muscles a good bit bigger than mine.

While I could outrun them, I could not outrun the Coast Guard, also on my radar, or the planes they could summon. I might make it back to the island, but it'd be the last run I ever made and I had no real intention of retiring just yet. If ever a person had a prime, I was in it. The engines behind me were a last ditch. To use them meant it would be the last time I'd ever run this boat, and at almost $500,000, I'd like to use it more than once. But that's the thing about owning a boat like this: If you're going to own it and stay in this business, you can't get too attached. That's pretty much true for anything. And anyone. No attachments. You've got to be willing to shove what you love off a cliff at the first sign of agents like Spangler and Beckwith.

In almost a decade of this business, I've learned much but one lesson guides me: I hold everything loosely. And that includes people. My life and those I value dangle on a knife's edge, a precipice where—if circumstances arise that are contrary to my freedom—one gentle nudge will send them cascading down. Gone. Over the falls at Niagara. This mind-set also governs what I enjoy and what I hope to enjoy. Even what I dream. As a safe-guard, I live with limited expectation. I tread cautiously. One foot on the bank. Cards close to my chest. I constantly calculate risk and reward because at any second, I may have to run, fold, or dive beneath the surface.

I own nothing and let nothing own me.

I checked my watch. A Marathon dive watch given to me by Shelly. She claimed I'd be late to my own funeral, so she'd set it five minutes fast. The hands were lit by tritium, which glowed brightly in the night air. I had time. I cut the engines and turned into the lights. Agents Spangler and Beckwith slid up alongside me, made all the easier in the glass-like conditions. Spangler's voice echoed across the water. "Hello, Charlie Finn. Imagine my shock at finding you out here this time of night."

I shoved my hands in my pockets and smiled at Agent Beckwith. Giving her my best Humphrey Bogart. "Of all the gin joints . . ."

She jumped onto my boat, tying off my bow to her stern. She smiled and said nothing. I nodded. "Looks like that weight lifting program is really paying off."

She pointed. "Stand there and be quiet."

The Drug Enforcement Agency and Coast Guard and Game and Fish Commissions possess expanded search authorities so they're a little more liberal in their violation of my constitutional rights. They also knew I wasn't about to take them to court or call my attorney. So they—and their German shepherd, Molly—spent the next thirty minutes tearing my boat apart. Sniffing for any-thing resembling residue. I folded my arms and watched with curiosity. I was really impressed when Agent Spangler slid into his diving gear and inspected my hull. About forty minutes in, the two agents disassembled my center console, leaving Molly sitting faithfully at my feet. I scratched her head and let her lick my hand. She put one paw on my thigh and leaned into me. When they weren't looking, I fed her dog bone–shaped treats. After almost two hours of grunting and sweating and finding nothing, they reported to someone in some office on the other end of their cell phones and then cast off my bowline and departed without a word.

Somebody had tipped them off that I was running tonight, and they were right—I was, but that same someone had also tipped me off that they'd tipped them off. It pays to pay more and Colin—my business partner—pays more. Spangler and Beckwith had been dogging me for the better part of five years. As had the team of Miller and Marks before them. And while I'd run enough to fill up this boat twenty to thirty or even fifty times, I'd never been caught. And I wasn't about to get caught tonight.

Casually, I cranked the engines and watched in muted amazement as Spangler and Beckwith disappeared north. Humming quietly to myself, "Na-na-na-na, na-na-na-na, hey, hey, hey . . . ," I slid silently into the maze of canals that fed into the bay. I slithered through the darkness past the hundred-foot yachts and $20 million mansions where the who's who of Miami parked their lives on display. I'd made drops at many of these homes, but one of the things that made me successful and still at it was the fact that what started with me stayed with me. I knew how to keep a secret, and I knew what to risk and how.

I serpentined through the maze, knowing that Beckwith had planted more than one hidden GPS receiver on this boat. They'd installed the first months ago, and we'd been playing this game of cat and mouse ever since. The show tonight was to plant a second as the first must have been giving conflicting signals due to salt corrosion. Of course, that muriatic acid I poured on it might also have had something to do with it. Never could really tell.

Miller and Marks had started this. That time I found it a few days later, so I sold the boat to a guy making a pass through the Panama Canal and up the other side. They thought I was making a pickup in Mexico. They sent boats and helicopters and planes, and that failed sting operation cost them a pretty penny. They were not happy. The guy who bought the boat said they were more than a little surprised to find him marlin fishing off the coast of Mexico and that Agents Miller and Marks had started throwing blows when they discovered it wasn't me. They were even more surprised a few hours later when, upon their return, they found me on my porch in Bimini, swaying in my hammock, staring out across the horizon with a cup of coffee in my hand and a devilish smile pasted on my face. "Coffee?"

Now I stared out across the water, the rumble of

the engines beneath me. While I didn't own this boat, I did possess a rather strong affinity for her so Colin had allowed me to name her. I called her the *Storied Career*. Tomorrow I'd turn forty, and if anything has been true about my life, it's been storied.

I tied off, checked the radar, and knew Spangler and Beckwith hadn't gone very far. They weren't the only ones with a GPS transponder. Two could play that game. We ran a tight ship, but our model was a little different. We ran a boutique firm, operated on the honor system—as much as there was honor among thieves—and worked to reduce the variables. We sold only to clients we vetted. We accepted payment only via wire transfer to offshore accounts. And we determined the drop point. And we never, ever, absolutely ever dropped it when they wanted it or where they wanted it, and we didn't tell them where it was until after we'd dropped it. If they had to have it right then and right there, we were not their supplier. This model had kept us in the business, and it had kept Beckwith and Spangler sniffing at our heels and always three steps behind.

I shut the engines and turned on the coffeepot. I knew they'd work up quite an appetite tearing up my boat, so I pulled a box of doughnuts from my bag and left it in a false floor in one of the forward hatches beneath a pile of greasy life jackets. Wouldn't take them long to find it. I sketched a smiley face on a yellow sticky note and wrote, "Help yourself." On the rear deck near the engine, located in another false floor beneath one of the live wells, I left a bowl of food for Molly. Her favorite—venison and lamb.

I pulled up the float indicating the crab trap and unrolled my wet suit. The water wasn't too cold, but the flat black color didn't show up as well under water as my pale skin. I slid into it, pulled the regulator over my mouth, slipped into the water, pulled on my fins, and began the half-mile swim. I took my time. My tanks had been retrofitted with dual Pegasus Thrusters. These were underwater propulsion devices that pushed me along at 170 feet per minute. Up top that equates to about two knots. I also held on to an H-160 thruster, which was similar to holding on to a torpedo. The combination of these sped me along underwater silently and unseen and kept my legs fresh in the event that I needed them.

I snaked my way through the canals, spotted the flashing beacon above me, dropped my gear, and squirreled out of my wet suit—letting it fall forty feet to the ocean floor beneath me—and surfaced next to the Pathfinder, which I'd packed and docked three days prior. I untied the bowline, shoved off. Thirty minutes later, I was staring at the dock where the basketball team, the rapper with his entourage, the pop artist with her management team, the hedge fund owner with all the girls he could buy, and one-quarter of Miami's elite were partying. If they wanted to suck their money up their noses, that was their right, their privilege, and their problem. I simply provided an overnight delivery service. If I didn't, someone else would. Supply and demand.

I slid up next to the dock beneath the rocking *boom-boom* of a party in the house. In the dark, I unloaded and stacked several packages inside a hidden floor cavity beneath a rolling locker on the dock. I'd been here before. A good customer. Having returned all the furniture to neat and tidy and just as I'd found it, I texted delivery confirmation, jumped back in my boat, and disappeared.

An hour later, I swam beneath the mangroves en route to the *Storied Career*. Four other DEA boats had surrounded her. She was lit up like a runway. As if the second search would turn up what the first did not. Staring from a distance, Agents Beckwith and Spangler marched about in a spitting frenzy, flinging four-letter words and whatever wasn't tied down in my boat. Molly stood on the stern, muzzle deep in a box of doughnuts. She must have gotten to the powdered first because her normally black nose and mouth were pastry white. A half mile down the street beyond the boat, the marquee of an all-night pizza joint flashed. I routed around the boats, bought a large pizza, and returned to the boat, holding the box on my shoulder. "Hi, guys. Pizza?" They didn't like that much, either. But since they had neither drugs nor cash nor evidence that I had or had had any of the above, there wasn't much they could do other than cuss a little more and tell me to get lost.

Which I did.

I snaked my way through the canals, docked at a marina, and then made my way on foot to my Beach Cruiser. A few miles later, I let myself in Colin's back door. When they built their house, Marguerite had custom cabinets installed in the back hall. Lockers of sorts for the kids, where they threw all their school and sports stuff, including smelly shoes or jackets, when they walked in the back door. Once I became family, Colin had one added for me. And like most everything Colin Specter did, there was more than one reason for this.

I slipped my hand inside the top shelf of my cubicle, in the back corner, where—invisible from the front—a small sleeve, or pocket, had been built. Just large enough for a cell phone—or a SIM card. It was one of many such places. My fingertips found the new postage-stamp-sized card; I quickly replaced it in my phone, dropped the old card in the trash can leading into the back of the house, and slid the phone back in my pocket.

Something I'd done a hundred times before.

Maria sat on the couch. Pigtails. Ribbons. Evidence of her mother's makeup. Pink leotard fresh from ballet. Knees tucked into her chest, popcorn resting on her knees, watching our favorite movie. I sat next to her as the nuns on the screen began to sing about their problem—Maria in the convent. The real Maria—the one on the couch next to me—sat, foot tapping, and did not need an invitation to join the singing now filling the airwaves of the living room and kitchen. Knowing full well she had our attention and that the curtain on the stage of her life had now parted, she stood on the couch and belted out the beginnings of a beautiful singing voice. Eyebrow lifted, a sly smile spreading across her face, her mischievous voice asked the nearly half-century-old question of the self-titled song regarding how one might solve a problem like Maria.

Maria and I first watched *The Sound of Music* when she was four. In a pinch, Colin and Marguerite had asked me to babysit, and knowing next to nothing about children, especially young ones, I plugged in what I thought would help pass the time. It worked and we've watched it a hundred times since. Now, at twelve, Maria knew her lines as well as the original cast members.

Jumping from the couch to the pool table, Maria spun, pirouetted, and pliéd herself across the tabletop, leaving petite, powdered footprints on the felt, quite oblivious to the effect her animated hands might have on the hanging light fixture. Her problem in gaining much reaction from "the crowd" rested in the fact that we adults had joined in so many times prior that we'd grown bored of the same and, in a desire for levity amid the monotony, begun to devolve into a confederacy of rhythm-challenged idiots. Doing so, we morphed into our own version of the now-hallowed song. From the kitchen, Colin and Marguerite sang out some sort of cheesy, offbeat rap duet while I feigned total beat ignorance, tapping and snapping badly out of time while singing with as much melodic acumen as a howling coyote.

Monkeys with pots and pans had more rhythm.

After little more than a single verse, Maria, hands on her hips and sensing that the room had descended into total musical chaos, raised an eyebrow, pursed her lips into a frown, and returned to her popcorn and the couch with a deflated exhale and a practiced look of measured disdain. Throwing a handful of popcorn into her mouth, she blew a strand of hair out of her face while texting a friend on her iPhone. Her fingers spoke one message, her mouth another. "You people are so old."

I laughed. "Yes, we are."

Cradling the popcorn bowl, she sat cross-legged on the couch, stuffed her mouth, and then rubbed her greasy hands on my shirtsleeve.

I scooted closer to offer some of my signature

comedic attempts, which once elicited bladder-busting belly laughter and tears, but now at the knowing age of almost-a-teenager, she would have none of it. She raised her maturing, stop sign hand and spoke without ever taking her eyes off her phone. "Talk to the hand."

I laughed, kissed her forehead, and turned toward the kitchen, but not before dumping the remains of the half-eaten bucket of popcorn on her head.

"Uncle Charlie!" She jumped up, stamping a foot. A vision in pink. "I cannot believe you just did that!" Eyes wide, she protested with a rather exasperated level of drama. "I just had my hair colored . . ."

I love that girl.

"Then I guess that proves what we already know . . . ," I said, laughing and walking backward toward the kitchen.

She looked at me confused. "What?"

I offered a fist bump to Colin, who knew what was coming next. "That you do, in fact, have a problem."

"Uncle Charlie!"

I escaped into the kitchen beneath a barrage of raining popcorn. I raided the fridge, ate some leftovers—which as godfather to both Maria and her older brother, Zaul, was my pseudo-parental right. Not one to stew long, Maria soon appeared, offering me a glance of—and the chance to admire

18

—her bedazzled book bag, which I appropriately praised. From there, she held my hand and led me around the corner to the door of the laundry room where, on a hanger, she had displayed a new bathing suit her mom had bought her. Hand on her hip, eyelids blinking in rhythm with her foot. "Dad says I have to take it back."

It was about the size of a napkin—more string than fabric. I turned to Colin and nodded. "Good call."

She gently slapped me on the shoulder. "You are not helping me."

I held it in my hand. "It doesn't cover anything. Besides, it's white." I stretched the fabric in front of my eyes. "Like almost see-through."

More eyelid batting. "That's the point. Have you seen my competition?"

I lifted her chin. "Honey, you have no competition. There's not another twelve-year-old on the planet that can hold a candle to you. Besides, you don't want the guys who only want you for how you look in this thing."

"It worked with Mom and Dad."

Marguerite laughed. "She's got a point."

Colin's voice again. "That is so untrue. I deny that completely. You hooked me with the way you play piano. I never even saw you in that white-and-blue-striped bikini with the little strings on the side."

Marguerite, over my shoulder. "Colin Specter,

you wouldn't know middle C if it hit you in the face."

Maria did not look convinced and stood waiting for me to join her side. I tried a second time. "Look at it this way: Skin cancer is a big problem these days and your dad and I are helping you with that."

She tugged on my hand, leading me toward her newest painting. "Yeah, you're helping me all right. Helping me become the biggest"—she formed an "L" with her hand and pressed it flat against her forehead—"loser on the beach."

Growing up in my family, life had been rather dysfunctional. In fact, I didn't have much family life. Walking through Colin's house, listening to the voices and the laughter, being accepted as one of the family, holding Maria's hand, and being asked by her parents to raise and take responsibility for her and her brother in the event of their death—these were the richest moments of my life. And every time I walked in here and ate the popcorn and kissed Maria's forehead and laughed with Marguerite at Colin and helped myself to any and everything in the fridge and propped my feet up on the coffee table and washed the dishes and took out the trash—I lingered and sucked the marrow out of it.

Colin and I seldom exited the same door, so when they left through the front, I slipped out the back hall, where I bumped into Zaul in the mudroom taking out the trash. "Hey, big guy."

I hugged him, or tried to. He was stiff. Distant. Thick with muscle and steroids and the stench of stale cigarette smoke. Just shy of eighteen, gone was the affable, curious kid. He was wearing a flat-billed ball cap cocked to one side. He raised his head in a half nod. "Charlie." Noticeably absent was the word "Uncle."

It'd been a while and I was genuinely glad to see him. "Your dad said you were hanging out with your sis tonight."

Zaul held the overfilled trash bag with one arm, and I realized just how muscled he'd become. A nod. "Thought maybe we'd go for a moonlight stroll or something in the Yellowfin."

The Yellowfin was Colin's twenty-four-foot flatboat powered by a three-hundred-horsepower Yamaha. Perfect for a glassy night like tonight. It also had state-of-the-art electronics so they'd have a difficult time getting lost. "Good choice. Love that ride. Especially this time of night."

He nodded and attempted a smile. He pointed above himself. "She likes to stand up in the casting tower and . . ." He shrugged. "Be Maria."

His shoulders were angling downward under the weight of something unseen. His eyes were dark circles and his voice raspy and tired. The trash was dripping on the floor. "I'd better get this cleaned up."

He disappeared into the garage while I exited out the back beneath the shadows. I stood long enough to let my ears and eyes adjust to the night and then crept down to the dock with the picture of Zaul weighing heavy on me.

I made the forty-four-mile crossing in *Storied Career* in a little less than an hour, slept fitfully, and as the sun rose over the Atlantic, I found myself on the porch, hovering over my coffee and staring both my fortieth birthday and my wedding in the face. While those were cause for celebration, a wrinkle had formed between my eyes as I stared at my left wrist. My naked left wrist. The watch Shelly had given me was gone. I'd lost it somewhere in the last twenty-four hours and I had no idea where.

And that was bad.

Chapter Two

I grew up with one single, overriding emotion. It drowned out all others. And it was this: that I was dirty. No matter what I did, how I tried to scrub it off, I was not clean and couldn't get clean. My mom seldom paid the utility bill so hot water was a scarce commodity. That meant on the rare occasion I hugged my mom, her hair smelled of stale cigarettes and beer. My clothes were constantly sour and soiled, and I was embarrassed at school. Our kitchen was piled high in weeks-old dishes, and the house was infested with roaches that used to crawl out of the woodwork and fall on me at night. I didn't have too many sleepovers as a kid. To mask my discomfort, I walked around in the shadows where the light didn't shine and people didn't pay too much attention. The last thing I wanted was attention. Doing so meant I got comfortable with the darkness.

And that's probably why I got away with so much.

I grew up combing the beach in Jacksonville, Florida. A barefoot, blond-haired beach bum without a curfew and with a disdain for shouldering responsibility. I had a bit of a Huck Finn childhood, and while that had nothing to do with my last name, I used to claim the connection. My mom and I lived across the street from the oceanfront property that blocked our view, so I watched a thousand sunrises from our second-story crow's nest.

I have no memory of my dad, a cabdriver, who died in an early-morning wreck when I was three. If Mom had a failing it was twofold: men and money. She knew this, so in a wise moment of self-awareness, she took Dad's life insurance policy and paid off the house. At heart, she was a gambler and a risk taker, which, she later told me, explained her affection for my father because he was a high-risk proposition given his love of gin. Paying off the house meant no one could take it from her—or me—and though we might not always have had food, we had a roof, albeit a leaky one. When the bank sent the deed to the house, she lifted my chin and said, "Never risk what you can't afford to lose." For my eleventh birthday, I got a job down the street at a restaurant, working for cash tips to help her pay the utilities. I think paying off the house allowed Mom to justify her other decisions, like stopping off in the slots room at the dog track after work or playing the lottery every week to the tune of fifty bucks. It took me a long time to realize that while it looked irresponsible on the surface, and we sometimes went a day or two without food in the fridge, Mom was searching for a way to give us the one thing our life lacked. The one thing that had been taken. The one thing we were chronically short on.

Hope.

I wouldn't say she succeeded, but she spent her life trying, and I loved her for that. With no dad and a mom who worked all the time, or was at least gone all the time, I was responsible for myself at an early age. While most kids' lives revolved around the requirements of school, mine revolved around the tides, swells, and direction of the wind—all of which determined the size and frequency of incoming waves.

In eighth grade, for every day I spent at school, I spent four at the beach. I didn't care. I hated school. Given my attendance, or lack thereof, the principal called my mother in for a conference and sat us down. He looked at a sheet of paper recounting my sins. "Ma'am, do you realize how many days of school your son has missed this year?" He chuckled. "It would be easier to tell you the number of days that he actually attended."

Mom raised an eyebrow at me and asked for the sheet. "May I?" He passed it to her, and her foot started tapping while she read it. Finally, she brushed her hair back and said, "So?"

"What do you mean, 'So?'" He looked at her like she'd lost her mind. "He'll repeat the eighth grade."

Mom dabbed the corners of her lips with a napkin. "Are we done?"

His face turned red. "'Done?' Lady, your son is behind. Aren't you worried about his future?"

Mom stood and grabbed my hand, leading me to the door, which was strange 'cause I was almost as big as she was. Reaching the door, she turned. "Sir, we're going to go eat a cheeseburger, and then I'm going to buy him a new surfboard because he evidently enjoys that a whole heckuva lot more than whatever you're doing here."

I smiled and waved at him.

He was dumbfounded. "And his future?"

She brushed the sun-bleached hair out of my face. "It'll be waiting on him when he gets there."

Mom died my junior year. I was sixteen. Heart disease aided by chain-smoking—a habit she adopted after Dad died. Alone and nauseated at the thought of answering to anyone else, I finished out high school working nights waiting tables, delivering pizza, and doing what I could. That "doing what I could" included selling as much marijuana as I could get my hands on to the surf junkies who were craving pizza. A convenient built-in audience.

Sam, my boss, used his pizza parlor as a front for his drug dealing and he dealt a lot. He brought it in on the shrimp boats out of Mayport and made me an independent contractor. He sold it to me at his cost, and I split all the profit with him. We made a good bit of money. I later learned that he knew the junkies and the amounts they were buying, so he knew exactly how much I was bringing home. When I presented him with exactly that amount, he learned he could trust me. I told him, "I'm not greedy. I just don't want somebody to kick me out of my house or ship me off to a state-run place." Every night when I handed him the money, he'd shake his head and mutter, "What is the world coming to? An honest drug runner." In a world devoid of meaning, I took what identity I could get.

In between deliveries, Sam taught me to play poker and soon discovered I was good at it. It doesn't take an education in Freud to understand this. I was attracted to risk and not attracted to anything resembling hard work that benefited someone other than me. If you were going to be dumb enough to risk your money in a card game, then I was going to be smart enough to take it from you. The same could have been said for me except that I won far more than I lost so— I argued—I was playing with other people's money. This would come in handy in the years ahead.

Team sports were contrary to my independence. Signing up for team sports meant that I was willingly joining arms with another group of people and stating that not only could they depend on me, but also that I would depend on them. Statements like "I'll show up for practice," "I'll be at the games," "I'll work hard" stood in stark contrast to my how're-the-waves-looking disposition. That said, I was rather competitive and competition did not scare me. In fact, I rather liked it. Solo feats like wrestling and running. Activities where the outcome resulted from me depending on me. This does not mean that I hunkered down and for the first time in my life learned to apply myself under the whistle-and-clipboard instruction of some guy in shorts pulled up to his armpits. Not at all. I rarely practiced, which drove them nuts, but I hated losing and seldom lost, so my coaches kept me on the team—which was interesting because I didn't really care whether they did or not.

Same was true for school. Homework seemed like a waste of time. My thinking was, *You've told me what you want me to know, now give me the test and let me regurgitate it.* I could remember most anything I saw or heard and scored well on tests so most of my progress reports read, "Charlie lacks work ethic but possesses great potential." I can't tell you how many times I've been called "exceedingly bright," "lacking drive," or my favorite, "bubbling with potential."

Whether it was two state wrestling championships, a sub four-minute, thirty-second mile, the death of both my parents before I was seventeen, or the fact that I was three questions shy of acing the SAT and had a guidance counselor who seemed rather keen on my actually attending college, I ended high school with excellent grades, multiple scholarships, and several higher learning options.

My senior English teacher told me I should consider the Marine Corps. I chose Harvard.

My graduating high school class voted me "Most Likely to Be Elected the First President with a Felony Record." My English teacher was big on knowing where you're going, what you're doing, "Have a plan!" Our final senior project was just that. Our plan A followed by plans B and C. I always thought he needed to let his hair down. Loosen his tie. Stop drinking so much prune juice. The paper was supposed to be eight to twelve pages with multiple supporting points. My paper consisted of one very short paragraph: "My plan A is to not have one. Which, by logical deduction, means there can be no possible plans B and C. My future will be there waiting on me when I get there." I failed that essay and he was incredulous at my choice of college—no, he was downright angry, saying I didn't deserve such an opportunity. He grew even angrier when he found out I'd be attending for free.

When I walked across the stage and he handed me my diploma, "With Superior Achievement," he mumbled something under his breath. I shook his hand, smiled widely, and said, "Does that toupee itch as much as it looks like it does?" His eyes darted left and right, and he smoothed his hair with his right hand. "It looks itchy."

My college decision process was simple. Harvard was expensive and an education there was "worth" a good bit. Again, if they were going to be stupid enough to give it to me, then I was going to be smart enough to take it. And I was smart enough to know that I'd never make it in the Marines with people blowing whistles in my face and screaming at me. Leavenworth did not appeal to me.

Besides, I'd never been to Boston.

• • •

I survived college in the same way I survived high school. I did just enough to get by without getting too caught up in any one thing. I'd always been good with numbers so when I declared a major, something in the world of finance sounded like a good idea.

By the middle of my sophomore year, I had grown tired of the track coach and his incessant need for me to train on his schedule, so following my four-minute, seven-second mile, I told him to take his clipboard and shove it in the same place I told him to put his stopwatch.

While my scholarship at Harvard paid for my tuition, room, and board, my stipend didn't go very far. Add to that the fact that I had never really enjoyed studying, and it's not too difficult to understand how many of my nights were taken up with poker.

I was a fair player, but I learned quickly that poker loves no man and good luck can turn to bad with no warning. Further, I detested losing. So I began looking for a way to tilt the odds in my favor. One obvious way was to cheat, which I wasn't opposed to, but that style of play has a limited shelf life, as does your career once you get caught. Then one night I was invited to a game where I discovered what I soon dubbed the "silver spooners." Trust fund kids who looked at poker as entertainment. They didn't really care if

30

they won or lost. They liked the reputation and action either way. Given their reckless behavior, I seized the opportunity and provided a service. By the end of my sophomore year, I had money in the bank and was making a name for myself.

As a player, I had two abilities that set me apart from most everyone else: First, risk didn't bother me and never had. I valued nothing, including money, so losing it didn't ding me like it did others. Second, I could read body language. Like Braille. Neither trait can be coached. You're either born with them or you're not. The higher stakes games were invite only and run by the son of a Silicon Valley tycoon. One night I cleaned up and ran the table. Took everyone's money. And it was a good night. Several thousand. One of my sore loser competitors suggested I cheated and manufactured evidence to support his claim. The invites quickly stopped. As a rising junior with few options, I was in a bit of a bind until he—a fifth-year senior—started running his mouth, so I challenged him to a public winner-take-all. Given his trust fund, he'd spent considerable time in both Vegas and Atlantic City trying to make others think he knew what he was doing. He liked to tell people he was a "professional cardplayer," but I had my doubts. Nobody as good as he said he was ran his mouth that much. Or if they did, they didn't run it very long. Sooner or later, poker humbles every man. His would be sooner.

Winning at poker is easy provided you know which hands to bet on and which hands not. Simple, right? Wrong. Wanting to rattle his saber and set me on my heels, he went all in on the third hand, but his bluff was ill-timed. I matched him, doubled up, and called. When the dealer laid down the river and he realized that a full house always beats three of a kind, the color drained out of his face. The pot sat at $17,000. Half of it was his. The girl propped beneath his arm all of a sudden found an excuse to visit the ladies' room. As his "friends" pulled away, not wanting to be associated with a loser, I saw the look in his eye and—so help me—I almost told him not to do it. But again, if he was going to be stupid enough . . .

He smiled around the room, trying to save face. "Double or nothing."

I scraped the money across the table. "What have you got?"

He dropped the keys to his Audi on the table. The "oohs" and "aahs" rose around the table. His friends patted him on the back, and his girl returned from her potty break to slide in alongside him. I didn't own a car and the thought of having one appealed to me. I nodded to the dealer, who dealt the cards, and the cards were not kind to him.

I walked out with not only his $8,500, but also the keys to his car and the beginnings of a storied reputation. Given that the car was his father's, his father quietly called the following day and offered me a check for the value, which I accepted. Sixty-four thousand dollars. A good night. Then and now, it wasn't about the money. It was about being told I couldn't do what I wanted.

Word spread and I got invites from all over to play. Problem was, I was getting invited by guys who'd done what I'd done—preyed on somebody with money. I could hear it in their voices and read it across their bodies. I played a few games and won a good bit, but they were marinating me. Slow roasting to tenderize and fillet me so they could take my last penny. I knew they were working me into a lather, waiting for their moment to pounce, but I never gave them the satisfaction. To their abject surprise, on a high-stakes Thursday night, I ran the table, cleaned up, and made enough to live on for a year. Collecting my chips, I kept my mouth shut but when I glanced at their eyes, I knew two things: that I'd stung them and that it would never happen again. Babysitting hour was over. Next week would start the reckoning. Having read the writing on the wall, I did what they never suspected. To everyone's disbelief, just when it was starting to get good and I was beginning to make a name for myself, I cashed in and walked away.

This did not make them happy, and as they had some pull in the city, they blackballed me in every game in and around not only Boston, but the

Northeast. It didn't matter. I'd tired of poker and I'd tired of Boston. My eyes had hit the horizon, and I was looking for a new game. And I found one.

In London.

Chapter Three

The water was waist-deep, gin-clear, and given no breeze, a sheet of glass. Deeper out, it faded from turquoise to midnight blue. Off to my right, the sun was falling en route to a beautiful setting. Twenty feet away, a lobster scurried to an underwater hide. A ray hovered just inches off the ocean floor. Two hundred meters out, a couple of boats were anchored. Kids in the water. Snorkels. Masks. Lobster bags. Laughter. Floating in circles around them, oil-soaked adults lay baking on rafts. The smell of salt, coconut oil, rum, and spent fuel suggested they'd been there the better part of the day.

Most every weekend, folks out of Miami motored out of Biscayne Bay, through Stiltsville, and across the forty-four miles between us, appearing early and packing this place with dozens of boats. At just over three miles long and a quarter mile wide—little more than a white speck in the Atlantic—the Bahamian island of Bimini is a blue marlin and bonefish hot spot, an offshore oasis for the Miami jet set, a famed Hemingway hangout, and one of the last vestiges of Her Majesty's empire. It's also a convenient escape for the disillusioned and a pretty good place for a rather successful drug runner to live uninhibited. The beach behind me sat bleach white and relatively untouched. The sand lay dotted with hundreds of conch shells. The northern tip of the island, including this beach, had been privately owned for a couple generations, but it sold last year to a casino, which was rapidly carving the landscape. In its wake, quaint fishing village had given way to the worst a casino has to offer. Local legend held that the lost city of Atlantis sat out in front of me just beyond the anchored boats. The legend held merit given the inexplicable geometric rock formations just below the water's surface. I guess you don't need me to tell you the name of the casino. The entrepreneurial owners had already cashed in on the legend and were ferrying visitors out to the rocks in glass-bottom boats. Not surprisingly, the legend had grown considerably. Mermaids had been sighted.

I landed on this island much like Columbus. By mistake. Been here a decade. Jimmy Buffett said it best: "Summers and winters scattered like splinters . . ."

Still no sight of her on the beach. My left foot was tapping on its own. She'd be here any minute.

Right? Right. The magistrate had first balked when I asked him to marry us on the beach at 7:00 p.m., but then I laid a wad of cash on the table and his entire countenance changed. Started talking about how he loved marrying folks on the beach at sunset. Still no sign of him, either, but he had a few moments to go yet.

In the moments following my not-so-romantic proposal, I'd asked Shelly where she'd like to get married. She pointed at her feet. "Right here." Which explained my present location. She wanted the setting sun on her face. Breeze in her hair. My hand in hers. She believed that our marrying here, in this turquoise water, would wash off the memory and pain of her first. I'd never been married, but that does not suggest I didn't have memory and pain. I stood there, ankle-deep, envisioning her, the wind tugging her hair across her eyes, her cheeks. Draping her cover-up across her bathing suit. Bare feet. Tanned. That smile. Wading out to meet me. Taking my hand.

Out of habit, I glanced at my wrist to check the time, but my watch still wasn't there. Nothing but the tan line noting its absence. Shelly was going to ask, and I had to think up a story without lying to her face.

Colin said he was coming over for the weekend on the Bertram—a sixty-foot sportfishing yacht powered by two supercharged Cat diesels producing more than a thousand horsepower each.

Given its tanks and capacities, the Bertram had a range of several thousand miles and was the perfect vessel for longer voyages down to the Keys or even Cuba and points south. With three staterooms, a kitchen and living area, not to mention expansive areas on both the bow and stern to stretch out and get away or sit in the fighting chair and wrestle a tuna or blue marlin, it allowed ample room for Marguerite, Zaul, and Maria.

While south Florida was beautiful in many respects, it suffered from one problem, which no politician could fix. In the event of storm or a natural disaster, there were only a few roads out. Which, when clogged with the millions who lived there, became a parking lot preventing a speedy exit. Colin had bought the Bertram more as a ferry for his family in the event that they needed to get out and could not. But, over the years, it had also become a great way to travel to the islands—which they did several times a month. Its forty-knot speed meant he could crank the engines, navigate out of the canals, skim across Stiltsville, and be in Bimini in less than an hour and twenty minutes.

Shelly had planned to make rounds this morning; she had a few surgeries up and through lunch, then she was going to run a few errands, shop for a few things, and meet Colin at the dock at 4:30 p.m.

I scanned the horizon for any sign of a boat, but still no Bertram.

I'd been there a while when a glistening speck crested the horizon, but it was not the Bertram. For Shelly not to show meant one of two things: She'd had second thoughts, which I rather doubted, or something at work—something she couldn't pass off to one of her partners—demanded she miss her own wedding. Colin, on the other hand, had been giddy at the thought of my marrying. Other than a pressing family need, I could think of no reason that Colin wasn't standing on this beach. The fact that he wasn't dropping anchor right now suggested something serious, and sudden, had happened to his family. For both of them not to show meant that "something" involved both of them: i.e, boat trouble, which was possible though unlikely, or Colin had need of Shelly professionally. As in, he needed a doctor.

After standing in the water for what felt like an hour, I waded onto the beach and asked an older lady walking her dog down the beach, "You know the time?"

She eyed her watch. "Quarter past eight."

Something was way bad wrong. I stood arms folded, lips pursed. I carried a cell phone, but I seldom dialed out on it and I hadn't the foggiest idea how to tell someone how to call me. Using the same phone on a regular basis was an occupational hazard because law enforcement agencies could use it to triangulate my position. Given this, Colin gave me a new SIM card every week—sometimes several times a week—and a new phone at least once a month. When I first got in the game, I tried to memorize each change, but after twenty new numbers and four new phones in less than four months, I gave up. Colin was the only one who knew my number, and as a testimony to his genius and his photographic memory, he never wrote them down. He stored everything upstairs. This pattern had been a major reason we'd stayed in the game so long and with such success.

The sun had fallen, and the moon was chasing the sunlight off the beach when I heard the rotors of the helicopter. Colin hated traffic—despised inefficiencies—so he used it routinely to check on locations for his import business or to hop to the island for lunch. The helicopter circled, landed, and Shelly stepped out, walking slowly. The light from the helicopter lit her approach.

She wasn't wearing her bathing suit.

Her medical scrubs looked like they'd been sprayed with tomato puree. She approached, arms crossed, and stood at a distance. She'd been crying. Still was. I reached for her and she stepped back, not making eye contact. When the helicopter had quieted, she glanced at me, looked away, then glanced again and held it.

I'd never seen such sadness.

The wind scraped the beach and blew the sand against my calves, stinging my ankles. After a minute, she brushed the hair out of her face and again crossed her arms. Holding herself tighter.

She retreated a step. The tears returned. She spoke without looking. "Last night, Life Flight brought in this little girl. A pit bull attacked her face. Lost most of her blood." She looked at me. "She got caught in the middle between bad people doing bad stuff." She stared at her hands, finally looking me in the eyes. "I spent eight hours trying to—" Shelly stopped. She was shaking. I tried to hold her, but she turned and slapped me as hard as she could across the face. Then again. She spoke through gritted teeth. "Get her smile back." She shook her head. "I'm not sure she'll—"

I waited. She shook her head and wiped her nose on her arm. She had finished with whatever she'd come to say.

Keeping her distance, she extended her other hand, palm down. Like she wanted to give me something. I responded, and she stared at her closed fist, which was shaking slightly. I touched her hand with mine, and she opened her fingers, dropping my watch in my hand. The watch was sticky and the face smeared. I couldn't read the time. She spoke while looking at it. "Maria was wearing this when they brought her in. It—" She cracked, then recovered. "Just dwarfed her little wrist."

Finally, it hit me. I pointed at my heart. My voice rose. "My Maria?"

Shelly swallowed but didn't acknowledge me. I'd already lost her.

I pressed her. "Will she live?"

Shelly only shrugged, nodded. She took one step toward the helicopter, then stopped and spoke over her shoulder. "Colin—" She hesitated and looked at her hands, finally continuing, "Told me . . . everything. Starting with the day you two met." She shook her head in disbelief. "I told him I did not know that man. Never met that man. That the man I loved would never lie to me. Never put me in danger." Her voice turned acrid. "Never use me like that." A pause. "When I left the hospital, three cops were sitting in their cars, typing reports. Tactical guys. Tattoos. Black clothing. They were with Maria when she came in. I asked them if they had any suspects. All they said was 'Corazón Negro,' and that they'd been chasing him off and on for a decade. Said he's a ghost." Eye contact again. A single shake. "You should have told me." Shelly had been in Miami for a long time, and her Spanish was very good. Far better than mine. She didn't offer a translation, and I didn't ask.

I knew what it meant, and I knew that she knew what it meant.

A wave spilled across our feet. She knelt, reached into the water, and washed the blood from my watch off her hands. The helicopter pilot read her body language and the rotors began spinning. Winding up. When she stood, she palmed the tears from her eyes and turned to look at me. Her face was puffy, shrouded in darkness, and her eyes looked like smoldering embers. She said, "Charlie, have you ever considered that life is *not* a poker game and that we aren't chips that you just toss about the table 'cause you feel like it?" A steeliness returned to her eyes and face. "There's an evil in you. And . . ." She waved her hand across the splattered blood. "It stains everyone but you." It was over. She stepped closer. "Don't ever contact me again." She turned, glancing out across the water. "Ever."

Arms crossed, wind tugging at her scrubs and hair, she stepped into the helicopter; it lifted off the beach and disappeared west with the night. I cannot say I was brokenhearted at her leaving. I'm not sure I wanted to marry Shelly as much as I didn't want to lose her. Marrying her said something about her. Losing her said something about me, and I was afraid to hear that indictment.

The truth of me had broken us.

Chapter Four

Given the size of Harvard's endowment and the immense block of recently freed-up time in my schedule, and having worn out my welcome in and around Boston, I began looking into study abroad scholarships and found one custom-made for guys like me—finance-minded juniors with off-the-charts test scores, all A's in math, no parents, no siblings, and no extended family. What the scholarship board called a "child of prodigy and hardship." Funny how there's so little difference between "prodigy" and "prodigal." The summer after my junior year, the Pickering-Kuscht Scholarship sent me to London, where I studied derivatives, leverage, and the emerald-green eyes of a goddess named Amanda Pickering.

Amanda was beautiful, self-confident, loved to run, and—fortunately for me—directionally challenged. After I quit track, I rediscovered my love of running—much of which I did at night, so while most of my classmates made the rounds of the British pubs sampling gallons of Guinness, I ran the streets of London. Incidentally, so did Amanda. Only difference was that I could find my way back to my hotel once I turned around. We'd been in a couple of classes together but given that she was a bit guarded, it was no wonder that we'd never said two words to each other. Amanda also had one other trait much talked about among the fathers and sons of the New England elite: She was the sole heir to the Pickering fortune. Her college experience was her father's personal talent search among the East's best and brightest to find someone to manage his precious money. One night, about 1:00 a.m., I found her—several miles from our hotel—standing next to an Underground sign attempting to read a map. She glanced at me but was too proud to admit she needed help.

It was pretty common knowledge that her father had put her up in one of those top-floor penthouses at the Ritz. I put my finger on the map. "The Ritz is here."

She glanced at me out of the corners of her eyes, nodded, and acted as though she were studying the map for an alternate route home. "Yep."

Her eyes still had yet to land on any one point on the map. I pointed again. "And . . . you're over here."

This only served to push the skin between her eyes closer and deepen the wrinkle, so I pointed behind her. "Which means you should run that way."

She tilted her head, still trying to make sense of the map and not admit defeat. Finally, she turned to me. "I'll bet you're good with a Rubik's Cube."

"Fifty-two seconds."

She shook her head and spoke, still trying to make sense of the map. "Been coming here my whole life but"—she wiped the sweat off her face—"looks so different in the daytime, and we always had a driver."

I pushed against the lamppost like I was stretching my calves. "Yeah . . . me, too. 'Cept mine would never shut up. Talked the entire time. Couldn't help but learn something. Knew this town like the back of my hand by the time I was eight."

"I'm lost, and you're making fun of me."

I shook my head and continued to poke fun at her. "Good help is just tough to find these days."

She smiled. "I've heard of you."

"Really?"

"You're that arrogant runner who's been taking everybody's money in poker. Even won a car."

I shrugged. "It was his father's and he's got several more."

A knowing chuckle. "Yes, he does." She continued. "Then you went in front of Father's scholarship board with some song and dance about how you're all alone in this world. Making everybody feel sorry for you."

"Father's?"

"You're Dad's scholarship pick."

"I thought a board decided that."

She didn't look at me. "You thought wrong."

"I spent over an hour answering their questions."

"Evidently, you answered them quite well."

"I have a talent for telling people what they want to hear."

"Are you always like this?"

"Like what?"

"Self-effacing."

"If I knew what that meant, I'd answer you."

She shook her head once. "An honest man at Harvard."

That's twice in my life I'd been called honest. Funny. I didn't feel it. I shrugged. "Sometimes being honest and telling the truth are not the same."

She sized me up. "Daddy will be so impressed."

"You tell him everything?"

"What I don't tell him, Mr. Pickering discovers on his own." A pause. "Money has its . . . responsibilities."

"A lot of guys would shoulder that burden for you."

A pause. "That include you?"

"I think whoever shoulders your financial burden will get your father's approval long before he gets yours, and I have no desire to play that game."

As one of the richest twenty-five and unders in the United States, my guess was that Amanda was not accustomed to being spoken to so plainly and with so little regard for how much financial leverage she wielded. I didn't know whether she believed me or not, but she perceived my honesty as a breath of fresh air. "And you'd be right about that."

"I'll bet your high school experience was a blast."

"It had its moments."

"How many times did you run away?"

She smiled. "Every night."

I chuckled. "Like now."

More honesty. Another nod. "Yes, like now."

I held out my hand. "Charlie Finn."

She held my hand several seconds. "Amanda Pickering."

I turned. "Come on. This conversation would've been over long ago if you knew your way home."

The best way to describe our friendship was one of curious amusement. Unlike the other guys who'd literally stalked her, looking for the opportunity to strike and share their résumés—and, hopefully, her money—I'd stumbled upon her, and rather than play the rescuing knight, I'd poked fun at her—which set me apart from everyone else and which I think she appreciated.

My reason for this was pretty simple. I'd been playing poker long enough to know that there's always somebody with greater skill, more chips, and better cards. This dictated that my chances with Amanda were zero, so why waste my time acting otherwise. As a result, we adopted somewhat of a take-it-or-leave-it attitude with each other. That meant unlike all the other guys lining up to take her out, we actually spent a good bit of time together.

The finance class I was taking culminated in a single project. On the first day, the professor had issued everyone a hundred thousand dollars in Monopoly money, then told us to create our own portfolio and keep him abreast of all trades. Stock picking had never really been my thing but research was, so I made some good decisions, shorted a few stocks, covered myself with some options and calls, and, as was consistent with my personality, held very few long positions. When the summer semester came to a close, my portfolio had outperformed my classmates'. This, more than my relationship with his daughter, caught the eye of Marshall Pickering. On the day before my return to Boston, Amanda offered to let me tag along on the family G5. A couple of other guys would be there. As tough as it was, I knew that if I wanted a chance with that girl I needed to *not* be like those guys. I needed to play it cool. I also had a pretty good idea the invite came through her father, given that I'd just won his portfolio contest. So I declined. "I've never traveled Europe much, so I'm going to take the train back through France and Spain. Get lost for a few days. Sample the beer and maybe the food."

I knew if I invited her that she'd come, and I knew she wanted to. I also knew that this relationship would never make the return trip across the ocean. Daddy would see to that. I waved her off. "I'll see you back in Boston." I smiled and then pointed west. "It's that way."

She laughed, held my hand for a second longer than she should, and that's when I knew she'd fallen for me. Amanda was strong, independent, highly intelligent, incredibly good-looking, and she had—or would have—more money than she could spend in ten lifetimes. She was also a pawn in Daddy's world. And while her dad loved her, I had a feeling he loved his money more.

The next two weeks were some of the loneliest I'd ever known. I forced myself to stay gone a week longer with no contact just to give an impression. The bluff worked. When I landed in Boston, her driver was waiting on me at the airport. He stood next to his limo. "Mr. Finn?"

The window behind him rolled down slightly and Amanda's emerald-green eyes smiled at me. We didn't leave each other's side for nearly a week.

A month later, she invited me to have dinner with her folks, private plane, helicopter, yacht, the Hamptons, all in a casual effort to meet the family. I was no dummy. Mr. Pickering had a file on me six inches thick. I was pretty certain he knew my grades in grammar school, how many pizzas I'd delivered, that I'd had my wisdom teeth pulled my senior year of high school, and he could recite my college transcripts from memory. He was either allowing me to come to dinner to publicly undress me in front of his daughter and show her the fraud I really was, or he was raising an eyebrow and wanting to know what I was made of. His future son-in-law might marry into this family, but he'd earn every penny of her money.

After kissing his daughter, he extended his hand and put his arm around me. "Charlie. Welcome. Come in. We've heard so much about you." He could not have been warmer. My first thought was, *This guy is good. Remind me to never play poker with him.*

Too late. We were already playing.

I chose my words at dinner, speaking only when spoken to, responding to Amanda's mom, who fired off most of the questions. These people had made up their minds long before I walked in that door, so I enjoyed my meal and answered honestly and casually. I figured that by *not* trying to impress her folks, I was actually doing a better job of impressing them—if that was possible. When asked, I gave the short details of my life— which I was pretty sure they already knew. Dad drove a cab but killed himself when he wrapped it around a concrete barrier with a blood alcohol of about .3. Mom worked two to four jobs to support us but followed Dad my junior year of high school. Three questions shy of acing the SAT. Harvard full ride. 4.0 GPA. Four-minute, seven-second mile. Would graduate a semester early.

Her mother raised a finger. "Following the death of your mother, who raised you? Supported you?"

"I did."

"How did you survive? Buy food? Pay the power bill?"

"I delivered pizza and sold drugs."

While she laughed at the joke, thinking I was making one, he sat back and smiled smugly—telling me he knew I was not.

Amanda's dad poured wine for everyone at the table and saw it as his personal mission to stoop to the level of a butler and make sure everyone was sufficiently happy with his "house" wine, which, Amanda whispered, wholesaled at $200 a bottle. I didn't touch it and every time he offered I declined.

He noticed my lack of consumption before we ate our salads and watched with curiosity as my wine sat untouched all night. When they lit the bananas Foster, he asked almost with disappointment, "Could we get you something else?"

This was it. His first push and I knew it. He was raising me. I shook my head and answered only what I was asked. "No thank you."

Another push. A raise. "You don't like my wine?"

I met his raise and raised again. "Don't know. Haven't tried it."

He waited, eyeing the cards in his hand.

Amanda sipped and smiled. More amusement. She tapped my foot below the table.

A single shake of my head. "Don't drink."

He knew this, but rather than admit that, he raised his glass and toasted me and then his daughter and finally his wife and their Persian dog. I wouldn't say that I won that hand as much as I had succeeded in earning myself a seat at the invite-only table.

Following dinner, we "retired" to his porch, looking out across the water. He offered me a cigar. Again, I refused. He rolled his around his mouth, lit it, and then sucked on it until the end glowed like a hot iron. Oddly, the color matched his eyes. Drawing several times on the Cuban, he exhaled and filled the air around us with a haze of smoke. "You don't appear to have any vices, Charlie."

I was in way over my head. Any idiot sitting in my chair knew that. This guy ate guys like me for breakfast and picked his teeth with what remained of our backbones. Somewhere around the third course, his stiffening body language told me that I'd be seeing less of Amanda following dinner. Little I could say or do would change that. He wanted someone strong but not someone who would so willingly challenge him—which is what I'd been doing all night. And he knew that. And he knew that I knew that.

Given that I could read the cards I'd been dealt, I again decided on the honest approach. I can't really tell you why other than I had a pretty good feeling that this guy could read my bluffs far better than I could make them. Besides, I'd never had dinner with a man worth almost a billion.

Halfway through his cigar, he said, "Amanda tells me you're a bit of a poker player."

"I've played some."

He pointed to a felt-covered table. An innocent fatherly face. "Shall we?"

I folded my legs and rested my hands in my lap. "No need."

He studied his cigar, drawing deeply. I think he was starting to get irritated. "Really?"

"I made money by playing trust fund kids who viewed poker as entertainment. And I sincerely doubt you brought me here to entertain you."

He chuckled, admiring the red tip. "You preyed on gullible people."

"I provided a service to kids who were burning through Daddy's money and should know better."

"And you know better?"

"I saw an opportunity."

He nodded. "And seized on it. I like that." The innocence drained out. "I pay a lot of money for people who can read other people."

"Mr. Pickering, I have the feeling you can read me a lot better than I can read you."

He smiled and grabbed his imaginary chips off

the table. "Touché." He may not have liked me, but he admired me for folding my hand when faced with someone who held better cards. He glanced at me. The smoke exited his throat like a chimney. "Marshall. Call me Marshall."

With her parents' apparent approval, Amanda and I "dated" through our senior year. Harvard seemed impressed enough with my under-graduate record that they offered to take me in the MBA program, and while I didn't know for sure, I was pretty well convinced that Marshall had more than just a little to do with it. After the first week of classes, Marshall called me into his office and made me a job offer I couldn't refuse. I decided to play another hand and accepted.

Marshall ran money. His and others'. He also owned companies around the world. The more I got to know him, the more I came to realize that the story about his net worth being a billion was off by about $2 billion. There was a lot at stake. He had three billion reasons to choose wisely. Knowing this, he'd staffed his "firm" with young guys like me under the guise of training us. Mentoring us. Showing us the ropes out of the goodwill of his heart. In truth, he meant to run us through the wringer and see what we were made of. Owners of horses do the same thing. Fill their stable with the cream and see which Secretariat rises to the surface. Butchers also do this with meat they are about to tenderize. Pickering and Sons was a highly successful hedge fund in an era when most were folding up shop. It was also Marshall's own private joke on the world. He had no sons. His entire life's goal after becoming otherworldly wealthy was finding the one thing he couldn't buy.

Someone to guard what he valued in his prolonged absence—i.e., his death.

He showed me around his office, introduced me to the guys, and then casually showed me my cubicle. Gone was the tender father from dinner, pouring wine and lighting cigars. "I have several hundred résumés, many better than yours, sitting on my desk. Each detailing why and how some young man is chomping at the bit to sit in this chair." He spun the chair around. "Why don't you take a turn?"

My mother was fond of saying something that had always stuck with me: *"Never look a gift horse in the mouth."*

So I started classes and, with Amanda dangling as the unspoken carrot, became Mr. Pickering's boy. His money also dangled—not so subtly—but unlike the other forty men who worked for him, I wasn't there for his money.

Amanda and I fell in love—at least as much as any two people can when they're separated by nine zeros and a father who is little more than a master puppeteer controlling everyone's motions with the strings between his fingers. For Christmas, we flew the family's G5 to Vail and then Switzerland. Venezuela for summer vacation and everywhere in between. I studied, managed to hover near the top of my class, and responded to Marshall's requests. Given my ability to read people and situations, I became his "assessor." Meaning he sent me into new territory, new acquisitions, and asked me to evaluate the three things upon which all businesses live and die: the balance sheet, the widget, and leadership. Harvard might have printed my sheepskin and been credited with my education, but I cut my teeth with Marshall.

Over the next two years, I got pretty good at it. Better than any "boy" he'd ever had. I graduated with my MBA and then the real work began. Marshall paid me a modest six-figure salary, which I didn't have time to spend, with the promise of a bonus at the end of the year based on production. He did this with all his horses. I owned a condo in Boston but lived on his Gulfstream. In the first year out of Harvard, I slept in my own bed twenty-six times.

Throughout all of this, I kept up my running. Not quite as fast as I once was, but pain needs an exit so my miles increased. Running was where I worked out my legs and feet what I couldn't work out of my mind. It was therapy. It was the bubbling effect of Marshall on me. Whether I was running to or from, I couldn't say.

My first bonus brought me mid-six figures. Sounds like a lot, and it was, except that my work had produced almost a hundred million in balance sheet revenue for Marshall. Upon one of my returns, somebody hung #23 above my cubicle. And they were right. In everybody's eyes but Marshall's, I was.

Remember how I told you I never played cards with people who were better than me? That works only if you figure out ahead of time that they're better. Brendan Rockwell was a pedigree kid, a standout on the Harvard crew team, and first in his Stanford MBA class. That in and of itself created immediate tension between the two of us. Stanford and Harvard have long disdained each other because they both do the same thing better than anyone. While I was traveling the continent and half the globe, Brendan had worked his way up Marshall's ladder, even earning the nickname "Papa Brown" because of his extensive work brown-nosing Marshall. Evidently, Marshall appreciated the fealty because I soon found myself working alongside him. Teaching him the ropes. He was tall, chiseled, highly intelligent, articulate, crafty, quick on his feet, as good if not better with numbers than I, and would not hesitate to slit my throat if I let my guard down. Brendan wanted one thing and it had nothing to do with Amanda—although he'd take her if she came with the package. He intended to get his money the old-fashioned way.

In Marshall's battle plan, I was the boots on the ground and he had no better field general than me, but the problem with that scenario is that I was always gone. Reporting in by phone. Brendan, on the other hand, reported in person and Brendan wanted that old man's money. Pretty soon, he weaseled his way into every reporting relationship and became the hand behind the curtain controlling the levers. Hence the revised nickname "Oz Brown." I told you he was a better cardplayer than me. He and Marshall were cut from the same cloth. I soon learned that Brendan would take my reports, study them, lift what he wanted, and later use incomplete facts to poke holes in my arguments. It's not the frontal assault that kills you. It's the flank attack. Death by a thousand cuts.

My second year in the firm, Amanda came to see me in my office. As she left, she lingered at the door. She was heavy. Anytime she left his office, she was heavy. She leaned against the doorframe and whispered, "You busy this fall?"

"Not especially."

"How would you like to go on an extended vacation—with me?"

I had a feeling she was talking about more than just travel. "Define 'extended.' "

She walked to my desk and kissed me, holding

her lips to mine for several seconds. "As in, 'the rest of our lives.'"

It was the first and only time we ever talked about getting married, but it also let me know that Marshall had bugged my office because after this conversation with Amanda, his interaction with me changed. More voice mails. Less face-to-face. The next morning I was on a plane for parts west. Of the next eight weeks, I was gone all but four days. Then came Thanksgiving, on which I was conveniently stuck on a well-drilling platform in the Gulf of Mexico with a bunch of sweaty Texans. Amanda called me and I heard Marshall laughing with Brendan in the background. I could read the writing on the wall. Amanda and I were caught in a machine and the gears were chewing us to pieces.

Given my experience with my office, I was rather certain Marshall listened to all our calls, so, in a sense, I was forcing his hand. I said, "Remember that vacation?"

"Think about it all the time."

"When?"

I could hear the smile in her voice. "Is this a family affair or just the two of us?"

"That's up to you."

"It'd kill Daddy."

"He'll get over it."

The following week, Brendan came to work to discover that his office, which had sat next door to mine, had been—wonder of wonders—moved upstairs. Same floor as Marshall. Just down the hall. Shouting distance. Further, while us boys had been working the chain gang, her father had continued to insert her in the public eye and Amanda had become the face of Pickering. That meant that Marshall began "requiring" more of her presence up front. More face time. Interestingly, those requirements, more often than not, conflicted with our plans.

Then came the Cinco Padres Café Compañía fiasco.

Chapter Five

The wind had picked up and created a six-to-eight-foot chop, which made the nighttime crossing challenging and not so fun. I'd done it before but bigger boats handle that better. I left *Storied Career* in her berth and motored Colin's sixty-foot Bertram out and into the open water.

As the bow rose and fell through a dark night and the spray from each wave swept across the glass in front of me, I kept one eye on the radar and the other on my rearview mirror. Staring back through the years. Colin and I had crossed some water together.

When the Miami skyline rose into view, the knot in my stomach told me how much the mess I was walking into was going to hurt—and how much was my fault.

Two hours later, I was on the floor of the Pediatric Intensive Care Unit at Angel of Mercy Hospital. The room was dark. Quiet. Colin was sitting in a chair, head in his hands. He was wearing what remained of the tuxedo he'd worn the night before. His coat, tie, and cummerbund were gone, and the front of his shirt was stained a deep red where he'd held and carried Maria. His black patent leather shoes were dull and smeared. Marguerite sat in a strapless, flowing gown. She was dozing in a chair next to the bed, resting her head on the sheets, holding Maria's hand in both of hers. Maria was connected to tubes, and her entire face was bandaged like a mummy except for a small opening where a tube had been inserted in her mouth. Other smaller tubes ran up her nose. An IV dripped over her left shoulder and into her arm. The bandages on her face were partially soaked through. Machines above her head beeped and flashed. She was asleep but her legs, fingers, and toes were twitching slightly. As if she were running.

I put my hand on Colin's shoulder but he didn't look up. He just put his hand on mine and shook his head. Marguerite stirred when I laid a blanket across her bare shoulders and then knelt next to her and put my arm around her. She leaned on me, resting her head on my shoulder. Maria lay gently jerking.

Marguerite began to relay the events of the night as two nurses walked in and began gently pulling the gauze off Maria's face. When they peeled away the soaked cloth, I could not recognize Maria's swollen and sewn face. The left half of her head had been shaved, and stitches covered the top and back of her head. When the nurses gently lifted Maria's head, Marguerite covered her mouth and turned away. Colin wanted to hold her but something stopped him. Maria remained unaffected in a medically induced coma.

When finished, the nurses left as quietly as they'd entered. Colin spoke over my shoulder. "After we left you last night, we attended a gala. Fund-raiser. Not gone more than an hour. Zaul had offered—" Colin's voice trailed off as incredulity set in.

Marguerite spoke from the bed without lifting her head. "We should have known better."

The dart stung Colin. He swallowed, and he continued, "I don't know how he found out about the drop." Colin was telling the truth. One of the signs of his genius was the amount of details, dates, and account numbers, which he kept inside his head—with no paper trail. There were account transfers, but that was easily "laundered" under his legitimate business interests. Regarding our business—the boutique firm, which sold and delivered high-quality cocaine to wealthy and elite members of society—no record existed. "After being so careful for so many years? Maybe . . ." He trailed off, continuing a moment later. "After we left, he told his sister they were going for a nighttime cruise." A shrug. "Something we've done a hundred times before. How was she to know? She loaded up. Put on her life jacket. They meandered through the canals."

Marguerite again. "We were glad just to have him—"

Colin closed his eyes. "About a year ago, Zaul began selling himself as a poker player. Looking for higher and higher stakes games. Where the buy-ins are five and ten thousand."

The knot in my stomach worsened.

Colin continued. Uncomfortable. "I've had to bail him out."

Marguerite whispered while not looking up, "Twice."

Colin continued, "The second time, I told him—" He sliced through the air with his hand level to the ground. "No more." A pause. "We don't know how much he owes but . . ." A shrug.

Marguerite added, "We were trying to set a boundary that we should have set a long time ago."

"How much?" I asked.

Colin shook his head and shrugged. "I don't know." He sat and leaned his head against the wall. "Couple hundred." Colin shook his head. "Somehow, he knew the location of the drop." A glance. Shrug. An honest admission that it was our—my—drop. "I guess he figured we could absorb the loss. Blame it on someone else. We'd make it good with the client. Move on. Problem was that whomever he owed money followed him. Surprised him on the dock." He glanced behind him. "Maria was oblivious, feeding the fish below the boathouse. Found your watch on the steps. Recognized the inscription. Was no doubt wearing it until she could give it to you."

That meant that whatever we were now in the middle of was far from over. I stared down at Maria and whispered more to myself than anyone else, "Somebody came to collect."

Colin whispered, "Zaul being Zaul tried to be tough. Fight back. Maria stood in the middle. Bread crumbs in one hand. Your watch in the other."

Colin nodded and Marguerite laid her head again on the sheets. I walked out into the hall and asked the nurse to roll in a second bed next to Maria's. When she did, I took Marguerite by the hand, and she climbed up into the bed, slid her right hand across Maria's bed where she could scratch her arm, and closed her eyes. I spread a blanket across her, and within a minute, she was dozing. I pulled Colin into the corner of the room and waited until his eyes focused on mine. Colin paused and wiped his forehead. He glanced over my shoulder at Maria. "Folks at a neighboring party heard the screaming. Said they found Zaul talking to 911 and carrying his sister to the street where Life Flight picked her up."

"Where is he now?"

"Both he and the boat have disappeared." A long stare at Maria's mummified form. He rubbed the bend in his elbow where the Band-Aid and cotton indicated he'd given blood. "She lost a lot of blood." Another break. "Shelly spent eight hours . . ." He trailed off. After a long minute, he said, "Charlie?"

I put my hand on his shoulder.

His voice cracked. "Do something for me?"

"Anything."

"Find my boy." He leaned against the wall and stared at the machines monitoring Maria's condition. "He raided the safe, took the cash and his passport. Two of his three surfboards are missing, and his credit card shows a charge from Delta. He's on a plane"—he stared at his watch—"to Costa Rica."

A year ago, Colin bought a summer home in Costa Rica. It cost him two and a half million dollars, but that much money buys a lot more house there than it does in the States. Twelve thousand square feet. Set high up on a bluff overlooking the Pacific. Private beach. Deep-water dock designed to harbor large yachts.

Boathouse with several boats. Both the pool and the hot tub had been built with "zero edges" so that they appeared to fall off into the ocean.

They'd spent all of last summer there, and when they'd returned, Colin thought he'd made real headway with Zaul. Colin continued. "Last summer, he met some guys. Surfers. Petty thieves and small-time dealers. They move up and down the coast, country to country, stealing or selling enough to chase bigger and better waves." He looked at me. "Given the amount of money he's about to surface with and given the way he spends it, they'll make him their new best friend, but that'll only last as long as the money. After that . . ." Another long pause. "The gangs down there will sniff him out. Then they'll call me. I don't think I'll ever see . . ." He trailed off.

The sting of Shelly walking away had festered and was growing raw. Looking down on Maria was like pouring lemon juice on that wound. It struck me that the only thing I deeply cared about in this life was lying wrapped in this bed, like a dead pharaoh, with the distinct possibility that she'd never smile again.

I nodded. "I'll go. Right now."

Ever the chess player, Colin was always thinking ahead. It's what made him good at his job. Both jobs. "You should take the Gulfstream."

Colin owned a G5, which he used solely for his legitimate import business. We never ran drugs on the plane because it was too predictable and because Marguerite and the kids traveled in it. Unlike me, he had never mixed the two. While the plane was faster, I knew once I made it to Central America that finding Zaul would not be easy if he didn't want to be found, forcing me to move around—possibly country to country—and I could do that a lot better and with more freedom by boat. Finding Zaul would be a problem—and a big one—but convincing him to return would be the bigger problem and that might take some time. He had left for a reason, and my presence didn't change that. While Colin wanted a speedy resolution, I could be gone months. "The Bertram's got the range and she'll fit in better with the culture. Make folks think I'm some guy in midlife crisis chasing marlin or something."

In the last decade delivering drugs, I'd developed a nagging itch in the back of my head regarding customs and immigration. Too many stamps on your passport—what I call "ins and outs"—and they start getting suspicious. Avoiding it altogether is better, provided you don't get caught in a country in which you hold no visa. I was pretty sure I could fly out of the United States, but given the events of last night and Shelly's final words to me regarding Corazón Negro, I wasn't sure I could get back in without being detained. Maybe imprisoned. I didn't know what they knew and I didn't want to assume they didn't. Also, if Zaul decided to move about, which I thought he would, I'd need to skirt country to country. I wasn't too sure how much Central American customs communicated with the U.S. DEA, but I had a feeling that checking in with customs every time I stopped in a different country would raise red flags. Water, while slower, was better than air. It also afforded me an escape route.

Colin's body language told me he had one more thing to say. Despite his success in an illegal world, Colin was not a good bluffer when it came to me. Never had been. He stared out the window, then at Marguerite and finally at Maria. His eyes fell when he looked at me. A single shake of his head. "I told Shelly." He glanced at me. "Everything. I'm sorr—"

"I know."

A shake of his head. His eyes watered. "I'm done." He waved his hand across the room. Across us. "Out." He moved his hands as if he were washing them. His eyes fell on Maria. "Price is too high."

I knew the tendency for anyone in a situation like this was to make a rash decision motivated by emotion. Colin and I had made good money selling drugs. Only problem with that theory was that Colin had never been motivated by money. He had plenty. He was motivated by the glamour, glitz, and people with whom it brought him into contact. Colin grew up working his father's grocery store, wearing an apron and pulling pickles out of the fifty-five-gallon drum by the front door for little old women and their cats. That perspective of himself had never changed. Colin was still the guy in the apron who desperately wanted to show his kids something else and convince his wife he was more than a pickle puller who swept the floors and stocked shelves. He used to tell me that when he was a kid, his hands always smelled like vinegar. To kill the smell, he would soak them in vanilla.

Colin feigned a smile, teared up, and sniffed his hands. "Never did get that smell out."

I reached into my pocket and handed him my cell phone. It was the string that connected us. No tether? No business. Maria lay twitching beneath the blue light above her. "I'll call from the boat."

I kissed Marguerite's forehead and she pressed her cheek to mine—a silent admission that we were standing in a mess of our own making. I stood over Maria not knowing how long it'd be before I saw her again. I held her small hand. The red-lit oxygen sensor had been taped to her index finger, reminding me of the night we watched *E.T.*—she had sat in my lap, spilling popcorn. I kissed the gauze covering her forehead and tried to speak but the pain in my heart choked the words out of my throat. I'd done this—I dropped the drugs. Had I not, we wouldn't be here. No, I'd not loosed the dog, but I had helped feed the evil world into which she'd innocently stumbled. Staring at Maria, the transparency of my life hit me. I had lived divided. Split time between two worlds—one foot in each. And I'd done so with a resigned indifference. The sight of the soaked gauze on Maria's face told me that the two had bled together.

I kissed her again, wiped my eyes, and disappeared down the hall.

Motoring out of Miami, I got a whiff of dried blood but couldn't determine the source. I smelled everything. Finally, I separated my watchband from the back of the watch and found a spot caked between the two. I washed it in the saltwater, scrubbing it with soap. It cured the smell but not the stain.

Vanilla would have been better.

Chapter Six

If Marshall and I shared one habit, it was coffee. We were snobs about it. Talking about coffee was the only time I found him remotely human. Somewhere in here, in my search for the absolute best cup of coffee I could find, I clued into the buzzwords "organic," "single source," and "fair trade." Pretty soon, Marshall and I were rattling off the names of farms in Africa and South and

Central America in the same way wine people talk about vineyards. We talked about them like we'd been there when, in fact, all we'd done was buy their beans and filter water through them. That changed when Marshall began his own research, and I soon found myself on planes bound for Central America. Marshall had found not only a way to drink great coffee, but to make a dollar. Or two. Or three.

Blame it on our taste buds, but for whatever reason, we both decided that we liked Nicaraguan coffee best. And specifically, Nicaraguan coffee from an area in the northeast center of the country that was rippled with primarily dormant volcanoes. Marshall described it as an "aromatic earthiness." I described it as the "nectar of God." Don't think we were chums or pals participating in blind taste tests. Far from it. I seldom saw Marshall at this point, and I was seeing less and less of his daughter. In truth, I was spent, washed up, and looking for an exit from the machine—an exhausted hamster. Problem is, it's tough to get off the exercise wheel when it's spinning so fast.

During this time, I hopped between New Mexico, Texas, Arizona, Oklahoma, Alaska, Canada. Mostly oil exploration and mineral rights along with a company that made racing tires for Formula One cars. Marshall had me in a new hotel every night. I was convinced that he'd hired two or three new people to simply manage my schedule and think up stuff for me to do. I was moving so fast that my body arrived in town three days before my soul.

Soon he began routing me through Central America, where research showed that in the several hundred years prior, dozens if not hundreds of eruptions had spewed from the mouths and sides of the volcanoes of the Las Casitas range. Doing so had deposited layer upon layer of rich minerals and nutrients onto the soil's surface that was found nowhere else on earth. Then, by the simple process of farming, all that flavor found its way to our taste buds through the lives and actions of some very poor subsistence farmers.

I spent six weeks on the back of a motorcycle on the dusty roads of Central America doing reconnaissance on who made what coffee, what made it great, and how it made its way to market. In each new town—Corinto, Chinandega, León—I'd call Amanda and ask her to take the jet and meet me for a long weekend, but Marshall had not only micromanaged my schedule, he'd configured hers as well. And nine times out of ten, Brendan would just happen to walk by Amanda's office the moment she was talking to me. *"Tell the rock star hello."* Uncanny how many times that happened.

Brendan was the best player of us all.

To take my mind off the growing anger and the

momentum of the wheel from which I could not escape, I studied the source, the first middleman, the second middleman, the guy who took a percentage of the second middleman's profits, the police who dipped their fingers just because they could, the politicians who brought in the international distribution company and took a liberal "consulting" fee for their efforts, and finally the shipping company that took what little remained. If I learned anything, it's that in all my business dealings, I'd never discovered anything more corrupt than the Nicaraguan coffee business and nobody, and I mean nobody, got more screwed than the farmer who grew the beans. On average, Nicaraguan coffee was sold to buyers in the United States and elsewhere for just over two dollars a pound. How much of that did the farmer make? On a good day, about ten cents.

That's right. A dime.

Then came the day that I happened upon the Cinco Padres Café Compañía.

Three decades prior, revolution and blood in the streets had solidified an agreement between five farms that, despite their personal differences, knew they had better join hands or what little they had would be ripped from their fingers. So these five fathers with farms of similar size and production, led by a man named Alejandro Santiago Martinez, joined forces and created a company that wielded enough selling leverage to eradicate some of the middleman nonsense. Alejandro owned a sizable plantation on the side of a dormant volcano, which, I later learned, was the single-most sought-after coffee in Nicaragua. Rumor had it that Alejandro, through years of buying, had pieced together his plantation on the mountainside leading down from the lake that had filled the crater atop the volcano. Further, Alejandro had planted hundreds of mango trees along the sides of the mountains, believing there was an intrinsic connection between his coffee and those mango trees—that the taste of one bled into the other and vice versa. I didn't know if it did or not but I could say beyond a shadow of a doubt that Alejandro's Mango Café was the best coffee I'd ever had in my life. For once, Marshall agreed with me.

Completely.

If Marshall had a personal motto, it was "Everything can be bought for a price." The unspoken half of that motto was "And if you don't like my price, I'll manufacture circumstances that will cause you to reconsider its attractiveness."

Marshall quickly sent me with an offer of ten cents on the dollar. I told Marshall that his price would never fly down here and he told me to remember whose money I was playing with, so I shut my mouth. In an effort to insulate myself from the backlash—because as dumb as I was, I knew enough to know that they might attempt to kill me if I delivered it in person—I contacted an attorney who, for an up-front cash fee, carried the offer to the Cinco Padres while I sat at a café watching the bank entrance from across the street. To no one's surprise, he entered and exited within the same five minutes, quickly returning with a no and a soiled dress shirt where one of the fathers had thrown his manure-stained boot at him.

No counter. No consideration. No conversation. No nothing.

About what I expected. The five fathers' farms had been in their families for two and three hundred years, and there was much more at stake here than profit and loss. These folks were tied to the land. It was as much a part of them as their black hair and suntanned skin. Simply put, it wasn't for sale. Not today. Not tomorrow. Not for any amount of money.

If Marshall had a firm grip on his money, he'd met his match in the actual five fathers, and in Alejandro, their leader. When he reluctantly increased his price to twelve cents on the dollar, they filled up two five-gallon buckets with fresh cow manure. The first they dumped over the attorney's head. They second they poured inside his car. All of it. And it wasn't the solid, pick-it-up-with-your-hand kind. It was the other kind.

Marshall didn't take too kindly to this form of

non-negotiation, and it didn't take him long to find the chink in their armor. Through a series of shell companies created for the sole purpose of bankrupting Cinco Padres, Marshall and Pickering and Sons, with Brendan driving the bus and me as their hatchet man, bought the entire year's production of several South American competitors and then began selling that coffee at a reduced rate to all the buyers of Cinco Padres coffee. Naturally, the five fathers had to follow suit. Wanting to inflict more and greater pain in the shortest amount of time, Marshall bought the bank that the fathers used to finance their operations during lean years. Given the growing losses and their weakening share of the market, their open lines of credit were "reassessed," and when the dust settled, they were required to put up twice the collateral for half the credit. The result reduced their buying power and hence their profit margin. It also meant that the bank owned more of their land than they did.

To Marshall, Nicaraguan coffee was a passing fancy. Idle thinking that filtered through the smoke-filled air of post-dinner conversations. It occupied his thoughts like golf or poker or the latest and greatest wine in his collection.

Marshall had little—correct that, he had no—regard for what he was doing to the generations of families in his wake. He couldn't have cared less because they, their lives, and their problems never occurred to him. He was sitting behind a desk in Boston wearing a $10,000 suit and $1,500 dollar shoes, picking out color combinations and textures for his next two-hundred-foot yacht. Their problems never entered his cranium—as was his right given his money. Or so he had convinced himself. In short, if someone else's life sucked, that was their issue. Not his. Welcome to Earth.

My role was a bit closer to the tip of the spear. I spent months in Central America, was constantly in communication with the people of Nicaragua, but I never once thought to learn Spanish. Had no intention of learning to communicate with these people. My thinking was, *If they want to do business with me, they can learn to speak my language. The only thing I need to know is how to count their money. I've got enough to worry about.* I dealt with those around me like crumbs on a table. Tasked with selling tons of coffee, I did. At the lowest rate I could obtain and to any-one who would buy it. Retailers loved me because I nearly gave it away. For the Five Fathers, my business method was death by a thousand cuts. I remember walking out onto the porch of my hotel room, propping my feet on the railing, staring out across León, and laughing when I received a report that they were now delivering coffee via horse-drawn cart as they couldn't afford gas for the trucks. Why? Because it meant I was that much closer to leaving this godforsaken place. When I called in to report, Marshall affectionately referred to me as "The Butcher of Boston" as I was "single-handedly gutting the Cinco Padres." He could almost taste the beans. I didn't really care what he called me or what happened to these people, and I didn't care about their Mango Café or their country.

I knew we had them on the ropes when I heard reports that Alejandro had stopped paying his workers and begun butchering his own cattle, pigs, and chickens to feed them. I did some digging and found out the size of his herds and the number of employees and figured he could last about another month, and then, without food, the people who worked for him—who were fiercely loyal—would have to seek work else-where as their children were starving. I was right; after a month, all work stopped, coffee production ceased, and living conditions on his mountain began driving people down and off. To add insult to injury, he was sitting on a fortune of coffee, as the best crop he'd ever planted hung from the bushes waiting to be picked. Staring at his own destruction, he and his wife and daughter and a few family members were single-handedly trying to harvest the crop of coffee in the hope that they could find a buyer. They could not, and it was a futile effort as doing so would have required hundreds of pickers, sorters, and a host of other people to pull it off. Problem was the workers could see the writing on the wall, and they knew that even if they picked and sorted and bagged, it would sit in those bags in their barns because some other company had sabotaged the market and now the bottom had fallen out. The old man would never sell that coffee. And every-one knew that. We all knew it. That had been the goal the entire time. To leave that man sitting in a pile of his own coffee beans.

Because Marshall prized information and always had, I paid a kid on a motorcycle to ride up the mountain and spend a day or two spying. I told him, "I just want to know what he's doing." He came back and told me that the old man had not slept in several days and had been working around the clock. News reports circulated of a coming storm. It had started raining and even the family had gone inside. Last he saw the old man, he was kneeling in the dirt, coffee beans sifting through his fingers, crying. He said he'd never seen an old man cry. Said he was screaming at the rain. Pointing his finger. Angry and sad at the same time. He said his daughter had climbed up into a mango tree to watch over him, and when he'd started to cry, she'd come out with a raincoat and put it over his shoulders, kneeling in the mud next to him. I remember laughing, thinking, *I bet he wishes he had sold when he had a chance*. I also remember thinking, *We broke him. We won.* And I took satisfaction in that.

Then came Hurricane Carlos.

Marshall could not have orchestrated a better natural disaster. It was as if he had bribed the hurricane because, for some inexplicable reason, it hovered over Nicaragua. For four days it stalled over Central America, and the rain never let up. In that time, Hurricane Carlos dumped over twelve feet of rain. That's right. Twelve feet. Doing so not only killed whatever crop was currently growing, but it filled up the lake atop a dormant volcano called Las Casitas. Once full, the weight cracked the mantle, causing a miniature eruption and mudslide. The thirty-foot-high, mile-wide mudslide shot off and down the mountain at more than a hundred miles an hour, cutting a thirty-mile swath to the ocean. Naval and Coast Guard vessels would later pick up survivors clinging to debris some sixty miles in the Pacific.

More than three thousand people died. From a sheer production standpoint, they'd been set back twenty to thirty years, not to mention the human toll on families and fatherless children and childless parents. As for the Cinco Padres Coffee Company, four of the five farms sat in the hurricane's path. Leveled. No more Cinco Padres Café Compañía. The lone padre teetered on the verge of bankruptcy.

I flew home. Rode the elevator to Marshall's office. My skin tanned from spying in the sun. He gathered us in his office—Marshall, Brendan, me, a few other guys. He asked my opinion. I told him there was an opportunity. Might take some time, but if he ever wanted a corner on the Central American coffee market, this was it. It struck me as I spoke that Marshall's attention was elsewhere. His head was aimed at me, but his ears were not. He'd checked out. Which meant he was three steps ahead. Whatever his next move was, he'd made it long ago.

He turned to Brendan. "Brendan?"

Brendan had developed a habit of pretending to shoot an imaginary six-gun when he spoke about stocks or decisions involving money. He'd practiced the whole routine: draw, cock, shoot, blow smoke off the barrel muzzle, and then holster. He thought it made him look like a gunslinger, which became his self-adopted nickname —because he didn't like "Oz Brown." Brendan brandished his finger pistol. "It's a loser. Close up shop. We've accomplished what we set out to do." He blew the smoke off the barrel. "Cut our losses and run."

The words *"We've accomplished what we set out to do"* echoed in my mind.

That's when it struck me how perfectly Marshall had played this hand. It was never about the coffee. In the last six months, he'd successfully removed me and inserted Brendan. My limited experience with Brendan told me that Brendan loved Brendan and would sell his soul for Marshall's money. Which he did. And it didn't take a genius to realize that while I'd been gone making them money, Brendan had been dating my girlfriend.

Overnight, Marshall called in the loans on the remaining family members of the Cinco Padres. Penniless and coffee-less, they and their families lost everything. The farms were foreclosed on and became the property of the bank. If the hurricane had set that region back two decades, Marshall's business tactics would set it back five more. Then, like a man who'd slept with the town whore, he took a shower and walked away. As was his right given him by his money.

Entire villages, dependent upon the plantations for work and sustenance, lost everything. And all for what? His money? His daughter? His entertainment? As the bitterness settled in my mouth, I realized it was about none of that. Marshall's life had one overriding urge—power. And this game he was playing, in which I was imprisoned and little more than a pawn, was how he wielded it.

The following week, I returned to Nicaragua to deliver the papers Marshall and his lawyers had signed and to clean out the hotel room in León, which I'd converted into an office and had served as my home. The night I left, I rode out of town on a rented motorcycle up into the mountains. Until then, I'd spent some time examining warehouses in town where the coffee was stored once it had been harvested, cleaned, and brought to town for sale, but I'd never actually made my way deep into the mountains—onto the plantations—where the coffee was grown. Where the people lived who grew it. Never gotten my hands dirty or talked to a single family working in the plantations. I can't tell you why I did. I just did.

Entire families were walking down. Mothers and fathers with three, four, or five kids. No shoes. No shirts. No food. No nothing. They carried their lives in sacks on their shoulders. I didn't know them because I hadn't tried. I didn't speak Spanish, nor had I attempted to learn. But something inside me, what might have once been called a moral plumb line, told me that I'd helped orchestrate their misery. No, I didn't create the hurricane, but they could have survived that. Rebuilt. What they could not survive was Marshall. Me. The empty and gaunt eyes told me that we'd broken these people.

One woman in particular still comes to mind. She was pregnant. Wore a black scarf that matched her black hair, her face ashen. She looked like she'd just lost everything that ever mattered. She stared down the road, numb to the tears shining on her cheeks. I cut the engine, crossed my arms, and watched as the line of people filed down the mountain like ants. Most didn't know where they were going. They were just walking until they got tired, then they'd sit down and sleep for the night. I cranked the engine, idled down the mountain, and put that place, those people, and that country behind me. I didn't want anything more to do with Nicaragua, its coffee, or the people who grew it.

I stepped onto the plane, buckled in, and within minutes we were climbing past ten thousand feet. I looked around me. Plush leather. An air conditioner control nozzle above my head. Food on the table before me. Drinks in the bar. In three hours, I'd touch down in Boston, where I'd eat sixty dollars worth of sushi—by myself. I stared out the window and down upon the lush, green landscape of Nicaragua still raw with a thirty-mile scar down its heart. I shook my head. I hadn't just robbed these people—I'd held them down while the classroom bully stole their lunch money and shattered their hope.

Sitting in Marshall's plane at forty thousand feet, I realized that Marshall's money was not worth what it was costing me. His daughter was, but by his own design, the two were inseparable. I couldn't have one without proving my worthiness of the other.

And I had not been found worthy.

New Year's Eve, Pickering and Sons met for their annual party. It was also the night Marshall handed out bonus checks. The week prior,

Marshall had me off "assessing" an oil exploration company in Texas, so I flew into town and Amanda was noticeably distant. Cold. Her eyes were red. We'd spent no real time together in months. Whenever I'd come home, she'd been busy. Or her dad had her off traveling. The "face of Pickering." Part of me hurt and I didn't understand why. It would take a few weeks for me to figure out that that painful aching place in my gut was my heart breaking.

My days with Pickering were numbered. I wasn't sure where I'd go or what I'd do, and I was pretty sure Amanda would not go with me. She loved me, but there was one thing she loved more.

I walked in the door and Marshall was warm as ever. Hugged me, introduced me to all the older guys as "his eyes and ears on the ground." An hour into the party, he put his hand on my back and invited me to share a cigar. Just the two of us.

After he shut the door, he offered and I once again refused. After emptying his lungs, he set an envelope on the table between us. A smile. "You've earned it."

I had a feeling it was a good bit of money. I also had a feeling it was more than a bonus. I was right. His tone changed. A glance out of the corners of his eyes. "Think of it as a 'going away' present."

I folded my hands, saying nothing.

I let him continue. "After tonight, you'll be

seeing less of Amanda." I sat with my hands in my lap. He wanted me to reach for the money. To take his deal. The problem with Marshall was that at the end of the day, I didn't want his money. Never had. That's one lesson he never learned. And the only card I had left to play.

A pause. "How so?" I asked.

He scratched his chin. One of his "tells" that he was about to lie. "She and Brendan are looking at dates now."

I smiled and nodded. "Does Amanda know this?"

He lit his cigar, drawing deeply. Exhaling, he spoke. "She knows her role."

I waited.

He stared at me through a cloud of smoke. "Brendan will make the announcement in an hour or so." He eyed the envelope and then me.

I stood, lifted the lid of his cigar box, took one, and cut the tip. I lit it, drew deeply, and stared over the end, catching a glimpse of Amanda in the mirror. She stood beyond the window just outside the room. I could see her; he could not. I turned the cigar down and placed the burning tip on the felt top of his table. The cigar burned through, curling up the edges where they rolled back. "Marshall, you're going to die an old, angry man." I turned and began walking out. When my hand reached the doorknob, I stopped. "Unlike you and unlike Brendan, it was never about your money.

It's always been about a girl with emerald-green eyes."

I could hear the smile when he spoke. "Then I have chosen wisely and you're a fool."

I turned and returned to the table, leaning in. My face inches from his. Amanda's reflection still showing in the mirror. "Yes." A long pause. "But whose fool are you?"

No job, no girl, and no future, I walked out, bumping into Brendan, who'd been standing behind the door. I stopped close. I wanted him to feel my breath on his face. "One of these days, you're going to discover that the bull's-eye you're shooting at is a moving target . . . and—" I glanced over my shoulder at the old man. "He'll never let you hit it."

I exited through the kitchen to my car, cranked it, and sat, letting the windshield defrost. Through the cardroom window, I could see Amanda standing in front of her father, envelope in hand. Shaking her head. She was screaming at him.

I pushed in the clutch and slid the stick into first. As I began easing off, Amanda appeared in my rearview. I stopped. Stepped out and brushed her hair out of her eyes. She was shaking her head. Lip trembling. Whatever cards she was now playing, Marshall had dealt her a long time ago. I wanted to make it easy on her.

To curb further losses, the best cardplayers know when to walk away. And I'd already lost a lot. What little remained lay in tatters. I kissed her on the cheek, said, "Call me if you ever find yourself lost at night on the streets of London. I'll always help you find your way home."

She nodded and a tear trickled down her face. It paused on her lips where I kissed it. Then her cheek.

It was the last time I saw her.

Chapter Seven

The Bertram is a sixty-foot sportfisher with three bedrooms, two bathrooms, a stateroom, kitchen, a captain's perch, and stainless tower. All in, she cost Colin nearly a million dollars. The back deck contains a fighting chair, a couple of downriggers, room to move around, and access to the engines. The Bertram was powered by two Cat turbo-diesel engines producing more than a thousand horsepower each. At forty knots, both engines consumed well over a hundred gallons an hour, but at a more modest cruising speed of twenty-five to twenty-eight knots, she burned only sixty-five gallons per hour. Cutting my fuel cost in half and nearly doubling my range.

The captain's watch, or control deck, looked like something out of *Star Trek*. Everything I needed at my fingertips except warp speed. All the com-ponents were new and came complete with built-in redundancy. Two of every gauge. Two radios. Two radars. The only thing not redundant was the satellite phone.

As the crow flies, the distance from Miami to the Panama Canal is a little over 1,100 miles. The problem is Cuba—you have to go around. From the Panama Canal to Costa Rica is another 250 miles north up the coast. A flight from Miami to Panama is two hours. In a sixty-foot boat with a cruising speed of about thirty knots, it's closer to the better part of five days—give or take—depending on weather. Just south of Marathon, I crossed over into the Gulf of Mexico where, traditionally, winds and waves are less than in the Atlantic. I set a southwest course, careful to avoid Cuban intervention. Then I turned south, Havana to the east, Cancún to the west, and crossed just north and within sight of the Cayman Islands. I overnighted in Montego Bay and took on fuel. I had enough fuel to make the entire trip, but I needed to rest and taking on fuel was always a good idea. The following morning, I set a southerly course for the Panama Canal. It had taken me two days to cross the six hundred miles of the Caribbean Sea when I finally entered Panamanian waters. Needing sleep, I anchored in a hidden cove, dozed until daylight, and on the morning of the fourth day out of Miami, I entered the fifty-mile Panama Canal. Eight hours later, I exited the canal, turned northwest, and traveled another long day up the mountainous coast of Costa Rica.

I knew Zaul would be looking over his shoulder a few days. Follow too closely and I'd end up pushing him. He'd simply duck and run and we'd never find him. I needed to let him breathe, let his guard down. I knew Colin well enough that he wouldn't cut off Zaul's credit card, allowing him nearly unlimited funds. Colin was not a good man and he was not a good dad—what man is who sells drugs?—but he did love his kids. And in order to pay for his own sins, he'd keep giving Zaul money. Buying his own redemption. In a way, credit card charges would allow Colin and Marguerite to track Zaul's movements. And as bad as that sounds and as much as they enabled Zaul to continue being Zaul, it was the only way Colin would be able to "follow" his son.

I talked with Colin every day, checking in on Maria. They had kept her sedated to allow her to rest and give her face time to begin healing on its own. He said Shelly had been by several times a day and that circulation looked good. She was hopeful, but she continued to caution that the nerve that controls the ability to smile had been severed. While she had reattached it, she told Colin and Marguerite to prepare themselves.

Time behind the wheel of a boat with nothing but water ahead gave me plenty of time to think. And the thought that kept playing over and over inside my head was this: What did I have to show for my life other than the scars on Maria's face? Like, what was the impact or influence of me on earth? While my destination lay in front, something kept drawing my eyes back. To the wake. The more I studied it, the more I realized that the wake was a good image of me. Angry at present, but once it settled, it smoothed over. As if nothing was ever there. No evidence. No permanence.

I had nothing to hold me and nothing to show for my life. No job. No wife. No family. One friend. Bimini felt empty. I had moved to an island and become one. I had a four-decade track record of playing my cards close to my chest and running from everything that hurt me.

With smooth water, I climbed up on the tuna tower. Two stories above the boat, I sat for hours just staring at the water. Before me flying fish jumped up out of the water and flew a foot or so above the surface for two or three hundred yards before diving back in. My left wrist wore the watch Shelly had given me. One more reminder of an angry wake.

I took my time. Conserved fuel. Soaked in the horizon. By noon on the fifth day out of Miami, I sat rolling in the waves offshore, staring at Colin's pool deck through a pair of binoculars. The porch doors were open, curtains swung in the breeze. Music played. Smoke from a bonfire trailed upward. Someone, or someones, had been there. I waited until evening, but in eight hours of surveillance, not a soul moved about in the house or on the deck.

Chapter Eight

In the days following my exit from Pickering, headhunters called nonstop offering me jobs of a lifetime. More money than I could spend. I sent them to voice mail. Amanda called twice but I never answered. Finally, driving south down I-95, I opened the window at ninety-seven miles per hour and tossed my cell phone into a concrete barrier. I was done. I wasn't sure who I wanted to be, but I was finished being whoever had worked for Marshall Pickering.

I floated south to Jacksonville and found myself in my childhood home sitting on the crow's nest with a cup of coffee staring out across heaven's reflection. Two weeks passed in which I slept most of the time. My body was so tired, when finally given the opportunity to sleep, it did. Days passed in which I slept eighteen to twenty hours a day. No drugs. No alcohol. I simply stopped long enough for my soul to catch up with my body, and when it did, it needed sleep. I didn't know what I would do or where or how I'd eventually make a living. I had some money saved up, but one day I'd have to get a job. Start over. The only thing I knew for sure was this: I'd never trust my heart to another.

It hurt too much. Despite all my tough talk about not risking what I wasn't willing to lose, I'd gotten in over my head and risked everything. And lost.

In the end, Marshall had won.

To add insult to injury, Marshall had given us, his "boys," the option of accepting our bonus in a year-end cash payout or equity shares in the firm. The "catch" was this: The year-end cash payout was at 50 percent on the dollar. It worked like this: If your bonus was $100,000 on paper, the cash payout was $50,000 minus taxes at 30-something percent. In brass tacks, that meant $100,000 turned into about $35,000 in less than a few seconds. Understandably, everyone took the equity.

The second catch was, to protect us from taxes, all bonuses were a gentleman's agreement written on paper. The only copy of that paper was kept in Marshall's office. He had us by the short and curlies, and we knew it—but it gets better, or worse. In another twist, if any of us wanted to buy something—say a house, a yacht, take our family on vacation, pay for private school, pay off college loans, or just "cash out" so that we controlled our own money—we had to take a loan against our personal balance. And while

Marshall never expected us to pay it back, he did collect interest on the loan—which he deducted from our principal equity or from next year's bonus. This ensured that Marshall didn't have to pay tax on our bonus money. He kept all the money, didn't pay tax on what he "paid" out, and earned interest on money that was rightfully ours. A genius scam. Really. Wish I'd thought of it. If anyone demanded all their money, Marshall never refused it and gave it with a smile and a pat on the back as he showed them the way to the door—*"Enjoyed you working with us. Let us know if there's ever anything we can ever do for you."* As a result, everyone was loyal to Marshall— they had to be. He had all their money. When I drove out his driveway, I left all that. I'd given up every-thing.

The only consolation I felt was this: Amanda knew that I valued her more than the million or so equity money. That left me with one problem— she chose the money over me. Maybe Amanda was the best poker player among us. As the weeks passed, that became tougher and more difficult to stuff.

I grew my hair, didn't shave, burned anything that resembled business attire, seldom wore a shirt or shoes, and reduced my life to a single suitcase. My motto became "traveling light." And while that was a good description of my physical appearance, it was a better description of my heart. No tethers. Nothing to encumber me. Nothing to hold me back.

I was getting a bite to eat one night on Third Street in Jacksonville Beach, a few blocks from my house, and overheard a guy talking about the Bahamian island of Bimini. Even though I'd grown up on the northeast corner of Florida, I'd never really realized that Bimini sits about forty-four miles off the Florida coast. People in Miami do it in a day-trip. Sometimes, several times a day. When he finished, I said, "Any chance you'd give me a lift over there?"

He sized me up. "Long as you don't mind working a few hours on deck before you get there."

"I don't."

He handed me a business card. "Boat leaves tonight at ten p.m. If you're not there at a quarter to ten, I'll figure you're not coming."

I didn't know how long I'd be gone or where I'd stay or what I'd do, but I had a feeling it would be longer than a few weeks, so I locked up the house, paid the property taxes a year in advance, and climbed aboard his boat.

It'd be years before I returned.

Once a British colony, Bimini is now a fishing island with a drinking problem. Given its resurgence in numbers and its appetite for fighting anglers, the bonefish rules the flats, but the top three blue marlin world records were caught in the deep waters within spitting distance of the beach. Sport fishermen catch everything in between. By boat, it's an hour and twenty-minute trip from Miami. Less if your boat is well equipped. Its culture is everything Miami is not and wishes it was—an island. The Bahamians are beautiful, laid-back, and the British influence exists in more than just accent. The north-south island is little more than three miles long, and at its widest point, it might be a quarter mile wide. There are essentially two parallel roads, there are about as many bars as homes, and if there happens to be a funeral, the streets will shut down along with much of the town. In its heyday, it was one of the sport fish capitals of the world. Hemingway frequented here. As did Zane Grey. Multiple movie stars. The water is turquoise, the beach is white, the women are bronzed, and the breeze always blows. Early in its history, the island of Bimini was populated by a colony of freed slaves. Many of the modern-day residents are direct descendants.

I fit right in.

I landed on the island, took a deep breath, and knew that I'd found the antidote to Pickering and Sons. I slung my backpack across my back, slid on my flip-flops, and pulled my Costas down over my eyes. After finding a hotel room "by the month," I began strolling the streets. A few blocks later, I stumbled upon Legal Grounds, the local coffee shop.

Jake Riggins graduated Miami Law two decades earlier. After an unsatisfactory decade practicing law, Jake, late forties, thumbed his nose at South Florida and took up residence on the eastern coast of Bimini, where he put his law degree to use making coffee and defending the occasional drug runner with enough money to bring him out of retirement.

Legal Grounds was a home run and exactly what I needed. Jake did coffee and he did it right. He started with good coffee—he had a thing for Tanzanian and South African but mixed in some Central American as well—ground it with a burr grinder, boiled water, let the boil run off, bloomed the coffee, and then slowly poured the water over the grounds to release the flavor. Perfection every time. Jake's nickname was "Picasso," and when it came to coffee, he was.

After a few weeks of sun, Jake's coffee, and a cool island breeze aided by not a single care in the world, I found my rhythm in Bimini. A month in and I bought a hurricane shack on the northwest corner of the island for a few thousand dollars. It sat up on a small bluff beneath some huge trees, and the sunsets from my porch were, hands down, the best on the island. I had to renovate pretty much the entire thing, including the walls and roof, but I was in no hurry. Six months in and I was actually sleeping in a bed with a roof over my head and four strong walls surrounding me. In my bedroom, I had an AC unit, although I seldom turned it on. The breeze across my bedroom was plenty. I would not say that I had a plan or a goal. Not in the traditional sense of "knowing where I wanted to go in life." I didn't. I just knew what I didn't want to be.

I wasn't running to, I was running from.

Working to get my house in order made me a regular at the hardware and lumber store, where I kept bumping into an old Bahamian man with gnarled hands, sun-weathered skin, white hair, wide straw hat, deep wrinkles, and a smile that just wouldn't quit. You know that thing that some old men have that makes everybody want to just sit and be quiet with them? He had it. He must have been eighty years old, but most every day we shared a "Mornin'" in the lumberyard or while staring at stainless steel screws in the fasteners aisle. Occasionally, he'd hold up a price tag and squint. "Forgot my reading glasses." I'd quote him a price, he'd nod, and then about once a week, I'd bump into him at Jake's, where he enjoyed a coffee while rolling his cigarette.

One morning while he sat with his right leg crossed over his left, trail of cigarette smoke rising up from between his fingers, coffee getting cold, hat sitting on the table, I walked up in front of him and extended my hand. "Sir, I'm Charlie Finn."

He stood, cleared his throat, and shook my hand. His grip was that of a forty-year-old, and there wasn't an ounce of fat on him. "James J. Hackenworth." A wide smile. "Friends call me Hack."

"Most folks call me Charlie."

Turns out Hack was the unofficial grandfather of Bimini. He knew everybody and everybody knew him. He was also born on the island, which made him a bit of a novelty in that he'd never left. Spent his entire life on these three miles of dirt and countless hundreds on water. He was a child of the water, not land, and I would learn this soon enough.

Months passed as my friendship with James J. Hackenworth grew. Hack invited me to his shop where he built wooden skiffs. Taped to the walls were yellowed articles from magazines and periodicals. Turns out he had a bit of a reputation around the United States and had been written up in *USA Today*, *Newsweek*, *People*, and *National Geographic*, to name a few. The wealthy elite from all over North America came to his shop to hire him to build them a wooden bonefish skiff. Over the last forty years, three sitting U.S. presidents had toured his shop and hired him to take them bonefishing. Hack was a living local legend.

A bonefish is one of the best fighting fish in the world. People come to the Bahamas from all over to try to hook one. While many game fish bite and run, peeling off maybe twenty or forty yards of line, a bonefish will strip a hundred before you have time to blink. They are highly sought after. They live on shallow flats, and consequently, getting to them requires a boat that can float in just a few inches of water. That type of boat is called a skiff, and nobody made a better bonefish skiff than Hack.

Hack had no family, no wife, and no children, which meant that the skill and artistry involved with building his skiffs would die with him. The more I got to know him, the more I realized that it was that fact that bothered Hack more than anything.

Months passed. Hack helped me with my house, and I helped him in his shop—learning what I could. One of the things that made Hack such a master craftsman with wood was his ability to seamlessly fit it together. While his boats may have required hundreds of pieces of wood, it was tough to tell that when you were sitting in one. So tight and smooth were his joints, it was as if he'd carved the thing out of a single tree. And if I had to state the one quality that made this possible, it was patience. Customers paid Hack $40,000 to $60,000 for one skiff. He made, at most, two a year. He wasn't in a hurry and wasn't motivated by money; he just loved building boats. Sometimes I'd catch him with his eyes closed, running his fingers along the wood he was sanding.

Bonefish braille.

One evening in his shop, Hack stopped sanding, ran his fingers along the lines of the wood, lost in the grain. His eyes a thousand miles beyond that shop. A whisper. "This is where I work out my anger. I rub this wood, and it forces it out, spilling it on the ground, where it drains into that water. The tide pulls it out to sea." He nodded, speaking not so much to me as the memory of something or someone. "My baptism."

A second passed before I asked my question. "How much anger is left?"

A smile. "Don't know."

"How will you know when you reach the end of it?"

"Never gotten there. But I guess I won't be angry anymore."

Tied hand in hand with his love of boats was his love of fishing for the elusive bonefish. Eighty years of casting for them meant that Hack knew where they were. Knew their patterns. What currents brought them where and what fly needed to be thrown when and how. Here, too, Hack gave me an education. And while I truly loved spending time with the old man, my gut told me that Hack was sharing what he knew with me, both about boats and bonefish, about coffee and cigarettes, about shaping wood and life in the

Bahamas, because he was alone in this world and had no one to share it with. I think Hack was looking at the end of his life and taking a lifetime's worth of experience and knowledge with him to a grave on the northwestern side of the island. This explained the resident sadness I experienced while around him. And while he knew some joy being around me, my presence did not redeem whatever he'd lost somewhere in his past. The more time I spent around him and the more I listened to him cough, the more I came to realize that Hack was saying good-bye to the world. I didn't know how long that process would take, but when Hack came to me and told me that he wanted he and I to build a skiff together—a skiff for me—I knew it was a going away present.

Hack worked most mornings before sunrise in his shop; then about once or twice a week, a client would show up and Hack would putter off in his skiff to some hidden bonefish hole. When he left with his clients, he left me alone in his shop so I met most of the guys with whom he fished. They were all the same. Überwealthy guys living the life I'd chased under Pickering, looking for peace of mind. Peace of heart. A break from the pace of their lives. They didn't love the bonefish, or Hack for that matter. They came here to conquer a bonefish so they could go home with pictures and a story and brag to all their friends. Hack knew this. He also knew that they needed what he had to offer, so he didn't judge them for their lack of character or the fact that they let their lives back home dictate the pace at which they lived. Rather than decide what pace they wanted to live and then live at that pace. When I realized this, it hit me. Hack was doing the same thing with me. He was readjusting my internal clock. The pace at which I lived. I realized this one morning sitting on my porch, staring west out across the Atlantic. My coffee had grown cold. I looked down and saw a half cup of cold coffee staring back at me. That meant, in my haste, I had not sucked it down so fast that I hadn't truly tasted it. Working with Marshall, I learned how to find and brew great coffee, but living with Hack, I learned how to taste it.

Big difference.

Somewhere in my second year with Hack, he double-booked clients for a day. Two guys show up, fly rods in hand, expecting the storied James J. Hackenworth to "put them on the fish." Hack turned to me and said, "You mind helping out an old man?"

Thus began my career as a bonefish guide.

When the guy protested, Hack backed me up. "He's better than me."

Setting out, it struck me how that was the first time anyone had backed me up in a long time. And as much as I guarded my heart from anyone, I felt a twinge toward Hack.

My client was the CFO of a Fortune 500 company with a Stanford MBA. Because I didn't want to answer a bunch of questions about how I ended up here, I decided not to give him my academic résumé. Figured it was just less complicated if he thought of me as an island bum who happened to know the location of the elusive bonefish. By the end of the afternoon, I'd put the guy on so many fish that he was rubbing his forearm to get the cramp out. Finally, he just sat down in the front of the boat, swallowed four ibuprofen, took off his hat, and shook his head. I asked, "You okay?"

"Best day of fishing ever. Period." He paid me $500 for the day, plus a $500 tip. I tried to split it with Hack but he just laughed. "What am I going to do with it? Can't spend what I got."

We sat, staring out across the water. Hack with his cigarette and I with my water. Seldom was I without a bottle of water in my hand. Hack noticed it. "You drink that a lot."

"Figure it's better than Scotch." I laughed. "Or the latest fad light beer."

"Why the bubbles?"

I glanced at the plastic bottle. "I guess I like the way it feels."

He took a long draw on his cigarette. He gazed out in front of us toward the coast of Florida some forty-four miles away. "I know you're here running from something that hurt you—from someone—but you need to know that to the folks you meet—" He pointed his cigarette at my water. "You're like that bottle of water." He squinted at me, and I thought I saw the residue of a tear. "Don't let the pain of whatever or whoever hurt you bottle itself up inside." A breeze rippled across the water and settled on us. "Everywhere on the face of this planet, water is life, and I don't know why, but you have that effect on people. They are drawn to it." He reached for my bottle and swigged from it. "They like the way it feels going down."

How I loved that old man.

Word spread and pretty soon Hack and I were both spending our days on the water. We built skiffs mornings and evenings and guided during the day. One morning I looked in the mirror, tanned, my hair turned blond in the sun, a few pounds lighter, and realized that the lifestyle agreed with me. I was reminded of the kid I once saw in the mirror. I don't know what my blood pressure was, but I knew it was a good bit less than when I worked for Marshall.

And Hack was right. Working that wood, drawing out the oil, pulled the anger out. I could see Marshall's face in my mind and not want to kill him or drive a fork through one eye and a spoon through the other. Between my folks, high school, being alone, Harvard, Amanda, her dad, I don't know how much anger I'd buried in my life, but working with Hack brought me up against the rock of it. I'm not saying that I had found a way to blast through it, but I am saying that for the first time in my life, I had pulled away the facade that masked it. If Hack had given me a gift, it was honesty with myself. Through his patience without expectations, Hack had dug down inside me and brought me face-to-face with the stone that separated me from my heart. And what he showed me was not a pebble, but rather the Great Wall of China. While I was more comfortable being honest with myself, I would not say that I grew to be honest with others.

This would come back to bite me.

One morning, a guy a few years older than me walked into the shop and started talking with Hack. He'd heard about the skiffs through some friends in Miami and wanted to know if he could order one. Hack informed him that his waiting list was now seven years long, and given the sight of Hack, the fellow could read the writing on the wall. That's when he spotted my skiff. "That yours?"

He wasn't unkind. Just curious. Opportunistic. He was also used to getting his way—or at least being able to buy it. "Yes."

"Any chance you'd sell it?"

"You like to chase bonefish?"

He shook his head. "Don't fish."

"You want to buy this skiff, but you don't fish?"

106

He nodded with a grin.

Hack smiled at me and raised both eyebrows. I wiped my hands on a rag and turned to admire my boat. "I just spent the better part of a year building it. Have had it out a half-dozen times. I don't mean to be ugly, but it would take a lot of money."

The going rate for a custom-built skiff from Hack was $40,000 to $60,000 depending on the finishings. He smiled. "How about two hundred fifty thousand? Cash."

I looked at him like he'd lost his ever-loving mind. "Are you on the level?"

"I'll have the money delivered this afternoon."

"A quarter of a million dollars? For some wood and glue and paint?"

He smiled. "And elbow grease."

Hack nodded several times and spoke out of the corner of his mouth. "Take the man's money before he changes his mind."

I looked at the boat. Then at Hack. Finally at the man. I offered my hand. "Would you like that gift wrapped?"

That afternoon, I found myself in a predicament. Just what exactly does one do with $250,000 cash?

Chapter Nine

Colin's house sat inside a gated community, the centerpiece of which was a resort hotel—a five-star-rated vacation. The resort also sold time-share condos with access to the hotel amenities, but the prizes of the community were the thirty or so ocean estates of which Colin's house was the pièce de résistance. A long driveway, nearly a half mile in length, wound out onto the rock point on which Colin's house sat, allowing for two points of entry from the water. The house faced the ocean and offered beach access down a winding path of rock and dune that led to a cabana. The back of the house led down to a deep-water port on a small, private cove—custom designed for large seafaring fishing yachts.

I docked the Bertram, tied her off, and inventoried the three other boats hanging on racks in the boathouse. I chuckled. Colin was a poor boat pilot, constantly running aground and knocking over pilings in the dock, but that did not hinder his ability to buy first-class boats. He had a great eye when it came to boats. Tiny lights had been mounted beneath every fifth step, lighting the way up the more than one hundred teak steps to the house. Whoever built this house had spared little expense. The smooth stairs wound up through the rock ledges, turning and twisting with several overlooks as I climbed higher. Off to my left, leading out of the boathouse, wound a cart path that serpentined its way around and then up the bluff. It allowed somebody with a golf cart or small car to shuttle necessities to and from the dock house without having to carry them up and down those steps.

The steps exited on the backyard, off to the side of the outdoor kitchen. Unnatural heat from the kitchen met me as I stepped around the stone wall serving as part of a chimney. One of the enormous gas grills—that could have doubled as a rotisserie —sat burning on high, and the commercial fan above it sucked up much of the heat. The residue and grease on and around the grill suggested that something had been burning at one time. I clicked off the grill and the fan, and then studied a margarita mixer, which sat mostly full and completely melted. The air smelled of rum and coconut oil. I circled the backyard and walked up onto the pool deck where the pool was lit. A couple of bathing suits and the halves of several bikinis floated in the water. Two lawn chairs sat at the bottom of the deep end. More than a hundred beer and whiskey bottles littered the backyard along with a couple dozen cigarette butts and almost as many marijuana joints, a couple of which were still stuck between paper clips. A hookah with several pipes lay on its side next to the pool.

The back of the house was mostly glass and the large doors had been slid open. One had come off its tracks and now rested on its side, crushing some bushes beneath it. Its partner had been broken and scattered in several large pieces off to the side. I stepped through a torn and flapping curtain and into the house to two smells: The first was of something having been burned in the oven. The second was something rotting in the main kitchen. Either oysters or shrimp. A glance in the sink and trash can confirmed both. If I thought the backyard was in disarray, I had another thing coming. The inside of the house was trashed. The stereo was pounding out something incomprehensible with a beat I couldn't follow, so I found the power button and killed it. Much of the furniture had been turned on end. The kitchen table sat at an angle as one leg had been broken off. Someone had punched multiple holes in the Sheetrock with something the size of an anvil. A green stuffed animal that looked like Kermit the Frog had been tied to one of the blades of the ceiling fan and was currently doing about 280 revolutions a minute. The TV had been a large flat screen before someone threw what looked like a lamp through it. The lamp was still protruding from the screen, which was now black.

The granite countertop covering the island in the kitchen had been cracked down the middle, but the most interesting "adjustment" made to the house on the first floor was that the kitchen sink faucet had been turned on and pointed away from the sink. A small river of water ran along the countertop, down the wall, along the tile floor, and down into the sunken living room, which now floated in eighteen inches of water—aided by water from a garden hose, which had been rolled in through the back door. The water had risen to the level of the top step, crested, and spilled over, cascading out a side door and onto the pool deck, where it emptied into the pool. The pool—aided by water from a second garden hose—had now filled and spilled over the zero-view waterfall that led into a smaller pool eight feet below on the second pool deck, which had also filled and was now spilling over the edge, creating a miniature waterfall down the craggy rocks leading to the beach some sixty feet below. I turned off the faucet and both hoses and then made my way upstairs. Someone had tied a curtain to the chandelier and had evidently been swinging on it from the stairwell, dislodging it from the ceiling. It now dangled by three electrical wires, threatening a dive into the recently added indoor pool below.

The seven bedrooms upstairs were no better. Each of the beds had been slept in or used by what appeared to be multiple people. One of the beds had been covered in plastic sheeting and soaked in something with the same viscosity as baby oil. Clothes and underwear lay scattered. The bath-rooms were soaking wet, and the Jacuzzi in the master bath had been filled with what was now stale and sour beer, as evidenced by the three empty kegs stacked next to it.

The master bedroom must have seen the brunt of the upstairs party because the mattress had been taken out on the balcony and someone had lit a fire in the middle of it with what looked like the remains of the master bed frame and head-board. The balcony was devoid of any other furniture. The sun had disappeared behind the Pacific and dark was falling, but one glance off the north end of the balcony proved that the furniture had been thrown down the cliff toward the boathouse. Most of it lay in splinters on the rocks.

Resting on a ledge above where the master bedroom had been sat a handheld video recorder. A cord tethered it to the master TV, which was the only piece of furniture or area of the house that had not been violated by the party. I was pretty sure I did not want to see what was on that recorder, but I thought it might help me determine if Zaul had been here and what his new best friends looked like.

The video recorder contained more than eight hours of unedited content. Someone had spent a good bit of time recording and narrating the events over what looked like three days of a rather epic party. The voice sounded female, but I couldn't understand a word as it was all spoken very fast and in Spanish. She did an excellent job of documenting the escalation of the party and the total destruction of Colin and Marguerite's house. A few minutes into the video, I heard a clinking of bottles behind me in the master bathroom. I paused the video and found a young man in what was once a tuxedo crawling out from underneath the laundry bin in the closet. He was in the early stages of waking up and experiencing the mind-splitting headache accompanying what was probably the worst hangover he'd ever known. His eyes were slits, one hand was attempting to shade his eyes, and at some point in the last day, he'd thrown up all over himself, which explained the smell. He was rank.

I looked at him and he grunted at me.

"Hi."

He lay his head back down on the floor, put one hand on the wall and one foot flat on the floor. He cracked a whisper. "Make it stop." His Spanish accent was thick and fell on the English words in all the wrong places.

I laughed. "Spinning a bit, is she?"

"Dude . . ." With that, he turned on his side and emptied what little remained in his stomach. It wasn't much. I turned the shower on cold, dragged him into it, and sat him up while the water ran down his head and chest. He might have been sixteen, and judging from his demeanor, I didn't take him for an invited attendee to the party. He looked to me to be someone who, at least initially, had worked the party.

While the water ran, I walked downstairs and scrounged up enough to make a pot of coffee. When ready, I carried a cup to the kid, who had now turned off the water and sat dripping in the shower. He accepted the mug with a thick-tongued "*Gracias.*"

I handed him some swim shorts and a T-shirt that might have been Colin's and then returned to the video. About fifteen minutes later, he stumbled out. The mug hand was both shaking and shading his eyes while the other felt and steadied his way along the wall. He began speaking in mumbled and nearly incoherent Spanish. Thirty seconds in, I held up a hand and spoke most of the Spanish I knew. "*No hablo español.*" He smiled, nodded, and began speaking slowly again in broken English. I managed to piece together that Miguel was an employee of the seafood caterer—or had been three days prior—and had accepted an invite when his shift ended to join the bartenders and work for tips. Sadly none of which were still in his pocket. But to his great pleasure, the alcohol had flowed, as had the tips, as had the girls dancing on the balcony. Following his tenure at the bar, he'd met a beautiful girl and they'd danced away the night—which he surmised was two nights ago—only to wake up in her arms on a lawn chair by the pool. They spent that day on the beach, partied into the night, and the last thing he remembered was pumping beer into the hot tub. As best he could recall, he'd been passed out in the closet for the better part of a day.

I clicked on the video and asked him to help narrate, which he did with animated delight. He told the stories of the girls and what they drank. Who liked rum. Martinis. Shots of tequila. He snapped his finger. *"Flor de Caña de bomb. E'body ly' fruit of cane."* We watched as the crowd grew and beer foam began to spew across the pool. Early on the first evening, some guy with long, sun-bleached hair dragged a hose into the house and started filling in the living room. Late into the night, bikini-clad girls swung from the chandelier. Soon, they were blindfolded, soaked in oil, and wrestling on the upstairs mattress. Somewhere in the middle of the night, another guy—a walking spark plug, muscled, bald— began breaking the teak patio furniture into splinters, which he promptly threw into a pile and doused with gasoline. The crowd of about a hundred danced around the fire, and most passed out within its glow. The second day followed much like the first, except a couple more sun-bleached and tanned guys showed up. Muscled, powerful shoulders. Not much fat. Four in total.

I pointed them out. "You know them?"

"Sí." He nodded as if it was a stupid question.

"Surfers mostly, but—" He mimicked smoking a joint. "You need som'sing, I hook you up. Dey ha' good produc."

Whenever Zaul showed in the video, one of the other four weren't far. I asked, "And him?"

He shrugged. "He new. Quiet. No smile much. But—" He rubbed the fingers together on his right hand. "He loaded."

With the video, I was able to put together a pretty good idea of Zaul's new circle of friends. Because Miguel also worked at the resort on weekends, he knew of most of the guys. Except Zaul. "No, he jes' roll in. Big wad of cash. Pay for whole party. Tip me . . ." He dug his hands into his tux pants and shook his head. "Hundred dollars."

When I asked him what had happened to everyone and their party, Miguel shrugged and pointed at the closet. His disappointment was obvious.

"Any idea where they went?"

He rewound the video and let a section play where the four surfers were talking with Zaul. They were animated, talking with their hands as much as their mouths, trying to persuade Zaul to come—and bring his money—to someplace where the waves were big and the girls were plenty and scantily clothed. Miguel translated. "Here, they talk about the surf being broken."

"Did they say 'broken' or 'break'?"

He rewound and listened again. Then he

nodded. "Break. Dey say 'break.' " He pressed play again. "Here, they talking about a resort. North o' Corinto. Son'sing about—" He shook his head trying to find the words. "A 'break' off the beach. At a reef. Thirty-foot wave. But—" He snapped his fingers and shushed me, listening another few minutes. He pointed at the TV. "First, go to León to party and stay at one of the guy's uncle's hotel where there is be a party."

"Does he give the hotel name?"

Miguel shook his head. At this point in the video, one of the guys points to Zaul, rubs his fingers together like Miguel had just done with me, and says something with a big smile at which point the other three nod. "What are they saying there?"

Miguel listened and tried to make it out. The music was loud and a couple of girls were singing in the pool, just off to the side. "Son'sing now how they meet him to '*el jefe.*' "

"They want to introduce him to someone?"

"*Sí.*"

"Who?"

"*El jefe.*"

"What's a heff-ay?"

He searched for the words. "E'body work for heem. He"—he held up a finger—"number one on flagpole."

I understood what he was saying, so I didn't bother correcting him. "Does heff-ay have a name?"

"No, but"—he pointed to one of the guys on the screen—"he know him." He kept pointing at the screen, using his hand to draw the words out of his mouth. "He think"—he pointed to Zaul—"he money be berry good. Make much more money. All around." He put his hand on the screen, covering Zaul's face. "He bank."

I was afraid of that.

I asked him if he needed a ride, and he lay down on the floor, closed his eyes, and said something about calling "his mu-herr."

Twenty minutes later, a girl riding a scooter zoomed into the driveway. The look on her face was not one of kindness. He walked outside, sort of circling her, when she promptly slapped him across the face, ushering another wave of vomit out of him and into the bushes. While he emptied himself, she continued with a verbal onslaught the likes of which I've seldom seen. I don't know if I've ever heard someone speak that fast before. After he cleaned his face with the hose, he eased onto the back of the scooter with his tail between his legs and then disappeared down the street. I don't think Miguel's wife was too happy to see him.

Around ten o'clock, I finally called Colin.

The doctors had slowly weaned Maria from her medications and brought her out of her medically induced coma. He lowered his voice. "A couple of times, we've gotten behind the pain curve. Had to play catch-up." A pause. "It's been . . . difficult." He whispered, "Especially on Marguerite."

I explained the situation with the house along with an assessment of the damage. Colin listened in silence. When I'd finished, he asked, "Any idea where he's gone?"

"I think he's chasing waves up and down the Nicaraguan coast with a group of guys who sell dope to support their surfing habit. First stop is a party in a little town called León."

Central America is a sliver of land that connects Mexico to Brazil on the northwestern tip of South America. It is bordered on the southern side by the Pacific Ocean and on the northern side by the Caribbean Sea, which fans out into the Atlantic. The countries of Central America are comprised of Guatemala and Belize on the northern tip bordering Mexico. Moving south, travelers reach El Salvador on the Pacific side and Honduras on the Caribbean. Nicaragua sits squarely in the middle with borders on either coastline before turning more due south and bleeding into Costa Rica. The last stop south is Panama—the most narrow of all the Central American countries, which explains the presence of the canal. Surf junkies had been known to chase waves from Panama to Guatemala. Nicaragua was a known surfing mecca and an obvious next stop.

"You know León?"

"Used to do business there in a former life."

"Any idea how he intends to get there?"

"Well . . . no, but he stole your truck so . . ." When Colin bought the house, he also bought a Toyota HiLux diesel four-door four-wheel drive truck and installed surf racks and oversized tires with a more Baja and aggressive grip. He and Zaul had used it to chase bigger waves up and down the coast.

I heard him mumble to himself, "I liked that truck."

I continued. "And there are no surfboards in this house."

He was quiet a minute. "Call us when you can."

"Might be a few days."

A long pause. I heard Marguerite talking in the background. Speaking over the phone, Colin picked up a conversation with her in the midst of ours. His voice lowered even more. "She does?" I heard some shuffling and Colin returned to me. "Maria wants to say hello."

More shuffling, then a garbled "Uncle Charlie?" Her voice sounded thick with sedation.

"Hey, beautiful girl. How you doing?"

"I'm—" There was a pause. Followed by some muffled cries. I heard the word "hurts" and Colin again.

"Hey. She misses you."

"How's she doing? Really."

Long pause. "Not too good." He was hurting inside. "Charlie?"

"Yeah."

"Thanks."

"For what?"

"For not constantly telling me that this is my fault."

"That's 'cause it's not."

A chuckle mixed with the hint of a muffled cry. Disbelief evident in his tone. Colin was holding it together by a thread. "It's not?"

"No." I stared out across the ocean. At the emptiness staring back at me.

"Then whose is it?"

If there was honor among thieves, Colin and I at least shared that. "It's ours."

Chapter Ten

Colin lived in Miami. He explained that he owned a fragrance company as well as a wine and spirits import company. This line of work brought him in contact with the Miami elite—athletes, movie stars, pop divas—who were often at his house. As a result, he'd turned his house into a bit of a museum and party destination. Said it was good for business. People liked to "ooh" and "aah" at his toys. He intended to put the skiff on display in his boathouse. The one stipulation to the deal was that I ferry the skiff to his house in

Miami. I looked at Hack who coughed, spat, and nodded. "For that much money, we'll paddle the sucker over there."

The following weekend, Colin sent his captain and first mate to lead us to his boat. We quickly learned that Colin kept a sixty-foot sportfisher yacht moored in Bimini. He used it to entertain clients that he would helicopter over from the mainland. While he liked boats and was attracted by the power and shine, he didn't know much about them or how to maneuver them, so he'd hire a captain and first mate to take them just offshore to find blue marlin, wahoo, tuna, et cetera.

Hack and I used the marina's crane to lift the skiff onto a specially built platform, which we anchored to his bow using some really heavy-duty tie-down straps. The following day, for the first time in almost three years, I returned to the coast of Florida.

We crossed the deep water, then through Stiltsville, Biscayne Bay, and into the lagoons that led to Colin's house. Hack sat up front, wrapped in the cloud of his own smoke, the view of the mangrove trees, and all the girls sunbathing in bikinis.

I dangled my legs over the edge and enjoyed the view of the world I'd left. Pulling up to Colin's house, Hack's eyes grew wide. It covered what looked to be three lots and must have had forty rooms. Hack flicked his cigarette out into the water. "You should've asked for more money."

I doubted he was worth more than Marshall, but he certainly did a better job of flaunting it. "Yep."

Mingling around the pool on the terrace above us, a party was in the early stages of getting cranked up. Beautiful bronzed women clad in string bikinis clung to hairy-chested men, some with massive biceps, wearing dark glasses and too many gold chains. A DJ had set up on the lawn beneath a tent and was performing a soundcheck. One girl, directly above us, leaned over the railing and winked at Hack. Hack shook his head and smiled. "I am definitely in the wrong business."

We lowered the boat and then set it on rollers that allowed us to move it at will. Same sort of idea that piano movers use. Colin's boathouse was larger than most homes and, as I would learn, was a bit of a museum for boats that other people valued. The inside was custom cedar from Canada and the lighting had been crafted like an art museum's. Inside, steel rafters had been hung that served as sliders with rollers and large hooks. He could move any boat in his house, in almost any direction. Up, down, sideways. Walking into his boathouse was like walking into the National Air and Space Museum in Washington, D.C. There were boats hanging everywhere.

He met us at the door, shook our hands, and gave us a tour, explaining his boats, their value, and what prompted their purchase. I quickly learned that my skiff was the least expensive—by a lot. I said, "You spend a lot of time in your boats?"

He shook his head. "Not really."

Finished with setting up the boat, Hack and I were loading back up on the sportfisher for the return trip when Colin asked, "You guys hungry?"

Hack stared at all the girls. "Starving."

I laughed. We made our way through the buffet, and while my eighty-year-old buddy introduced himself to every girl at the party, Colin introduced me to his wife and two kids. With black hair and eyes, Marguerite was a Spanish knockout an inch taller than Colin. She was also a concert pianist, which explained the Steinway in the acoustically perfect auditorium built as a wing on their house where she gave private concerts. Colin had met her at the Miss Universe Pageant where she'd been a contestant. Gonzalo, or "Zaul," his ten-year-old son, was wearing a T-shirt that read I'M WITH THE BAND. He was handsome, had his mom's eyes, shook my hand, and then disappeared to the backyard, where he shadowed the DJ. Colin then introduced me to his four-year-old daughter, Maria Luisa. The apple had not fallen far from the tree. She was wearing a princess dress, lipstick, her mom's high heels, and a tiara. And while Zaul's smile warmed me, Maria melted me and stole a piece of me. I knelt down and straightened her tiara, which had slid to the side. "Hi."

She had the most beautiful smile and blue eyes I'd ever seen.

Colin and Marguerite gave me a tour of the house while Maria slipped her hand in her dad's and gave me color commentary about "her" house. When we reached the theater, Colin convinced Marguerite to play. She sat and her hands rolled across the keys, producing quite possibly the most beautiful thing I'd ever heard, while Maria twirled onstage beneath the spotlight.

Later, we ate lunch and laughed at Hack, who was surrounded by every girl at the party. Late in the afternoon, Colin tapped me on the shoulder. "Got a second?"

This was not my first rodeo. I knew there was more to this tour and boat delivery than met the eye. A guy like this could have had his people deliver this boat with a snap of his fingers, but for some reason he wanted us, and I suspected me more than us.

He led me to the boathouse, where we climbed the crow's nest to the third floor and stared out across Key Biscayne. Below us, the DJ was getting the party cranked up. He was covered in rings, gold, and tattoos. Colin said, "He's a rapper. Known as 'Liv-ed.' That's devil spelled backward." Colin shook his head. "His real name is William Alfred Butler, and he's currently number one on the charts. We're rolling out his fragrance line this week."

"You like rap?"

Colin shook his head. "No, but"—he pointed to the people attending his party—"they do."

"How'd you get him here?"

"Same way I got you."

I decided to skip all the BS, so I said, "You always buy your friends?"

"My friends? No. But the people at this party? Yes."

On the lawn below us, William Butler was instructing Zaul how to hold the microphone, how to wear his hat, and then what to do with his hands while he screamed into the mike. Most gestures gave the indication that he was angry and had something to do with adjusting his groin. His hat sat off to one side and his pants had been lowered down below his buttocks. Whenever he wanted to make a point with emphasis, he held his hand up in the air, like he was holding a gun turned on its side and pulled the trigger. Zaul mimicked as best he could. I watched in mild amusement. "What's the name of his fragrance?"

"Incarceration."

A moment passed while the breeze dried the sweat on our skin. I figured I'd take the lid off. "What's the real reason you've got me three stories up staring down on the world you created and yet the one you care very little about?"

A smirk. "Perceptive." He pointed at Marguerite and the kids swimming in the pool. "They're the only ones I really care about." He waved his hand across the landscape below us. "The rest of this is just noise."

"Why do you listen to it?"

"It's necessary." He shrugged. "Which brings me to you. I don't know you from Adam's house cat, but I've a pretty good idea you didn't set out in life to build skiffs. You're running from something, and from what I can tell, you're really good at the two parts of that vocation."

"What parts would that be?"

"The first part is cutting all attachments."

I pointed at Hack, who now had a six-foot blonde sitting on his lap. He was liberally rubbing suntan oil on her shoulders. Others were waiting in line for him to do the same. "Except him. And the second?"

"The ability to keep a secret."

"How do you know that?"

"I'm pretty well connected on Bimini, and yet I can find no one who knows anything about you, other than that—after almost three years—you seem to get along well with the island legend there and that you keep to yourself. No friends. No girlfriend. No family."

I didn't respond.

"Am I right?"

I chuckled. "Answering that would sort of negate the idea behind it."

He paused. "Let me cut to the chase."

I waited.

"I'd like to hire you. On the side. Won't interfere with anything you've got going on with Hack. And you'll make more money than you can spend."

I didn't look at him. "Money is not a carrot to me."

"How about adventure, fast boats, and helicopters, seeing different shores and getting away with something."

"That would depend on the work."

"Well, to begin with, it's not legal." He waited. "Are you opposed to illegal?"

"I'm opposed to jail."

He chuckled. "Me, too. If you don't want me to go any further, you're free to enjoy the party and the guys will take you back whenever you like."

Between the bronzed girls with long legs; Hack's easy laughter; the lobster; the smells of coconut oil, rum, and spent diesel; the flashy boats; the movie stars; and pop divas walking around below me, I was drunk on the atmosphere, intrigue, and mystery.

"I'm listening."

"My dad came over from Cuba. Started with one corner grocery store. Built several. Then moved into distribution. Trucking. Warehousing. He owned everything from the field to the table. He kept his costs low, smoked out inefficiencies, and made a pile of money. He brought me in early, taught me the business and how to deliver a good product to people. I have no college education, but I know how to run a business. My dad left me $50 million, and because people like to smell good; drink fancy liquor, wine, and champagne; and suck white powder up their noses, I'm now worth close to twenty times that. I don't need money, but I do like the life and the people, and to be honest, I like the identity that comes with it. I've been poor, and given the choice, I prefer wealthy." A shrug. "That said, my business is a mix of legitimate and not. I need a runner. Someone I can trust in a business where no one is trustworthy."

His story intrigued me. I watched Marguerite walk across the backyard carrying a plate of food to a guest. "She know?"

He nodded. "I have no secrets from her."

"How is it that your father was legal and you're not?"

"You're assuming he was legal. My father started with one grocery store, and for my first few years of life, we lived in the back of it. I can remember sleeping in the big walk-in refrigerator where we kept all the produce during the August heat. Then my dad figured out how to import rum from his brothers and sell it out the back door. Soon, we were selling it out of the back of his truck, then trucks, then stores—plural." He smiled. "Dad was mostly legal. More than that, he knew how to make a dollar."

"Cocaine and rum are two very different things. That doesn't bother you?"

"If you're a drunk, don't blame the man who sold you the alcohol. I'm an entrepreneur. I provide a service. If not me, then someone else."

The problem with his line of thinking was that I completely agreed with him. "How's it work? Pragmatically. Like what's your business model?"

"Spoken like a man with an education."

So I showed Colin one of the cards I was holding close to my chest. "Harvard MBA."

He smiled and nodded. "Those people down there are just junkies with money. They think their money insulates them. Only difference is that they don't want their bad habits paraded across the front page of the newspaper, so they pay me to provide them what they want and keep their secrets. And they pay me a premium to keep it that way. They place an order, a minimum of fifty thousand—some are much higher—they transfer the money to an offshore account, and I make the delivery. Or drop. I have several runners in major cities across the country. I need one around here and up the East Coast."

"What happened to the last one?"

He pointed at a tall, thick Mr. Clean sitting off to one side with an Amazon on his lap. "He's moved into trucking. Wanted to own and run his own business, so I set him up. Sent him on his way."

"No hard feelings?"

Colin shook his head and offered nothing more.

"How about competition?"

"Competition exists when others know what need you are meeting. Others don't know of"—he waved his hand across the crowd—"their need. So, I have little—if any—competition." He shrugged. "I don't sell on street corners. Don't employ men with guns."

"If you, in fact, operate this way, then your buyers trust you."

"It also means that if I don't deliver on what I promise, that my boutique model will come crumbling down. While I possess what they want, they possess the ability to tear down my house of cards with just a few aptly spoken words. It's a"—he weighed his head side to side—"delicate relationship. So, I do what I can to massage it and make them feel at ease with me. Reassure them that they can trust me because they trust very few people. My legitimate business provides us with a fine life. All the money we want. My illegitimate business provides us with the life-style, entertainment, and adventure that my wife and I enjoy."

"What would I do? How would you pay me? I imagine I wouldn't see you too often."

He set a cell phone on the railing in front of me. "I'll get you a new SIM card with every drop. It'll either be in the boat or some place we designate. You'll never make two drops with the same SIM—"

I interrupted him. "That might make it difficult to remember the number."

"I didn't get this good and stay in this business this long by getting lazy or being stupid. The law around here knows that I exist, but that's about it."

"You keep your hands clean and I get mine dirty."

"We're all dirty. Anyone that tells you otherwise is selling something." He motioned to the phone again. "I'm the only one who will ever know this number. You don't give it to anyone. Not your mother. Sister. Hack. And certainly not your girlfriend. Keep it on 24-7."

"Sort of like a tether."

"Exactly. I'll send you coordinates, you plug them into the GPS on the boat, follow my instructions to the T, and leave the package exactly where I tell you. You never handle the people or the money. Just the drop. You're in, out, and you get to see some beautiful places and people in the process."

"What's my percentage?"

"Ten percent of whatever you're carrying with a five-thousand-dollar minimum."

"That seems like a lot of money to drive a boat."

"You won't think that if you find yourself

staring through bars. In a sense, I am buying your silence. Both now and if and when you find yourself staring at prison walls." He let the truth sink in. "I treat my people well. I'll wire the money to your offshore account before you make the drop."

"You'll pay me before I drop?"

He nodded.

"You trust me that much?"

"I need you that much. If you want to burn me? Great. Keep the money. Even in this business, loyalty means something. If you want to make a lot of money, then do what I ask, when I ask, every time I ask." He shrugged. "In some cases, because of the various businesses people are in and their desire to eliminate a paper trail, people pay me only in cash. When that occurs, I'll pay you in cash. But there will never be cash and dope in the boat at the same time. In those instances, I'll arrange payment separate from the drop, and I can't promise you it'll occur before you run." He held a finger in the air. "What you do with the cash is your business, but you do realize that if you want to continue in this line of employment you can't just go deposit it in a bank."

The pendulum had swung. I was no longer delivering pizzas, but I was back doing something I was good at. "When would I start?"

He pointed below us at a sleek black Intrepid that looked to be about forty-five feet long and powered by four outboard engines. Each engine had 350 horsepower. That meant the boat had 1,400. "I need that in the Abacos by tomorrow evening."

I slid the cell phone into my pocket and shook his hand. "I've been wanting to see the Abacos."

It was the beginning of a beautiful and profitable relationship. Colin made me an employee of Specter Import Nationale. He said the acronym didn't occur to him until after he'd filed the corporation papers, but he never changed it. From a certain perspective, it fit.

Before we left the crow's nest, he whispered, "One thing you need to know from the beginning. This business has a definite life span. There is a ticking clock for every guy like me—and now like you—who steps into this. The trick is pushing the envelope just far enough—enjoying the life and making all the money we can—and then getting out before the clock strikes twelve." He stared out across the canals and the neighborhood filled with $10 million and $20 million homes. "There will come a day, and it will come in a flash, when this will end. When this ride is over. When the only business that remains is legitimate. When the pool deck is empty. And when that day comes, you have to be willing to walk away. Period. We are simply riding a wave."

Chapter Eleven

I slept in a hammock hanging on the balcony of the master bedroom. The breeze was cool and the sound of the ocean reminded me of my hurricane shack on Bimini. I thought of Hack; his laughter; his love of boats, bonefish, cigarettes, and women —all women. From there I wandered to Shelly and the pain etched across her face when she'd met me on the beach. It was the same look of pain worn by Amanda the last time I'd seen her standing in the snow outside her parents' house. What was it with me and women standing in some form of water, experiencing pain of my doing? I left and wondered what sick scheme Marshall was up to and just how miserable Brendan had become now that he was waiting for the old man to die so he could get his money. I ended, as I did most nights, staring into the emptiness that had become my life. At the series of disconnected events that marked moments of direction in my life. I often tried to connect these dots. To see one event through the meaning of another. I could not. They shared no relation. They did not connect.

I woke at daylight desperately craving a good cup of coffee. Rummaging through the kitchen, I found some frozen beans in the fridge and managed a cup. Staring across the mug, I decided to leave the Bertram at anchor and set out across land. I needed to get to León, then Corinto, and while she could certainly get me up to Corinto, she'd be no good to me once there. Colin's home had a well-protected and safe berth. I just needed transportation.

Standing in the kitchen, I pulled down a framed picture of Zaul where, undoubtedly, Marguerite could look at it while washing dishes. I removed the picture and put it in my wallet.

The garage was empty, but there was a single room next to it that looked like it might house the lawn equipment. I tried the handle, but several locks barred the door. Evidently, the partygoers had not bothered to open these. I found Colin's keys, unlocked the doors, and smiled at Colin's good taste. "Bingo."

Colin's house bordered a Costa Rican national park. Mostly dunes, it contained miles of sandy roads and was an ATVers paradise. Obviously, Colin and his family had bought the truck to chase waves and the ATVs to ride the dunes. This room was where he kept all these toys. Complete with three four-wheelers and two motorcycles, one of which was a KTM 600 with a few modifications. Essentially, an Enduro dirt bike bred for long stretches on the desert or back roads on which someone had slapped a tag and two turn signals thereby making it street legal.

Perfect.

I grabbed what I needed from the boat, stuffed it in a backpack, and hid a key for Colin's workmen who would arrive throughout the next week and begin repairing the house. Then I hopped on the back of the motorcycle, pulled down my Costas, and turned north.

Six hours later, I was circling the cathedral in León, searching for both a hotel and a really good cup of coffee.

I stepped off the bike, blanketed by humidity and a sweltering mirage of heat. Hotel Cardinal promised air-conditioning, hot water, and Wi-Fi. I paid cash for my room, and the tall skinny guy at the counter led me through a lounge, down a long hall, around what looked like a communal kitchen, out into an open area filled with enormous trees, and finally to one of two rooms in the rear of the property. It was large and did in fact contain AC. I dropped my bag, set the air control on "snow," and set out on foot in search of a café.

León has sixteen churches, but the largest single structure in León, and most of Central America for that matter, is the cathedral. Rumor holds that when the Spanish landed here almost five hundred years prior, they thought they were in North America. Wanting to stake their claim to the land and establish the new national religion, they set out to build the largest cathedral in the Americas. To their credit, they succeeded. Problem was they did it in the wrong Americas.

I walked the sidewalk next to the cathedral and spotted a café kitty-corner to the entrance. The café offered umbrella shade and oscillating fans, which served to move the heat from one table to the next. I chose a table with a good view of the front of the flowing fountains.

Once seated, I began to detect a smell that did not agree with me. I first blamed the sweaty guy next to me, but then the fan oscillated in my direction and pushed it back at me. I checked my shoes. Nothing. I checked the table. Under the table. Still nothing. Finally, my nose convinced me that I was what I was smelling. I was ripe. And I was in desperate need of a shower and some deodorant.

The kid waiter stood in front of me and tapped a pencil to a pad of paper. While I didn't speak Spanish, I knew enough to say, *"Café."*

He smiled and said, *"Con leche?"*

I knew what that meant and had heard it before, but the words weren't taking shape in my mind. I shrugged and shook my head. He began making hand motions like he was milking a cow. *"Vaca. Leche."*

I smiled. "Milk would be great."

He returned in a few minutes with a very hot and very good cup of coffee.

I didn't know where to start, but I had a feeling that if I waited until dark, I could find the party by the sound. My experience with folks in Central

America was that they loved music. But more than that, they loved it loud. I finished my coffee, ordered a second cup, and watched the city unfold around me.

The fountains fed out from the front steps of the church and serpentined through an open park for the better part of a city block. In terms of volume of water, they certainly contained more than an Olympic-size pool.

Sipping my coffee, I noticed that several cars had pulled up to my left and parked with an advantageous view of the park. The drivers had exited and were now sitting on top of the hoods of their cars. Next to them, several police cars did likewise. The officers were now standing, tapping their hands with their billy clubs and making light laughter as they waited for something to occur in the park.

The police didn't look like cops in the States. Their clothes were disheveled, unkempt, shirts untucked, no pistols on their belts. A few rested shotguns on their shoulders, but they didn't look all that ready to use them. One of them had a radio, but it looked as if the three of them were sharing it or the other two didn't care enough to carry it. Their vehicles looked much like they did. Dirty. Hadn't been washed in a while. Little tread on the tires. Numbers and emblems faded. The manner in which they held a conversation with the guys in the cars next to them gave me the impression they had not so much accepted their task to "enforce or keep the peace," but rather to "observe the festivities until they got out of hand, at which time they could either join in or quietly disperse." Their friendly, just-one-of-the-guys banter gave me the impression that they were friendly with whom they wanted to be friendly.

While I observed them, one of the guys started snapping his fingers and pointing in an attempt to get the attention of all the rest, which he promptly got. Before me, something of a loose crowd, maybe fifty or sixty people, had gathered at the park. All eyes were trained on the far end of the fountain where a young lady, probably early twenties, was standing on the edge of the fountain wearing a trench coat.

She had dark hair to her shoulders, no shoes, and her hands were perched on the belt of her coat. She twirled once, then a second time, and began what can only be described as a ballet on the edge of the fountain. This continued for a moment or two while the jeering and catcalls increased. Judging from her appearance, something was a little "off" in her expression. She neither heard them nor cared. She wasn't performing for them.

With little notice, she unbuckled her coat, slipped it off her shoulders, and continued her dance.

Completely naked.

The boys around me watched in marked fascination, but there was nothing seductive about it. The more I watched her movements, the more it became obvious that she was not mentally functioning on the same level as everyone else. Dancing for an audience of one, her ballet continued. Her spins were not fluid, turns not complete, not beautiful, nor was she or her figure. She would have never graced the cover of a women's fashion magazine. None of which mattered to her.

She continued spinning and turning like a top out of balance. While I say she wasn't beautiful, she was very much a woman and—despite her deficiencies at dance—that was what the crowd had come to see. Spinning her way toward the middle of the park and the fountain, she dove into the water and frolicked about like a dolphin, baring every side and end of herself. People stared through binoculars, long camera lenses, and inched closer for a better look.

While this was occupying center stage of the park, some seventy-five yards away, several hundred husbands, wives, and children were climbing the steps into the cathedral for Friday evening Mass where the organ was ushering the call to worship.

With the organ music filling the air, offering auditory bookends to the verbal calls for more jumps and movements where she threw one leg

141

high into the air, the ballerina climbed back up onto the ledge of the fountain and pirouetted her way closer to the steps. The closer she danced to the doors, the more obvious it became that she was listening to music that none of the rest of us heard and dancing to a beat we couldn't follow.

A short distance from the entrance to the fountain, she dove back into the water, spun on the surface, and then performed handstand after handstand, which worked the crowd in a foaming frenzy. As more and more churchgoers walked up the steps, I began to notice that the entirety of her dance was serving to move her closer to the front of the cathedral and something about her timing was, either purposefully or not, structured to land her on the front steps about the time the Mass started.

Which begged the question, What were the priests going to do when that naked woman walked into their church?

I didn't have the answer but I was going to find out. My waiter returned with my check and didn't seem too interested in the dance, suggesting that he'd either seen it before or he'd been sufficiently warned by his mother not to let his eyes wander. Either way, unlike half the police force of León, he went about his business, busing tables. I paid my tab and stood as the ballerina danced herself out of the fountain and onto the first step. She then performed a rather awkward approach toward the door. Had anyone in their right mind attempted her movements, it would have been described as "erotic," but when added to the disconnected look on her face and her disjointed movements, my overriding emotion was not excitement or titillation, but sadness.

She danced herself up the stairs to the front door. We heard singing and prompted recitation echoing from the inside. She continued to dance between the doors, kicking her legs here, throwing her arms there. Then, just as quickly as she'd appeared, she disappeared through the front door of the cathedral. Disappointed that the show had come to a close, the crowd began to disperse. I crossed the street, went up the steps, and through the giant wooden doors some twenty-plus feet tall. Inside, I found that most of the congregation had already filed down the center aisle for Communion. Many knelt or prayed, both at the altar or back at their pews. The priest stood center stage, bread and wine in his hands. Offering to all takers.

Including the ballerina.

I arrived in time to witness her finish her dance down the center aisle directly in front of the priest who, to his credit, was staring into her eyes. I leaned against a column wanting to see how this would play out. Just how would "the church" deal with someone like her?

Standing at an angle to the priest, she

genuflected and stuck out her tongue. He dipped the bread in the wine and placed it on her tongue, prompting a second genuflection. About this time, two more priests appeared from the left with a long red robe, which they quietly wrapped around her shoulders as she moved to the altar. While she knelt, eyes closed, lips moving, they stood silently by her side, offering prayers of their own.

Standing there scratching my head, a priest tapped me on the shoulder and ushered me forward in his best broken English. "You?" He motioned toward the railing. "Go."

I shook my head. "No."

He smiled. "You welcome. We welcome you."

Another shake. "You don't have enough bread."

"You hungry?" He smiled, but his eyes told me that the question he asked wasn't the question he was asking.

I shook my head.

He pointed toward the altar and nodded excitedly. "*Redención.*"

I stepped aside; he smiled, nodded, and walked around me toward some other folks standing in the rear of the church.

Dark had fallen outside as I returned to the hotel. I stood in the shower, smelling of clean soap and thinking back to that bread. The woman in the church was naked. That's all. I was dirty. The water turned cold as I listened to the echo of the priest's voice.

I had my doubts.

For whatever reason, I hadn't eaten in almost forty-eight hours so I stepped out into the streets and followed my nose to a roadside café. The owner was round; wiping her head with a towel, she smiled and handed me a menu printed in both English and Spanish. When I worked for Marshall, I'd learned to order only cooked food and not drink anything that doesn't come in a can, which you see opened, and never anything with ice. I pointed at items on the menu. Beans, rice, and some cooked meat. She nodded, punched numbers into the cash register, and motioned to a table where I sat waiting, sipping from a water bottle. The food appeared a few minutes later. The smell was intoxicating, and the meal hot and delicious. I ordered a second plate and ate until I was thoroughly stuffed.

The young guy working the desk at the hotel didn't know of any parties of note, but he told me that the nightlife of León occurred about seven blocks "da' way."

I had parked the bike behind the hotel in a locked area where guests kept their cars. The area was very small and crowded bumper to bumper with cars. In order to get my bike, which was jammed into the far corner, my young friend would have had to move the five cars in its way. When I saw what was required, I waved him off. "I'll walk."

• • •

I had walked three blocks away when the first wave hit me. The nausea came, followed with little warning by projectile. I had enough time to turn my face toward the street before the contents of my stomach exited my mouth. This occurred several times, dropping me to my knees. Once my stomach was empty, the urge reversed course and hit my bowels with the impact of a train. Had I been in my own home, I would not have had time to get to the bathroom. This expulsion was also projectile, and I was powerless to control it.

Seconds later, I found myself kneeling in the road, both hurling and soiling myself. I don't know how long this lasted, but my guess is several hours. The result left me exhausted and teetering on delirium next to the curb. I do know that several people walked around me, holding their noses and speaking in hushed tones. I held out as long as I could but finally collapsed next to an old building, a trail behind me. I could control no aspect of my bodily functions and curled up in complete weakness and a foggy semi-consciousness.

Some time later, a man with a broom poked me and said something in Spanish. I had no idea what he said, but his tone told me it was not positive. With his broom in my ribs, I crawled a block and up next to an even dirtier old building. Somewhere in the middle of the night, I felt a hand tugging on my arm and another rifling through my pocket. I grabbed it and tried to hold on but was unable.

Daylight bore through my eyelids and warmed the air around me, stimulating the unbearable smell of myself. I was weak. Could not stand. Could barely open my eyes and the cramping pain in my stomach was excruciating. The only relief came in those moments when my body relinquished control of itself. I was aware that people were walking around me and probably talking about me, but I did not care.

The only thing I knew for certain was that I was unable to help myself.

I passed out again. Above me, church bells rang and woke me. When I opened my eyes, my vision was blurry, but I could detect two people walking from my left to my right. One was smaller than the other. I think they were holding hands.

I reached out my hand and they circled around me. From one of the figures, I heard a small, quiet voice. The voice spoke in Spanish. I heard the word "*borracho.*" Then a pause. Then another voice responded in Spanish. I don't know what they said and I didn't know if they spoke English, but I'd been around enough to know what *borracho* meant. As the voices and the feet that moved them shuffled by me, I extended my hand and said, "I'm not drunk." They slowed but didn't stop. I whispered again, "I'm not drunk."

A pause.

She was small. A child. She knelt, lifted her shirt to cover her nose against the stench, and with one finger lifted my eyelid. A larger shadow fell across me, and then I felt a finger, stronger and more purposeful, on my carotid. Another pause. The voice belonging to the large shadow said, "How long have you been like this?" Her English was as good as mine, but her accent was thick.

"Last night."

"When did you arrive?"

"Yesterday."

"Did you eat?"

"Yes. A café."

"You remember the name?"

"No."

"What'd you eat?"

"Beans, rice, and meat."

"Was it steaming?"

"Yes."

"What'd you drink?"

"Bottled water."

She paused another second. "You eat any chips?"

"Two or three bowls."

I could hear her smile when she spoke. "You eat any salsa with that?"

That's about when the truth hit me. Salsa is made with fresh and often uncooked vegetables. "Two or three bowls."

She covered her nose with her hand. "Wow. You really stink."

She pulled out a cell phone, called someone who responded; she spoke in Spanish, and within a few minutes a truck pulled up next to the sidewalk upon which I'd soiled and sprawled. The truck backed up, a man exited and lowered the tailgate, and the woman said to me, "You want my help, get in the truck."

I crawled along the street, pulled myself up on the tailgate, and was physically unable to get myself inside, prompting the driver to lift me in.

I lay down in the back of the truck; the engine whined, clutch slipped, and I fell asleep beneath the smell of spent fuel and the heat of a rising sun.

During my sleep, I remember cold sweats and fever. More vomiting and diarrhea. Then I vaguely remember a sting in my arm, and later someone telling me to roll over and relax and then shoving something up my rectum to which I was powerless to object.

I woke to the soft light of evening. Above me, in the gap between the concrete block walls and the tin roof, I could hear dogs barking, a pig grunting, several birds singing farther off, kids playing what sounded like soccer, someone chopping wood, a fire crackling, and the sound of a passing car. I could hear food simmering close by and could smell the wood fire and coffee, which helped leverage open my eyes.

My room was hot, ninety degrees or better, and my skin was painted in my own sweat. I lay naked beneath a sheet, but I was clean. I could smell soap. The oscillating fan to my left clicked, paused, and began its return in my direction, pushing the wave of heat across my skin. An IV bag dripped over my left shoulder, running down a clear tube that ended in a needle that had been inserted and taped into my arm. I reached to touch it, but a hand rested gently on mine. "Antibiotics."

It was the same voice I remembered hearing on the sidewalk beneath the bells.

She spoke again. "Think you could hold down some water?"

"I don't want to put anything near my mouth. Ever again."

Her laughter was easy and quiet. She held a cup to my lips. "Come on. Sooner you start drinking, the sooner you get that needle out of your arm."

My stomach felt better and I was very thirsty. I lifted my head and sipped.

She had black hair tied up in a bun. Dark skin, toned muscles, and sweat on her top lip. She wore a long skirt to her ankles, sandals, and a loose short-sleeve shirt. She said, "It's water, lemon juice, honey, and a touch of salt."

I swallowed and sat back, coming to grips with

the realization that such a small effort required so much of me. I was exhausted. My tongue felt thick as I licked my lips. "Tastes like bleach."

She held the cup again to my lips. "Least we know your taste buds still work." A pause. "It kills bacteria. In the water and in you."

I sat back and closed my eyes. "What happened to me? And where am I?"

"Amebic dysentery. You're in Valle Cruces." She held out her hand. "Paulina Rodriguez Flores." The way she said Paulina sounded like "Pow-leena." "You're in my uncle's house."

"Are you a doctor?"

"Nurse. But around here, those two occupations are a bit blurred." She crossed her legs. "Want to tell me what you were doing out there? I'm assuming you were mugged because your pockets were empty."

For the first time, I noticed my left wrist. There was no watch on it. Again. "You didn't happen to notice a watch on my left arm, did you?"

She shook her head.

"I remember someone tugging on me, but it's all a little hazy. I'd had a bite and went out for a walk after."

"What are you doing in León?"

"Your English is good."

"College in Virginia. Studied medicine at the University of Miami. And you didn't answer my question."

"It's a long story, but I'm looking for a kid."

"Is he in trouble?"

"If he's not, he will be." I continued, "And not to be indelicate, but did you shove something up my butt?"

She laughed. Easily. "Suppository. I was tired of cleaning up your mess."

I tried to counter with humor. "You do that with all your guests?"

"Nope. You're the first." She stood and walked to the curtain that acted as the door. "Get some rest. You've been asleep for over two days."

I pointed out the single window. Several miles in the distance sat a volcano. It stood three to five thousand feet above us. Its shoulders were green, lush, and a second smaller volcano sat off to its right. "What's that?"

Her Spanish accent was thick when she spoke the name, proving that she moved fluidly between English and Spanish. "San Cristóbal."

"It's smoking."

"He does that."

"Why?"

"He likes to remind us."

"Of what?"

"The fact that he's in control and we're not. Life around here is like that."

"Why do you call it a 'he'?"

She laughed easily. " 'Cause a 'she' would never do that to these beautiful people that she loves."

"Are you one of those women who doesn't like 'hes'?"

"No, I like 'hes' just fine. Used to be married to one, but if you look closely enough around here, you'll find that the source of ninety nine percent of our problems are 'hes' and that's not just the 'she' in me talking." I decided to shut my mouth before I got myself in trouble with a woman who had no problem shoving something up my butt.

"Yes, ma'am."

She continued. "You should sleep. You were pretty close to being in a real bad way."

Sleep fell heavy on me, but my mind was spinning. I couldn't help but think of the time I'd lost. Any trail I'd had that might have been hot regarding Zaul had long since grown cold.

Before I dozed off, I heard the sound of a young girl speaking Spanish with Paulina. I also heard the sound of water being poured over someone, which suggested she was bathing just beyond the wall. Later, maybe early morning, I heard the deep tone of a man's voice whispering with Paulina. And while I didn't understand a word he said, his tone toward her was tender. Almost fatherly.

Chapter Twelve

In the beginning, most of my drops were South Florida. Eventually, Colin stretched me to the other islands and points south. Given my stellar six-month record, Colin called. "You mind making a few pickups? You can say no, but . . . the money's pretty good."

Like it or not, and despite my denials, money had become the carrot. As had getting away with something few were willing to risk—and every time I hopped in that boat, I was risking my freedom. As much as I denied and tried to act like it was not, money gave me the one thing nothing else did. Control. It allowed me to trust and depend on no one.

"A pickup is just a delivery in reverse. I'm in."

He laughed.

I had also become an adrenaline junkie. I knew more about boats than the people who made them, and given my rather advanced woodcrafting skills after working with Hack, I got pretty good at retrofitting boats with compartments that were almost impossible to detect. Soon I was driving drug-laden boats real fast between Miami and Cuba, the Cayman Islands, Jamaica, El Salvador, Honduras, Puerto Rico, and Nicaragua. Sometimes as far north as Savannah and Charleston.

Colin kept a fleet of about ten boats. Give or take. And he was always trading. Always buying and selling. Seldom, if ever, did I drive the same boat a second time to any location. His entire fleet was seaworthy, and most were worth a half million or more, averaged forty-fifty feet, carried a lot of fuel, and were deceptively fast. As in, when fully fueled, which they were, they could maintain 100 miles per hour for several hours. The trick—and it was why I stayed in the game so long at such a high level—was never using all that speed. Look like you're out for a Sunday stroll, and people believe you are. It was just one more bluff.

High risk, high reward. Running drugs was an adrenaline rush and I loved it. I also kept it entirely to myself. I talked to no one about it. Not even Hack. I had a sense that he suspected something, but he never said anything. We continued building skiffs, and I helped him guide when he needed help. But at night, when he'd go to sleep, I'd leave Bimini churning in an angry wake. And I got really good at traveling by chart, radar, and GPS. Sometimes, if the drop was close and the weather agreed, I'd return at midnight. Sometimes I was gone a day. Sometimes two. Given all my Central American travel, it would have helped had I learned Spanish, but I managed. I could find a bathroom or order bottled water, but that was about it. My best talent was learning how to be visible yet invisible, not draw attention, how to "fly under the radar," how to not look guilty, and how to avoid detection.

I had one problem. So did Colin. And if we were riding a wave, our problem was a tsunami and it was gaining quickly. And that was the idea of control—which was an illusion—and there was nothing we could do about it.

Colin and Marguerite had adopted me as family. As did the kids. I taught Maria how to tie her shoes, jump rope, whistle, drive a boat, and bait her hook. I knew which rib was the most ticklish, that she liked ketchup and mayonnaise but hated mustard, and I'd attended all twenty-one of her dance recitals. I'd helped her with her math homework, picked her up from school, run with her the first time she ever ran three miles without stopping, and of all the stuffed animals on her bed, the fluffy monkey with the long tail that I'd given her was the one tucked under her arm every morning.

If I'd ever been committed to one woman in my life, it'd been Maria and every time she said "Unca Charlie," I melted.

At least once a week, I drove her to school, but not before stopping off at Krispy Kreme where the HOT NOW sign was flashing glow plug red. "Uncle Charlie" became the de facto babysitter and I loved it. Maria followed in her mother's footsteps, and Zaul fell in love with two things: surfing and the life—and look—of a rapper.

While Maria owned the spotlight, Zaul shared his mother's gift of music and, at one time, could make a piano sing. He had his father's quick mind—a whiz with math, could solve complex problems with relative ease, and had always disliked school. I was with him when Colin took him to his first Dolphins game, and I got to sit courtside with him at his first Heat game. We caught umpteen lobsters together both in Bimini and around the Keys, snorkeled around dozens of wrecks, and speared some really big fish in forty to sixty feet of water. Unlike Maria, Zaul wasn't friends with the masses, but he was good friends with a few.

Despite mine and Colin's best attempts at influence, Zaul was attracted to two things: others' attention and things that glitter. Especially people.

To insert himself, to get noticed, he'd jump off the dock house—three stories up. Then he'd jump off and do a front flip. Then a back. Then two backs. As he grew older, he constantly ramped up his appeals to impress people. Soon he was trying to impress the attendees at his dad's parties. And while that was cute at first, I saw Colin begin to wrestle with how to control a son who was growing out of control. And the effect showed on Marguerite's face. The wrinkles above her eyes. If my life with Colin was a controlled burn, Zaul's life was a smoking heap and had the possibility to become a wildfire out of control.

Shortly after I met him, Zaul began hanging with the wrong crowd. Sneaking out. He changed his clothes. His mannerisms. He spent his days and most of his nights, 24-7, calculating how to be or become cool in other people's eyes. Everything he did, every action he took, had been precalculated to draw, and hopefully keep, attention. He was driven by bitter envy and selfish ambition. Where Maria had gravitated toward beauty, Zaul was attracted to power—and wielding it. He saw his father, the circles he walked in, the money he spent, and somewhere in that mind of his, he decided he wanted it. He spent less time at home, snuck out more, had three tattoos before his folks knew about the first. He was buying, selling, and smoking dope before he was twelve; cussed out his mom when he was thirteen; had a diamond stud earring by fourteen; and, following his sixteenth birthday, had wrecked two new cars before the permanent tags had arrived in the mail.

Colin and Marguerite were not unaware. They knew they were losing or had lost control of Zaul, but the seeds of that were sewn long ago. They'd given him a generous allowance since he was ten. Pampered. Enabled. Made apologies for. Rolled out the silver platter. Let him do as he pleased. If he wanted something, he demanded and they gave. They erected no boundaries in his life, and hence, he operated by few, if any. A few months ago, he bought himself a $20,000 gold Rolex with a diamond bezel. A month later, when he turned up one morning with a black eye, a busted lip, and no watch, he hopped in his car and bought another.

The last real glimmer of light I'd seen with Zaul came just after he'd turned fourteen. I'd been sitting on the dock with Maria, feeding the fish, when Zaul appeared with a stack of playing cards. "Uncle Charlie . . . you teach me how to play poker?"

Zaul had so retreated into his own world and I saw him so seldom that interactions between us were scarce. And conversations with his folks were almost nonexistent. His sudden interest in me surprised me. I could tell Colin and Marguerite were worried, so I was looking for a way, any way, to engage Zaul. When he invited me in, I jumped on it.

Zaul and I met in his dad's boathouse and played every week for the better part of six months. And I think in his own way, he began looking forward to our "weekly game" as he called it. He listened, learned, and got proficient, but he wasn't any good. The only part of the game he was good at was losing money. Which he could do as well as the best of them. And he couldn't bluff to save his life. His greatest strength was also his greatest weakness. Despite his tough exterior, Zaul had his mother's heart. Tender and honest. That may make for a good human being, but it makes for a very bad poker player. To compensate for this "inadequacy," he kept wanting me to teach him how to cheat. In order to keep him in my life, I taught him two or three tricks—real novice stuff—but I never thought he'd actually try to use them in a real game.

Then about a year ago, he quit showing up at the boathouse. I hadn't seen him much since.

One interesting development occurred during this time. American distilled spirit consumption changed and grew at the same time, and people's desire for rum doubled and tripled overnight. Colin was pretty well connected in the legitimate Central American rum trade. So while I was a drug runner, I became a legitimate rumrunner. Sugarcane production in Central America was at an all-time high, as was rum production. People couldn't get enough of it, and while our margins on rum weren't what they were on cocaine, good rum business allowed Colin to launder more money through SIN. While we imported some through legitimate channels in and around Miami customs, we also hired barges and floated some north to the islands, where we unloaded and stored it until I could carry batch loads over. I soon found myself making the forty-four-mile crossing every other day. Sometimes every day. A few times I made it twice a day. Colin and I knew this had to be attracting attention, and his two well-paid contacts in the DEA confirmed this. So I never drove the same boat twice and never dropped at the same place twice. On three occasions, we got a tip that law enforcement was waiting on us in a canal en route to the Keys. I anchored just off-shore, thumbed a ride back to Miami, "borrowed" one of Colin's museum boats, and made my way home by tacking north some ninety miles and then coming in on the eastern "back" side of Bimini. The "abandoned" vessel was reported on the news along with the suspicion of drugs, but they found none because—with Colin's full agreement—I'd fed the fish.

The Bahamian police soon clued in to the fact that we were running rum through the island, and they wanted a cut. Gladly. By the caseload. We gave them all they and their families could drink. We wanted to keep them as happy with us as possible, and they were. They never bothered us. Didn't check our boats. Didn't wake me up in the middle of the night. In fact, they ran interference for us when the larger U.S. agencies came knocking.

Given my special set of skills, Colin leaned on me more and more. On the surface, Colin and I ran a successful business. Beneath the surface, we sold and delivered a lot of cocaine to very wealthy people, who paid us a lot of money to keep their identities and habits hidden. Which we did. Business grew. When I hadn't seen Hack in a week, he came knocking and found me asleep. I'd been out all night and returned only about an hour before he shook me.

He held a cup of coffee next to my nose and said, "Come on. Your porch is calling you."

I sat and he jumped right in. "I was once crazy like you." An exhale and a smile. "I ran rum before it was legal. I told you once I'd never been off this island." He shook his head. "That's a lie. I been over a good part of this hemisphere and bought and sold more rum than most companies." He lit a second cigarette with the dying embers of the first. "I don't fault you for what you're doing. If people want to blow that white stuff into their lungs, so be it, but let me offer you one bit of advice." He turned to me. "I have love one woman in this world." Hack often dropped the "d" on his past-tense verbs. "Love her with all of me. One night pirates wanted our boat. A lot of rum. I tell them they no can have it." He sucked through his teeth. "So because they could not take my boat, they took her. Shot her." He pointed at his stomach. "Painful. I buried her at sea." A long pause. "It's been over forty years and the hurt hasn't gotten any better." A nod. "So, you do what you want. You've a right to that, but just know that the business you're in does not have a happy ending. No one . . ." He waved a finger in the air.

"And I mean no one, no matter how smart, ever stays in and escapes what they got coming."

I nodded. I knew I was pressing my luck. But while getting in was one thing, getting out was another.

At the age of thirty-five, I checked my offshore balance and found I was sitting on an excess of $2 million. And while it wasn't "about the money," it sure beat working for Marshall. Later that week, I woke early and en route to the bathroom tripped over a bag holding several hundred thousand in cash. That had me a bit stumped. Where could I put that much money where no one would ever think to look for it? Not knowing, I asked Hack and he showed me with a smile. "Same place I hid mine when I was your age."

Colin and I ran a tight operation. We didn't run volume. We ran quality. And using some well-placed and well-paid law enforcement contacts, we ran it only to folks Colin vetted. We charged a premium, but what we offered in return was a product seldom equaled with the added bonus of complete anonymity and the promise that the buyer—who was usually extremely wealthy—didn't get noticed on some ransom checklist or written up in the paper after he was busted by some high-tech narcotics unit. Our job was made all the easier in that most of our clients were public figures. We knew who they were because we either saw them on TV, bought their albums, read about them in the paper, or listened to them make public speeches. This made us very profitable, successful, and busy.

One of the perks of running drugs from Miami to Central America was how much time it afforded me in Costa Rica, Honduras, Guatemala, and Nicaragua. I'd take one of my boats south out of Bimini, set a course around Cuba for a destination given me by Colin, dock the boat, and either make the drop at the dock or, if the customer preferred, travel inland. I traveled light, alone, and saw some beautiful country.

Another year passed. Then another. And another.

To justify my life, I began having conversations with myself. Long, drawn-out arguments where, eventually, one side told the other side to "shut up." I didn't realize it, but my inner turmoil was ramping up and whatever peace I'd found on Bimini was leaking out. I figured people could string themselves out all they wanted and it had little to do with me. If you drive a car that burns gas, don't blame the petrol company for the pollution you make. I'm not saying this was right, I'm just saying it's how I thought.

There were three bright places in my heart. Hack, Maria—who was budding into puberty and a beauty that surpassed that of even her mother— and Zaul, who continued to push the envelope. Where Maria was her parents' joy, Zaul kept them up nights. First, he'd started with one earring, which his mother thought was cute. He followed it with another and then a third. Body piercings appeared soon thereafter. Soon he delved into tattoos. And like earrings, one was followed by two and three and so on. At last count, he had eight and was making plans for two more.

Zaul routinely reeked of marijuana and alcohol, and for every one night he spent at home, he spent four or five elsewhere. He skipped the last quarter of his sophomore year in high school, resigning himself to spending his days practicing his rhymes and lifting weights. He spent his nights hopping from underground rap scene to strip bar. I know because I followed him. Given Spanish genetics, a five o'clock shadow at 9:00 a.m., and what I guessed were healthy amounts of growth hormone, he looked twenty-five. He denied it when I asked, but the sight of his biceps suggested he was shooting steroids. I told him it would wreak havoc on his kidneys, and while it might swell his arms and make his shirts tight, it would shrink him in other areas. He laughed and said, "Wives' tale." I knew better. He was huge.

One morning, I searched his car while he was passed out in his room. Given the new tattoo of a Glock pistol on his chest, I was looking for anything resembling a firearm beneath his seat. I didn't find one, but I did find a spent shell casing for a .40 caliber. I tucked it in my pocket and made an honest attempt to spend more time with Zaul. While his exterior had become angry and prone to showy bouts of violence, I knew better. Zaul was a tenderhearted kid trying real hard to show everyone, starting with his dad, that he was cool and worthy of their admiration and respect. He had grown up in a world where everybody around him was "somebody" and yet he—in his mind—was a "nobody." Little more than Colin's son. With zits and an occasional stutter. Problem was, Zaul—the kid who once asked me to teach him how to finish a Rubik's Cube, bait a hook, and steer a boat—was getting his affirmation in all the wrong places and from people who were just as lost and insecure as he.

Colin and Marguerite had a problem, and it wasn't just the cocaine or cash buried in their underground bunker. Zaul had everything. And he had nothing. He presented to the world that his life was bubbling over. In truth, he was desert dry. North Africa wrapped in skin.

Zaul was the most popular guy in school. Wild parties, famous movie stars, singers, rappers, fashion designers. His dad's driveway was always filled with guests' Lamborghinis or Ferraris or the latest Porsches. Zaul's house was every kid's dream. Problem was that all that glitter and gold was merely a mask for the shells that owned it.

I was the exception and the only person in his life who saw beyond his facade and loved him anyway. While his parents were ready to ship him off, I saw a kid who was a lot like me and on whom I'd had great influence.

I never talked about my "work" with Zaul, but he wasn't stupid. While the rap lifestyle faded, the angry, tattooed surfer, who drove expensive cars and wielded power because of the money he had, grew more and more attracted to the life I led. He saw the boats I drove, the fact that I seldom wore anything more dressed up than flip-flops, that I always carried cash and that I went where I pleased. That I punched no time clock. That while I worked with and for his dad, I answered to no one, and if I had an office, it existed on the water.

One night I found him drunk, passed out on the dock. Alone. I couldn't carry him, so I set a pillow under his head, covered him with a sheet, and sat nearby for a few hours while he slept it off. Somewhere in the middle of the night, he woke in a drunken and fearful stupor. When he found me next to him, he pointed in my general direction and with barely discernible words said, "Of all the people in this world I'd like to be—" He shook his head. "It's not my dad." He tried to touch my nose with his finger.

Zaul was nose-diving, so I suggested to Colin and Marguerite that they take the family away for the summer. Buy a house somewhere in Central America and spend the summer chasing good waves with Zaul and looking for shells with Maria. Given the nature of our business, I knew Colin could run SIN from anywhere as well as he could from his desk. Plus, a break would do him good.

To his credit, he did.

Colin bought a home in Costa Rica—on the coast. Made-to-order waves right out the back door. I ferried the family down in one of his boats and dropped them off. I'd done some research and found this board shaper who lived a few hours away. Made boards for all the pros. I paid him to be there when we arrived and spend some time with both Zaul and Colin and then craft the board or boards they wanted. The trick worked. On the surface, Zaul forgot everything about the Miami party scene, and from the sound of Colin's communications with me, Zaul was in a good place. Actually eating breakfast and dinner with the family. Colin sent me a series of sundown pictures of Zaul, Maria, and Marguerite. They were walking hand in hand down the beach. Looking for shells. Maria was sitting up on Zaul's shoulders. They were laughing. On the phone, Colin sounded happy. Content.

It was one of the only really good things I'd ever done or had a part in, and because of it, my soul smiled.

It was also short-lived.

Chapter Thirteen

The rooster woke me, but it was the smell of coffee that got me out of bed. I walked out of the single-room shack occupied by the bed I'd been sleeping in. Two parallel walls of concrete block. Plastic sheeting on the other two. Rusted tin roof. An orange extension cord snaked out of the main house, across the yard, and under the door where it powered a light above my head and the oscillating floor fan. The door was made of horizontal slats with an inch or two of space between. It wouldn't keep out much. Stepping back, I realized I'd been sleeping in a converted chicken coop.

I shuffled across the yard and onto the porch wearing another man's shorts. From what I could tell, she'd already swept the dirt porch, washed and hung the laundry, fed the chickens, and cooked breakfast—which looked like beans, rice, and fried plantains. A pot filled with what looked like milk sat simmering on the stove. The smell of it wafted from steam off the pot and hung in the air. I waved and my voice cracked. "Hi."

She was standing next to a large, waist-high concrete sink. The left side of the sink was a rippled section on which to wash clothes. The right side looked like a drain for clean dishes.

The middle was a deep sink. She was hovering over the middle sink, pouring water from a bucket over her sudsy hair. When I first met her, her hair had been pulled up and back. Now it was wet and hanging nearly to her waist.

She rinsed again, then wrung out her hair and began brushing out any tangles. She pointed with the brush. "Breakfast there if you feel like eating."

I pointed to the coffee. "May I?"

She nodded. Something about her body language told me she was in task mode and that I was one more task getting in the way of several others. She wasn't unkind, but I could tell she was trying to figure out what to do with me.

I poured myself a cup from an old percolator, sat at the worn wooden table, and hung my nose over the mug. I was hungry enough to eat the table, but that coffee smelled so good. When I sipped, it did not disappoint.

She noticed my reaction. "Good?"

I nodded while the taste swirled around my mouth. The caffeine buzz was immediate and satisfying.

"You like good coffee?"

Another sip. "I'd let you put it in my IV."

Over her shoulder, San Cristóbal sat smoking. She pointed to the smaller volcano, lush and green, that sat to the right. "Grown right there."

The coffee was intoxicating. "The flavor is, well . . . wow."

She nodded knowingly. "It ought to be." She finished brushing her hair, then spun it into a tight bun at the back of her head. She poured herself a cup and sat.

I extended my hand. "I think we've already done this, but I'm a little hazy. Charlie Finn."

She nodded and bowed slightly. "Paulina Flores." She waved her hand across the neighborhood. "Around here . . . Leena."

"Thank you." I waved my hand across myself. "For everything. I don't remember much, but what I do remember tells me that it wasn't pleasant."

Her daughter appeared, sleep in her eyes, hair in her face. She walked up to me, extended both hands, pressed palms together—like she was swimming the breaststroke—and held them out, bowing slightly. She held the pose for several seconds. Waiting. Paulina said, "She's honoring you."

I cradled both her hands in mine. "Hello, beautiful."

Paulina spoke softly over my shoulder. "*Hola, linda.*"

The girl listened to her mother, and a smile slowly spread across her face. I had a feeling she understood me, but she was waiting for her mother to give her permission to respond to a stranger.

"What's your name?"

Her mother prompted her. "It's all right."

Her voice echoed inside me, taking me back to the sidewalk outside the cathedral. "Isabella."

"Good morning, Isabella. Thank you for allowing me into your home."

She puffed up as though she had information I did not. "You're not in my home. You're in the chicken coop. Momma put you in the chicken coop so the neighbors don't start talking." Her index finger started waving like a windshield wiper. "It's not—" She put her hands on her hips, letting me know that she was about to unleash a grown-up word on me. Her lips moved slowly around the letters as she made the word. "Appropriate for you to sleep in our house."

Look up the word "precocious," and you'll find her picture. I asked Paulina, "How is it that her English is so good if she's grown up here?"

"Life is tough here. It's a good bit tougher if you don't speak English. I knew she'd get Spanish by default, so since she was born, I've spoken English with her."

Isabella smiled wider, grabbed a red plastic mug, dipped it gently into the milk, and climbed up into her mother's lap where she sipped on the milk, painting her upper lip in a mustache while her mother brushed her hair. Leena spoke over Isabella's head and eyed the pot of milk. "Help yourself. We own one cow. Half Brahma. Half India. The Brahma half is strong and can survive the conditions around here, namely the heat and drought, but generally gives little milk. The India half is weaker but gives good milk. More *robusto*. Put them together in one cow and . . ." A shrug. "We drink milk on a regular basis."

I hefted my coffee mug and smiled. "Why'd you help me?"

"Couldn't very well leave you." An honest shrug. "You'd either be dead or about to be."

The little girl spoke up. "You looked drunk. Were you drinking?"

I laughed. She smiled again, leaned against her mother, and tucked her knees up into her chest. Her hair matched her mother's, as did her eyes. Jet-black. I chuckled. "No."

She didn't skip a beat. "Do you drink?"

I shook my head. "No."

"Are you telling the truth?"

"Yes."

"Why not?"

"Never really started."

"Then you're a good man?"

So much wrapped in so small a question. I'd lied for so long. The memory of my parting with Shelly on the beach was still raw. I had no desire to suffer another self-inflicted wound in such a short amount of time. I shook my head. "No. I'm not."

Paulina broke the awkward silence. "We didn't know where to take you in León so we brought you here."

"Where is here?"

"Valle Cruces. Forty-five minutes west."

"I know I owe you some money. Everything's in my hotel room in León."

"No hurry."

"Any idea how I might get back there?"

"Bus leaves in a few hours. Cost you a couple of dollars."

I patted the pockets of my shorts. "Not a penny to my name."

"Truck leaves in two days. You could hitch a ride then."

"Truck?"

"Belongs to my uncle. He's working today and tomorrow, but he can drop you in León day after tomorrow."

"Any other option?"

She pointed to the road. "You can walk. Although thirty miles in flip-flops might leave your feet in worse condition than when you started." I eyed my feet. She continued. "You can hitchhike, but unattended gringos with an 'I'm lost' look pasted on their faces have a way of disappearing around here."

She could see my wheels spinning, but she said nothing. My options were few. "Mind if I stay until the truck leaves?"

She shook her head once. "We'll be gone most of the day, so you'll be on your own."

I eyed her cell phone. "Mind if I call my hotel?"

She slid it across the table and helped me contact the young man at the desk. He answered and was glad to hear from me. I told him to hold my room and I'd pay him when I returned day after tomorrow. He agreed, said it was "no problem" and that my bike was still parked out back. It would keep.

I returned to Paulina. "I feel a bit guilty sitting here doing nothing when it looks like you've been working since you got up. Can I help?"

She pursed her lips and the space between her eyes narrowed as she considered this. She looked at Isabella, who was smiling and nodding. "You think he should go with us?" Armed with the ability to determine the course of the day, Isabella raised an eyebrow and considered me. Finally, having given it enough time, she nodded. Paulina pressed her nose to Isabella's. "He could carry the backpack."

Isabella laughed an easy laugh.

Paulina looked at me. "If you feel up to it."

"Seems the least I can do."

"It's a long day, and in all fairness to you, it's a lot of work for a guy who's been as sick as you. If you go, you need to let me know how you're feeling. Okay?"

"Deal."

She filled a gallon jug with water, poured a few drops of bleach into it, and set it in front of me. She walked to a plant, twisted off a few stems, and shoved them into the water. "You need to drink most of this before we go. I doubt you'll get your strength back for several days, but this will help. You took four bags of IV fluid, but I doubt that was enough." When I lifted it to my lips, the water smelled of mint. "We'll leave soon as you're ready."

The sun was rising and I was already sweating. I drank the entire jug, which seemed to make her happy and did not make me need to pee, which told me that I really needed it. We refilled it, and she began shoving medical supplies and food into two large backpacks plus a third, which was much smaller. She handed me a worn-out baseball cap and said, "You'll want this in a few hours. The midday sun around here will bore a hole in your head if you let it." She also handed me an old pair of tennis shoes. They were too small, but the ends had busted open, allowing my toes to stick out the front. "Where we're going, those will be better than flip-flops."

I shouldered the backpack, which felt heavy, and we began walking. Isabella hopped along in front of us. Her backpack was loaded with a bottle of water and a bag of candy. Both Paulina's bag and mine had been loaded with medical supplies, medicines, rice, beans, and oil. My bag might have weighed ninety pounds. Eyeing the mountain in the distance, I shifted under the weight of the straps, knowing that in about two hours ninety pounds was going to feel like two hundred.

Paulina put her hand on the pack. "Is it too much? We can leave some here."

I ran my thumbs below the straps that were knifing into my shoulders. "No, I'm good."

"You sure?"

"No worries." In truth, it was pile-driving me into the earth, but this lady had just nursed me back from the dead. What else was I going to say?

She smiled and walked on ahead of me, her skirt waving in the hot breeze.

Walking out of the yard, Isabella routed us past the corner of the chicken coop. She leaned over and stared into a small area protected by chicken wire. Inside sat a duck, staring quietly up at us. Isabella poked it with her finger, prompting the comfortable duck to exit her perch and waddle a few steps away, revealing the four eggs beneath. Satisfied, Isabella shouldered her pack and continued walking. I had never seen anyone raise ducks, so I asked, "You guys raising ducks?"

Leena spoke over her shoulder. "No. They're chicken eggs. We're just using the duck to hatch them."

That prompted the next obvious question. "Isn't that confusing to the chicken?"

She laughed at me. "The duck doesn't know the difference."

"Whose duck?"

She pointed to a house on her left without looking. "Neighbor's. It's on loan."

I wasn't prepared to argue this. "What happened to the chicken?"

A shrug. "Don't know. Woke up, found four eggs in the nest and a bunch of feathers out here in the yard. Haven't seen the chicken since."

"What will you do with the chickens?"

"Hopefully produce more eggs. Isabella likes them scrambled."

The simplicity and matter-of-factness of life around here was striking.

The road wound along a riverbed. A man, woman, and two kids passed us riding a motorcycle, as did several pickup trucks overloaded with people. Most of the trucks were Toyotas. Older versions of the one Zaul took from his father. The cabs were loaded with six or eight people, and the beds were filled with fifteen to twenty each. Most were headed up the mountain. A few were headed down. Young barefoot boys, wearing tattered straw hats and riding horses, whistled and herded their cows along the road, most of which was lined with thick rows of sugarcane almost fifteen feet tall. As we walked, crosses—the size of a man—rose up out of the earth and dotted the woods on either side of us. There seemed to be no pattern. But we couldn't walk fifty yards without seeing another cross. Some were next to the road. A few were nailed to trees. Many had been stuck in the mud of the riverbed and surrounded by rocks. Most were in clumps. Three or four together. In one spot, I counted nineteen. Singles spread out like bread crumbs. I pointed and the tone of my voice asked the question. "Valle Cruces?"

She nodded and felt no need to explain. A few steps later, she turned to me. "Charlie?"

"Yes."

She waved her hand across the road and kept walking. "You might want to use another name."

"Why's that?"

"It's English for Carlos, and that name isn't real popular around here."

A young boy, maybe five, wearing only underwear, ran barefoot up to Paulina. His face and hair were filthy. As was his entire body. His nose was running and the snot trickled down his lip. His right ear was crusted with yellow dried wax and a dark ooze. He held out his hands to Paulina. *"Buenos días."*

He responded with a muffled *"buenos días."*

She reached in her bag and handed him a banana, which he gladly took. Then he turned to me, held out both hands, and bowed like Isabella had. I took both his in mine and said, "Good morning."

Feeling released, he turned and took off running back toward a plastic-wrapped structure beyond the trees. A man in a hammock waved at Paulina as we passed. She returned the wave. She spoke to me while looking at the man. "Don't touch your mouth with your hands until you've washed them." Her eyes followed the boy. "People around here don't have toilet paper."

I tried to make conversation. "How often do you make this trek?"

"Every Wednesday. Sometimes on the weekends."

"How long is it?"

"Six miles."

"Up and back?"

She shook her head once. "One way."

I considered this. "Why all the crosses?"

She spoke without looking at me. "Something happened. Years ago." She lifted her head and spoke while surveying the landscape. Her voice betrayed a sadness. "And it is happening still."

We walked in the quiet—the river slipping silently on one side, and on the other, sugarcane groves that exploded in tight clumps like giant porcupine quills. Soon the landscape shifted, turned uphill slightly, and the trees returned. Tall trees, some nearly eighty or ninety feet tall, grew up and covered the road. Other trees, mostly fruit, filled in the shady space beneath. On a slight incline and bend in the road, Leena reached up, grabbed the low-hanging fruit with one hand and with the other she unsheathed a machete from her pack. The machete had been sharpened many times, and the rounded blade had been replaced with a long stiletto. She placed the fruit on a rock. Isabella waited patiently. Paulina reached in her pack and then squirted hand sanitizer into my hands. Isabella held out her hands, and she did likewise. Then Paulina cut the fruit, which was about the size of a football. The inside was a deep purple and orange and looked like a distant cousin to a cantaloupe. She sliced the fruit, then stabbed it, and, careful not to touch it with her hands, she gave it first to Isabella and then to me by holding out the flattened machete blade, which acted as a skewer.

She noticed me eyeing the blade and smiled. "I washed it. And hold it by the rind. Never touch what you eat with your hands no matter how clean you think they are."

I slid the fruit off the blade. "Good call."

The fruit was sweet, and we ate it as we walked, pitching the rinds in the woods alongside us. Behind us, a kid on a squeaky bike approached. He spoke to both of them in Spanish, tipped his hat to me, and gently rolled past. As he did, I noticed that he'd replaced the entire front axle of his bike with a short piece of rebar held in place by two pieces of thick shoe leather.

Finished with the melon, Leena walked to the side of the road, and with a swiftness and strength I'd not previously noticed, she cut a piece of sugarcane at the bottom, trimming off the leaves as we walked. Once trimmed, she peeled off the outer protective skin and held it out to me. "Just pinch the end with your fingers." I did as instructed, and she brought the machete down quickly, leaving me with a ten-inch section of cane. As I stared at it, she said, "You suck on it." She did the same for Isabella and herself, cutting several pieces for all of us as we walked uphill.

It tasted like candy, and I sucked it dry.

To our left, in an open field, two boys watched over a small herd of cattle, letting them graze. The boys were playing catch with two worn-out gloves that had long ago lost the stitching. As I looked closer, they were using a large lemon for a ball.

Finally, the road turned up steeply, and Isabella returned to her mother and handed her pack to her. I offered to carry it and she gladly agreed. It was a pink Dora the Explorer backpack. The water bottle was empty and the bag of candy had been opened. We climbed up through the trees and eventually into the coffee groves Paulina had pointed to this morning. "Paulina, is this the coffee—"

"Leena. And yes, this is the coffee you were drinking this morning."

"What makes it so good?"

A smirk, but she did not answer.

By this time, we were several hours into our

hike and several miles up the mountain. She stopped, breathing heavy, and turned. She pointed northeast to the smoking volcano a few miles in the distance. Between us and the active volcano sat a dormant volcano. Its sides were lush green and the crater atop was well-defined except for what can only be described as a scar coming down one side. The scar traced the lines of the mountain, rolling along the shoulders, winding like a serpent just below us, where it then descended into the valley. I remembered staring out Marshall's plane and seeing the scar leading to the ocean. The pieces began to fall in place. "A decade ago, Huracán Carlos hovered over Nicaragua for several days. During that time, it dumped twelve feet of rain." She turned in a slow circle. "Here." Her eyes lifted toward the Las Casitas crater. "There was once a beautiful lake up there. The rain filled it to overflowing. The weight cracked the mantle, caused a miniature eruption, blew out the side of the mountain, and created a mudslide that ran—" Her finger began tracing the lines of the scar. "Down here. A mile wide and over thirty feet high, satellite imagery down-loaded days later showed that it was traveling in excess of a hundred miles an hour." She turned and pointed behind us where the world had opened. We could see for miles. She pointed. "All the way to the coast. Some thirty miles away." She paused. "Coast Guard vessels would later pick up survivors floating on debris some sixty miles out in the Pacific."

"And the crosses?"

"Over three thousand died that day. The crosses represent places where we found either bodies or parts or a piece of clothing or . . ." She trailed off. She turned and began slowly stepping forward, saying no more, and letting the story hang in the distance between us.

"Your family?"

She spoke without looking. "Twenty-seven members of my family." Smoke from cooking fires hung in the trees above us. She waved me on. "Come on. We're late."

We climbed quickly through coffee plants as tall as me. Leena ran her fingers through the leaves, plucking a few beans. She spoke over her shoulder. "They started picking them last week." Isabella ran ahead. Laughing in the bushes ahead of us. Leena climbed effortlessly up the steep incline. I had not regained my strength, and it was showing. I doubted I could run a six-minute mile right now. I lagged behind, slowly plodding forward. With each step, my pack felt like it was driving me deeper into the ground. She stared down at me. "What'd you say you did?"

"I didn't, but—" An awkward chuckle. "In a previous life, I worked for a man up north. Boston. He ran a private investment firm. Which meant he—"

She spoke without looking at me. The tone of her voice told me the smile had not left her face. "I know what it means. I'm poor. Not ignorant."

"Sorry. My bad. I didn't mean to—"

This time she turned to look at me. "Judge a book by its cover?"

Leena was easy to talk to, and while what she said was true, she didn't speak it in such a way that it pierced me. She wasn't trying to one-up me. "That bad, huh?"

She raised both eyebrows and then extended her hand, offering to help pull me up a steep step. I took it. "Anyway, he had a lot of money. I was something of an errand boy. He was always hiring and firing—"

She interrupted me. "That include you?"

An honest shrug. "Eventually, yes. Pretty much. Anyway, when he would interview guys who had either been fired from their previous job or somehow found themselves between jobs, they would all use the same buzzword. Each would sit in that interview, cross his legs, and hope he couldn't see through their polished veneer as they said, 'I'm in transition.' I can't tell you how many times I heard that spoken across the table with such rehearsed polish." I nodded as I tried to catch my breath. "But climbing up this Mount Everest with five hundred pounds on my back, I now understand what they meant because that feels about right. I'm in transition."

She laughed and pressed on, winding through the trees.

We turned a corner on the road and were met by an old wooden sign overgrown with vines. The sign was five or six feet wide and just as tall. The paint had faded, chipped, and a few of the boards had fallen off, suggesting it had not been maintained in a long time. The name on the sign read, CINCO PADRES CAFÉ COMPAÑÍA. Below that, an older sign, with hand-carved letters, read: MANGO CAFÉ.

I stumbled and caught myself. Leena turned. "You okay?"

I stared at the sign, the color draining from my face. "Yeah."

She returned and placed her index finger on my wrist, quietly counting. After fifteen or twenty seconds, she let go but her suspicion had returned. "You sure?"

I waved her off. "Yeah. The truth would take too long."

"Let me know if you're feeling faint."

I was feeling a bit more than faint, but I decided not to let her know that.

Moments later, we cleared the trees and walked out onto what would become the plateau on the shoulders of Las Casitas. Before me stood two tin-roofed, barnlike wooden structures. Two stories and thirty doors on a side. Leena spoke as we walked. "Families work the coffee. They make a dollar and a half a day. The skilled workers, the sifters, make two dollars." She pointed at the buildings. "They live in these rooms. Sometimes as many as six to eight people will live in a six-by-six space. No ventilation. No heat. No cooling. They have no school here, no medical care, and most will never leave this mountain. But it's better than the alternative."

"I'd hate to see the alternative."

She echoed my words. "You've been sucking on it the last hour or so."

"Sugarcane?"

"The curse of Nicaragua."

"How?"

She waved me off. "The truth would take too long." She pointed to the work ahead of us. "We collect medical supplies and food from churches from Valle Cruces to León and then bring them here. It's not much so we stretch it."

"Is that why you were in León?"

"Yep." She pointed at a small table beneath a gigantic tree off to our left. "We'll be here for an hour or so. Let the healthy come to us. Once they thin out, we'll go to them."

By the time we took off our backpacks, a quiet and well-mannered line of about sixty people trailed off around the tree and toward the closest building. Most of the adults were looking at me. Paulina picked up on it. "Most have never been this close to a gringo."

The first woman had a gash in her hand. Dirty. Paulina spoke to her while she washed the woman's hands in warm water. As she spoke to the woman in Spanish, she translated for me. "I'm telling her that she needs to wash it in warm water several times a day. She doesn't really understand germs so it's an uphill battle." While she worked, a group of twenty or so kids circled me with quiet fascination. Leena said, "You're probably the first white man some of these kids have ever seen."

Most of their noses were snotty. The mucus ran in streaks down their faces. "What's with the runny noses? Seems like everybody around here needs an antihistamine."

She laughed at my ignorance. "They live in homes where everything is cooked over wood-stoves. They don't ventilate them because the smoke keeps out the mosquitoes, so most kids around here grow up with an excess of smoke inhalation. Most of their lungs are inflamed, and about half are asthmatics. We're working with them to ventilate the smoke, but they say ventilating a house lets in the ghosts on this mountain." She pointed to the kids milling around me. "You can't tell, but they're actually a good bit healthier now than they have been in recent years."

"How so?"

"Their stomachs. They're not swollen."

"What'd you do?"

She pointed to our water jug. "Added bleach to their water." She eyed the mothers. "Educate the mothers and the entire plantation changes. A few years ago, I started bringing bleach and slowly adding it to their water. They didn't like it, but then the worms stopped showing up when they changed diapers and the kids' stomachs returned to normal. Now, they listen to me and add bleach to everything."

A pregnant girl—maybe fifteen—walked up and spoke quietly to Paulina. Paulina listened, holding both her hands, and spoke in hushed tones. She gave her a bottle of children's aspirin and the young mother walked off. An old man stepped up and began pointing at his hip. Leena again listened, her eyes staring intently into his. Isabella sat just to her left, giving each patient a piece of candy. The kids were milling around her, taunting her for candy, but she paid them no attention whatsoever.

"Where do they get their water?"

She pointed to a creek that ran through the property. "Who really owns this place is a bit of a mystery to all of us. We do know the planting rights are leased, but to whom is anybody's guess. Whoever it is employs a foreman to run interference. Over this hill, whoever it is pastures his cattle—and his pigs. Every horrible thing known to man floats down that creek and right through here. Including some really nasty parasites. The families who live up here have to walk several miles down to get clean water, and then they've got to climb back up here, and when they get done working, most don't have the energy to do that so they drink what's at hand."

"What about a well?"

She pointed to our left. "Just over that rise. Took two men more than a year because they had to dig it so deep. Used four lengths of rope making it over three hundred feet deep, which is a long way for a hand-dug well."

"Was the water any good?"

"Some say God himself drank from that well."

"What happened to it?"

"Charlie's mudslide."

"Why don't they just dig it out? Seems like the hard part's already been done."

"Awful dark for the man at the bottom of that well, and nobody wants to be the man at the end of the rope. Besides, people here think the devil will own their soul if they dig out a well that God filled in."

"You don't believe that, do you?"

"I believe there's a connection between that well and this mountain."

I scanned the squalor walking around me. "But wouldn't it help these people to have clean water?"

She answered without looking. "Yep."

I spoke as much to myself as her. "That doesn't really make much sense."

A chuckle. "Welcome to Nicaragua."

The third patient was a woman who might have been in her fifties. She was skinny, had lost about half of her teeth, and she had been beautiful before the sun weathered her. Her hair was turning gray, and whenever she smiled, her lips hooked on two of her remaining teeth. Paulina hugged her when she saw her. The woman spoke quietly but quickly. Leena listened and then reached for me. She said, "Charlie, I'd like you meet my good friend Anna. She's lived here twenty-seven years." I held out my hand and she shook mine. Her hand was frail, calloused, and tender. Leena handed me a pair of needle-nose pliers and ushered Anna toward me. "She's got a tooth that's giving her some trouble. I'm going to run in here and check this little pregnant girl to see how far along she is, and Anna needs you to pull her tooth."

With that she turned and began walking off. "What!"

She laughed over her shoulder. "Don't worry, she'll show you which one hurts." She held up a finger. "And don't pull the wrong one. She doesn't have too many left."

Leena disappeared through one of the worn wooden doors, and Anna stared up at me with beautiful blue eyes and hands crossed. I held up the pliers and asked, "Which one?"

She wrapped her hand around my hand, which held the pliers, and gently pointed to a top rear molar. Then she opened wide and stood waiting. Isabella stared up at me, sucking on a piece of candy. Paulina had disappeared, and a line of hopeful, tired, and sick people waited on me to pull Anna's tooth so that I could get to them. I opened her mouth wider with my left hand and gently placed the pliers on the tooth in question. "Is that the right one?"

She made no response.

I asked again. "*Sí*?"

She nodded.

So I gripped what remained of the abscessed tooth and tightened the pliers as best I could. The smell coming from her mouth could have gagged a maggot. I held my breath and tried not to. Careful not to hurt her, I pulled gently. Thankfully, the pliers gripped, and the rotten and infected tooth slid from its hole in her jaw. As the blood and pus drained, she took the tooth from the jaws of the pliers and slid it into her pocket. Smiling, she spat, patted my shoulder, and walked off. Over the next hour, I pulled nine teeth while Isabella watched in muted curiosity.

As the line dwindled, a small boy came to me limping. His big toe was red, infected, and there was a hole in it about the size of a pencil lead. I asked him to sit and poked around a bit. He tried to act tough, but I could tell it hurt him. Leena encouraged him to let me look at it. He stiffened and gritted his teeth. I felt like there was something stuck up in his toe, but I couldn't get at it without hurting him. Seeing the muscles of his jaw flex, I squeezed his toe like I was popping a zit. At first, nothing. I stopped to get a better grip, and he took a deep breath and held it. I knew it was hurting him, so something had to be stuck in there. Finally, I pressed with both thumbs, and he let out a small cry. When I did, pus oozed and the tip of something stuck through his skin. His eyes were teary, but I showed it to him and asked Leena to ask him if I could keep going. He nodded and pointed at his toe, then poked me in the arm and nodded some more. I took that as a good sign and squeezed one more time. This time, white-and-green stuff shot out followed by a thorn. I took Leena's tweezers and slowly pulled it from his toe. His eyes grew wide as I held the thorn—nearly three-quarters of an inch long—in front of him. He smiled wide. We bathed his foot, massaged as much antibiotic ointment into the hole as we could, and then wrapped it in a bandage with strict instructions from Leena not to walk barefoot for at least a week. He nodded and carried the thorn in the palm of his hand to show his mom. When he walked off, his chest had puffed out a bit. He looked up at me. *"Gracias, Doctor."*

The words swam around in my head. When they

came to rest, so did the meaning. I turned to Leena. "What'd he just call me?"

Leena whispered, "I think you've made a friend." A sly smile. "And more than one."

"What do you mean?"

"Anna is quite taken with you."

"That's some . . . lady."

"Let me tell you something about that lady. When her husband was sick last year, the medicine he needed was very expensive. Most people in his condition die. But Anna would work all day in the coffee plantation, then walk down the mountain at dusk to the peanut fields and work all night, by moonlight, digging up peanuts with her bare hands. She slept in the field for an hour or two before dawn; then she'd hide her peanut bag and walk back up the mountain to check on her husband and then make it to work on time. It'd take her three to four days to fill a hundred-pound bag with peanuts, and for that bag, they'd pay her ten dollars."

"And her husband?"

"Healthy as a horse—thanks to her."

When we'd finished, we packed up and moved toward the dwellings. The dwellings were about the size of a closet. Bunks on one side. They were made years ago from raw hardwood. Over the years, use had smoothed the wood, and oil in hands and bodies had turned it dark. People in the States would have paid thousands for the beauty of this wood. Those living in it would have paid thousands to be rid of it. The plantation filled a small shoulder off the southern end of Las Casitas. The owner's house was a large plantation house equal in size to Colin's house on the coast. Paulina walked me toward the middle of the building where a channel or walkway cut through the middle proving that just as many people lived in the middle as on the outside. The air was still and the heat oppressive. She waved her hand at the dirt, grime, shoeless kids, and snotty noses. "Don't let your eyes fool you, these are proud people. They have nothing, but what they do have is kept. The dirt is swept in neat lines, they've sought out and placed smooth river stones at their front doors to wipe their feet and welcome guests, fresh bananas are hung above their beds, their clothes may be dirty but they're folded neatly. The men wear belts, they remove their hats when they meet you, and the women wear scarves to cover their heads."

I understood what she was telling me. I just couldn't understand why. "Why're you telling me this?"

"I am pointing out the difference between poverty and squalor."

"How so?"

"You can be poor without living in filth."

We walked into the row houses, which were more like a giant barn with dozens of stalls barely wide enough for a single horse. She explained, "These are for the younger workers with less seniority. Or"—she pushed on a door—"older ones who sell their homes on the outside when they are too old to work."

Inside, a hammock stretched from wall to wall. In it sat what was once a man. Skin draped across bones. Barefoot. His shirt lay unbuttoned, pants were pulled up to his thighs, but his groin and bottom were exposed. His hands were large and had been muscled at one time. On the floor next to him sat a half-full bottle of water.

The door swung and light slowly entered the room. When the old man saw Paulina, he smiled and his eyelids closed and opened slowly. His lips were chalky white, and his tongue seemed swollen and stuck to the roof of his mouth. He made an attempt with his hands to pull his shirt-tail over his groin but was unsuccessful. Judging by the soaked hammock and the smell permeating the room, he'd been too tired to rise so he'd urinated on himself. She pulled off her pack, held his hand—letting her index finger rest on his pulse—and knelt on the ground next to him, whispering quietly and never letting her eyes leave his. Every few seconds, he would nod and his lips would move, but I couldn't hear him. Isabella stood behind me outside the door, listening but not looking.

Keeping her eyes on the man, Leena pulled

some baby wipes from her pack and began to gently bathe the man's torso, arms, groin, and legs. Then, with delicate tenderness, she bathed the man's bottom and penis.

When she finished, the old man patted Paulina's hand and then placed his hand on her forehead as though he were giving her a blessing. She rose, kissed his forehead, his cheek, and then his hand.

When she walked out, a tear trickled down her face. She stopped at a basin to wash her hands, but collecting herself, she said nothing and offered no explanation. In the ten minutes she was with him, Leena's smile never left her face, yet in that room I saw nothing to smile about. Finding him naked, she'd dressed him in honor and dignity. And in dressing him, she'd undressed me.

I've seen a lot of things in my life, many I'm not proud of, but until that day, I'd never seen the face of an angel. Maybe for the first time, I saw one in that room. Sadly, if the angel of mercy had visited him today, I had a feeling that the angel of death wasn't far behind. I think he knew that, too.

And the tear trailing down her cheek told me that Leena knew that most of all. She caught the disconcerted look on my face. "You want to say something?"

"No, well yes. It's just that no one seems overly affected that that man is lying there dying right in front of their eyes. As if they're not surprised."

"People here don't feel entitled to perfect health."

"Yeah, but shouldn't they? I mean, isn't it a worthwhile goal?"

"Sure. But at what cost?"

"Well, at any cost."

"That's where you and them differ." She held up a finger. "I'm going to let you in on a little secret. When I first traveled to the States to study, I was struck by how everyone I encountered spent their days working feverishly to make enough money to buy a better tomorrow. Here, people are content—they buy what they need today and leave tomorrow to God. These people don't have a death grip on their life here. They hold it loosely because they're not in control of it in the first place, and—" She paused, weighing her words. "In their experience, it can be ripped from their hands no matter how tightly they squeeze it."

Somewhere in there, I clued in to the fact that for people like me, there is an undoing that occurs here. A breaking. Like dropping a glass rod. It is the sound of the shattering of our assumptions when we learn that our pretending, our masquerading, is all vanity. As if we have any control over any of this. I, like most everyone I've known, spent most of my life furiously attempting to protect myself from the truth, from the undignified bottle beneath the hammock. Truth is, we can't protect us. These people don't suffer from the illusions that I have built up to insulate myself—namely that death won't come for me on a hammock in Nicaragua when I don't have the strength to stand so I pee in my pants. That somehow I deserve different. As if my money or social status could buy me, could guarantee me, a dignified death. These people know that they are born, they might grow up, might be given in marriage, might live long, might laugh, and might know love, but they all know that they will die. That what they see here is fleeting. I, on the other hand, don't think much about it. I looked around me, at all the eyes staring down on that skeleton of a man, knowing they don't have that luxury. Nor do they pretend to. The contradiction was striking. I have lived my life fighting against a tidal wave of forces that I am powerless to defend, like a man standing at the ocean's edge, swatting at the waves. I can no more turn back the tide than I can light up the sun.

She knocked on a few more doors and poked her head into rooms where two women nursed babies. Leena smiled widely as the babies gorged on their mothers' milk, and the tired women made no effort to cover their breasts in my presence. I stood back until Leena beckoned me forward. She then dug into my pack and left several large bags of rice and beans and several bottles of cooking oil. The mothers nodded and smiled and repetitively thanked her. One of the girls had the remains of a black eye, which she was careful to hide from me. For the next hour, we stopped, Leena talked, and we unloaded rice, beans, and oil. The only thing better than the feeling of less weight in my pack were the smiles that small portion of food produced in those who received it.

Woodsmoke wafted through the interior. Dogs watched from a distance as Isabella led us through the living quarters. Finally, we turned toward the kitchen, a large building centered around an enormous wood fire. Large pots of rice and beans and corn sat simmering on iron grates suspended over the fires. Large, sweaty women worked the pots and poked the fires with long sticks. In the corner, two teenage girls worked feverishly making tortillas. A second fire glowed beneath a sheet of steel. The girls would dip their hands into a bucket of what looked like cornmeal and water, pound out a flat cake-like thing, and then drop it onto the hot sheet. They'd let it sit sixty to ninety seconds on one side and then flip it.

Paulina hugged the women and the girls and spoke quietly with each, listening and nodding. When they offered food, she refused, but when the young girls pointed toward the tortillas, she looked at me and must have seen my mouth salivating. She nodded; the girl quickly picked one off the hot sheet using only her fingers and handed it to me. Paulina nodded. "It's okay."

One of the women dipped a large spoon into the boiling beans and offered. I held the tortilla under while she dribbled goodness on top. Then I folded it and sank my teeth into it. I guess my smile betrayed me because the women laughed loudly, and evidently the delight on my face and absolute approval of their cooking made me an instant friend. They offered more, but Paulina quickly shooed them and ushered me out, laughing.

We continued walking out of the living area into what looked like the working part of the plantation. Large warehouses, tractors, and various pieces of oiled and rusty heavy equipment lay scattered about. Above us, huge trees shaded our walk. Flowers bloomed like peacock wings in the branches, and as I stood mesmerized, I noticed the birds shooting like F-16s between the branches. I shaded my eyes. "What are they?"

Isabella answered me. "Parrots."

Farther off to my right, maybe several hundred yards, I heard a strange sound that was loud and can only be described as a howl. "What was that?"

Paulina spoke as she walked. "Howler monkeys. There's one directly above you." I stopped and stared upward, where I was met by two eyes staring back at me. Paulina snapped her fingers and made some whistling, clicking noise with her mouth that I'd never heard. The monkey jumped as if shot out of a cannon. It danced from tree limb to tree limb until it landed on the ground, where it ran across and, to Paulina's great delight, climbed her like a tree and perched on her shoulder.

I adjusted the pack on my shoulders and shook my head. "This place should sell tours."

Behind me, the little boy who'd had the thorn in his foot appeared from around a tree. He was dragging his mother—a skinny young woman carrying an infant. He pointed at me and proclaimed loudly, "*El doctor*!" He tugged on his mother's shirt. "*El doctor*!"

I waved and she eyed me from a distance.

Paulina nuzzled and spoke quietly to the animated monkey, who drifted from shoulder to shoulder to arm and then to the top of her head. He was constant motion.

With another click of her lips, she set him down and he disappeared into the trees, swinging from limb to limb as we walked.

"I guess you and he have done that before?"

"No." A knowing smile with a single shake of her head. "Just met."

We walked into what looked like a garage where they repaired the tractors and heavy equipment. A man working on a large tire, with an enormous wrench in his hand, smiled widely when he saw Leena. He limped around the tire, and she extended her hands in the same way Isabella had with me. He bowed slightly and then she hugged him. His eyes lit.

She spoke, he nodded, and after a second, he sat in a chair while she knelt and began rolling up his pant leg, exposing a nasty wound. She rinsed it with bottled water, then cleaned the wound. Finally, she gave him an injection above the wound, covered it in a greasy antibiotic ointment, and wrapped it in gauze. She finished by giving instructions, which included politely, and with a smile, pointing at him to do exactly what she said. He nodded and pulled a small bag from next to the chair and gave it to her. She rolled it up and stuffed it into my pack, then kissed his hand and walked me through the back of the warehouse.

Beyond us, a large concrete world—half the size of a football field—opened up to us. Huge sheets of black plastic had been spread across the concrete, and men with brooms and rakes were spreading coffee beans in single rows across the sheeting. Leena spoke. "The first harvest of beans is coming in. They'll spread and sort across these sheets, where they will dry. Then"—she led me by the hand—"they are bought in here." We walked into a separate building where a huge belt-fed machine shook large sifters filled with beans. The noise was deafening, and the air was filled with dust and pieces of hull. The earth vibrated with the movement of the machines. "Where the husk is broken, leaving only the bean." She continued walking, leading me by the hand out the back where a row of a dozen or so people sat sorting beans into bags between their legs. "They are then sorted into grades of bean. The best are sorted and sold as single source, organic, and fair trade, although I find little that is fair about the trade that occurs here." When she said this, her tone turned acerbic. She continued. "The lesser or imperfect beans are sold to larger companies for ground coffees throughout the Americas."

Leena spoke to several of the workers sorting beans, who waved or smiled at her. We exited out the side and down a hill that took us through a chicken coop holding several thousand chickens.

The sun was falling as Leena led me to a pot of water sitting off to the side of a fire where the embers glowed red and white. She touched the water with her finger, then pulled a bar of soap from her pack, and we washed at the water. She made me scrub my arms nearly to the pits, my face and neck. Isabella, too. When finished, we shook dry, shouldered our packs, and began descending the hill through the coffee plants. With the smell of the plantation still wafting around us, Paulina stopped and listened. The sound of an engine. A diesel. Grew closer. Paulina pulled us behind a large tree, and we squatted as a newer white Toyota 4-wheel drive HiLux with roof racks and aggressive tread mud tires climbed up the mountain. Leena leaned around the tree to get a good look at the driver. She whispered, "That's the foreman." Her face grew tight, and she spat, "Can't afford clean water for his workers, but he can drive a new $20,000 truck." She paused, shaking her head. "He doesn't allow us here. Says we're bad for business. For morale."

"You're doing all this, and they don't want you here?"

She shook her head. "Nope." She listened again. "He fancies himself a cardplayer, so he plays a game every Tuesday night in León. Sleeps off his hangover until Wednesday about noon. Pays his whores. Returns here about dinnertime." She weighed her head back and forth. "He's early today. That means he won, and he's back in time to show off."

I spoke while watching the truck ramble over the rocks. "Did you say he likes to play cards?"

She looked irritated, and the veins in her arms had popped out like rose vines. "Yeah."

"And you say that truck is new?"

She watched with disapproval as it rolled and bumped over the rocks and roots. "He wasn't driving it last week. Why?"

"Just curious."

I'd only seen pictures of Colin's truck, but I doubted there were two just like that. And if the foreman was driving it, that meant Zaul had lost it in a card game, which made me wonder what else he'd lost. León was not a big town, and I'd be surprised if there was more than one high-stakes poker game on Tuesday night.

She stared up through the trees at the plantation, which was now out of sight. She spoke quietly. "The two young nursing mothers are his—" She spat in anger and shook her head. "And he makes no provision for them. He feeds them scraps from the table when they do what he wants, but they just gave birth two and three weeks ago so they can't"—she held up her fingers like quotation marks—"do what he wants."

Isabella tugged on my shirtsleeve and waved her index finger. Wiper again. "That means they don't do any kissing. 'Cause kissing makes babies. Then when the babies are big enough, they pop out the zipper." She poked me in the side. "I have a zipper 'cause I'm a girl. And momma has a zipper 'cause she's a girl, but you don't have a zipper 'cause you're a boy."

I nodded and looked at Leena. "Zipper?"

Leena shrugged. "You have a better explanation?"

"No. No, I do not."

We continued walking. My pack was empty, for which I was grateful. As we walked, I heard a thud, followed by a second and a third. Finally, I saw the cause of the noise—something orange and yellow falling from the tree above us.

Leena picked one up. Cutting a slice, she handed it to Isabella, who shoved it in its entirety into her mouth. She smiled widely, pushing the juice out the sides of her mouth, which did not go unnoticed. Leena smiled, and the look spoke of healing of a deep wound. She offered one to me and I accepted. "I've never eaten a mango that I can recall."

"Never?"

"Certainly not like this."

She shoved a section in her mouth and spoke around it. "It's the taste of Nicaragua."

My teeth sank deeply and the juice exploded. I'd never tasted anything like it. Leena enjoyed my reaction. "Good, huh?"

I nodded but didn't speak, trying to keep the juice in my mouth. Isabella retrieved four more, and while Leena peeled another, I asked her, "Tell me about the man in the hammock."

She paused. "Roberto. He used to feed me mango when I was Isabella's age." She looked up. Eyes red. "He's dying."

"Can anything be done for him?"

She shook her head. "He has a disease in his kidneys. It is caused from pesticides, which are sprayed on the sugarcane. They aren't legal in any civilized country, but here in Nicaragua they are used in plenty. Before they cut the cane, they burn it. Making it easier to harvest. Burning it does something to the pesticide, turning it into some other chemical or something that is even more harmful. The men working the cane breathe it, and it is filtered by their kidneys. There are scientists here from America studying it, but even they have no idea what's going on. All they know is that what is sprayed on the cane is killing the men that work it. Roberto started working in the cane when he was five."

"How long have you known him?"

"My whole life."

"Does he have family?"

She shook her head. "They were either killed by Carlos or left for Honduras."

Either the heat or the insanity of this place was starting to get to me. "So, he's going to die alone in that dark, hot room, soaked in his own urine, and all he has to show for his life is half a bottle of water and one piece of candy?"

She stared at me. A long pause. Her head tilted as she considered me. A tear accompanied her whisper. "Yes."

We walked down the mountain in the dark. Isabella got tired halfway down and reached for my hand. We walked a few hundred yards like that, and when she stumbled, I picked her up and set her on my shoulders, which seemed to wake her momentarily. When we reached the road beneath, Isabella raised her hands high in the air and stared up at the stars. "Look, Mom, I can touch them."

I'd never seen so many stars.

We got to their home sometime after nine. Isabella ran inside, where I heard a man talking. Leena walked to the hand pump attached to the well and began filling a bucket. When full, she dropped a smaller bucket into it and slid the whole thing next to a black plastic curtain. "I'm going to heat up some dinner. You shower first."

She pointed to the building where I'd spent my recovery. "Should be some more clothes in there. Wear whatever fits."

Leena broke some sticks in half and shoved them into the embers of the fire in the corner where she intended to heat dinner. Then she disappeared into the kitchen, where again I heard a man's voice. I stepped behind the curtain, stripped, found the soap, and took a bucket shower. Cold at first, it felt divine. Dumping water over my head, I took a look at myself. My arms and legs were filthy to where the line of my clothing had been. My ankles and feet were white. Relatively clean. Then the tips of my toes were dark and caked in mud and dust.

Outside, Leena poured water over a naked and sudsy Isabella who was squatting on the concrete sink.

In my room, I found a pair of cutoff jeans and gray T-shirt that fit. When I returned to the kitchen, Leena stuck her soapy head out of the plastic sheeting. "Dinner's on the table."

"Thank you."

I walked into the kitchen and found Isabella laughing at the table with an older man, maybe sixtyish. He stood, shook my hand, and tapped his chest. "Pow-low." He had, quite possibly, the strongest hands of any human being I'd ever met. Not to mention his forearms. He was a walking, talking Popeye.

Paulina shouted over the edge of the curtain. "Charlie, meet Pow-low. It's spelled like Paulo but"—she laughed easily—"we say it a bit different around here." She said matter-of-factly, "He helped me lift you into the back of the truck."

I tapped myself. "Charlie."

He smiled, exposing gums missing more teeth than he owned. He pointed at his truck, sitting in the backyard. "You vomit and manure my truck."

"I'm sorry?" He pointed matter-of-factly to the bed of his truck, then to his mouth. "Vomit. You." He shook his head and held his nose. More hand motions. "Truck." He pointed to my shorts. "You . . . dirty . . . smell very much bad."

I heard Paulina laughing from behind the curtain.

Paulo evidently didn't speak very much English, but I understood what he was saying. I shrugged. "Yeah, about that. I'm sorry."

He smiled kindly, as if it happened every day.

"*No problema.*" He acted as if he were emptying a bucket. "I water."

Dinner consisted of rice, beans, a fried plantain, and some water. I was hungry enough to eat the table, the neighbor's dog, and the chair I sat in, but when offered seconds, I declined. Leena watched me with quiet amusement. Paulo hovered, elbows on the table, and spoke quietly with Leena and Isabella. Leena translated his Spanish to my English as he spoke, not wanting me to feel excluded. He told her about his day working in the sugarcane fields, and she scolded him and told him he shouldn't have worked there today. He waved a finger and said something that she didn't translate.

Finally, she turned to me. "Thanks to you, we were able to see about four times as many folks. Thank you." A genuine smile. "You make a good mule. The truck leaves tomorrow a little after noon. Paulo is going to work in the morning, and when he returns on the noon work bus, he'll take you to León."

Her tone of voice told me that something occurred before noon, which prohibited him from driving me. "Anything I could do to be useful?"

She spoke to Paulo, who weighed the question and then nodded. Leena returned to me. "You could work with Paulo. It would double his daily rate." A shrug. "It'd help pay for gas."

"Seems the least I can do."

Paulo seemed to appreciate the gesture and poked me in the arm. "I wake. We work with me. It's good. Very good. Work not hard."

The night was quiet, and people had returned to their homes around us. The smell of smoke was constant. Somewhere a pig grunted and two dogs fought. In the distance, I could hear singing.

Paulina cleared the plates. "He'll wake you in time to leave." Isabella stood from the table, sleep heavy in her eyes, and hugged Paulo and then her mother. Finally, without giving it a second's thought, she hugged me and then climbed into the bed. It was the only bed in the small space, so she must share it with her mother. She was asleep by the time Leena pulled the covers up over her shoulders. Leena returned and began washing the plates in the concrete sink when I stood next to her. "I'll wash."

She shook her head. "Nicaraguan men don't do dishes."

She was tired and hadn't stopped moving since before I'd awakened. She had to be dead on her feet. I offered a second time. "I am not Nicaraguan."

She nodded, dried her hands. Retrieving the bag from my pack that had been given to her by the man at the coffee-sorting house, she poured its contents onto a large cloth napkin and sorted through them.

She picked through the beans as one who'd done it before.

"Will you roast them?"

"If there's time . . . this weekend."

Paulo had gone to bed in the room next to theirs. I could hear him snoring quietly. When I finished the dishes, Leena chuckled. "I don't know what you do for a living, but if it doesn't work out, you make a pretty good *el doctor* in the volcanic mountains of Nicaragua." More laughter. "You got skill."

I looked at my hands in the growing moonlight. She followed with, "I set a jug of water next to your bed. You need to make yourself drink it. You'll need it tomorrow morning."

"Okay."

"And fill it again before you leave."

She was walking away when I asked her the question that had been on the tip of my tongue since I saw her kneel next to that man's hammock. "Can I ask you something?"

She turned. Waited.

I glanced up at the coffee plantation atop the mountain. "How do you do this? Day in and day out."

She paused, stared up at the mountain, and then answered the heart of my question. "I love them without trying to change them. I look at their suffering, their hopelessness, and while I'd like to wave a wand and fix it, I can't, so I do what I can."

"Which is?"

"Climb down in their misery and love them where they are." She waved her hand across the landscape. "People would much rather die holding someone's hand than live alone."

"How do you not let it taint you?"

A shrug. "Never said it didn't."

She disappeared inside as I whispered, "Sure fooled me."

I walked to my little plastic-wrapped shed and lay on my bed in the dark. The mosquitoes were buzzing my ears, so I turned on the fan, opting for the lion breathing in my face instead of the buzzing horde.

As the fan oscillated, I kept asking myself how I got there. The world had turned upside down and yet something about it felt completely right. The problem of Zaul seemed a long way away. Colin. Maria. The Bertram. My shack in Bimini. Shelly. Drugs.

As sleep pulled heavy on my lids, one image would not retreat. The sign that read, CINCO PADRES CAFÉ COMPAÑÍA. As I tossed and turned, an image returned. When I worked for Marshall and he'd dismantled Cinco Padres, I had returned to my office in León to close up. My last afternoon, when I'd taken a motorbike up into the hills, I remembered stopping and watching families walk down—carrying their lives on their backs. That road was the same we'd walked up and back today.

I whispered to myself, "Those people were these people."

Chapter Fourteen

By the time I turned thirty-nine, Hack and I had finished two more skiffs and I noticed him slowing down. Hack's cough grew worse and began producing more. Often at night, when we were working in his shop, he'd get to coughing and have to step outside to bring that stuff up out of his lungs and spit out whatever came up. One night, after a rather violent coughing fit, I noticed his handkerchief was tinted red. I told him, "You better let me take you to a doctor."

He nodded, holding his rib cage. "Maybe it's about time." Given that he hated doctors, I knew it was serious.

The next morning, I borrowed a neighbor's golf cart and carried him to the Bimini Clinic toward the northern end of the island. If Bimini has anything resembling a hospital, it's this. For reasons unexplained, a CLOSED sign hung on the door. I muttered to myself, "How do you close a hospital?"

Hack laughed. "Easy. It's Bimini."

He was right. This was typical Bahamian lifestyle. If something better presented itself, work could wait. The island had a limited drugstore, but only one doctor, who was more often than not drunk, so the idea of "emergency medical care" didn't really exist. That made it tough to get a prescription for anything while he was passed out. We stepped back into the cart where Hack started one of his coughing fits. Minutes passed while he coughed up a lung and spat the remainder out on the ground around us. This was not a pretty sight and, sitting there with my hands in my lap, it made me feel rather helpless.

While Hack retched, an attractive lady walked by. Bathing suit, hat, flip-flops, designer shades. Bag over her shoulder. Big wide hat. In truth, her legs caught my attention. While her face was beautiful, the look blanketing it was one of resignation and depression. Her shoulders looked like they were carrying a thousand pounds. But despite the small planet that was weighing her down, when she passed Hack, she stopped and listened to his cough. Then she turned to me. A switch flipped and professionalism replaced the heaviness. "Does he belong to you?"

"I'm not sure he belongs to anyone, but yes, I'm his friend."

"Sounds like he has walking pneumonia. And currently, it's winning. You'd do well to get him to a doctor."

I pointed at the CLOSED sign on the clinic door.

Her eyes narrowed, and she then rested a hand on her hip. After a minute, she pointed to her hotel a few blocks up the street. "Follow me, I'll give him a look."

"You a doctor?"

One ear still trained on Hack, she nodded and held out a hand. "Shelly Highsmith." Hack bent over double, clutching his ribs. "You better follow me."

We followed her to her hotel, where I sat Hack on a bench and we waited. She returned from her room with a stethoscope draped around her neck and a cold bottle of water in her hand. She sat next to him, gently put her hand on his back, and began listening to him breathe. He winked at me. The resulting look on her face did not encourage me.

After a minute, she turned to me. "You live nearby?"

I nodded. Hack was in the process of rolling a cigarette. She touched his hand. "If you want to see tomorrow, you better hold off on that."

Hack slipped the rolling papers back in his pocket and leaned his head back.

Shelly turned to me. "He's carrying around a rather nasty infection that's probably been in there a while. He's pretty weak and extremely dehydrated—which isn't helping matters. He needs intravenous antibiotics and fluids. Like right now."

I glanced down the road. "I imagine they have that at the clinic, but we'd have to break the door down to get it."

Hack spoke up. "Doc leaves his back door unlocked. He's got some medicines in there. If you let yourself in, get what you need. I can pay him when he wakes up."

We couldn't leave him in the hotel lobby, so we took Hack to my place and set him on the lounger on my back porch with Shelly's water bottle. He promised to stare at the waves and not smoke while we drove the golf cart to the doctor's office.

Shelly Highsmith was a plastic surgeon. And

evidently a good one. She was the chief of cleft and craniofacial surgery at the research hospital in Miami where she specialized on children. "Every kid should have a beautiful smile." Four years younger than me, she was in her mid-thirties, and yet unlike me, she was visiting the island for her first vacation in eight years, prompted by an ugly and unexpected divorce. Said she was sitting in her office, staring out across the bay, when the papers came to finalize it. She signed and realized she'd never made the crossing. Lived in Miami a decade and never ventured across the water to the island.

The doc was in fact passed out on his couch next to an empty bottle of our rum. I didn't bother Shelly with that detail. We raided his medical cabinet and fridge, getting what we needed. Shelly said she'd like a drug more specific to his condition but broad-spectrum would work.

We found Hack where we left him with an unlit cigarette in his mouth. She sat next to him and swabbed the vein on his arm. When she did, the short, thin, see-through skirt she wore to cover up her bathing suit fell off her thighs and slit to her waist. Hack rested his palm on her thigh.

She eyed his hand and held the needle where he could see it. A smile cracked her lips. "You want pain or no pain?"

Hack put his hand back in his lap and spoke to me. "I like her."

Shelly spent the weekend checking on Hack, and consequently, based on the tilt and angle of her shoulders, not to mention the disappearing wrinkles on her forehead and the way the edges of her mouth began to turn up every time Hack started telling her a story, the effect of the island, along with us, was good for her.

Being a doctor, she was naturally curious. About Hack. The skiffs. Our fishing. But mostly about me. She also had a thing for good coffee, so I introduced her to Legal Grounds. Sunday afternoon, I took her out on the skiff and helped her catch a few bonefish. She enjoyed that.

She told me more of her story, about medical school, marriage, and why she chose to specialize on kids and their faces: "There's something special about a kid's smile. I see in their faces what we all used to be before the world got hold of us." I liked her. And I liked being around her.

She asked me about me and I told her my story. High school. College. Playing cards. London. Amanda. Marshall. Landing here. Hack. And I told her about "my business partner, Colin." And how we were in the fragrance and spirit and wine import business. And yes, I left out one important detail.

Before she left, I said, "I'm in Miami about every other week, mind if I check in on you?"

"I'd like that."

On our first official date, Colin let me borrow

his Mercedes because I didn't own a car, so I took her to my favorite restaurant, Ortanique on the Mile, on the Miracle Mile in downtown Coral Gables. She ordered a mojito and I ordered water. She eyed my decision. "You really don't drink, do you?"

I shook my head.

"Ever done drugs?"

"No, but I was a miler in college and running is a pretty strong drug."

"Ever done anything you regret?"

"Sure."

"Such as?"

She waited. Shelly had a strong intuition and suspected something about me was not on the up-and-up. I didn't flaunt money and I didn't spend a lot of money, but she saw the boats I drove. Colin's Mercedes. She knew there was more to my story than I'd admitted.

"I have not been truthful when I should have."

"Have you been truthful with me?"

"I've not lied to you."

"There's a difference between not lying and being totally truthful." Another sip. "So, have you been totally truthful?"

There are several moments in my life that hurt me. This is one of those. I looked her straight in the eyes. "Yes, I've been totally truthful."

"And you're not into something that could come back to bite you?"

The problem with being a good cardplayer is that I held my cards close to my chest and I could bluff most anyone. "No."

She crossed her legs, sipped again, and her foot nudged mine. "Good."

When I look back across the war-torn landscape of my life, at the people I've hurt, those I've taken advantage of, and those I've betrayed and lied to, I think back to that afternoon with Shelly. I'd like that one back. I'd like to tell her that I'm sorry. Really. Poker players are some of the most constantly optimistic people on the planet. No matter what you lose, it can be won back, and double, at the next deal. Nothing is ever truly lost forever.

Problem is, people are not cards or the chips we bet with. Neither are the relationships we share across green-felted tables and smoke-filled rooms.

A blissful year passed. We were happy. I never took Shelly on a drop, but I'd pick her up on my way back and we traveled a lot by boat. Spent lots of time on all the islands. She'd hop in the boat on Thursday or Friday afternoon with nothing but a small bag and say, "Which island?" We became island hoppers. Then we started venturing farther. Central America.

What Shelly didn't know was that loaded in the belly of our vessel, in specially crafted holds made to look like the hull or engine or anything but a storage department, was enough cocaine to put us both in jail for several lifetimes. There were times when I thought she suspected, but if she did, she kept it to herself.

And yes, I was risking her life, which was a risk I was willing to take. Which should tell you everything you need to know about me.

One Friday afternoon, I was late picking her up. Again. I hadn't worn a watch in about eight years and other than my schedule with Colin had become chronically late in pretty much every other area of my life, so whenever we made plans and I told her I'd pick her up at a certain time, she'd ask me, "Now is that 'real time' or 'Charlie time'?" When I slid up to the dock almost two hours late, she stepped into the boat, both eyebrows raised, and handed me a small wrapped box. A present.

I was about to say, "I'm sorry," when she shook her head and pressed her finger to my lips. "Don't. Just shhh."

I opened the box to find a beautiful Marathon dive watch. It looked bombproof and was reported to be waterproof to over a thousand feet. She took it from my hand and rolled it in hers. "I found these guys online: topspecus.com. Couple of self-described 'gearheads.' So I called them on the phone and asked them what was the toughest, most accurate watch they sold. They say this thing is nearly indestructible and only loses like a second every hundred years or something." A playful smirk. "I had them set it five minutes early. So . . ." She was smiling now. Wrapping my arms around her waist. "You should never, ever, as long as we live . . . be late again." A tilt of her head. Half a smile. "Right?"

I nodded obediently. "Right."

She put her hand on my head and turned it left and then right, prompting me to repeat after her. "Never again."

I continued moving my head left to right. "Never again."

She turned and sat in the captain's chair next to me. "Good. 'Cause if you are, you're going to need more than just a good plastic surgeon." A smile. "You're going to need a donor."

I laughed.

"And just so you don't forget"—she pulled the band away from the back of the watch—"I had it inscribed."

Chapter Fifteen

I had just closed my eyes when Paulo woke me. He whispered, "*Vamonos, el doctor.* We go."

I heard myself mumbling something about not actually being a doctor, but he was gone. I stood and pulled on my shoes, whereby my toes poked out the ends. When I exited my shed, he put his hand on my chest and motioned back in my tent. *"Agua."*

I grabbed the water jug, we refilled it, and then he handed me a long machete. I followed him out the yard and down the road beneath a dark sky. We walked in silence for almost thirty minutes, returning in the same direction we'd walked yesterday—uphill toward the volcano. When the sugarcane rose up on our right, he took a hard right turn and I followed him through the cane. We walked down long rows and were soon joined by other men, silently stepping through the night. Each carried a machete with the same ease that men carry umbrellas on Fifth Avenue.

It was still dark. Well before daylight and yet people were alive and awake and moving and working. Fires were lit, people were chatting, men were hurrying to work, and all before the first ray of sunshine had cracked the summit of Las Casitas or San Cristóbal. Unlike the world I came from, these people were on the earth's schedule— the earth was not on theirs.

We exited into a clearing where a large cart, about the size of a railroad car, sat empty. A man sat on the cart, waiting. Smoking a cigarette. When we appeared, he spoke in harsh and muffled tones to the men, pointing in various directions and splitting the men into teams. Paulo pointed his machete and directed me toward a row of cane.

When we reached the beginning of the row, he walked in front of me and demonstrated how to grab the cane with my left hand, how to cut it low on the stalk with the machete in my right, and then how to throw it in parallel piles alongside us. He did this quickly and, despite his diminutive size, with great strength. I nodded. He stepped to the row beside me, motioned with his machete to my row, and then he began his assault. Only then did I notice how much larger his right forearm and biceps were than his left. Nearly half again as large.

We worked in tandem until daylight, when we stopped for about thirty seconds to swig from our water jugs. We worked in like fashion throughout the morning. He worked fast and with the strength of several men. I kept up as best I could. By midmorning, my hands had blistered, popped, and oozed. Raw like hamburger meat. Every pull on the sugarcane ripped more skin loose. If he noticed, he said nothing. Neither did I.

With an hour until noon, he had finished his row and returned to help me with mine. By noon, we came to the end of it, and that was good because I could barely swing the machete. He pointed with his machete again, and we walked down the same row we'd just cleared. When we reached the superintendent's cart, we found him where we'd left him with another cigarette in his mouth. I could not lift my arms above shoulder height. He surveyed our work with little interest, placed two bills into Paulo's hand, and we began walking home. Paulo turned to me and handed me one of the bills, but I declined, waving him off, and said, "No, no. You."

He folded the money and said, "*Gracias.*"

We took a different route home, swinging wide around the cluster of homes known as Valle Cruces. We came to a building and he pointed. "*Escuela.*"

I didn't understand, so he folded his hands like he was reading a book. "*Escuela.*"

"Oh, you mean school."

We walked up next to the door and found Paulina teaching math to a classroom full of kids of various ages and sizes. Isabella sat in the front row, her heels tucked under her butt to lift her up to the level of the desk in front of her. She twirled her hair with her left hand. With her right, she scribbled on a sheet of paper. The chairs and desks were all handmade from the same wood used in the tenement dwellings up on the mountain. The seats and desktops were worn and oiled. The sides were unfinished and splintery.

When she saw me, Isabella hopped down out of her seat and danced toward us. The measured speed with which she gallivanted across the room told me that she wasn't so much glad to see me as she wanted to be recognized by the other kids that she—and not they—was on a first-name basis with the gringo. Moving slowly made her point all the more poignant. When all eyes noticed her familiarity with me, she returned to her seat. Sitting a little higher. Task accomplished. Paulo said something to Paulina, who then ended class. Isabella appeared at my side and slid her hand into mine. When she sensed the blisters and raw skin, she turned my hand over and eyed it with tenderness. She ran her fingers around the edges of the blisters that had popped. "Do they hurt?"

I shook my head.

When we returned to the house, Paulina pointed to the sink and said, "Better wash those in the *pila*."

"The what?"

She pronounced it more slowly. "*Pee-lah*. It's the name for that concrete sink. You don't want those getting infected."

I did as instructed while the three of them loaded the truck.

I watched Paulo hand the two bills to Paulina, who placed them in her pocket. Quickly and showing no sign of fatigue, Paulo backed the truck up and began honking the horn, drawing Isabella and Paulina out of the house. Isabella climbed into the cab with Uncle Paulo while Paulina sat with me in the back. He eased off the clutch, which was slipping, and revved the engine, which blew white smoke out the exhaust, suggesting that it was burning nearly as much oil as gas. Grinding the gears, we eased out of Valle Cruces en route to León.

Paulina and I sat on the wheel wells as the heat and dust and humidity pressed against us at forty-five miles per hour. Along the roadside, all the brilliant Technicolor flags and homes and cars and people stood still as we sped by. Occasionally, I'd catch a glance of a vine-covered fountain or an old home or chapel or some prior remnant of beauty buried beneath a caked layer of dirt, exhaust, and disrepair. After a few minutes, she reached for my hand, turning it in her own, studying it. She offered softly, "My uncle says you work hard."

"Twenty years older, he did twice as much work. Came back to help me when he finished."

She laughed. "He said he kept waiting for you to fall over, but you never did."

"I wanted to."

"Well, thank you."

"How much did we earn?"

"A hundred córdobas."

I calculated. "Seems like a lot of work for three dollars and eighty cents."

"It's twice what he normally makes."

I spoke out loud to myself. "I spend more than that on a latte at Starbucks. There was a time in one of my former lives when I'd spend a hundred times that on a lunch and not think twice about it."

She stared out in front of us as the wind tugged at her hair. She nodded but said nothing. We rode in silence. I turned to her. "How come you haven't asked me anything about me?"

She grinned and pointed to Isabella in the front seat. "I let her do my dirty work."

"Seriously. I could be an escaped convict, and you wouldn't know it."

She shrugged. "An escaped convict wouldn't have been found on the sidewalk covered in his own excrement."

"Good point."

"You did carry a ninety-pound backpack six miles up the side of a mountain."

"You sure it wasn't heavier than that?"

She smiled, proving that Isabella had not fallen far from the tree. "Since you're offering, can I ask one favor of you?"

"Anything."

"Pan y Paz is a bakery in León. Isabella's favorite. They make these chocolate croissants. Do you—?"

"Done. Anything else?"

"The bakery is plenty."

I pressed her. "Are you one of those people who's good at offering help but not so good at accepting it?"

She nodded and tucked her skirt under her thighs as the wind pulled at it, momentarily exposing long, muscular quadriceps and toned, beautiful legs. Then she pulled the hair out of her face. "Yes. Yes, I am."

"What are you three doing for dinner?"

"Driving back."

"Before you go, will you let me buy you dinner?"

She hesitated. "When I found you, you had nothing. And unless something's changed, you still have nothing." She lowered her voice. "How're you going to buy dinner?"

"I left my money in the room."

"Can you afford to buy us dinner?"

"Yes. Please. It's the least I can do."

Paulina considered this. And the look on her face told me that she was not accustomed to accepting help. "As long as you let me pick the restaurant."

We reached León and the Hotel Cardinal, where the young man was glad to see me and seemed proud that he'd guarded my room and everything was just as I'd left it. When he left, I turned to find Isabella staring at the peephole in the door. Paulina was smiling. "She's never seen one."

I lifted her so she could press her eye against the door. Paulina stood outside the door and waved. Isabella jumped back in shock at her mother's distorted image, then giggled and tried to make sense of the illusion.

Paulo was a quiet man. Few words. He watched, listened, and was purposeful in all he did—wasting no movement. I attributed it to years of conserving his energy for whatever unknown came next. His unwritten response to life was one of crisis management. While Isabella entertained herself with the peephole, he waited quietly in a chair just outside the door.

We left the hotel on foot, following Paulina's finger, and arrived at Meson Real fifteen minutes later. It was a "locals" joint and the smell coming from the kitchen was divine.

The waitress came and took our orders, and given that the menu was written on the wall—in Spanish—Paulina asked, "Want some help?"

I tried to make sense of the wall. "Yes."

"You want real Nicaraguan or tourist stuff?"

"Real."

She raised an eyebrow. "Might be kind of spicy."

"I'm game."

While we waited on our food, I tried not to pepper Paulo with too many questions. He told me he had been born just a mile or so from where he now lives, but he had traveled a good bit to find work in both cane and coffee plantations.

When he said he'd worked in coffee, I began listening a little more attentively. "You've worked coffee?"

"*Sí.*"

"Where?"

"Honduras. Costa Rica." He tapped the table. "Nicaragua."

"Where in Nicaragua?"

He pointed west. "Las Casitas. Near *mi casa*."

"Any one place in particular?"

He shook his head. "No understand."

"What plantation?"

"Jus' one." When he said it, there was a sense of warmth and affection I'd not heard before. "Cinco Padres Café Compañía."

I swallowed hard. "What'd you do there?"

He made a circle around the table. "Manage workers." He tapped himself on the chest and smiled. "*El jefe.*"

I shook my head and was in the process of saying I didn't understand when Paulina put her hand on mine and said, "He managed all the workers. The plantation. Everything."

"He was the foreman?"

"Before this foreman . . . yes, that was *part* of his job."

"Why did you leave?"

He paused. "Jus' too many events."

I pointed at Paulina, acting as if I didn't know. "Was it the hurricane you mentioned?"

He sliced his hand across the table in a level motion. "Hurricane Carlos bad. Very bad. Kill many. Kill my brothers. Their wives. My wife. Many family, but . . ." He shook his head. "We survived Carlos."

My voice quivered. "What . . . happened?"

Paulo paused, crossed his hands, and then

spoke, almost in reverence. "American company." Paulo made a fist as if he were crushing a cracker. "They squeeze us . . . require us to pay back loan. Have no way to pay. But after Carlos, we has nothing. All gone. So, when we no pay, American company take."

Something about my complexion must have startled Paulina because she put her hand on my forearm. "You okay? You're doing that thing again." Her index finger rolled around the underside of my wrist and landed on my pulse where she held it.

"No, I'm good." I wiped the cold sweat off my face. "What'd you do?"

He shrugged. "Many empty homes in Valle Cruces. We move in. I return to sugarcane."

"Do you rent?"

He shook his head. "No one to pay rent."

"Who owns it?"

"My cousin." He said the name proudly. As if he were honoring it. "Saulicio Mares Estevez."

"Where is he?"

"Beneath the mud."

"I'm sorry?"

Paulina spoke. "His family in Managua lets us live in it."

The pieces of this puzzle were floating around my brain, and I was having a tough time putting them together. I scratched my head. "Where were you living?"

He looked at me, surprise covering his face. He pointed at Paulina. "*El casa.*"

I turned to Paulina. "Whose house?"

She brushed the hair out of Isabella's face. "My father's." She turned to me, and for the first time, she fingered a polished stone hanging around her neck. She said his name slowly and with great affection. The words swam around my head, finally settling on the memories attached to them: "Alejandro Santiago Martinez."

I swallowed hard.

"He, along with four other men, started Cinco Padres." She pointed across the table at Paulo. "Paulo married my father's sister. So while he wasn't one of his brothers, they trusted him. My father was the businessman. Dealt with the banks. The buyers. Paulo was the people's man." She smiled at Paulo. "He kept everybody happy. And"—she laughed—"he kept everything working. Tractors. Trucks. Conveyor belts. Even delivered babies. Didn't you?"

He laughed as if the memory were pleasant.

When the food arrived, steam lifted off the overfilled plates, and everyone ate and savored it with great delight. My meal looked like steak fajitas with everything in the kitchen thrown on top. And while it tasted and smelled wonderful, I didn't so much eat it as push it around the plate. Halfway through his dinner, Paulo said something to Paulina in a hushed tone, which she acknowledged quietly. I wasn't sure what to make of it, so I asked if he was okay. She said, "He asked if you liked your food, because you're not eating."

Following her dinner, Isabella eyed the offering of ice cream listed on the wall. Paulina quietly scolded her in Spanish. I had a feeling she was telling her that we weren't ordering dessert. When the waitress returned, I asked Paulina, "Would it be okay if I ordered her some ice cream? Really, it'd be my pleasure." She turned to Isabella, who nodded excitedly. Isabella held up three fingers and said, "Cho-co-la-tay."

The image of Zaul entered my mind and the ticking clock I'd been hearing since I sat in the hospital room beside Maria's bed returned. I needed help yesterday, so when everyone had finished, I spoke to both of them. "I'd like to make you a proposition—if you'll allow."

Paulo nodded. "Of course. Please."

"I'd like to hire you. Both of you." Paulina stared at me with a growing suspicion.

Paulo shook his head. "No need to hire. You ask. We help."

"What I'm about to ask is no small thing. I'd feel better if you'd let me pay you."

Paulo shook his head, and for the first time, I saw a shadow of pride I'd not seen before. He waved his hand across the table, palm down, slicing through the air. "No pay. We will glad help."

The job for which I wanted to hire them would mean he'd not be working in the sugarcane fields. Which meant a loss of income. Which meant their meager existence was about to get worse. I said, "I am here looking for someone. A sixteen-year-old kid. He's sort of like my nephew. He got mixed up in some bad stuff, ran away from home, and came here. His name's Zaul, and his parents asked me to bring him home before he gets him-self hurt or disappears forever. He's hotheaded, tempestuous, and as much as he would deny it, he's a bit naive as to people and their intentions. He thinks he can read people, but he can't. I know he came to León, and he's a surfer, so I know he intended to chase big waves along the coast, but I have a feeling his fortunes have reversed since arriving because the foreman at Cinco Padres Café is now driving his truck."

Paulina looked surprised. "That new truck?"

I nodded. "My business partner, Colin, bought it last year. Zaul's his son, and he hoped it'd bring them closer as they chased waves up and down the coast."

"That's an expensive truck."

"My partner inherited a business from his father. They started poor, then struck gold when his father realized how to import rum. He picked up where his father left off and has done very well since."

Paulina raised an eyebrow. "And you?"

"I work for him." I emphasized the word "for."
"I handle deliveries." It wasn't a complete lie.

Paulo lit. "Management?"

"No. I'm a solo act. Work alone. It's just the nature of my business."

Paulo nodded. "No matter. We will help."

"I'm afraid it will require a lot of your time. At least half the day. Sometimes all day. I'd be keeping you from your work."

Paulo asked, "How long?"

"I'm trying to find a kid who doesn't want to be found. A week? Two? Maybe a month."

Paulo paused. I could see him calculating the cost. "I work *la caña* in the morning, and we go with you after lunch."

I shook my head. "From what I know about him, he surfs in the mornings and they travel or sleep in the afternoons. Our chance of seeing him in any one place would be the time until noon. If we wait until after lunch to get started, our chances will be slim." I pointed at him. "I need a driver who speaks the language, and I'll pay for all your gas." Paulo calculated again. Paulina sat uncomfortably quiet. I offered, "Whatever you miss in income, I'll pay."

Paulina spoke up. "If he doesn't work, if he misses a day, he loses his seniority. That means when he returns, he won't be guaranteed work."

I began to see how I was upsetting the balance of their lives. How one missed day, one cold, one sickness, one injury, one missed bus or just over-sleeping by ten minutes could alter the fortune of their lives for a long time.

She leaned forward on the table, trying not to be unkind but wanting to make sure she got her point across. "Seniority in this part of the world is a commodity. Worth more than the money we make."

She had found me on the street. Naked except for my underwear. In her experience, I was not a solid bet.

"How will you pay?"

"With money?"

"Whose?"

"Mine."

"Why do you want to hire me, too?"

"To translate and, no offense, to be a woman."

"What do you mean?"

"In my experience, sometimes a woman can get information that a man cannot."

That common sense seemed to satisfy her, yet she still looked incredulous. She sat back. "And you can afford to pay us?"

In her eyes, I was nearly as poor as she, so I wanted to be careful here. "Yes."

She crossed her arms. "If Paulo misses a single day of work, what we call 'getting out of line,' he loses his place of seniority, which has taken him years to build. That means that like all the other men now waiting for a chance to work, he has to get back in line. Wait his turn. It could take him weeks to get a single day of work. It's how things work around here."

"I'll pay for those days as well."

More disbelief. "Until he can get work again?"

"Yes."

"Every day?"

"Yes."

I placed a single twenty-dollar bill on the table. "I'll pay in advance." That got both their attention. "I need you to drive me up and down the coast, looking for Zaul. We may have to drive a long way. I'll pay you this in advance, I'll pay your daily work rate, plus all your gas, plus any wear and tear on your vehicle, plus every day that you have to wait in line."

I set another twenty-dollar bill on the table and turned to Paulina. "I'll pay you the same."

She pursed her lips as her mind wrestled with whether or not to believe me. They spoke in muffled tones to each other. Isabella looked like a kid sitting next to a Ping-Pong table keeping her eyes on the ball. Hoping to sway Isabella, I set a single dollar bill in front of her. Her small hand crept up over the top of the table and was reaching to retrieve it when her mother put her hand on hers and shook her head. Forty-one dollars sat on the table uncollected.

I set another twenty-dollar bill on the table. Paulo was now paying closer attention. That was more money than he'd make in a month, and depending upon work, maybe two months. I knew I needed to be careful. I wanted to buy their time, not shame them, and I had a feeling that there was a point at which too much money meant shame. "And I'd like to rent the chicken coop." I licked my thumb and counted out another twenty. "And pay for all my food in advance."

Eighty-one dollars sat uncollected. I looked at Paulo and held a finger in the air. "And if we find him, I'll pay a hundred-dollar bonus." Paulo was listening now. "That's nearly as much money as he can make in a year."

Paulina's voice turned edgy. Almost cold. "You always buy what you want?"

"No. But I can't do this on my own. I need to hire someone. I'd prefer it be you three."

Paulo spoke a few harsh words to Paulina, which had the effect of quieting her and preventing her from asking me any more questions. He pointed at the money as if he didn't need any more reason. He folded his hands. "I help you? You help me." I wasn't sure where this was going, but I knew I needed their help. He pointed at my watch. "I help you to lunch. You help me to dinner."

Sounded fair. "Okay."

Paulo stood, folded the money, and slid the wad into his pocket. He extended his hand. "We are very happy to help."

Paulina stood as Paulo led us to the door. His body language told me he wanted to get us moving before I changed my mind—or before someone spotted all that money and robbed us. He pointed to the street. "*Sí. Muy bueno. Vamos.*"

Out in the street, Isabella slid her hand in mine and looked up at me—a chocolate mustache dripping off the edges of her upper lip. Content to be, she said nothing. When I looked down, she was cradling my heart in her hands.

It was late when we returned to Hotel Cardinal, so I rented them the rooms adjacent to mine, for which they were thankful. Isabella had never spent the night in a hotel, and the cold air blowing out of the two square holes in the wall was an amazement beyond words. As was the little box with blue numbers that makes the air colder or hotter. Followed closely by hot water and the idea that someone other than her mother had washed and dried the towels and sheets. Further, the fact that that same someone had then hung the towels on a bar in the bathroom and made the bed with clean sheets and left free soap in the bathroom and that the water coming out of the faucet was clean enough to drink was just more than she could wrap her mind around. When her mother tucked her in, she said, "Mami, I feel like a princess."

I was sitting on the porch outside my room when Paulina turned out Isabella's light and sat beside me. "This kid you're going to find, he's not a good kid, is he?"

I shook my head. "No. He's not."

"Why does he matter?"

"By his own admission, his dad is something of a nerd. Good at counting beans and entertaining the wealthy. Me? Not so much. So, I picked up where his dad left off and taught him a few things his dad had neglected."

"Like?"

"How to ride a bike, tie double knots in his shoes, brush both his teeth and his gums, drive a boat, then a stick shift."

She pointed to my lips. "When you speak about him, there's a tenderness in your voice."

It was a question posed as a statement. "When he was young and his folks would host a party, he was often overlooked. I have some experience with that, so we'd fish off the dock." A shrug. "I'd bait his hook. Taught him how to throw a cast net, the difference between deodorant and antiperspirant." A chuckle. "Why girls say one thing when they mean another."

She was quiet several minutes. Before she spoke, she pushed her hair out of her eyes that the wind had loosed. "I need to say something to you and I don't know you very well and you're being very kind to us, so it may come across as hard or ungrateful. I don't intend that."

I waited.

She waved her hand across the air in front of us. "There is a thing in this country called 'the

Gringo Effect.' It's when white people like you—no offense—come in and wave a little money around people like me and my uncle who live on two to three dollars a day, and we jump like circus monkeys doing whatever you want us to do because we've never seen that much money. My country is dotted with gringos; many like you cash in their 401(k)s, buy a little place, and live out their days in relative ease, thinking that their money buys them the right to live or act however they want or that they can own us because we need what they have. I'm not a rich woman, but I was educated in the States. I've not always been poor. There was a time when I could afford groceries with enough left over for ice cream. Maybe even a movie ticket. Or a new razor when the old one pulled out the hair on my legs rather than shaved it." A pause. "I don't have a lot of experience with men who so easily buy the services of others, but I've lived enough to know it's not common."

Her statements were leading, but I wasn't sure where. "So—"

"So, I can't figure out why you just hired us to do for you something you could very well do on your own."

I threw an answer out there, doubting it would satisfy her. It was more of a question than a statement. "Because I need help."

She shook her head. "I doubt you've needed

help in a long time." She pursed her lips. "Just curious, but how much would you have paid?"

I shrugged. I didn't want to answer her.

"Five hundred?"

I nodded, hoping it would satisfy her and end this line of questioning. It did not.

"A thousand."

Another nod. Same hope. Same result.

She sat back and crossed her arms. "Five thousand?"

My eyes met hers. "Yes."

She considered this. "I don't know you well enough to say, but I can't figure something."

"What's that?"

"I can't figure if you're a good man—the likes of which we seldom see around here." She paused.

"Or—?"

She never hesitated. "Guilty."

An uncomfortable silence settled. She turned her chair toward me, inched forward into my personal space, spread her legs like a man, and rested her elbows on her knees—an athlete on a bench. I was not totally unprepared for this. I'd just bought them, and I had a pretty good idea that didn't set well with her. "Charlie?"

I made eye contact but said nothing.

"I need to know . . ." She reached in her pocket, pulled out the wad of cash I'd just given them, and held it before me. "If we take this, are you putting us in danger? Of any kind?" She glanced at Isabella's window, shook her head, and proffered the money. "Because if you are . . ."

I held out my hand like a stop sign. "I owe you more than that for taking care of me while I was sick. It's the least I can do."

"You didn't answer my question."

"To my knowledge, I am not putting you in any danger, but there is the possibility that Zaul is messed up with the wrong people. If in helping me, you ever get the slightest hint that I've put you in danger, you're free to walk with no explanation."

She sat back and returned the money to her pocket. Our rooms were on the second story, as was the porch. This gave us a limited aerial view of the lights of the city. She stood, dusted off her skirt, and waited several seconds. "The bakery opens at six, and that's when everything is hot and the little chunks of chocolate are still soft. You don't want to miss that. Almost a religious experience. Paulo will get on the phone early and make some inquiries. We'll get moving after that." She put her hand on my shoulder. The first time she'd touched me in tenderness. "If he's within a hundred or so miles, Paulo will find him. We'll do what we can." She turned and walked to her room, stopping at the door. She weighed her head side to side and said, "For the record, we'd have done it for nothing. All you had to do is ask."

"I figured that."

"And yet you offered anyway?"

"I have my reasons."

"Which you still don't care to explain."

"You won't like me when I do."

She leaned against the doorframe and nodded, finally turning and partially closing the door. "There's a seasoned old man and an innocent little girl, both asleep in here, who find that hard to believe."

"And you?"

"I think that may be the most revealing and truthful statement you've made since I met you." With that, she shut the door and turned out the light.

And she was right. It was.

Chapter Sixteen

Colin moved his family home after that summer in Costa Rica while keeping the house, swearing that he and his family would return there for all eternity. That he and Marguerite would retire there. Colin had found a home. As had his family. Life was good.

In the coming weeks and months, I introduced Shelly to my family. To Colin, Marguerite, Zaul, and she-who-holds-my-heart-in-her-hands, Maria Luisa. Every time we saw them, Maria would run, jump up in my lap, throw her arms around my neck, and speak in a voice that could melt titanium. "Uncle Charlie, what'd you bring me?"

I'd hold her in my lap, tickle her, sing "How Do You Solve a Problem Like Maria?" And then after ignoring her long enough, I'd snap my fingers and circle back around to her question. "I knew I forgot something."

She'd try to search my pockets, and finally I'd pull a wrapped package out of a hidden place in my shirt or shorts. A necklace or a ring or something glittery from some foreign soil. The first time Shelly met her she shook her head. "Least I know who the competition is." She smiled. "She's got you eating out of the palm of her hand."

I nodded and said, "Hook, line, and sinker."

The more time Shelly and I spent with Colin and his family, the more I could see how the absence of children in her own life was affecting her. There was a joy missing. And she knew it. She sensed its absence. She also saw that I was good with kids, that I loved them, that they loved me. Add to that her love for me, and it wasn't tough to see that coming freight train in the tunnel.

One night, walking hand in hand in the surf along our favorite part of the beach, on the northwestern tip of Bimini, Atlantis buried in the waters over my shoulder, she asked me, "Can I ask you something?"

I had a feeling this was coming. It'd been on the tip of her tongue for weeks. "Yes."

"You ever think about getting married?"

"No."

She poked me in the ribs. "I'm being serious."

This was one of those conversations with which I wasn't entirely comfortable. The kind where we talked about things of the heart. Where we leaned over the green felt and showed the other the cards we were holding. Where the mystery, the fun and games ended and the playing stopped. Where we held our chips loosely. I swallowed. "Yes."

She tucked her arm inside mine. "Ever think of someone you might like to do that with?"

I nodded. "Yeah . . . Maria."

She punched me in the arm and pointed to the water rolling in gentle waves around our ankles. "You want to go swimming?"

I laughed.

She continued. "I'm serious."

It was time. I'd put it off long enough. The game had brought me to this place. Either I was all in or I needed to fold. I turned, held both her hands, and knelt. As I was about to open my mouth, a wave crashed just beyond us and the whitewater rolled me over. Tumbling me. She laughed. A lot. Maybe it was an icebreaker I needed.

I stood. Soaked. And wiped the sand out of my face. She stood in front of me with her hands behind her back. "You were saying?"

"You're really going to make me go through with this, aren't you?"

She nodded.

Shelly had made it pretty clear in previous conversations that if and when she remarried she didn't want the big diamond. Been there and done that. She wanted a simple gold band. Something with some history that meant something.

About two months prior, we'd been in León, Nicaragua. Shelly thought we were there to pick up rum and some raw coffee beans. Which were. We were also there to pick up a lot of cocaine. One afternoon, while the boat was being loaded on the coast, we were walking the streets and passed a shop that advertised jewelry made from shipwrecked gold. She eyed the window and talked mostly to herself. "That's about right. Ship-wrecked gold." The owner was a bit of a local legend, a salvage diver and a weekend shipwreck junkie. Through the years, he'd discovered several small Spanish ships off the coast and managed to sift a little gold from each. From that, he'd had a few rings made. I don't know if his story was true, but his rings were custom and the gold as beauti-ful as I'd ever seen.

Maybe it was the breeze, maybe it was Shelly's see-through chiffon, maybe it was island life, or maybe it was the sight of my fortieth birthday not too far in the distance, but as we stood outside that store and museum, I actually heard myself say these words: "Doesn't hurt to look."

I pushed open the door. Shelly eyed the CUSTOM-MADE JEWELRY sign and said, "Doors like this are usually one way. Once you go in . . ." She held my gaze and waited.

I led her to the counter where the rings were displayed beneath the glass. She clasped her hands behind her back and leaned over the counter, the gold glistening off her eyes. She was waiting on some signal from me. I struck up a conversation with the man who lifted the trays from the display case and shared with us the stories of his treasure hunting. Shelly listened with one ear, but her focus was wrapped around her finger. We tried a few, thanked the man, and then walked out. The following day, while she napped in the hotel, I returned to his store and buried the resulting purchase in the bottom of my pocket.

I enjoyed Shelly's company and I liked her a lot, but I can't tell you that I spent a lot of time dreaming about sharing the rest of my life with her. I didn't dream that way with anyone. I know how that sounds, and no, I'm not real proud of it. I enjoyed her company and I wanted to be with her, but I wasn't looking so much long term as I was short. My motive was simple: I didn't want to live without her. Not because I couldn't. I'd been alone a long time. I was good at it. But because of what "being without her" ultimately said about me.

The moon was high. Bright. Clear. Full. Trailing

out across the water. I picked her up and she swung her arms around my neck. The vein in her neck throbbed. Her body might have been relaxed, but her heart was pounding. I walked her out through the waves to the clear, warm calm water just beyond the break. "Shelly?"

Years of shattered dreams and a painful first marriage were dissolving with every word. Her face lit. I slid the ring from my pocket, pulled her hand from around my neck, and placed the band in her palm. "Marry me?"

Looking back, it was probably not the proposal she wanted. No girl, no woman, wants a half-spoken, somewhat guarded proposal. The whole down-on-one-knee thing? The whole all-in thing? It matters. She smiled, closed her palm, and kissed me. I can still taste the saltwater. I didn't see it then, but she had resigned herself there— to take what she could get.

Sometimes I wish the story ended here.

What I didn't realize at the time was that my half-fast proposal had cheated Shelly out of a marriage proposal that lived up to her hopes and closed the door on the pain of the first. That brought healing. Her first husband had not been faithful, not cherished her, and not been truthful until caught. He'd left a bitter taste. While never spoken or expressed, she was hopeful that I would remedy this. And that remedy started with a proposal that lived up to her idealized and romantic notions of marriage. Notions that I fed and encouraged.

I had cheated her of this.

It would not be the last time.

Just off the northern tip of Bimini, some two hundred yards from the beach, a huge, flat piece of limestone—about the size of a fishing boat—rises up out of the water some six or eight feet. Some believe it's included in the Atlantis formations. On several occasions, Shelly and I had swum out to it and rested or hunted for lobster, then swam back. Following my lame proposal, Shelly stated she wanted a beach wedding. Barefoot. Preferably on that rock. We'd meet on the beach and swim out together. Small. Just "family." In the time I'd known her, Shelly had grown close to Hack, Colin, Marguerite, and the kids—who weren't really kids anymore. She'd grown especially close to Maria. Even taught her how to French braid her hair. Given their inclusion in our lives, it was important to her that they share that moment with us. We booked a justice of the peace and set a date for a month in the distance.

My fortieth birthday.

The following morning I walked to Hack's shack at daybreak to share the news. Normally, I walked around the corner to the aroma of coffee and a lit cigarette. This morning, I experienced neither. "Hack?"

No response.

"Hack?" I said a bit louder.

I found him in bed. No shirt. His feet sticking out from underneath the sheet. He was staring out across the water. He was not smoking. Not drinking coffee. Just staring east across the Atlantic. I knew when I saw him that Hack had folded his cards. He was done. He would never leave port again.

I sat and his eyes moved while his head did not. He whispered with a forced smile, " 'Bout time you got here." He tried to whisper again, but doing so dislodged something in his chest, causing a coughing fit he was too weak to fight. His lips were tinted red. His mouth dry. I fed him a sip of water and he asked for a cigarette. When I started to argue with him, he whispered, "What? You think they're going to kill me?"

I lit it and hung it from his lips where it dangled. Hack was pale and his breathing labored. I think he'd hung in there as long as he could. Long enough to have one last talk with me. I repositioned the pillow behind his head and then slipped my hand inside his. He smiled and nodded. The muscles felt deflated. The decades' worth of calluses not so thick. Life was fading. Draining out. Only a trickle remained.

His voice was weak when he spoke. "I'd like to ask a favor."

I leaned in. Closer. "Anything."

He was staring out beyond the sheet of glass that had rolled up nearly to his back door. "I want you to"—he gestured with his right hand—"bury me at sea. With my wife." A pause.

I swallowed. Then nodded.

He tapped two sheets of paper next to him. "Instructions." He closed his eyes and rested the papers on his chest. "Signed. Made it legal." He shook his head once. "Nobody'll bother you." His eyes turned to me. "You're all the family I've got."

I lifted the cigarette, flicked the ash, and returned it between his now blue lips. He drew, held it, exhaled, and spoke. "Don't let that girl slip away." A single shake. "Lonely is no way to live." He tapped me on the chest. "And you been lonely since the moment I met you."

I nodded. The thought of one more loss was sinking in. Another someone I loved being taken from me.

He continued. "You, me, her. We need each other."

A tear trickled down my cheek.

He noticed it and one side of his mouth turned up. "Glad to know you've got a heart."

I thumbed the tear, lit a new cigarette with the glow plug end of the other, and hung the new one from his lip.

A slight smile, he filled his chest and focused on his breathing, the smoke trailing out his nose. Finally, he handed me the papers, closed his eyes, and then reached for my hand. Held it between his on top of his chest. A few moments later, he drew in half a breath, stopped short, and then his body relaxed, his hand fell limp, and he exhaled long and slow, filling the air around us with a cloud. When he didn't inhale, and he didn't move, I sat back, breathing in the cloud.

I crossed his arms over his chest and pulled the sheet up over him. As I did, I noticed something in me hurt. Deeply. Something I'd not felt in a long, long time. It was my heart. And it was aching.

I buried Hack at sea, as detailed in his last will and testament. Strangely enough, it'd been witnessed by the island doc who'd come to check on Hack the night before. Turns out he'd been making house calls the better part of the last few weeks, upping Hack's morphine each night so he could handle the pain from the growing mass in his chest. He later told me that when he'd signed the papers, he was pretty sure that Hack would not live out the night. He was surprised he'd hung in there as long as he did.

With a signed affidavit from the magistrate, I laid Hack's body in the coffin and loaded him into the *Storied Career* and then slowly motored out to sea. I had plugged in the latitude and longitude coordinates into the GPS and followed the arrows. When I crossed the "X"—with nearly 1,900 feet of water below me—I cut the engine, said my good-byes to Hack, and then lifted the box and his body over the ledge, gently sliding it into the water. The box filled and the weight of it pulled against me. I held on several minutes, unwilling to let go. Finally, having to strain to keep it afloat, I released my grip and it slid like a torpedo out of my hands and out of sight.

I sat there, tears streaking my cheeks, rolling in gentle waves on the stern. Needing to hear his voice, I unfolded the letter he'd left me to read at this moment:

Dear Charlie,

Looking back, I've lived a long life. A good life. But looking back, I do have a few regrets. If I could give you anything, I'd spare you the pain of those. I'd tell you to grab that woman and don't let go. To find another business 'cause the one you're in is too dangerous and you don't need the money. Especially now that I'm giving you mine. You'll find it when you unearth yours. Spend it on something worthwhile. Something beautiful. Something bigger than you and me. Life is more than bonefish and skiffs and coffee and cigarettes and island sunsets. Those things are good and I've enjoyed my fair share, but I've enjoyed them with an empty heart, which means they didn't fill me. But my wife? She filled me. In the more than forty years since her death, I've been with no other woman. Couldn't. She's been here by my bedside lately at night. She's younger. Smiling again. Looks better than the last time I saw her. Took me a long time to get the image of the blood puddling on her stomach out of my head, and seeing her here the last few nights, all dressed in white and clean and pretty and not poked full of bullet holes, has pretty much erased it. I've missed her smile. In forty years of penance, I have paid for my sins. There were lots of them.

Charlie, don't be me. Don't die this way. It's no way to go.

Thank you for being my friend. For coming by and checking on me. For letting me teach you about skiffs and working with wood—which you have a pretty good bit of natural talent for.

Thank you for not letting me die alone.

Sincerely,

James J. "Hack" Hackenworth, Jr.

Sitting there wrestling with his words and the weight of his letter, I realized that I'd never told him about Shelly. About us. About us getting married tomorrow night. I cranked the engine, turned west, and pushed the throttle three-quarters forward. The boat shot out beneath me, and 1,400 horsepower lifted the boat up on plane like a 100-mph water-skimming rocket en route to Bimini some twenty miles in the distance.

The problem with driving west in the afternoon was the sun. I pulled down my Costas, the water leveled out, and I pushed the throttle against the stop as the wind dried the tears streaking my face.

I needed to get moving. The wind was picking up and so was the chop. I had a drop to make in Miami.

Chapter Seventeen

The three of them were dressed and ready when I walked out at six. We exited the hotel front doors and walked a few blocks down the street until we caught the smell of fresh baked bread. When it grew stronger, we turned left, and by the time we reached the door, my salivary glands were pumping double. We walked in, were greeted by a fair-skinned, blond-haired woman who looked Swedish and was sliding steaming trays into a glass counter display. Paulo and Isabella sat while Paulina ordered for each of us. Within a few minutes, one of the kids behind the counter delivered three delicious cups of coffee along with an entire tray of croissants and Danishes.

I ate six.

Isabella and I laughed as the chocolate crusted the corners of our mouths. Starting on my seventh, I stared at the croissant and said, "I think they just dip the whole thing in butter."

While we were eating, the busboy began clearing the tables around us. A good-looking kid, clean-cut, apron, hard worker, looked like he'd lifted a few weights. But that wasn't the feature that caught my attention. I asked Paulina to call the owner to our table. She did and the Swedish lady appeared. "Everything okay?"

I pointed at the kid. "How well do you know him?"

"Mauricio?"

"If that's his name."

"He's my nephew. Worked here two years. One of the more reliable kids I have."

"You ever caught him lying to you?"

She raised an eyebrow. "No."

"How about stealing?"

Her face tightened. "Why?"

"You mind bringing him over here?"

"Sir, I'd prefer you speak to me first—"

"Just call him over, please."

"If you have a complaint—"

"Please."

She did and he appeared at our table wiping his hands on his apron. *"Sí, señor?"*

I pointed at his watch. "Nice watch." I said it that way because I wanted to catch him off guard and gauge his reaction.

He smiled and nodded proudly, holding it out for me to see. If there was guilt, he was a better actor than most Academy Award winners. The owner watched without comment, but she looked ready to pounce. I asked, "You get it locally?"

"Sí, señor. I buy from"—he pointed at the floor—"here. Man who eat here say he no need and sell me less money."

Everyone's attention at the table was glued to his wrist. "You like it?"

He nodded, but then frowned and began to wonder. *"Señor?"*

"On the back, beneath the band, some words are written. You know what it says?"

He looked at the owner, then back at me. He shook his head. *"Señor?"*

The owner broke in. "He says he bought it, sir. If you think—"

I wrote on a napkin, folded it, and set it on the table in front of them. "Five days ago, I was mugged, stripped, and everything I had taken as I lay sick in the street." I looked at the kid. "Now, I doubt you had anything to do with that, but whoever you bought it from may have well taken it off me, and unlike everything else, it can't be replaced. I'd like it back."

He frowned. The owner said, "Take it off, Mauricio. Let's see."

He unbuckled it from his wrist, pulled the band away from the back, and read the words. I opened the napkin and spread it across the table. He read it out loud. "Never again."

I pointed to the grooves of the inscription. They were stained and dark, as was the back of the watchband. "That's blood. It belongs to someone I love."

He turned the watch in his hand, touching it lightly, as if it were delicate.

The owner's look of suspicion transferred from me to Mauricio. I said, "Mauricio, I want to ask you a question."

He straightened and nodded. "*Sí, señor.*"

"Did you take that watch off my arm?"

He tried to put the words together, but I apparently spoke them too fast so Paulina quietly translated. He shook his head. "No, *señor*. I buy it right here." Another point.

Fortunately for Mauricio, I believed him. The owner waited quietly, wanting to see how this was going to pan out. I said, "How much you pay for it?"

He looked at the owner and then back at me. When he said nothing, I asked again. "How much?"

After a sideways glance at the owner, he looked over his shoulder and lowered his voice. "*Catorce dólares.*"

The owner looked at him with surprise. "Mauricio?" Her tone turned motherly. "You know how many days it takes you to earn that!"

I said, "Will you sell it to me?"

He extended the watch to me, shaking his head. "*Señor*, if it belong to you—"

I showed him twenty dollars. "Will you sell it to me for that?"

He nodded quickly. "*Sí. Sí . Muy bueno.*"

I turned to the owner. "That okay with you?"

She smiled, exhaled, and put her hand on the back of my chair. "Would you like some more coffee? I think Mauricio can brew you up something hot. He makes a pretty mean latte."

I handed him the money, which he folded and stuck in his pocket. After shaking my hand, he returned to the coffee machine. The owner spoke to all of us. "Please let me know if there's anything else you need."

Paulo stared at me over his coffee mug. Isabella sank her teeth into another Danish, and Paulina watched me with a suppressed look of curiosity. I strapped the watch on my wrist and was finishing my croissant when a wrinkle appeared between her eyes. A slight shake of her head accompanied by the beginning of an amused smile. "You're an interesting one."

"How so?"

"You could have easily taken that watch from that kid."

"I could."

"Why didn't you?"

"I have, or had, a friend in Bimini named Hack. He's dead now. Used to tell me that people spend money on three things: what they love, what they worship, and what helps ease their pain."

"Which of those does that watch represent?"

I ran my thumb along the bezel of the watch. "The third."

"What else do you spend money on?"

"Good coffee, bottled water with bubbles—and Costa Del Mars."

She pointed to the glasses resting on the top of my head. "Like those?"

A nod. "I have about sixty pair at my house in Bimini."

"Sixty? As in six-zero?"

"My partner, Colin, is married to a lady named Marguerite who has a bit of a shoe fetish. Something like two hundred pairs. Had a cedar closet built just for her shoes. We often compare notes about our latest purchases. I guess we're cut from the same cloth."

She eyed the kid making my latte. "I think you made a friend."

"That's good 'cause I don't have too many of those."

• • •

Paulina and Paulo shared a cell phone with prepaid minutes, which they used only in emergencies. Paulina explained that they seldom, if ever, used it. Regardless, Paulo had been on it all morning. One call leading to another. He was talking on it as we left the café, and Isabella began steering me through the streets. Walking by the cathedral, she turned to Paulina, tugging on her arm. "Mami, can we go see Dadi?"

"Just a few minutes. We can't stay long."

Isabella jumped and climbed the same steps the naked dancer had pirouetted up a week earlier. Paulina noticed the strange look on my face but said nothing. We followed Isabella inside where it was quiet. And empty. Paulo dipped his finger in some water on the wall and genuflected. Paulina did likewise, although she added a bow, or curtsy, when she crossed in front of the center aisle. Isabella ran down the aisle and turned right, near the altar. Just above her, a lectern had been built on the side of a huge column that supported the ceiling. Stairs led up to a platform where the priest gave the sermon.

Isabella ran to the stairs, and when she reached them, she slid on her knees on the marble. Coming to a stop, she crawled on her belly beneath the stairs. When I reached her, she was propped up on her elbows speaking to a stone plaque. It simply read: GABRIEL.

Paulina pointed. "My husband is buried here."

I nodded and said nothing.

Paulo sat behind us in the second row. Hands folded.

I sat on the stairs and could understand nothing, as Isabella was talking a hundred miles an hour in Spanish. Paulina sat opposite me on a pew and listened. "She's telling him what's happened since we were here last week. About finding you; you sleeping in the chicken coop, which she thinks is funny; about pulling teeth; and"—she smiled— "about last night." Isabella said more but Paulina didn't translate it.

We sat quietly, listening while Isabella rattled on—talking to the stone just inches from her face. I pointed behind me to the vault where her husband lay. "When?"

"Ten years ago. I was pregnant." A single shake. "She has no memory of him."

I rested my elbows on my knees. "How?"

"He was a doctor. Made house calls. We worked"—she waved her hand in front of us— "out in the villages. He contracted a virus that attacked the lining of his heart. Grew weak. We took him to a specialist, but he had self-diagnosed and knew there was no cure. Six months later, he died at home." She looked around the church and waved at a priest. "He took care of all the priests. Many of the parishioners. He started a clinic"— she pointed to the back of the cathedral—"which continues to this day. About ten well-trained doctors volunteer their time here—a day here every two weeks. Some more than others. Because no one wants to anger the Catholic Church, hospitals donate medicine—and a lot of it. Some of which they give me when they can spare it. It's where I get most of the medicine I need for my work. Barring a trauma, it may well be the best clinic in Nicaragua, and in some ways, it's better than most hospitals in Central America. The church honored us by burying him here because he was beloved of the people." She pointed to Isabella, who was whispering, her lips brushing the stone. "Still is."

"I'm sorry."

"Me, too." She waved her hand across the walls around us, which were full of dead people who had been entombed in the walls and beneath the floor. "They paid over a million córdobas to be buried here. It's a very great honor." Her eyes fell on Isabella. Who was still talking. "She talks nonstop whenever she walks in here." A pause with half a smile. When she spoke, she wasn't looking at me. She was looking through the stone. "Every girl should have a daddy."

Paulo clicked the phone shut and slid it in his front pocket, waving us onward. "*Vamos.*" He pointed. "*Vamos al océano.*"

I turned to Paulina, who was listening to Paulo.

When he finished speaking, she turned to me. "Your friend has been seen around the ocean not far from here."

"Really? Just like that?"

She held up a finger. "He's been seen." She stood. "Not found. Evidently, he likes to leave an impression wherever he goes."

We drove west out of León toward the Pacific. Isabella slept up front, coming down off a sugar and carb high, while Paulina and I sat in the back. When we were out of town, she said, "Your friend played a card game here a week ago. He was drinking a lot and is not a very good cardplayer. Paulo talked to a man who tended bar in the game. You were right, he lost his truck to the foreman. Later in the game, in a—" Her face contorted. "Twice or zero?"

"Double or nothing?"

"That's it. He was caught cheating, tried to run and steal back his own truck so the foreman—who is a big strong man—roughed him up. After that, your friend went to the beach. He was there yesterday. That's all we know."

San Cristóbal loomed behind us. White smoke spiraling through a blue sky into the stratosphere.

She pressed me. "Does that sound like your friend?"

I hesitated. "Yes."

"He does not sound like a good man."

"Sometimes . . . people have some help becoming like that."

Leena chewed on my answer, which I was learning was her process. She thought before she spoke, although I didn't confuse thoughtfulness with hesitancy. She was not afraid to speak. The wind tugged at her hair and skirt and dried the sweat on her skin. I'd not told her this—as I had no reason—but Leena was one of the more beautiful people I'd ever known, much less seen, and I'd known some beautiful women in my life. Amanda was petite, polished, fashion minded and design savvy, quick to speak, and striking. Shelly was taller, more natural in her appearance, more attracted to the shadow than the spotlight, comfortable in loose-fitting scrubs, and well-suited to both the operating room and the beach. Leena was something of a combination of the two. As tough as her environment demanded, tender at the drop of a hat; quick to speak but more apt to listen; modest in her dress but also comfortable in her confidence; beautiful not only in silence and passing glance, but even more so in action. Leena also possessed the one thing that neither Amanda nor Shelly did: presence. She commanded authority because she was first and foremost ready to serve those around her. She'd earned it. Her willingness to kneel down and clean the groin and bottom of a feces- and urine-soaked man, then kiss his forehead, put her on a pedestal unlike any other. I did not feel comfortable around her not because she made me feel uncomfortable, but because I felt counterfeit. Her willingness to stop, kneel, and serve amid filthy, embarrassing, and uncomfortable situations jarred something loose in me because I wasn't. I'd spent my life pursuing my comfort, not others'. Leena had not. A strange emotion shadowed me as we bumped down dirt roads in the middle of nowhere. I did not know what to call it, but "unworthy" came about as close as anything. The second emotion was a question: How could someone so pure and selfless sit inches from someone so stained and selfish?

After an hour's worth of driving dusty, potholed dirt roads, lined mostly with sugarcane nearing twelve feet high, we turned down a coquina-layered drive where the smell of salt and the sound of seagulls wrapped around us. A half mile later, we arrived at a small resort on the beach: a row of concrete bungalows, hammocks stretched between the columns, surfboards leaning against every available wall, various bathing suits hung out to dry on laundry lines, a man and woman floating on inflatables in the pool, cold beer in their hands with limes in the tops and condensation running down the sides, four tanned guys with sun-bleached hair sitting on chairs staring out across a relatively flat ocean. An American guy about my age—beer belly, reading glasses on his nose, bathing suit faded, barefoot with Hawaiian shirt unbuttoned—was scurrying between the rooms and serving patrons in the pool. When he saw us, he raised a hand and said in a Midwestern accent, "Be right with you."

While we waited, Isabella walked around the pool. Eyeing it. Paulo, Paulina, and I stood beneath an umbrella, waiting.

Moments later, the guy appeared in front of me, sweating, breathing heavy, and smiling. "What can I do for you folks?"

I showed him the picture of Zaul that I'd taken from the kitchen sink at Colin's house. "You seen this guy?"

He nodded and palmed the sweat off his head, flinging it onto the ground. He was not happy to see the picture. He squinted at me. "Sure have."

"Mind telling me when?"

"Most of last night. Then this morning."

"Here?"

He pointed at one of the bungalows, then around the pool. "He and his friends—if you can call them that—trashed my villa, partied at the pool till almost daylight, and ran off a couple of my guests. I'm just now getting the mess cleaned up."

"Is he still around?"

"I sincerely hope not."

"Any idea if he plans to return?"

"I told them if they did that I'd shoot them on sight."

"That bad, huh?"

"They destroyed a brand-new flat screen, and I lost three extended-stay couples. Two had booked for a week. One for a month. I don't do business with kids like him as I can usually sniff them out, but the girl that works for me took the reservation."

"Any idea where they went?"

He pointed out in the ocean. "They hired a charter to take them to the reef. Some big swells out there the last few days. Almost twenty feet."

"You know where they caught that charter?"

"Nope."

"Do you know if they had transportation? A car or anything?"

He stuck his thumb in the air. "Best I could tell, they were hitchhiking, which can be tough when you've got five guys with boards."

"Would you mind calling me if you happen to see them again?"

"Not if you don't mind if I shoot them first."

I turned to Paulina. "Can I give him your cell number?"

Paulina gave the man her number and he returned to his office. Paulo turned the truck around, and we were loading up when Paulina discovered that Isabella was not in the truck. We turned toward the water and found that she'd walked across the sand to what looked like the end of the yard and the beginning of the dune before the beach. Paulina hollered and told her to get in the truck. Isabella stood, staring at the ocean.

Paulina hollered again, but still no reaction.

I said, "She okay?"

"Yes, she's just never seen the ocean before. I told her we'd come back when we had more—"

I hopped out of the truck and walked up next to Isabella, who was wide-eyed and chewing on a fingernail. The wind was blowing in her face and amplifying the sound of the waves crashing on the beach. I held out my hand. "Come on." She took it and we walked the well-worn surfer's path toward the beach. When we got there, I kicked off my flip-flops, as did she, and we walked down toward the water. The surf pounded the sand and, to her amazement, rolled up and across her toes, bathing her feet in sand and small shells. The Pacific was cool, dark blue, and she stood speechless as the water washed up and back. Wave after wave. A moment later, Paulina stood to her left and whispered, "Careful. She can't swim."

I'd never considered that. Isabella walked a few feet toward the waves. Knee-high. Almost midthigh. I spoke more to myself than Paulina. "What kind of kid doesn't know how to swim?"

Paulina spoke to me while staring at Isabella.

Ready to pounce. "The kind who's never had access to water and never been taught."

Isabella turned, delight on her face, and walked out of the water.

I spoke again. "We need to remedy that."

Paulina glanced at me but said nothing.

We climbed into the truck and were rolling out the driveway when I tapped on the hood of the cab and said, "Give me one second." I found the man in his office, talking on the phone. When he hung up, I asked, "How much do you figure that crew cost you?"

He was still irritated but he calculated anyway. "Four-hundred-dollar TV. Two of the couples were a week at sixty dollars a night. Other couple was here a month. I gave them a rate." He tilted his head. "Two thousand seven hundred dollars—give or take."

I counted out thirty hundred-dollar bills and handed them to him. He looked at me like I'd lost my mind. "I'm . . . sorry for your trouble."

Eyes wide, jaw hanging halfway open, he stuffed the money in his pocket and followed me out to the truck. "Mister?"

I turned.

He pointed to the picture of Zaul in my pocket. "You know that kid?"

"Yes."

"He important to you?"

"Yes."

He squinted against the sun and hesitated before he spoke—as if doing so was painful. "You know, he's real different than you."

"I had a lot to do with making him the way he is." I waved my hand across his resort. "If you want to blame someone for this, you can blame me."

He held up the piece of paper on which he wrote Paulina's number. "I'll call if I see him again, but chances are—" He shook his head.

After Paulo had shifted into fourth, Isabella had fallen asleep in the front seat, and the wind had dried the sweat and salt and sun on our faces, Paulina nodded back toward the resort and asked through hand-shaded eyes, "What'd you do in there?"

"Asked him a few questions about Zaul."

"And?"

"He told me."

"And?"

"That's it."

"You sure?"

"Yeah."

I don't think she believed me, but I wasn't willing to tell her the truth.

At my hotel, I paid my bill, tipped the attendant twenty dollars, and pulled my bike around front.

Isabella's eyes grew wide and round when she saw me sitting on it. She turned to Paulina and asked without asking. Paulina tried to shake her head without my seeing, thinking I'd be bothered by her. I spoke softly. "If you don't mind, I don't."

Isabella needed nothing further. She stood next to the bike with her arms in the air. I asked Paulina, "You know how to drive?"

"Yes," she said matter-of-factly.

I stepped off the bike and held it by the bar, motioning for her to ride. She smiled, stepped out of the truck, and straddled the bike, hiking up her skirt and then tucking it tightly beneath her thighs so the wind didn't pull a Marilyn Monroe on her. I lifted Isabella up and she sat on the indentation between the tank and the seat. I gave my Costas to Paulina and buckled my helmet on Isabella, pulling the shield down over her eyes to keep the bugs out.

Paulo drove the speed limit while Paulina followed us. Isabella's smile covered the entire inside of the helmet and Paulina's spread nearly as wide. I sat up front in the truck with Paulo—in the cab with no air-conditioning. Where it was a hundred and twenty degrees if it was anything. My sweat—trickling down my face, neck, back, and calves—stuck me to the seat like honey while Paulo, seemingly unfazed, drove in relative comfort.

Halfway home, he pulled up near a roadside store advertising cell phones and prepaid cards. He motioned for me to follow. I did. When we reached the counter, he bought a new prepaid card for his own phone and then pointed at the phones in the counter. "You buy?"

He was right. A good idea. Paulo helped me negotiate with the man for a new phone and a calling card. After we'd paid, he dialed my number in his phone and watched as my phone rang. Knowing he could now get in touch with me, he nodded and waved me onward. "*Vámonos.*"

Paulina was right. If you needed something done, Paulo was your man.

Back in the truck, the heat returned and stuck my clothing to my skin beneath a layer of sweat. Paulo was growing more comfortable with me so every few minutes, he'd point through the windshield at something he wanted me to see or know or understand. And while I didn't understand a word he said as he unconsciously rattled off in Spanish, I do know that the words he spoke were beautiful. Tender. Paulo was attempting to share his world with me.

Over the next thirty minutes, I kept an eye on the girls in the rearview, listened to Paulo, nodded as if I understood completely, and lost five pounds in sweat.

It was a great conversation.

• • •

After dinner, I used my new phone to call Colin's house line. He picked up after the first ring. I said, "Ronnie?" and hung up.

Colin got a new SIM card every couple of days and nobody ever knew the number—because it wasn't intended for incoming calls. If I needed to talk with him, I called his house number and said the name of any president and hung up. That left him to call the number on his caller ID. Which he did. We'd had a decade's worth of practice. Seconds later, my phone rang and I answered. "How you guys getting along?"

"Better." His voice sounded different. Even some levity. He also spoke softly, which led me to believe that someone was sleeping nearby. He was almost whispering. "Small progress, but it's progress. Any luck?"

"Some." I backed up and told him about León. About Isabella, Paulo, the coffee plantation, his truck, and then the beach resort. He was quiet when I finished.

He said, "Any idea what's next?"

"Tomorrow I thought I'd get on the bike and ride up and down the coast. Surfers are particular about their waves so it shouldn't be too tough. Find good waves and I should find some surfers. Provided he's still with them."

"You think he's not?"

"I think Zaul will be of use to these guys as

long as he has money. He's lost his transportation and I'd bet he's running low on money, so I'm guessing his usefulness is running out—if it hasn't already."

Colin mumbled in agreement. I tried to change the subject. "Any sign of Shelly?"

"She's been to see Maria every day. The reconstruction of her face was nothing short of miraculous. She stops in on her way home."

That sounded strange because Colin's house wasn't on Shelly's way home. My silence told Colin I was trying to figure this out. He picked up on it. "She's . . . spending some time with an orthopedist from the hospital. When I asked about him, she said, 'He's a safe bet.' He's got a place down on the canal."

I did not see that one coming. "I hope she's happy."

Colin cleared his throat. "He heard she'd called off the wedding and showed up at her work. Took her to dinner. All the nurses say she seems happier."

"I hope she is."

"She looks different. Peaceful."

I could hear a noise in the background. I was scratching my head when Colin said, "Hold on. Somebody wants to talk to you."

He handed her the phone. Maria sounded sleepy. Her words sounded thick, like she'd just come from the dentist and the Novocain had yet to wear off. "Hey, Uncle Charlie. I miss you."

"I miss you, pretty girl. How you feeling?"

"Okay. It hurts less. You find Zaul?"

"Not yet, but I'm looking. He was always pretty good at hide-and-go-seek."

She chuckled. "I remember. Uncle Charlie?"

"Yeah, baby girl."

"When you find him, hug him for me. We all miss him. Mom cries most of the time now."

I swallowed hard. "You heal up. I'll see you soon."

"You bring me something?"

"You bet."

She handed the phone back to her dad. Colin and I sat in silence. After a minute, I broke it. "That one's special."

He sniffled. Blew his nose. "I been thinking a lot lately and I can't figure something."

"What's that?"

"Why was one like her given to someone like me?"

It was a good question, and I'd been wrestling with many of the same emotions. I had no answer for him. "I'll call when I know more."

I hung up, lay on my bed, and listened to the night. People talked in hushed tones in their homes around us. Dogs barked. Pigs grunted. A horse neighed in one direction and a noisy cat screeched in another. Every few moments, I heard a thud on the ground outside. Finally, I heard one on the tin roof of the chicken coop, which, when it landed, sounded like a bomb going off above my head and levitated me about four feet above the bed. I walked outside in the moonlight and stared up into the tree. A monkey was pulling on the mangoes and dropping them to the ground where several dogs had gathered. When I walked beneath the tree, he sat up straight, staring down at me. I picked through the mangoes, finding one that felt ripe, and washed it in the *pila*. After washing Paulina's knife, I peeled it, placed the slices on my tongue, and let the taste swirl around, filling me. Between the aroma, the taste, the juice, the texture, it was an all-encompassing experience.

That mango was a mirror image of my last few days. Once beautiful, placed on display for all the world to see, it had been ripped from its perch, thrown to the ground, rolled in manure and squalor, and left to rot. While that might have bruised it and soiled its skin, it didn't change its nature or what it freely offered, for once I peeled it back, an inexplicable sweetness was waiting to be discovered and tasted and consumed. There was just one catch—you had to be willing to get your hands dirty. Even sticky. To pick through it. Bathe it. Peel it back. And for so much of my life I had not.

The second train of thought coursing through my mind was a quiet nagging. Whether I found

Zaul or not, what was I going to do? At some point, this search would end, and when it did, where would I go? What would I do? Who, if anyone, would I do it with? Hack was dead. Bimini held nothing for me. Miami had never been my home. While I'd been born there and while I still owned a house, Jacksonville wasn't my home. I felt no tug anywhere in the States. No one was expecting me. No one was waiting by the phone. If I didn't show up somewhere, no one would know or care.

The fruit of my life was that there was none.

I finished the mango; climbed up on the tin roof, which was still warm from the day's heat; and lay down, staring at the stars and counting the satellites that screamed overhead.

An hour later, I climbed down, having never felt so full and so small at the same time.

Chapter Eighteen

Monday morning daylight brought with it the glorious smell of coffee. I followed my nose and found Paulina and Paulo sitting on the back porch. The back porch was a compacted area of dirt next to the house where the tin roof had been extended like a stiff tent over two posts. It was both a shelter from the rain and half a hot box. While Isabella slept, they were talking about the day. She told me Paulo's idea was that while Isabella was in school, we'd break up into two "teams." Divide and conquer. He'd take the truck and go one way; she and I would hop on the bike and go another. He felt we could cover more ground that way. We'd start at the northern end of the coast and move south, and he'd return to León, across to the coast, and then north. That way we could cover the entire coastline, and by the end of the week, we should meet somewhere in the middle. Granted, Zaul could move around and to places we'd already covered, but at least we could get some info from the locals who might have seen him.

Sounded good to me. I asked, "You don't mind sitting on the back of a bike?"

She smiled. "I'm used to it. Or"—a shrug—"I used to be."

Paulo asked, "We meet back here after noon. Then you help me?"

I wasn't quite sure what he was asking. Paulina offered, "He wants to ask a favor of you." She paused. "He's hesitant because it's different than working in the sugarcane."

I turned to Paulo. "Sure. Anything."

Paulo nodded and left while Paulina readied Isabella for school, which left me savoring my coffee. I'd had some good coffee in my life, and I'd often considered myself a connoisseur in much the same way people prefer wines, but as I sat there, the flavor of those beans and that resulting coffee struck me as possibly the best I'd ever had.

She smiled. "Good, isn't it?"

I spoke staring at my mug. "Not sure I've ever had better."

"You must mean it. That's the second time you've said that." We walked Isabella to school and then stood in the backyard staring up at the mountain several miles in the distance. She pointed. "You see that dark spot below the crater. Where it's real lush?"

I nodded.

She shaded her eyes. "My father was walking up there forty years ago and discovered that the lake atop the crater spilled into that area. Natural irrigation that deposited all those minerals into the soil. He also found wild coffee. The land wasn't very valuable; no one wanted it because no one believed you could do anything with it, but he felt differently, so he bought that plateau with his life savings and then cultivated the coffee. He felt there was something special in the combination of that volcanic water, the shade from those ancient trees, and that soil. I was born a few years later, and by then we had coffee plants popping up out of every thing or container that wasn't nailed down." She shook her head. "I have walked up that mountain a thousand times and planted ten thousand coffee plants myself. By hand." A pause. "What you are drinking comes from some of those original plants." A smile. "Provided you know where to look and do so when others are not."

"You stole these beans?"

She considered this. "How could I steal what was given to me?" She pulled on my helmet and began buckling the strap. Then pulled on a backpack filled with a few snacks and water. "My father was very successful. Bought more land. Planted more coffee. And employed hundreds of people in this valley, but the economy he created affected thousands. If the head of household makes money, the community grows, and the men walk with their heads high because their family eats at night. At one time, he was the largest grower and supplier of coffee in the northern half of Nicaragua. We shipped all around the world. Europe. Africa. North America. There were larger farms who produced more, but they weren't family owned." She smiled. Her eyes glistened. "My father paid good wages, gave hand over fist, created good working conditions, shared profits, started a school and taught the kids for free, brought in doctors and provided health care." She laughed. "He even helped birth a few babies, and there are more boys and men in this valley named Alejandro than anywhere. My father was unlike anything these people had ever seen. His goodness shocked them because for so long they'd been beat down so far that they'd lost everything. What's worse, they'd lost the most important thing and he gave it back to them. He loved this country, he loved these people, and he loved my mom and he loved me, but that didn't earn him his legacy. He is still talked about today because he gave these people something no one had ever offered before. No government. No military. No warlord. No rebellion." A nod. "He gave them hope—the currency of love—and they loved him for it." She shook her head, laughing. "He had this crazy idea that mangoes and coffee, if planted together, shared their taste with one another. So he planted hundreds of mango trees across this mountainside and then, as they grew, thousands of coffee plants beneath them. Oddly, he was right. Add to that the rich volcanic soil, natural irrigation from the crater lake, and our coffee has a hint of mango in it and our mangoes have a hint of coffee in them. Only place in the world. And my uneducated father, who quit school the third day of second grade, figured that out."

My voice stuttered when I asked, "What happened?"

"Two things: First, an American company wanted to buy my father's business for pennies on the dollar, and when he wouldn't sell, our guess —and we don't know this for sure—is that they bought the competition and unloaded the coffee at ridiculous prices, bloating the market with cheap coffee with which we could not compete. They couldn't have us, so they destroyed us, giving it away in order to bankrupt my father. It worked. Feeling indebted to his workers, he borrowed to the hilt and mortgaged his mountain to pay and feed his people. Then, when every ounce had been squeezed out of him and he'd lost forty pounds working his fingers to the bone, trying to resurrect something from nothing, Carlos happened."

Her voice fell quiet and soft. A long pause. "We were all gathered in the house together, and Papi said he needed to take food to the people down the mountain. To the few that remained. He knew they were wet and hungry and afraid. Mami went with him. I remember staring down after them, watching them walk away. And I knew that the food in his backpack meant that he would not eat for a week. He reached for her, grabbed her hand as they walked in the rain. Happy." A nod. "I remember that despite hardship untold, they were happy." She shook her head once. "They walked down the mountain in the rain on the road that passed the well, and I never saw them again. Next thing I knew, we heard a noise like helicopters and then . . . all the world changed. Mudslide. In the months that followed, my husband, Paulo, and I tried to resurrect what we could, but so many people died. Ninety percent of our workforce had been killed. My husband was a doctor, so he and I spent weeks tending to the sick and wounded. Paulo began building coffins and he quit counting at two hundred. Coffee production came to a standstill. We had no thought of producing coffee when we were trying so hard just to survive and help others do the same. There was"—she wiped her hands in a large swath across the entire valley between us and the mountain—"death everywhere. The smell of it lasted for weeks. At one point, it was so bad we just had to stack and burn the bodies of both people and livestock to kill and stop the spread of disease. These people who worked for us weren't just paid workers. They were family. We paid for more than two hundred funerals and paid to help rebuild Valle Cruces. So the remaining families had a roof and a place to live. Because my father would have wanted it this way, we gave what amounted to life insurance policies to the families who lost anyone." She shook her head. "How do you value a human life?"

Another long pause. She continued. "Somewhere in there I got pregnant. My husband, Gabriel, wanted to name her Isabella because it means 'devoted to God.' I remember him standing not too far from here up on a shoulder of the mountain, staring at a wall of mud one mile wide and thirty miles long, stretching to the ocean, and saying that something or someone in the midst of this hell needed to be devoted to God because nothing else had been. We worked around the clock. He went for days without sleep. With a weakened system, he contracted the virus that attacked the lining of his heart. We buried him six months later. One more death amid a sea of others. I was pregnant and brokenhearted, I tried to pick up the pieces. I went to the bank, took out one more loan—basically on my father's good name because we had nothing left except the homestead—and in so doing leveraged what had once been the heart of Alejandro's Mango Café and Cinco Padres Café Compañía. While I have my father's heart for these people, I don't have his business savvy. I was desperate, didn't read the fine print, and then the bank sold and the new owner"—she held up her fingers like quotation marks—"called in the loan. When the bank called to tell me, I had to ask. I had no idea you could 'call in a loan.'" A painful shrug. "The foreclosure was quick and decisive. We walked down that mountain three weeks later having lost everything. If it hadn't been for Paulo, I'm not sure where I'd be. He's . . . special to me. To Isabella."

I wanted the earth to open up and swallow me whole.

She continued, "Losing my father's mountain was tough at first, but it's been a decade so sometimes my life there seems like a distant memory."

"Why did you stay? Why not move? Start over someplace else?"

"I love these people. Losing the farm changed how I do that. Not the fact that I do." She pointed to a small rise on the lush plateau once purchased by her father. "The well that my father dug is there. He dug it when I was just a kid. Younger than Isabella. He would be digging by an oil lamp, some three hundred feet down, and sending up buckets of dirt that hung suspended over his head. Which is why you need to trust the man holding the rope. Anyway, he'd be down there all day, digging, sending up buckets, and I'd pull one off the rope, drag it to the garden, and by the time I got back, Paulo would have lifted another for me. Late in the afternoons, when I got tired and wanted to play with my friends or do something, anything, other than haul a five-gallon bucket of dirt over my shoulder to some hot garden, he would write a note and attach it to the bucket. I'd read it when it came up."

"What'd the note say?"

"*Este es el amor con las piernas.*" She then translated without being asked. " 'This is love with legs.' My father used to say that you can tell someone you love them until you're blue in the face, but until they see that walked out, they have no idea what it means. Hence, 'love with legs.' "
A wide smile spread across her face. "Every day he'd climb out of that hole covered in mud from head to foot. The only thing you could see were the whites of his eyes. When he finally hit water,

Paulo pulled him up, and my father stood under the wellhead while Paulo showered him. The water was muddy and brown at first, but the more he pumped, the more pure and clear it became. Finishing the well, with a concrete cap and hand pump, he was so proud. While the concrete was still wet, he took a stick and carved deep into the side, "*Agua de mi corazón.*" She pointed with her toe. "It means, 'Water from my heart.' " A warm breeze washed across us and cooled the sweat trickling down my back. "Whenever he would walk me to school, we'd pass by that well, and he'd hold my hand and point with an ear-to-ear grin. 'That's love with legs. That's love with legs.' My father was proud of many things, but he was especially proud of that well."

"I understand you love these people, but with so many hard memories, how can you stay here?"

"I, like Paulo, like Isabella, am a child of this land. My soul breathes here. It doesn't breathe in town. I've tried it."

"You could make more money in town."

"Money doesn't buy the air I need." I had no response to that. She eyed the valley, the mountainside, the homes dotting the landscape, and continued, "We, all of us, have been affected by war, hurricanes, drought, economic hardship. The result is a disease—an epidemic—called 'hopelessness.' It's carried on the air around here, and I am fighting it."

My voice dropped to a whisper. The enormity and impossibility of her task weighing on me. "How do you plan to do that?"

She didn't look at me. "With the antidote."

I'd never felt this passionate about anything in my entire life and I knew it. I spoke slowly. "Which is?"

Her eyes found mine and in them I saw no pretension. No quarter. "With my life." She straddled the bike and waited for me. "It's the antidote. And it's all I have to give."

I swung my leg over, careful not to kick her in the chin, and cranked the bike. We sat idling, staring up at the mountains. She spoke over me. The tectonic plates of my life were shifting with every word she spoke. Nothing felt certain. She continued. "Every now and then, somebody will be working a garden or digging a well, and we find another body or a bone or something that some-one can identify as having belonged to someone they love. When they do, we erect another cross. Hold another funeral. We pause. Dead a decade, the pain is very much alive. Sometimes I remind myself when I'm walking up the mountain that my father bought with his blood and sweat that my dad's looking down, watching my sweat mix with his. I hope he's pleased with what I've poured out." A smile and a single shake. "But I will admit, I sure do miss his coffee."

We drove north out of Valle Cruces onto the main highway, and then I followed Paulina's finger down dirt roads toward the coast. We stopped at every surfing destination, dive, and hangout we could find—and there were many. Nicaragua is a surfer's Central American paradise. We talked to a dozen tanned and bleached surfers carrying boards of different lengths and sizes. None had seen or heard of Zaul. Evidently, he'd not made it this far north.

We returned after lunch and met Paulo at the house. I was anxious to get back out on the road, but Paulina reminded me of my deal with Paulo. Paulina picked up on my anxiety. "Nothing happens in Nicaragua between lunch and dinner other than a bunch of naps. Besides—" She motioned to Paulo, who was holding three new coils of rope and a rather stout-looking harness. "*Jefe*, will you dig?"

I turned to Paulina. "*Jefe*?"

"Boss."

I pointed at the ropes. "He wants to drop me down in that hole, doesn't he?"

She nodded. "He thinks if he can show the people that you're not afraid to go down there—"

"Seeing as how I'm an ignorant gringo."

"Pretty much. They'll have no reason to be afraid."

"You mean, my corpse hanging on that rope will shame them into digging it out themselves."

The purity in her laughter was unlike any I'd ever heard. "Yep. Something like that." She shrugged. "You can say no." A pause. "But . . . you can also say yes."

"What happened to 'nothing happens in this country after lunch'? I was thinking about a nap."

"It's ninety-six degrees in that chicken coop. You think you can sleep in that?"

I fingered the ropes, as if I knew some way to test the strength. As if holding them would convince me that they were strong enough to hold me. Paulo stretched a length between two arms. "Strong. Very strong. No concern." He grabbed my forearm with his hand, squeezing it. The effect was that my hand latched onto his forearm where the muscles rippled. He held it there. Popeye with skin. "I hold the rope." He smacked his forearm with his other hand in order to bring attention to his strength.

I didn't take my eyes from his. "You hold the rope?"

"*Sí.*"

"Okay."

He smiled, exposing his few white teeth. "*Vámonos.*" He shouted loudly and with growing excitement toward the house, "*Vámonos.*"

Chapter Nineteen

The truck wouldn't make it up the mountain, but the bike would. Paulo hopped on back and we climbed our way up. Paulina and Isabella took the truck until the tires began slipping and then followed on foot. I told Paulina that I was okay and that there was no need, but she just shook her head. "Are you kidding? I'm not missing this."

We stood next to the wellhead. Below me, the words were worn but I could still read them. "*Agua de mi corazón.*"

The mudslide had removed the concrete cap and cracked the top of the well. Through the years, someone had bordered it or attempted to keep people from falling in by placing trees next to or over it. We cleared those. I stood over the dark hole and dropped a small rock. I did not hear it land below me. Next to me sat the dormant pump. It was a seesaw-looking apparatus about five feet long, a handle on either side, connected to a PVC pipe with a four-inch diameter. Paulo pointed. "This well one time flow over. Up. Out. Rise from ground. Then one day, mountain move—" His hand gestures suggested an earthquake. "Not so much water. Then more people live on mountain. More coffee plant in ground.

More cows. Everyone use more water. Need more water. Put in pipe." He imitated the motion of pushing down and pulling up on the arm of the pump. "We bring water up. Very good water."

Around us, kids came out of the trees. First two, then three more. Pretty soon, a crowd had gathered, and they were whispering among themselves.

Maybe the most striking feature was not what lay below, but what grew above. The largest mango tree in Nicaragua had grown up around the well. Literally. It was ginormous. Paulo pointed to the treetops and then to the roots below our feet, leading my eye to how the roots had encircled the concrete cap of the well and grown over. He pointed to the corner of his eye, to his tear ducts. His English was broken, long vowels were short and short long. He sounded more American Indian than Spanish. "Long ago, tree cry in the water. Roots make many tears. Water taste like mango. Very very good. Very very sweet." He made an aggressive blender motion with his hands. "Mango clean water. Good medicine. People walk long way drink here."

At the moment, I didn't care too much about the water or how it tasted; I cared about the harness, so I pulled on the webbing and buckled myself in. Paulo tied the rope to the tether behind my shoulder blades and I pulled on his headlamp. Paulo held the rope and demonstrated, pulling on the rope twice: "I come up." He pulled a single time: "Give loose." Then he pulled for a prolonged time: "I come up right now fast."

"Got it."

Paulo threw the rope over the rusty wheel above me and fed the rope through the grooves. Then he wrapped the rope once around a nearby tree to cause friction in my descent. He then handed me a five-gallon bucket and tethered it to my harness. He placed a notepad and pen in my hand and said, "For talking." Last, he handed me a small trowel, or shovel, and a hammer and patted me on the back, followed by a not-so-gentle shove. "You go."

I stood over the opening as he tightened the rope, pulling his end up close against his hip; the four hundred feet of rope was neatly coiled at his feet. As Paulina and Isabella cleared the crest of the hill, I spoke to Paulo. "You'll hold the rope. Right?"

He nodded. And eyed the hole. "You go."

I sat in the harness, testing its ability to hold me, squatting over the hole. Then very gingerly, I pulled up one foot and then the other until I was suspended over the hole, sitting in my harness like a hammock. Holding my bucket, I nodded at Paulo and he slowly began lowering me into that hole. My last image of daylight was Paulina staring down on me. She spoke over me as the well covered me up. "I might have not been entirely truthful about people's reasons for not going down there."

"Oh, really."

"Yeah, we have these snakes up here that—"

"Don't. Just don't."

"They like the cold."

"You're serious, aren't you?"

I couldn't see her nodding, but her tone of voice told me that she was. "But don't worry. They're not poisonous."

The hair rose on my neck and arms. "Now you tell me."

I was thankful for the headlamp. As I descended, it showed the painstaking work that Paulina's father had done and what he'd had to cut through to put in this well—much of which was rock. Every foot or two, I found an indentation in the wall. Large enough for a man's hand or foot.

It took several minutes for Paulo to lower me to the ground floor—or what had become the ground floor after the mudslide and what had been thrown on top since. I had a feeling that the actual floor of the well was still another hundred or so feet. And to my great delight, before I set my feet down on the dried and hardened mud, I searched and found no snakes. Which was good because I wasn't quite sure what I was going to do had I found one.

I worked through the afternoon, sending up a bucket—on a second smaller line—every few minutes. Through the afternoon, we passed the bucket back and forth thirty or forty times. The mud was dense, full of rocks, and in many places, hard as rock. The moisture added with the pressure had turned volcanic mud into nearly impenetrable rock. I sent up a note, asking for something that I could work like a pick in such a small space. They sent down a dull hammer.

Breaking through that rock took a long time.

After about six hours, I was exhausted and the harness was cutting into my hips and armpits. I'd also lost count of the number of buckets I'd sent up. Toward what felt like dinnertime, I tugged on the rope twice and Paulo began the long pull upward. I did what I could to help by climbing up the small "steps" Paulina's father had chipped into the wall decades ago. When I reached the surface, a crowd of fifty or so people had gathered. Paulina covered her mouth and laughed at my appearance. I was covered in dirt from head to foot. Many of the kids laughed. A few ran away, afraid. One of them walked up to me and touched me—poking me as if to determine if I was truly a man or if the devil had stolen my soul.

Paulo asked, "Good?"

I nodded.

He patted my biceps. "You strong dig. *Bueno*. Much distance."

Paulina appeared. "How you feeling?"

"Like a shower never sounded so good."

She laughed at my appearance. "There are a lot of women who pay a lot of money for that kind of mud bath."

I pointed at the rope. "How far down did I go?"

Paulo waved his hand side to side. "Two hundred."

"How far did I dig?"

"Six. Maybe eight feet."

That was discouraging. "Felt like fifty."

Paulina rode Paulo and Isabella down the mountain on the bike to the truck. Then Paulo drove Isabella home and Paulina returned for me.

Back at the house, Paulo had filled two buckets of water for me behind the plastic curtain. Most "showers" require about half a bucket. I guess he was trying to tell me something. It took me twenty minutes to get clean. Staring down at the muddy water swirling the crude concrete drain, it struck me that more than volcanic mud was coming off.

I devoured my rice and beans and must have eaten a dozen tortillas followed by two plantains. I heard some rustling out back, and then Leena poked her head in the door and beckoned with a curled finger. When I walked outside, she was resting one hand on a hammock stretched between the mango tree and some other large hardwood. "You need to learn how to swing in a hammock."

"Seriously?"

She smiled. "Park it, Charlie."

All I wanted to do was climb in my bed, but I

straddled the hammock, sat, and then lay back. She was right. Everything about it was divine. She sat next to me in a plastic chair, gently rocking me back and forth, and as she did, every pain and weight lifted off me with the gentle sway of the canvas hammock.

I was having trouble keeping my eyes open, but I had a feeling there were dishes to do or clothes to wash or some responsibility I was shirking. I offered, "Aren't we supposed to be doing something?"

She propped her feet up on the end of the hammock and chuckled. "We're doing it."

I doubt I'd ever been that tired. And it'd been a long time since I'd felt that good.

Chapter Twenty

Paulina woke me with a steaming mug beneath my nose, then set it on the table next to me. She said, "Paulo's already gone and Isabella's at school. We should get moving." I glanced at my watch. It was already eight o'clock. I'd slept ten hours.

We piled onto the bike and resumed our search, starting where we'd left off yesterday. My hands and forearms were sore from digging, as was most everything else in my body. Our path paralleled the coast, and much of the time was spent rolling down dirt roads just inside the dunes with the sound of the waves on the other side. We stopped in several gas stations, places to eat, bars, any-place where someone might have reason to stop. No one recognized his picture. At noon, Paulo called. He said he'd talked to a manager at a seaside hotel who had kicked out five guys who trashed two of his rooms and broke a bunch of bottles on his pool deck. He said they were traveling in an old Chevrolet convertible. He also said one of them had been pretty busted up, one eye was swollen shut. When asked what he looked like, the man described Zaul.

Paulina and I shared lunch on the dunes beneath a mango tree that had been picked clean except for the shade. The breeze felt good and I actually dozed. When I woke, I found Paulina walking in the waves, a faraway look in her eyes. She said nothing to me upon her return. I got the feeling it'd been a long time since she'd done anything like that. That in itself got me thinking. As did the fact that Isabella couldn't swim.

Other than a single necklace, Paulina didn't wear jewelry. Few women around here did. Granted, it cost money, which was in short supply, but I got the feeling it was more cultural. The necklace she wore was a long chain, which seldom showed unless you were looking. And I admit, when it came to Leena, I found myself looking more often than not. She also let her hair grow—as did every other woman. While they wore their hair all rolled up in a bun, none cut it. Most hung at waist length when they let it down, which was usually after a shower or when they brushed it just before going to bed.

She sat down next to me beneath the mango tree, and I asked about it. "Why do you keep your hair so long?"

"It is believed here that a woman's hair is her crown. Where God bestows his glory."

"Then why do all of you pull it up in tight buns that pin your ears back?"

She laughed. " 'Cause it's hot and all that hair on your neck only makes it worse."

"All function. No form."

More laughter. "Something like that."

"What about jewelry? No one here wears any."

"We are taught not to bring unnatural attention to ourselves. To let our natural beauty do that. To not attempt to improve on what God made perfect."

I pointed at her necklace. "And that?"

She smiled. "That is the exception."

"I noticed."

She placed the polished and worn stone that hung on the chain in her palm. "One evening, when my father was at the bottom of his well and had been digging for months, thinking he'd never strike water, he found two polished stones. When he picked them up, water began seeping in from the edges. To anyone but us, the stones are worthless, but he had them made like this; the chains are made of Nicaraguan gold. He gave one to my mother, one to me. In over thirty years, I've never taken it off. My mother did the same. Worth nothing, yet to me, it's priceless." She crossed her legs and her face turned curious. "Tell me more about you. How you got here. Your work. What you do when you're not here."

"In college, I spent some time playing poker for a living, but I realized there were people better than me so I cashed in my chips."

"Smart."

"Doing so caught the attention of a man who ran a venture capital firm. So I spent some time in the financial world but was fired when I didn't want to play ball with my boss."

"Why?"

"Let's just say he wanted to own more than just my time."

"What'd you do for him?"

"Traveled a lot. I evaluated companies. Tried to figure out which were worth keeping and which were worth breaking up into small pieces. Depended on which made him more money."

"Did it pay well?"

"Could have, but he kept it all when I left."

"Sounds like a story there."

"Just a bit."

"You ever work outside the States?"

"Yes."

"Where?"

"Europe. The islands. Asia. Some in Central America."

"Ever come here? To Nicaragua?"

I casually looked away. "No."

"How'd you get to Bimini?"

"When I left, I wandered some. Eventually, I found myself on a shrimp boat headed for Bimini, where I gutted a hurricane shack and began working with an old man to make specialized wooden skiffs. We built about two a year."

"You work with wood?"

A nod. "I do seem to possess some talent there."

"Well, aren't you just a Renaissance man."

"Not too sure about that." I wasn't comfortable talking about me, so I tried to speed the conversation along. "From there, I began guiding people fishing for—"

"You're also a fishing guide?"

"It's not too difficult in Bimini. The fish are rather predictable."

"You're starting to get interesting."

"I met my current business partner when he came to fish. He told me his family owned an import business, and if I ever wanted or needed a job, he'd put me to work. So Colin put me in charge of import logistics and transport. Primarily acquisition and delivery."

"Wow, listen to you with the big words." She was smiling now. "What did you import?"

"Primarily wine and spirits. Lately, he's been moving into olive oil."

"Ever been married?"

"No."

"Why?" She smiled. Playing with me. Growing more comfortable. "You seem likable enough. You wear deodorant, trim your fingernails, not too much stuff hanging from your teeth."

I rubbed my front teeth on my shirt. "Can we talk about you a while?"

"But you were just starting to get interesting."

"I'm afraid the interesting part is over."

"And your friend, Zaul?"

There was more to her question. "What about him?"

"What kind of kid is he?"

"He's had a cell phone and a credit card since he could crawl. His parents have, admittedly, enabled him so he knows next to nothing about responsibility. He's also grown up around the überwealthy and social elite so he has a skewed view of reality."

"Sounds like a bad recipe."

I pointed at San Cristóbal smoking in the distance. "Yep."

"Why'd he come here?"

"I'm not sure, other than they own a home in Costa Rica and he knows the surf."

"Why'd they send you? Why not his dad?"

"You sure do ask a lot of questions."

She smiled. Beautiful white teeth that filtered laughter with nothing to hold it down. The tension here was to satisfy her without giving up too much or getting too close to the truth. "When he left, his sister, Maria, was in the hospital. He feels responsible for her being there. He thinks his parents feel that way, too."

"Is he?"

"Ultimately, no. But that's why I'm here, because his father wouldn't be able to convince him of that."

"Can you?"

A shrug. "Don't know, but my chances are better than Colin's. If anyone has Zaul's ear, it's me, but that's a big if."

"One more question?"

"Sure. You seem to be on a roll."

I had a feeling she'd been baiting me, asking me a bunch of questions until she got to the one that mattered—the one she'd been wanting to ask me for a few days. Her eyes told me this was it. "When you find him, how do you know he's going to let you take him home?"

It was a good question and I'd been asking it myself. "I don't."

Her eyes didn't change. "And yet you're here anyway."

It was a question posed as a statement. "Yes."

"What motivates a man to do something when he knows he's got almost zero chance of succeeding?"

I answered, hoping she accepted it. "I love the kid." She did not.

"I bet his dad does, too." She paused. Considering me. "If I knew you better, I'd say there was something you're not telling me."

She was a good reader of people, and she was reading me like a book. There was a tenderness to her that drew me. More than that, I liked being *known,* and for the first time in my life, I was *known* by another. I'm not saying I liked what she knew about me, not proud of the bits and pieces, but somehow she was standing inside my skin and yet I didn't experience shame at her reflection. I feigned. "Have to try."

I don't know if I satisfied her or gave rise to more questions, but for the rest of the ride back, she eyed me, studying my face and saying nothing more.

Chapter Twenty-One

We returned to the *casa* in time to pick up Isabella from school. Paulo and I quickly loaded up and returned to the well, where he patted me on the back and once again dropped me in the hole with a smile that spoke volumes. Before I kicked my feet loose, suspending myself over the hole, a crowd had gathered. Kids. Old folks. And it'd grown. Paulo said, "Word spread. Gringo digging Alejandro's well."

I worked through the afternoon, robotically filling buckets and driving the hammer down into the mud and rock as deeply as I could in such a tight space with limited swing arc. My headlamp was growing dim. As was I. Between the sugarcane, the heat, and this well, I was tired.

Around dinner—or to be more honest when I couldn't lift that hammer one more time—I tugged twice and Paulo lifted me to the top, where he patted me on the back approvingly. It'd been a good day. I'd dug another twelve feet.

After dinner, Paulo gave me the information I'd requested and even told me he'd been able to secure my seat at the table. I didn't speak with Paulina before I left, knowing that her look of disapproval would affect my ability.

I arrived in León forty-five minutes later and hunted around until I found the restaurant where the game was played. La Playa was an upscale restaurant in León. White tablecloths. Waiters with starched shirts. The works. The restaurant had a private room around back entered via a staircase. I parked the bike just below the stairs and noticed Colin's HiLux parked in the shadows along the fence. I climbed the steps and a young man in a suit and sunglasses, which he didn't need at 9:00 p.m., stepped in front of me. He pointed around front and said nothing. I said,

"Poker? Card game?" and pointed to the door behind him.

"*Su nombre?*"

"Charlie."

He held out a hand and said, "Five grand."

I placed $5,000 in his hand.

He nodded approvingly and moved aside. I stepped into the smoke-filled room to find seven men sitting in a circle around a large table. Two scantily clad women were serving drinks while a third sat on the lap of the most puffed-up man in the place. Apparently the foreman. High off his win from the week prior, he had returned the conquering hero. I didn't know anything about his ability to play, and even less about his ability to cheat, but I knew his arrogance was my asset. I was here because I wanted two things: information about Zaul and Colin's truck.

Being the "new guy" and speaking little Spanish, the crowd of regulars nodded at me and spoke in Spanish—solely. I was ripe for the picking and they, a pack of wolves, smelled fresh meat.

I played dumb, lost early, and fit the description of "ignorant gringo" to a T. The liquor flowed, laughter ensued, and for three hours, I lost several thousand dollars. As did many of the other players. No one at the table was an especially good cardplayer, but the foreman was an exceptionally good cheater—which meant they were going to lose anyway.

A few hours in, the foreman was rolling in chips and the three "girls" were taking turns either sitting on his lap or rubbing his shoulders. One by one, and with some help from me that he didn't realize, the table dwindled. One of the men turned out to be the chief of police. Another was the mayor. By midnight, we were down to three players. The foreman, myself, and the restaurant owner, who was the biggest loser of the night and too stupid or prideful for his own good.

Pretty soon, I realized they were speaking about me and, I felt, making a comparison between me and another player. Presumably Zaul. If I had envisioned obtaining any information, I was misled. They spoke about as much English as I spoke Spanish. But the truck was still in play.

At 1:00 a.m., I quit losing chips, put the restaurant owner against the ropes, and took everything he had in three hands. The foreman watched me out of the corner of his eye, but he'd had so many drinks by this time that I knew he was foggy. And while the number of players at the table had dwindled, no one had gone home. Each had lost some or all of $5,000, so no one was eager to get home. That meant that we at the table had an audience of eleven other people. The dealer. Six other players. The three girls. And the guard. When I finished with the restaurant owner, the foreman switched to water and asked for a cold rag.

By 2:00 a.m., we were even, and by 2:30 a.m., he was swimming in doubt. I had twice as many chips, and he was sweating despite the air-conditioning. Close to 3:00 a.m., I shoved; he went all in and my straight beat him on the river when the dealer dropped a king.

Beaten, embarrassed, and broke, his eyes narrowed and he cussed me. I smiled—which only made him more angry, which was exactly what I was hoping. I needed him mad if he was going to risk that truck.

I cashed in my chips with the dealer, placed a thick wad of cash in my pocket, and stood as if to leave, paying him absolutely no attention what-soever. When I did, he sat back, slammed down an empty glass, and spoke loud enough for the room to hear. I didn't understand what he said, but every eye in the place was looking at me. He said it a second time. This time louder. "*Doble o nada.*"

While I had a pretty good idea what he was saying, I shrugged as though I did not. "*No hablo español.*"

The guard stepped forward. "Double or nothing."

I laughed mockingly, keeping my eye on the foreman. "With what?" I patted my pocket. The message was clear. I had his money.

The foreman, looking to save face and praying for one more lucky hand, which he was not going to get, stared around the room, making sure he had everyone's attention, and then with great machismo, reached into his pocket and dropped the truck keys on the table. That was his version of throwing down the gauntlet.

And it accomplished exactly what he wanted—it got everyone's attention. One by one, they inched their chairs closer to the table. All eyes on me.

I shrugged, as if I didn't know what vehicle the keys fit. To suggest that I hadn't heard the story. That his fame hadn't reached me.

I pointed at the keys and then shook my head at the parking lot as if I didn't know. The foreman waved off the guard, who propped open the door, descended the steps, and cranked the HiLux. When he returned, I said, "What's it worth?"

He looked at my pocket. "All."

Actually, it wasn't, but I didn't argue with him. I wanted the stakes higher because I was not only about to take his truck, I was going to take his reputation—and consequently, his power.

I also had a feeling that he'd paid off the dealer. Too many hands had gone his way. That meant that the flop, turn, and river would "tell" me what hand they'd predetermined to play.

When the dealer set to deal, I waved a hand and said, "No." Then I turned to the owner and said, "You deal?"

I knew he wasn't happy with me, but he wasn't happy with the foreman either so his deal would be as fair as any. A vein popped out on the foreman's temple, throbbing like a balloon, but wanting to save face, he backed off.

Because the bets were already made, there was no reason to check, push, or raise. We knew what was at risk. Everyone around the table knew. The owner dealt us two cards apiece. Then he laid down the flop, a king of diamonds, followed by a pause. Then the turn, a four of spades, followed by an even longer pause. Finally, he laid down the river—an ace of hearts. Sweat was dripping off the foreman's dark eyebrows. Seeing the third card, the foreman smiled, showing stained teeth and bloodshot eyes. It had been a long night and it was about to get longer. Breathing easier, he sat back and lit a cigar, drawing deeply and filling the air around us in a haze of smoke. As there was no need to bluff, I knew he had to be sitting, at least, on a pair of aces.

Lucky.

The dealer asked to see our hands, and the foreman slowly laid down a seven of hearts and an ace—giving my ugly friend a pair of aces.

Very lucky. Also predictable.

I kept my eyes on the foreman because I wanted to see his reaction. Even on a rigged Tuesday night game.

When I laid down my cards—king, ace—he turned ashen and began spitting venom at me because two pair beats one every day. I couldn't understand the curse words coming out of his mouth, but I had a feeling he was cursing not only me, but the five or six generations behind me.

I hefted the keys in my hand—giving him one last look—and then slid them into my pocket. Spittle had gathered in the corner of his mouth. I had not taken time to count it, but having started with eight people at $5,000 each meant I had $40,000 cash in my pocket. Wanting to add insult to injury, I removed the fat wad from my pocket and counted out $10,000—my $5,000 and the foreman's $5,000. This got everyone's attention in the room, but what really got their attention was when I handed $30,000 to the restaurant owner and told him to "give it back to everyone but him." Interestingly, everyone's English improved miraculously, and they understood me well enough to know exactly what I'd said.

The foreman stood, slammed his drink glass against the wall, and stormed out—without any of the girls. I think his good thing had just come to an end and he knew it. I wasn't naive enough to think I'd just made a roomful of friends but they certainly weren't my enemies, and I'll bet if I'd wanted dinner right then, the owner of the restaurant would have cooked it for me.

When I pulled in behind the house with the bike tied down in the truck bed and parked next to the chicken coop, I stepped out and a weary shadow appeared from next to the mango tree. It was Paulina. She'd been sitting in a plastic chair, leaning against the tree. She pushed the hair out of her eyes and flipped it a couple of times, tying it in a knot. "I guess you won."

"Yes."

She ran her fingers along the sides of the truck. "The foreman was there?"

I nodded.

"Did you shame him?"

I paused. "Yes."

She stepped closer. "Badly?"

I tilted my head side to side. "That's one way to put it."

"That may not bode well for the people that work for him." One of the things I'd grown to appreciate about Paulina in the short time that I'd known her was her fierce protection of those she loved. "Were others there?"

"The owner of the restaurant where we played, the chief of police, and the mayor, to name a few."

She shook her head. "Charlie, people know you're here." She looked exasperated. "You stick out. People like the foreman will take out on us what you inflict on him. There are ripple effects. You can't take like that from people around here."

"Then they shouldn't risk it."

"You're preying on them."

I didn't answer.

"Did you cheat?"

"No, I got lucky with the cards. But you should know that I would have. I wouldn't hesitate."

"Learn anything about Zaul?"

"No."

She shook her head and walked toward the house. "Sun'll be up in a few hours."

Chapter Twenty-Two

Unlike most of the women I'd known, Paulina did not own many articles of clothing, and what she did have she wore several days in a row. As best I could tell, she had three pairs of shoes: running shoes that looked several years old, flip-flops that had been taped back together, and a pair of sandals, which doubled as her "dress shoes."

She woke me yet again with coffee and a smile. Flip-flops and yesterday's dress. She set the coffee down and pulled a chair up next to the bed. "You want to walk me back through that poker game last night?"

I sat up and rubbed my eyes. Based on our last conversation, I wasn't sure where this was going, so I wanted to offer as little as possible.

She continued, "You left out a few details."

"Such as?"

She crossed her legs. "How you won all the money and then gave it all back to the losers—save one."

I sipped, trying not to make eye contact.

She stood. "Word is that you're crazy."

"What do you think?"

"I think you have your reasons that reason doesn't understand."

"Paulina, I'm not trying to prey on these people. I'm trying to find Zaul."

She nodded. "We might be closer than you think." She walked out, talking over her shoulder. She was chuckling. "Breakfast was delivered this morning."

I splashed my face and walked into the kitchen, where Paulo was beaming over a cup of coffee. He pointed to two bags on the floor and a cage outside that was clucking. One bag was full of mangoes. The other was full of coffee. The cage contained twelve chickens.

Paulina pointed. She was giddy. "Laying hens." Her face lit. "Do you know how long it's been since we owned chickens? Chickens mean eggs! Every morning."

I rubbed my eyes. "Where'd they come from?"

"Your friends at the coffee plantation."

"What?"

Paulina stepped toward me—into my personal space—put her hand on my shoulder, and kissed me tenderly on the cheek. Paulo was nodding and smiling larger.

"What's that for?"

She explained, "The foreman did not come to

work this morning. Seems someone exposed him as a first-class cheat. Given that he took a lot of money from several high-ranking officials, chances are likely that he won't ever return."

"What's that got to do with me?"

"Conditions in the plantation mirror the foreman. If he sneezes, the entire plantation gets a cold. If he smiles, everyone laughs. If he's gone, they take a deep breath and throw a party."

We dropped Isabella at school, and the three of us took Colin's truck to the coast. I let Paulo drive. Paulina leaned forward from the backseat and whispered in my ear, "It's been a long time since I've seen him so happy." I handed him my Costas, which he accepted and wore proudly.

We returned due west to the coast to an inlet on the beach where several companies ferried surfers to offshore reefs to surf waves often reaching twenty feet in prime conditions.

Like yesterday. Palm trees dotted the dunes and a frayed hammock rocked between two. An American guy was sitting in an old Ford van topped with eight surfboards of varying lengths. He was reading a paperback novel. Led Zeppelin spilling from the speakers. Long bleached hair. Bronzed skin. Skin and bones. Bare feet propped on the dash. Life was good, but currently slow.

He hopped out of his van when we pulled up. "Help you?" he asked.

I showed him Zaul's picture. "Seen this kid?"

He studied it, finally nodding. "Yeah. Yesterday."

"Where?"

He pointed at the swaying hammock. "Right there."

"Talk to him?"

He shook his head. "No. I took his four friends" —he pointed toward the reef—"out for a few hours. Gnarly action. Epic."

"He didn't go with you?"

"Nope. Lay right there." He placed his hand on his rib cage. "Dude was hurt. Took a spill or something. Walking pretty slow. Limping around. No shape to surf."

"Anything else you can tell me about him?"

He chuckled. "Yeah. When we got back, he was gone."

"Where'd he go?"

"No idea. His buddies didn't know, either. They seemed happy to be rid of him. No love lost there."

That meant the money had run out. "Any idea where they're staying?"

He shook his head. "Sorry."

I strode over to the hammock, and while I couldn't find anything that belonged to Zaul, one thing stuck out. Blood. Soaked through the fabric and caked on the right side of the hammock. And a good bit of it, too. Paulo rubbed his finger across it and smelled it. Paulina looked concerned but said nothing. We drove the coastline until lunch but discovered nothing. Paulina checked in with the hospital in León, but no patient had checked in fitting either Zaul's description or wound.

We returned to the house at lunch. Feeling helpless and knowing I could do nothing to help Zaul, we drove Colin's truck to the plantation, where we were met by a smiling and growing crowd. More than a hundred waited in line. She turned to me. "Looks like you have a fan club."

"Why?"

"They want to meet the man who did to the foreman what they always wished they could."

"Which was?"

"Shame him."

Paulina began examining the people in line while Paulo uncoiled the rope and held out my harness. I buckled in and descended into my hole, spending the afternoon digging, worried about Zaul and wondering how I would explain to his mother how I found him dead in a ditch. Or worse, didn't find him at all.

Paulo pulled me out at dark, when I discovered the crowd had not abated, but grown. Torches lit the night. Paulina was talking to a young mother and rocking a sleeping baby. When I climbed out, they inched closer. Paulo patted me on the back and showed me the rope. Fifteen feet. He nodded. "Good dig."

While the crowd watched from a safe distance, Anna Julia, the woman whose tooth I pulled last week, walked forward smiling a nearly toothless smile. She held out her hand and placed a single piece of hard candy in my palm, then closed my fingers around it and patted my hand.

I didn't want to get Colin's truck dirty, so I climbed into the back of the bed while Paulo turned the truck around. As he did, people began climbing on or getting in the vehicle. One by one, the men slung themselves up with the gringo while the older women or nursing mothers climbed in the backseat. By the time Paulo began rolling down the bumpy six-mile road, there were nine mothers in the cab with Paulo and eighteen men sitting with me on the rails or just standing in the back of the truck. Each talked to me, speaking in fast Spanish— none of which I understood. What I did understand, what I interpreted completely, was Paulina's laughter spilling out of the windows up front.

When I was studying in London, Amanda and I took a weekend trip to Vienna to hear the Three Tenors. Specifically Pavarotti. I'm not much of an opera fan, but when that man sang "Nessun Dorma," something in me responded, awakened, that had been asleep for all of my life prior. When he opened his lungs and belted out that last high C, there was a voice inside me that despite the fact that I can't sing my way out of a wet paper bag wanted to. I wanted to stand up on that stage and sing with all that I am. I wanted to join that man. Join my voice with his. Not because I could or would have added anything. Certainly, I wouldn't have. I'd only have taken away, but that's not the point. The point is, I wanted to. That "wanting to" was the effect of that man and his song on my soul. Julie Andrews had the same effect, which might explain why Maria and I shared so much from *The Sound of Music*.

I've only had that response one other time in my life, and it was coming down that mountain in the back of that truck, covered in volcanic mud, surrounded by a bunch of sweaty Nicaraguans I couldn't understand, and listening to the most beautiful laughter I'd ever heard coming out of the front seat.

If ever a soul was alive, it was hers. There. In that moment. When her soul sang.

In my entire life, I don't ever remember crying. I may have shed a tear or two, but I'm talking about crying—tears dripping from a heart that feels. I did not cry when my dad died. Not when my mom died. Not when I lost Amanda. Not when Hack died. Not when I lost Shelly. Not when Maria cried out to me from the hospital bed. Not ever. The part in me that felt, where my soul and my emotions crossed, had been disconnected from the part that poured. Tears have to be broken loose and mine had not been.

Until my ride down that mountain.

Whether it was my helplessness regarding Zaul or Maria or Hack or Shelly or the emptiness that had become my life . . . I rode, moonlight shining down, wind in my face, a stream of tears cascading down my cheeks. I wouldn't call them tears of joy or sorrow. I don't really know what to call them. I just know that they flowed out of an emotive response—they carried with them a feeling or emotion or something and that something was aimed at someone other than me. The proof lies in the source. They did not fall from my head. They poured up and out of my heart.

Big difference.

I rode those six glorious miles, shoulder to shoulder with a truck bed full of men who would do well to take a shower and put on some deodorant, but to be honest, I don't know if I was smelling me or them. Oddly, that thought never crossed my mind. I blended in. What struck me was a feeling, and it was a feeling I'd possibly never known. It was the feeling of something in me coming clean. That ride bathed me in laughter, in moonlight, in my own tears, and in the singular and surprising thought that maybe my cold, dead, calloused heart wasn't as cold and dead as I'd long believed it to be. The type of bath I needed —that my heart craved, that could wash off the stain of me—was not of water acquired from an external source, that came from a bucket or tub or even the kind that you dove into, but water that rose up from a source on the inside.

My life had been characterized by emptiness the size of the Sahara but there, in that moment, in the back of that truck in the armpit of Nicaragua, I wondered—for the first time—if there wasn't a river flowing down deep inside me.

If so, the water that would cleanse me was not water from my head—where I'd learned to rationalize my indifference.

But water from my heart.

Chapter Twenty-Three

The euphoria of the previous night was muted early the next morning when Paulina woke me, crying. I checked my watch. It was 3:17 a.m.

She said, "You mind driving me up? It's Roberto. He's . . ." She trailed off.

I jumped out of bed. "Sure."

Paulo asked a neighbor to sit with sleeping Isabella, so the three of us climbed the mountain in Colin's truck. Thirty minutes later, we walked into Roberto's room, where a vigil was under way. Candles had been lit, and beneath the whispers, I heard singing. Soft and angelic. Coming from the voices of the mothers and several of the children.

All the women wore scarves, covering their heads.

I held back while Paulina and Paulo tiptoed their way through the crowd to Roberto. Another woman sat next to him, waving a fan while a second woman gently swayed the hammock. He was pale in the dim light, his eyes half-open. Paulina tied a scarf around her head, and then she and Paulo stepped through his door, but they weren't the only ones to do so. Death was there, too.

Paulina knelt next to him and slid her hand in his. The right side of his face twitched upward and held for a second. At one time, that would have made a smile. His clothing was dry. As was his skin. Without moving his head, he held up his right hand, beckoning her. She leaned in, placing her head on his chest, where he rested his hand on her head. The movement exhausted him, and he lay several minutes catching his breath. Finally, he whispered. Faint. She nodded. Crying but trying to smile. He whispered some more. She cried harder and the pain peeled the forced smile off her face entirely. Tears streaming, she lifted her head; he placed his right thumb on her forehead and crossed her. Three times. Sobbing, she held his emaciated head in her palms and kissed his forehead, then his cheek. When she kissed his cheek a final time, he relaxed, exhaled, and died—his hand inside hers.

She hugged him several minutes while the

crowd continued to sing. Paulina knelt on the floor, buried her face in her hands, and cried. Out loud. The cries were deep, echoed across the room, and I had the feeling that more than the pain of Roberto's death was leaving her body.

After several minutes, Paulo lifted her to her feet where she stood along with the rest and sang a quiet song. When the song finished, someone stretched a dirty, tattered sheet over Roberto, covering his body and face. Silently, each person filed out of Roberto's cramped room and the hallway that led to it.

Outside, Paulo asked, "*Mi hermano*—" He searched for the words. "Please, may I drive?" He pointed at Paulina. "She asks you to walk."

I gave Paulo the keys and followed Paulina off the mountain. She had wrapped her arms around herself as if cold in the hot night air. I walked alongside. Saying nothing. Stepping around the rocks, which were difficult to see in the darkness of the new moon. She was sweating and her soaked blouse stuck to her back. The first several miles, she said nothing. Halfway home, she stopped, stared up at me, then off toward Las Casitas in the distance. She stood, shaking her head. Tears drying on her face. Every few seconds, another would trickle down, hang on her chin or the side of her lips, before finishing its fall. Unaware, she didn't bother with them.

Around us, swarming in the trees, parrots and

howler monkeys lit the early morning in a cacophony of sound and prelight activity. Either unable or unwilling, she didn't speak on the way home until just a few hundred yards from the house. Finally, after a silent six miles, she turned. Her face looked tortured. She said, "I wonder if I could trouble you."

"Anything."

"We need to build a coffin. This morning. Would you help Paulo?"

"Certainly." A pause. "Anything else?"

"I—" She searched my face. "I'd like to . . . we used to . . . a funeral—"

I handed her two hundred-dollar bills. "What else can I do?"

She held the money in her hand and choked back a sob. Collecting herself, she said, "Thank you."

When Paulo showed me his rudimentary tools and a coffin, which he had built months prior for a man who had yet to die, I asked if there was a hardware store close by. He said, "León." We drove to León, I bought the tools we needed, and then Paulo led me to a lumberyard, where we bought planks of seasoned Nicaraguan hardwood. It was some of the most beautiful wood I'd ever seen, and Hack would have really appreciated it.

When we returned, Paulo clued in to the fact that I had some experience with wood, so without steamrolling him or making him feel like his coffin wasn't good enough, he and I set out to build Roberto's coffin. When I fashioned my first dovetail together with seamless edges, Paulo sat back and patted me on the shoulder. "You finish."

By midafternoon, I'd finished the coffin. Paulo ran his fingers along the smooth edges, along the rounded corners, the cross that would rest above Roberto's face and nodded. "*Mi hermano*, you honor us."

The four of us drove up the mountain for the beginning of the procession. The women—each head covered—had prepared Roberto's body, dressing him in a white dress shirt and pants, which Paulina had bought with some of the money I'd given her. Then they laid him on top of a thin mattress covered with a blanket hand knit by one of the older women in the plantation. When the women began singing, the procession of almost two hundred lifted Roberto onto their shoulders and began walking down a path that led toward the remains of the mudslide. The younger men carried Roberto, sharing the load, passing him from shoulder to shoulder. Other than the almost subaudible singing from the women, the procession walked silently. Stepping quietly. Reverently. While Paulina and Paulo walked up front, alongside Roberto, Isabella remained next to me and slipped her hand in mine.

When the path leveled out, we walked out from

the trees and into a valley spiked with several dozen tall white crosses. A cluster of three sat off to one side, and alongside them, someone had dug a hole. When the young men reached the hole, they laid the coffin on top of the boards that crossed it. The soft-spoken preacher spoke several minutes, followed by Paulo, who said a few words. Finally, Paulina stepped forward, and without saying a word, she opened her mouth and sang a song I'd never heard but will never forget. It was beautiful, mournful, and the other women joined her in the chorus.

Without being instructed, the young men slowly lowered Roberto into the hole and, one by one, each individual in the crowd crossed themselves, whispered words I could not understand, and dropped a gentle handful of dirt onto Roberto's coffin. When they'd finished, Paulo handed me a rudimentary wooden shovel, and I helped him fill the hole. When we'd finished, the crowd had filed out of the valley and back up the hillside. Silently.

When I turned around, Paulina, Isabella, and the rest of the crowd had disappeared while one older woman stood next to me. It was Anna Julia. She tugged on my shirtsleeve and looked up at me. Paulo listened as she spoke. When she'd finished, he nodded, and she turned and followed the others uphill. Then he turned to me. "It was the most beautiful coffin. She's never seen its equal. She say God will surely accept him and the angels will be jealous."

I didn't know Roberto but evidently everyone else did, and the fact that he was beloved by young and old was evident by the reverence with which they handled him. Seldom, if ever, had I seen such tenderness toward the living or the dead.

When we returned uphill, we found the beginnings of a banquet in full force. Huge pots of steaming rice, beans, and hundreds of handmade tortillas lay mounded on tables. A rather large pig hung roasting over a spit, where four boys took turns turning it, and greasy, sweat-soaked women began pulling the meat off the bone.

The subdued party continued long into the night as everyone ate plate after plate. Isabella conscripted me to help her make coffee and stir the punch in coolers and then pour it into paper cups. Near midnight, I took a break from cleaning up, from carrying food, from pouring punch, from doing whatever was needed. When I stopped to drink some punch and wipe my head, Paulina appeared next to me. Dripping with sweat, her scarf soaked to her forehead, a satisfied and weary smile on her face, she hooked her arm inside mine, leaned on me, and said nothing as we stood staring at the party around us. Several older folks came up to her, speaking quietly, nodding, and holding both her hands in theirs. She spoke softly as well, nodding to each one and hugging several. When they'd left, she turned to me. "Thank you for this."

I'd known beautiful women. But I'd never known a human being whose inward beauty had the effect Paulina's had on all those around her. Her outward beauty was unequaled, but it was her inward beauty that left me speechless. I said nothing.

She waved her hand across the dwindling crowd. "They've not eaten like this . . . since my father. They were thanking me for that." She turned to me. "So thank you."

It was nearly 3:00 a.m. when we got home. Isabella had been asleep on Colin's front seat for the better part of three hours. Paulo carried her to her bed. I stretched out in the chicken coop and was too tired to kick off my flip-flops.

Chapter Twenty~Four

Friday morning appeared and only Paulo woke before me. We shared a quiet cup of coffee while Paulina and Isabella slept, and then I called Colin. Time to check in. I told him about the poker game, the truck, and about finding someone who'd seen Zaul—and about the blood on the hammock. I thought about not, but it's not my place to with-hold from Colin. Zaul's not my son.

Colin listened quietly and then agreed that if Zaul was out of money, and possibly hurt but unwilling to go to the hospital, chances were good he'd return to the house in Costa Rica to rest, heal up, get whatever money he'd left there, and put together plan B since plan A had failed. I told him I was heading out in a few hours and that I'd be there tonight. We talked about Maria, her improvement, and he told me they were scheduling a follow-up surgery with Shelly to reduce some of the scar tissue. They had yet to tell Maria.

Before he hung up, I said, "Wonder if you'd do me a favor."

"Sure."

"You have any attorney friends in this part of the world?"

"You need one?"

"Maybe, but not for anything criminal. Least not yet." I told Colin what I needed, or wanted, and when I finished, he was quiet a minute. Finally, he said, "Give me a few days."

Sometime after 11:00 a.m., Isabella woke, shuffled out her door, climbed up into Paulo's lap, and fell back asleep. A few minutes later, Paulina appeared. She didn't look much better. Coffee only raised her eyelids to half-mast.

"I have an idea I'd like to run by you."

She and Paulo looked at me agreeably. Isabella

cracked open her eyes and stared at me with little interest. "I think Zaul may be returning to his parents' house in Costa Rica. I need to check it out. If you're not opposed, I'd like to show it to you. There's a pool where maybe we could teach Isabella to swim, and there's a beach with miles of sand in either direction."

Uncharacteristically, Paulina rubbed her face and consulted no one. "I think I'd really like that."

Paulo and Isabella nodded. We left at noon. The problem I had with this excursion is that while I could pass myself off as a vagabond in flip-flops and cutoffs who had a little cash to flash around, Colin's house would not let me get away with that. It was one of the nicer homes in Costa Rica. By taking them there, the disparity between my life and theirs was about to become apparent and that would give rise to questions that might be tough to answer.

We drove the shoreline. Paulo played the role of tour guide and showed me the facets of his country that never make the travel books. He was right. It was beautiful—and nothing more so than the smiles of the people. For nearly seven hours, we stirred up dust on dirty back roads and drove on the asphalt only long enough to cross over it en route to another dirt road. Never once did he consult a map. Paulo knew this country like the back of his hand.

We arrived at the house a few hours before

sundown. If passing through the security gate itself wasn't an eye-opener, then driving through the gate and down the long drive was. When we pulled up before the front door, Paulina spoke through an open mouth. "What business did you say your partner was in?"

Isabella's eyes were large as silver dollars. Paulo sat speechless with both hands on the wheel.

I laughed. "Come on."

The house was clean, dry, and mostly put back together. Some finish work remained but it was livable. Looked like a contractor had yet to clear out the punch list. I gave them a tour, during which they were mostly silent and afraid to touch anything. The house was much as I'd left it, only cleaner, and unless he was hiding, Zaul had yet to show. I showed them their rooms and then told them I'd meet them at the pool. Paulina spoke up. "I don't own a bathing suit."

I hadn't considered that, so I took her to Marguerite's closet. "Probably find something in here. I'm not an expert judge of size, but you and Marguerite look to be similar."

"Marguerite is your partner's wife?"

"Yes."

"She won't mind?"

I shook my head. "No."

Paulina pointed to a picture on the wall hanging in the closet that depicted Marguerite in her bathing suit, wearing a tiara, after having just won one of many pageants. "That's her?"

"Yes."

"Great."

It didn't take them long to change.

Isabella, wearing a suit that was two sizes too big and sagged in the butt, walked up to the edge of the pool, where I was standing in the shallow end. I held out a hand. "Come on."

She shook her head.

"I'll catch you."

She leaned, her feet weighted to the pool deck, and fell forward into my arms. As I held her afloat and talked to her about kicking her feet and pulling with her hands, Paulina walked out wearing a rather modest one-piece and a chiffon wrap tied around her waist. In my defense, I was holding it together pretty well until she untied that chiffon, folded it, walked to the steps, and stepped into the pool, where I guess my jaw was hanging open. She reached up and closed it with a smirk. "Haven't you ever seen a girl in a bathing suit?"

"Not like that I haven't."

I don't know if she was flirting with me or if I was flirting with her, but somewhere in those few seconds, we passed from woman helping man find kid to woman allowing herself to look appealing and wondering if man was interested.

And he was.

Paulo joined us a few minutes later, we swam, I tried my best to teach Isabella to swim, and at sundown we all walked down the steps to the dock, where I gave them a tour of the boathouse and Colin's Bertram. Paulo ran his fingers along her clean lines and loved every minute of it. From the boathouse, Isabella led us out onto the beach, where the tide was low and the breeze was welcome and cooling. We walked until the sun disappeared behind the edge of the sea. Living on Bimini, I've seen some beautiful sunsets, but I've never seen one more beautiful.

I cooked dinner—spaghetti—and the conversation while we ate was relatively muted. After dinner, Paulina pointed at a door we'd not entered and said, "What's in there?"

"That's the theater."

"Theater?"

I led them into Colin's twelve-seat theater. I don't know the dimensions of the screen, but it was the size of the wall, which was huge. The chairs were plush leather, stadium seating with motorized recline, massage, and footrests. Paulina pointed at the wall of DVDs. "Will you pick us your favorite?" I made my selection, started the video, and left as the nuns began lamenting the problem that was Maria. The three of them were glued to the screen.

● ● ●

I checked in with Colin, reported on the condition of the house, and told him there was no sign of Zaul but that we'd stay through the weekend. Talking about Zaul was painful for Colin as it was a constant reminder of his failure as a father, so to deflect and change the conversation, he told me I should take my three guests on the ATVs tomorrow. The trails leading out the back of the house go for miles along the ocean. "It's one of the more beautiful vistas in Costa Rica."

When I first went to work for Colin, Zaul was just a ten-year-old kid. He always saw me as the guy coming and going in his dad's boat, so it was only natural, when he was about eleven, for him to meet me on the dock of their house in Miami one morning and ask, "Can I drive?"

I loaded him into one of Colin's smaller boats, a twenty-four-foot Pathfinder, because it's more maneuverable, and we eased off into the canals that led out into Stiltsville. Zaul stood at the console, up on his toes, staring through the windshield, craning his neck, one hand on the throttle, the other on the wheel. I stood beside him, watching. He was a natural, and unlike his father, he was good with boats. Coordinated. He was good with his hands, and when you could get him to, he would work hard and wasn't afraid of hard work. He drove us out of the canals and between the homes that make up what's left of Stiltsville.

Off to the northwest of us, several kite surfers rode the famous break that existed about a mile offshore. It was breezy, not a cloud in the sky.

I remember him staring at those homes, mesmerized by how they rose up out of the water and rested on stilts, at those kite surfers suspended in the air flipping and spinning with ease, at himself driving that boat, at the blue water and the porpoises rolling nearby, and I remember him being happy. I remember him smiling. I remember a kid at play. The problem is, I don't have too many memories of him being happy after that nor of him playing. And that's what I was sitting there thinking about, staring out across the ocean below, when Paulina snuck up behind me. I don't know how long she'd been standing there, but when I turned around, she asked, "What're you thinking about?"

"Enjoying the view."

"You're not a very good liar."

"Thank you, but the truth is I'm an exceptional liar. I've made it an art."

She sat next to me. "Well, then tell me one thing that's true about you. What do you remember about life as a kid?"

I thought about this a second. "As a kid, I don't ever remember not feeling dirty. It wasn't so much feeling dirt on my skin as a sinking in my gut. A resident weight. Something I was born with or that woke up with me every day. To combat it, I surfed a lot—thinking the ocean might wash it off. When I got to high school, I ran a lot, thinking I could sweat it out. Same in college. After college, I lived on planes and in hotels, thinking if I didn't stop moving, I could outrun it. That the newness of my environment would replace it. Finally, when none of that worked, I moved to the ocean and bought a little place where I could watch the sun go down every day and sleep every night under the sound of constant waves crashing."

"Did it work?"

I shook my head. "No. And you want to hear something funny?"

"Yes."

"In all my life, my work, my travels, my attempts not to work, in all my going and doing, I've never felt more 'clean' than when covered in volcanic mud, hanging from Paulo's rope in the bottom of that dark, damp well."

Unlike at the hotel in León, she didn't press me but just sat with me. Enjoying the view. After several minutes, she offered, "Thank you for today. It was special. Especially to Isabella."

I smiled. "You would do well not to take advice from me, but if I might—you should think about wearing a bathing suit more often. It suits you."

A chuckle. "It's been a long time."

"Doing so would really spice things up in Valle Cruces. Spend about thirty minutes walking around in that, and you'd have more men knocking down your door than Paulo could keep away."

"That's not the kind of man I'm looking for."

"You mind if I turn the tables and ask you something?"

"Sure."

"You've been a widow more than a decade, and you don't seem to be trying to change that. You're beautiful, you laugh with an easiness I don't think I've ever known, you bend over backward to serve folks, you are constantly pouring out, so—"

She interrupted me again. "What's wrong with me?"

"Yes." I laughed. "For the life of me, I can't find anything wrong with you."

"I have my moments."

"Well"—I scratched my head—"I have yet to notice any. Seriously, what kind of man are you looking for?"

"Not the kind who is solely attracted to me because of how I look in a bathing suit."

"I hate to break it to you, but . . . you do look good in a bathing suit and I'm not apologizing for recognizing that."

More easy laughter. "I guess that's some relief. It's been so long since I've tried to get noticed."

"So, without getting overly personal, have you dated?"

"There have been guys."

"That's not an answer to my question."

She smirked. "You're perceptive."

"Don't let the flip-flops fool you."

"I'm beginning to see that."

"You're stalling. What kind of guys?"

"The kind that never call when they find out I have a daughter."

"Okay, let's say you could script the perfect guy. Order á la carte."

She considered this. "Seriously?"

"Yes."

"The kind I can walk beside, lock arm-in-arm with, who's not afraid to pull teeth, drop down into a well, work with Paulo, hold hands with my daughter and it not be weird, who doesn't complain about a bucket shower, who would stand up to the neighborhood bully and then give back more money than I've made in most of my adult life and"—she held a finger in the air and grinned with a wide smile—"one who can definitely ride a motorcycle. For starters, a guy like that."

"And how many guys do you know like that?"

She turned away. "A couple."

"Oh, really. What are their names?"

"Well, okay, maybe it's just one, but I don't know him very well and something about him tells me there's a whole lot I don't know."

I didn't hesitate before this flirting went much further. "And you'd be right."

"So maybe we should just leave it right there

before we uncover the truth and you disappoint me."

"How do you know the truth of me would disappoint you?"

"Your face tells me every time I look at you."

If I'd ever had a gift when it came to poker, at bluffing, at not showing my hand to another, it was gone. Talking with her on the deck over-looking the ocean was when I knew I'd never play cards again. The other players would read my face and take everything I held dear.

She sat back, crossed her legs and her arms, and stared out across the water. "I'm just guessing, but I'd say you've lived most of your life acting as though you don't care. As though you don't con-cern yourself too much with matters of the heart. But I wonder if you don't feel them more deeply than others."

We were starting to get a little close to home. Where I'd always been rather good at reading people's weakness, Paulina was good at reading people's pain. The difference between the two of us was glaring.

We spent all the next morning on the ATVs. We rode miles up the coast, returning through the trees and then out onto the beach and up and down the dunes. Paulo had never ridden an ATV, but he took to it quickly and with great fervor. And while Paulo feared no hill, Paulina— prodded by Isabella—was the speed demon.

We returned for lunch, a dip in the pool, and then I took them out on the Bertram for an afternoon on the Pacific. The seas were glass, and we stayed well within sight of the coastline, which kept their dizziness at bay. I threw the cast net and caught some baitfish, dropped a few baits in the water, and helped Paulo catch a few wahoo and several tuna. Throughout the afternoon, he'd set the hook, and then he and Isabella would reel them in accompanied by much high-pitched squealing from an exuberant Isabella, who desperately desired to see the fish but not necessarily touch them. Paulina sat up top smelling of coconut oil, wearing Marguerite's bathing suit and my Costas, and laughing at the festivities below.

Toward evening, Paulo filleted the fish with a speed and proficiency that would have rivaled Hack, and then we grilled the fish on the pool deck along with some vegetables that Paulina picked up at a market down the road. As the sun went down, we reclined at the table with full stomachs and easy smiles. Isabella stood in the shallow end of the pool, testing her newfound boldness. Paulo finished his third serving of fish, scraped his plate, and wiped his mouth. His satisfaction was palpable. He patted me on the shoulder, then tapped himself on the chest and said, *"Mi corazón está lleno."*

He knew I didn't understand, but I got the feeling that he said it in Spanish for emphasis.

I shrugged and he said the words again.

When they still didn't make sense, Paulina translated, "He said, 'My heart is full.' "

It was quite possibly the most fun I'd had in recent memory.

Sometime after 9:00 p.m., Isabella fell asleep and Paulo carried her upstairs to bed. Paulina followed, giving me a chance to check in with Colin. I told him about the day, the house, the progress of the cleanup, and that we'd still found no sign of Zaul. I explained how now that Zaul was separated from his friends we were looking for the proverbial needle and—as difficult as it was—our best bet was to wait right here. He agreed and then fell quiet. Heavy, not saying much. Finally, he said, "You remember that favor you asked of me?"

"Yes."

"I've got some information for you . . ." I listened while Colin reported on what he'd found.

And the news was not good.

We hung up and I sat staring at the moon on the water. After a few minutes, Paulina returned and sat. Closer this time. "Where were we?" There was a childlike playfulness in her voice and an innocence in her eyes that told me she was enjoying her time here and, more important, me. I also got the impression that it wasn't something she did with every guy she met. I admit, I was drawn to her. Maybe a lot. Well, okay, more than a lot. But I had a track record of hurting people, and something in me did not want her to be one more. I wanted to spare her from me.

Sitting on that pool deck, I was staring back over the wake of my life and the thing that struck me was how the churn and chop was littered with relationships. With people I'd used to get what I wanted. I didn't know much about my present life or where I was going or what would happen to me when we found Zaul and I returned him to his folks, but whatever happened, I knew I didn't want Paulina to be one more casualty in the war that had become my life. Maybe pain does that, and while I tried to mask it and pretend that I couldn't or didn't feel it, I was in pain. My pain painted me and was the source of what made me feel dirty. I was rarely self-aware, but somehow at that moment, bathing in the smell of coconuts and sweat and the utter delight of a woman in full bloom, I was lucid enough to know that Leena deserved better than me, and while I might not be able to get clean, I didn't have to drag her down in the mud with me.

I turned to her. "When I came here, looking for Zaul, I didn't expect you. This. I am having some trouble wondering what I'm going to do when I or we find Zaul and I have to leave here. I've enjoyed the last several days with you, but before

I go any further and make you feel I'm one kind of person, I want to tell you exactly what kind I am. And if you'll let me, I'd like to get it all out before you walk away. Because you'll want to; you should, and when you do, you'll be showing good sense." I swallowed. "When I said I'd made an art of lying, I was actually telling the truth." I took a breath and tried to figure a way in. Not finding one, I came right at it. "Paulina, I'm a drug dealer. Or I was." She didn't flinch, so I continued, "I've dealt and delivered more cocaine than most any one individual in South Florida save the Mafia and cartels. My partner and I run, or ran, a boutique purchase and delivery service. It was easy money and we've made a good bit. A few years back, I got up one night to go to the bathroom and stumbled over several hundred thousand dollars in plastic bags in my house in Bimini and had to figure out where to hide it because I couldn't just walk up and deposit it in the bank." I turned one thumb over the other. "I've never considered myself an evil man, but I'm not a good man, either. Good men don't live life as I do. A couple of weeks ago, on what was to be the night before my wedding to a woman who loved me—or what she knew of me—I made a delivery. Same type I'd been making for a decade. A few kilos to a party in Miami. Zaul got mixed up in it, and as a result, his sister—the closest thing I have to a niece and maybe the only female on this planet who loves me with any real sincerity—got between him and a pit bull." Paulina winced. "The dog attacked her face and neck, severing the nerve that allows her to smile. My former fiancée was the doctor that patched her back together, and until that moment, she had no idea that I did what I did. I'd lived two lives and she never knew of the second. I have no family, one friend, no real occupation, and I've contributed nothing to this earth other than broken businesses, shattered relationships, increased addictions, and greater pain." I shook my head. "The other night I stood in the hospital room while the nurses pulled the bandages off Maria's face and realized I don't know how to make good on a life like mine—I doubt it's possible—but if I could, I'd find Zaul and return him in one piece to his mom and dad and sister. And if that takes every penny I've ever made, and I've made millions, then—" I pulled a wad of cash totaling several thousand dollars from my pocket and placed it in her palm. "I'd gladly give it all and steal ten times more." The suspicion drained out of her face and something akin to compassion took its place. I sat back. "At night, when I get angry, I think about the man who released the dog, but in my mind it's my hands I see on the leash. I try to shower, to get clean, but I can't." I palmed my face. "Right now, out there is a kid trying to act tough and mimic all the gangster icons of the silver screen, and he's in a really bad place. He's hurt, scared, and angry. I don't want to sugarcoat this—Maria's face. I did that. And I did this to Zaul. So, when you look at me and we talk, you need to know who you're looking at, where he's come from, and what he's brought with him."

She leaned back and crossed her arms, but she didn't look scared or concerned. She looked thoughtful. After a moment, she asked, "What's one thing you're proud of?"

"Did you hear anything I just said?"

"Answer my question."

I shrugged.

A smile. "Just one."

"You sure you want to go here?"

"Yes."

"About six, no, seven years ago, I was picking up a load in Cuba. A day run. Down and back. I was literally pulling my boat out of the dock when a man wearing a dirty suit showed up at the docks with a bag of cash, his wife, and three kids. He waved the cash in my face and told me in broken English that they needed to get out right then. I asked if he had papers and he shook his head. Ninety miles away, in Florida, my partner Colin had a 'friend' who made papers for people. For the right amount of money, he could make you well established as a citizen of the United States. So, I looked at this scared woman, these frightened kids and this sweating man, and I asked the man,

'What'd you do?' He looked at his wife, then at me, and shook his head. He said, 'I didn't give in.' So, I pointed to my boat, wherein they immediately disappeared below. I had no idea what I was going to do with them, but I got on the phone and talked to Colin, who met us with his friend. Last I heard, Juan—as he is now called—was selling Oriental rugs in South Florida. Doing quite well, too. Every now and then, when I'm buying my coffee at this Cuban bakery in south Miami, I bump into him. He smiles, buys my coffee, and tells me how his daughter is studying to be a doctor at UM. Every time we part, he holds my hand just a second longer and his eyes well up." I nodded. "I'm proud of that."

"And the worst thing?"

I sipped from our water bottle. "Paulina, you're talking to a professional dealer."

"Pick one."

"Colin was having trouble getting a load in from Argentina through customs. So I flew down and bought a hundred head of Argentinian beef cattle headed to the U.S. for slaughter. Paid a premium for the beef, but it was nothing compared to what we stood to make on the drugs. So before we shipped them over, I wrapped the drugs in heavy plastic and then inserted the drugs into the females and placed them on a barge. We took delivery of the cows, retrieved the drugs, and sold the cows to a Florida cowboy who owned a chain of steak houses throughout the southeast."

"Other than the whole delivering drugs part of that, what's the bad part?"

"During transit, a couple of my bags burst so the deckhands fed the sharks . . . I'm not real proud of that."

"You're okay with people sucking that stuff up their nose, but you feel guilty when a few cows die who were weeks from dying anyway?"

"I don't feel particularly good about either one, I'm just telling you the first thing that stood out in my mind when you asked me what I wasn't real proud of. I want you to know that, until recently, I have viewed what we do as simply providing a recreational drug to recreational users. In order to protect myself from the ripple effects of what we do, I routinely—and with great numbness—turned a blind eye to those whose indulgence surpassed recreation. If they couldn't handle it, that was their problem. Not mine. I've viewed our business as a couple of bootleggers outrunning 'the man.' Truth is, we're peddling strychnine. And it poisons everyone but us. Somehow, we're immune. Or were."

Sweat beaded across her top lip. "Charlie Finn, you don't scare me. Who you see in the mirror and who I see are not the same man. There's a disconnect. A contradiction. Several times in the last few days, I've watched my daughter slip her hand in yours as she walks downhill or climb onto your shoulders like a human jungle gym. I watched you pay a man for damage at his resort with no plans of ever staying there."

"I didn't know you saw that."

"I told you before. I'm poor. Not ignorant. His face told me when he walked out. I've watched you hang from a rope and dig a well with no intention of ever drinking the water when for more than the last decade not a man around here has been willing to do that. And every day I watch you scour a country for a kid that's not your own. And then I watch you stare at me and wonder if a girl like me could ever fall for a boy like you. So you'll forgive me if what I see disagrees with what you tell me."

I eyed my watch, loosening and fastening the band. The proof of my skill as a liar and deceiver was evident in her innocent belief in me and my innate goodness. The fact that she was still standing there. The truth of me—of my role in the failure of Cinco Padres Café Compañía —sat on the tip of my tongue, and yet for reasons I cannot articulate, I could not spit it out of my mouth. I guess maybe I didn't tell her the truth because I couldn't stand the thought of losing one more woman to the truth of my life. Maybe I could change. Maybe the truth would hurt too much, and it'd be better to hold it. Keep it where it couldn't hurt her, as she'd already suffered enough. No need to go picking off the scab. So many times I'd wanted to look back at my relationships and ask, "What's wrong with them?" but every time I did, the only common denominator between me, Amanda, Shelly, and now Leena was me. Sooner or later, the problem is not them.

I kept my mouth shut.

She stood, leaned across the space between us, and kissed me. First on the cheek, then she stepped back, cradled my cheek in her palm, and kissed me on the side of my lips, and then on my lips. She held there. Tender. Soft. And inviting. While her lips were pressed to mine, the argument inside my head was raging. Some part of me wanted to save her from me.

I knew better and she didn't—which was the growing source of ache in me.

Slowly, she pulled away, wiped her thumb across my lips. A satisfied smile. She whispered, "I want you to know I haven't kissed a man since my husband died. For years, I didn't want to, and for several more I couldn't find anyone worth it. I've been holding that a long time."

When she turned and began walking inside, I watched her—her shoulders, the vein throbbing on the side of her neck, the small of her back, the angle of her hips, the lines of her calves. She wasn't inviting me to follow her, but she wasn't wishing I'd look away, either. In her own way, she was allowing me to look—to soak in the sight of her, appreciate her as a woman, and I was pretty certain she'd not allowed that in a decade, either.

My emotive response to both Amanda and Shelly was a deep desire to ease their pain, to not regret, to not be alone, to not have to face life without them and what that said about me. Of course, I cared for them. Deeply. And not all of my reasons for being with them were selfish but many were. What I felt for them can best be described as "deep affection." A product of convenience. Of geography. Of my own need. Watching Leena climb the stairs inside, I couldn't honestly tell you that I loved her—I'm not sure I'd know that if and when I felt it—but whatever I felt for her was different. At every level, and the depth of it convinced me that while I'd told both Amanda and Shelly that I loved them, I knew then, sitting on that pool deck overlooking the Pacific, I had not.

Not even close.

I sat by the pool a long time. It was close to 2:00 a.m. when I thought about going to bed. I walked to the edge of the pool and was about to turn out the light when I heard a stick crack, followed by footsteps, a shuffle, and a guttural grunt. Then another footstep. Another shuffle. Another grunt. I stepped into the shadow and watched as a lone figure walked up the steps from the side of the house toward the pool. He climbed the last step, leaned against the railing, and steadied himself. I was moving toward him when he took a step and fell headlong into the pool. His still body floated facedown as a cloud of red spilled out of his side and into the water around him.

Chapter Twenty-Five

I was screaming for Paulina before I hit the water. I dove in, caught Zaul by the shoulders, flipped him, cradled his head, and began pulling him to the side. By the time I got him to the steps, she'd turned on the light and was standing at the railing—her gown flowing in the wind. She saw us and disappeared.

I dragged his body from the water and laid him out on the pool deck. His face was busted up. Whatever piercings he'd once owned had been ripped out. His ear had been torn. Eyes were swollen. Had a nasty cut over one eye and beneath another. Someone had carved on one of his arm tattoos with a sharp object and one shoulder seemed out of place and resting lower than the other. He was clutching his rib cage, and when I pulled up his shirt, I could understand why. Deep black-and-blue contusions surrounded his entire torso. One leg seemed limp and weak. A couple of his fingers were swollen and one looked broken. But that was not the worst of it.

The worst was an open gash on the side of his stomach that wound around his back. Infected and actively bleeding—it was an ugly wound. He'd stuffed it with paper towels and a piece of cloth I couldn't make out. Based upon his ashen appearance, he'd lost a lot of blood, and based on the caked stains on his clothes and skin, he had been for a while.

Paulina landed next to me about the time I figured out he wasn't dead. Least not yet. He was delirious and fading in and out of consciousness, muttering words I couldn't understand. Her finger immediately landed on his carotid while the other hand propped open an eye. Didn't take her long. She checked his injuries, including his side, and shook her head. "He's very weak. Fighting infec-tion." She pointed to his face, arm, and side. "He needs about a hundred stitches. He's dehydrated. He needs a hospital, but—" She held up a finger. "If we put him in a hospital and he's done any-thing deserving arrest since he's been here, the police will arrest him and put him in a Costa Rican prison, and you and his mother and father will never see him again no matter how rich they are."

Blood was trickling out of his face. I pulled my cell phone out of my pocket and began dialing Colin. I spoke as I dialed. "Colin can be here in an hour and either find an airport close or land his jet on the highway a few miles from the house.

This time of night there won't be anyone on the road."

As soon as I said this, Zaul's hand came up and covered both mine and the cell. He held it there, shaking his head, preventing me from dialing. His words were muffled, and I couldn't understand what he said the first time but I did the second and third. "Not going home."

I leaned in. "Zaul, you may die tonight if we don't get you to medical care."

He nodded. Then he shook his head again. "Not going home." He laid his head back, but his hand remained on the cell phone.

While I sat thinking how to circumvent Zaul and get him home, Leena spoke. "If we can get to a pharmacy, I can get enough medicine to inject him and get us to León, where he will need some time to recuperate."

"How about here?"

"His injuries are serious. Even if you could get the plane here, I'm not even sure he should fly. His blood pressure is dangerously low. He needs an IV. Antibiotics. Fluids. Morphine. X-rays. A check for internal injuries. A lot of stitches. And I can't get that in Costa Rica because they don't know me, but I can get it in León. And by the time we wait through the crowded emergency room anywhere close to here, we could get in through the back door in the clinic at León and then, if needed, right into the hospital. The doctors know me there." Her intensity grew. "He needs care right now. And the only way I know to do that for certain starts in León."

Zaul's eyes were closed and his breathing shallow. "Get Isabella. I'll get him to the truck."

I carried Zaul to the truck while Paulina woke Isabella and Paulo and then brought me some blankets and several pillows as well as an armful of towels. Ten minutes later, Paulo backed us out of the drive and was headed north up the highway to León. The highway was dark, and there wasn't another car in sight. Isabella stared through the back glass while Paulina huddled in the back with me. While I cradled Zaul and kept him from bouncing around, she did what she could with what little first aid we had to pack the gash on his side and wash his wounds. The look on her face told me she was worried. I held the flashlight and helped her as best I knew how. For his part, Zaul was mostly unconscious, which was good. If he were awake, he'd feel the pain, so unconscious was better. The last hour, she checked his pulse every few minutes and grew increasingly worried. "His fever has spiked." She was right; Zaul was on fire and his skin was hot to the touch and his lips were blue. Paulo stopped at a gas station and bought a bag of ice, which we packed behind Zaul's neck, in his armpits, on his stomach, and around his groin.

Driving in the dark, staring back and forth

between Zaul and Paulina's eyes, the occasional house light passing in the trees off the side of the road, clarity settled on me.

But the clarity did not bring me peace. How I got where I am in life was not the result of much thought or planning on my part. Nor can I tell you it was always the path of least resistance, although that was sometimes the case. More like the path of "that looks interesting" or "why not" or "wonder where that goes." I've checked no moral compass and until recently never considered myself evil. Sitting in the back of that truck, Zaul bleeding in my arms, his life draining out of him, the whole of me pressed down on me and my reaction to the timeline and consequences of my life—and my choices—was one of disdain. Of bitterness. Of an acrid taste in my mouth. My sin had not been outright murder. I'd not defrauded millions. Not caused a holocaust. Not shot a dozen kids in a school. Not raped. Pillaged. But as I looked across my history, I wondered for the first time if my actions might be even worse.

I didn't need to ask the question. I knew the answer.

I might not be in league with other evil men, but over my life, I'd looked away, gone on my merry way, done nothing to prevent or hinder—or rescue. While not an active instigator, I'd been passive. An accomplice even. That passivity had only served to multiply. Maybe that was the toughest thought to swallow. The effect of my life had been to multiply evil, not fight it. Not eradicate it.

If my life had been spent sifting through a fog that did not allow me to see, there in the back of that truck, it lifted and daylight cracked the skyline. I could define me in one word.

I was "indifferent."

Staring at Zaul, at the crimson stain of my decisions, I knew I could no longer claim ignorance and manifest indifference. My sins were many. I glanced at my watch to check the time, but the face was smeared and the time covered over.

As I looked at Leena and felt in my heart an ache for something more than what I'd known and maybe what I hoped for what remained of my life, I was left with only one question and I had no answer to it.

When we reached the cathedral in León, Leena ran inside, leaving me alone with Zaul. With no movement, his eyes popped open and he stared at his hands. He shook his head. "What a mess I've made."

My words were an attempt to take his mind off the pain. Anything to divert his mind from the moment. I said, "You really went out of your way to follow in your dad's footsteps."

His head swayed, and eyes rolled around. Forcing himself to return, he focused on me and tugged on my shirt, pulling me toward him. Through gritted teeth and a growing gurgle, he spoke, "Wasn't trying to be my dad." A single shake. He tapped me on the chest. "Was trying to be you." He laid back, exhausted from the effort of pulling himself up. He whispered through closed eyes, "Like you."

I did not bother to palm away the tears as Leena returned with two priests in flowing brown robes tied with white rope. I lifted Zaul from the back of the truck, carried him inside and down a tile-covered walkway into the medical clinic full of stainless implements where a bed had been prepared. Leena immediately prepped Zaul's left arm, inserted a needle, and handed me the bag of fluids. "Squeeze this. Force them in." As she began cutting off his clothes, she said, "The doctor will be here shortly. They have an outdated X-ray machine, but it works well enough. He's bringing some film. Between now and then, we need to get him clean and start stitching him up."

An hour later, she and I had bathed and scrubbed most every square inch of Zaul—who was sleeping peacefully under a haze of morphine. Once clean and disinfected, she began stitching, starting with his side. Doing so required her to stitch both internally and externally. Her hand was steady and her stitches near perfect. She worked like an experienced surgeon. "Your husband teach you that?" I asked.

She shook her head but kept her eyes on her work. "No. Necessity."

From there she worked her way up to his face, eye, and his arm. She set his broken finger and worked his dislocated shoulder back into its socket. When it popped back in, I said, "Necessity teach you that?"

She almost smiled. "No." She massaged his shoulder to manipulate the bloodflow. "My husband did."

When the doctor showed with the unexposed film, the priests rolled in the X-ray machine, flipped the camera head horizontally, and I helped position Zaul to get the best pictures, of which they took several. Once developed, she and the doctor examined them and determined he had four broken ribs, but they had cracked along the line of the rib and not across, which meant that while painful, they weren't poking into his lungs and demanded no treatment other than rest. The doctor also felt rather certain that Zaul did not appear to have multiple internal injuries other than severe contusions, but time would be a better indicator. At first, given the sight of his torso, he feared a burst spleen but that did not materialize. For the next hour, she and the doctor gave Zaul a rather thorough exam from head to toe, which was made all the more difficult by his being asleep, preventing him from answering the "Does this hurt?" line of questioning.

By 10:00 a.m., Leena and the doctor had done what they could. Zaul needed rest, fluids, antibiotics, and freedom from the fear of further harm. "And make no mistake," the doctor said, holding a finger in the air. "Someone has caused him great bodily harm." The doctor lifted the sheet off Zaul's stomach, exposing deep blue-and-purple contusions. He waved his hand across Zaul. "Grey Turner's and Cullen's sign."

"I'm not familiar with either of—"

"Intra-abdominal bleeding caused from blunt trauma. May indicate hemorrhage." He turned to Leena. "Monitor carefully."

Leena nodded as if she understood. The doctor returned to the hospital, promising to check on Zaul later that evening. Walking out, he turned and cautioned us that Zaul would be laid up a while. And that we should make plans for an extended recuperation.

I stood over the sink, scrubbing my arms and watch. Trying to get the blood out of the cracks in the bezel where it had caked and dried. Again. While we'd found him, things had gone from bad to worse.

Time to check in.

Chapter Twenty-Six

I put in the call, said "George," and waited a few seconds for the return call. When he did, I answered, "We found him. Or rather, he found us. Anyway, he's here."

"How is he?"

"Well . . . he's alive and he'll recover, but he's in pretty bad shape."

"I'll send the plane. I can be there—"

"I don't think that would be helpful."

He was quiet a moment. "You need money?"

"No. I'm good. The doctor just left. Leena is taking care of him. We're probably looking at a week or two of bed rest. Somebody really worked him over. He's in a bad way."

"You talked with him?"

"Not much. He's been in and out. Sleeping now. Doc gave him a pretty heavy dose of something to help him sleep." I swallowed. "He's got a bit of a recovery ahead of him so rest easy. I'll take some pics with my phone and send them your way over the next few days. Give you something to have hope in."

"That'd be good. That'd be good."

"I'll be in touch."

He cleared his throat. "You know that other matter?"

"Yeah."

"It's complicated."

"How so?"

"You can get it, but I'm not sure you're going to want to go where you're going to have to go to get it. Or, that you can afford it."

As Colin explained, I sat quietly listening while the ramifications of his explanation settled in me and the ripple effects spread out across my mind.

When he finished, he said, "Send us some pics if you think about it. Marguerite will like that."

Colin hung up and I sat there with my head in my hands, certain that I'd never felt so empty in my entire life.

Leena spent the day by Zaul's bed, charting his progress—temperature, blood pressure, medications administered, and any change in his condition. Paulo, seeing he could do nothing here, took Isabella home, leaving the two of us at the cathedral, where we would spend the night before trying to move him tomorrow.

Toward evening, my stomach reminded me that we hadn't eaten all day. I stuck my head in the room where she was listening to Zaul's heartbeat with a stethoscope. "I'm going to get some dinner. You want anything?"

She nodded, smiled, and said, "Yes, but stay away from fresh salsa."

I held up a finger. "Note to self."

She laughed.

I struck out, walked the streets of León, bought two to-go plates at Meson Real and a couple bottles of water, and then returned to the dark clinic. Paulina was asleep in a cot next to Zaul's bed. I left a plate on a table next to her and covered her with a blanket. From there, I walked into the cavernous cathedral. I picked a pew that lined the back wall and sat, staring at all the stained glass, and picked at my dinner.

Across from me hung a painting. Maybe eight or ten feet tall and half as wide. It was old, cracked, and had been poorly repaired. It depicted a slave market where a naked man, bloody with the stripes of a scourge, stood on a block, the auctioneer next to him. A bloody spear hung horizontally above his head. It dripped into the dirt at his feet. Around him, angry men shouted bids while he stood helpless. At the bottom, a plaque had been engraved: SOLD UNDER THE SPEAR.

I lay on the bench. Another painting hung above me. Below it, some words had been carved into the massive stones: YOU HAVE SOLD YOUR-SELVES FOR NOTHING. AND YOU SHALL BE REDEEMED WITHOUT MONEY.

I closed my eyes and shook my head. I could not wrap my hands around that. Couldn't see how that was possible.

Leena shook me some twelve hours later. A

priest was mopping the floor nearby. She was smiling. "He's asking for you."

Zaul was sitting up when I walked in. His face was still puffy. He spoke when I walked in. His voice was ragged. "How's Maria?"

"She's better. Been asking for you."

"How's her face?"

"Your dad said Shelly did a really great job. Can hardly tell."

I stood next to him, letting him speak, not pressing him. He looked away and tears cascaded down his face. "You tell her I'm sorry?"

"You can tell her yourself."

"I'm not going home."

On the surface, Zaul was a muscled, tough-talking seventeen-year-old. Inside, he was still very much a kid. I pulled the cell phone out of my pocket. "Little over a hundred years ago, some really smart guy invented a thing called the phone. It's been through a few versions but I have one here. It allows you to talk to people who are a long way away." I pointed to the earpiece. "When you put your ear here, it sounds like they're sitting right next to you. And when you talk in this part"—another point—"you can tell them things like you're sorry and that you love them . . . That you hope they're okay."

He nodded, laughed, nodded, wiped the tears on his sheet. "Guess I made a mess of things."

I rolled the stool up next to the bed and sat.

"You did." I put my hand on his shoulder. "But if we're comparing messes, mine's bigger."

As tough as he liked to pretend to be, Zaul had his mother's heart. He tried to mask it with steroids, tattoos, piercings, and four-letter epithets, but all that had been exposed for what it was. Just a cover. Something to mask his own insecurity. The kid sitting before me was none of that, and his hard shell had been cracked. Exposed for what it was. He was like the kid who walked into the living room wearing his dad's robe and slippers. It just didn't fit.

He shook his head, exhaled, and clutched his ribs. "I feel like I've been hit by a Mack truck."

"Want to tell me what happened?"

"Where do you want me to start?"

"How about the beginning. After I made the drop."

Zaul glanced at Leena, not knowing how honest he could be.

"She knows about me. I told her."

Zaul explained how he'd been tracking my drops through his dad's phone. Learning where, when, how much, etc. I made it a lot easier for him one afternoon when he saw me lift the SIM card out of my locker in the back hall of their house and then drop the old one in the trash can. I'd never known he was there. Since then, he'd been following me, trying to learn how I did what I did. He was also trying to figure out where his dad kept the bulk of his drugs, so he could skim a little off the top and make some money on his own. He thought, after all his many screwups, that his dad would appreciate his entrepreneurial efforts. He also explained how when his losses mounted and he realized he wasn't all that good at poker that he started hanging out with some guys who ran a dogfighting operation. Hence, pit bulls. Easy money. Thought he'd pay one gambling debt with another sure bet. So he bought a dog and paid some guy to train it, but when he put it in its first fight, it lost badly. As did he. He'd bet a good bit at bad odds. Poker losses compounded with dogfighting losses meant they'd come to collect. So on the night he took Maria for what he told her and us would be a moonlight stroll, they'd followed him and caught him off guard. The dog was meant for him. He called 911, then waited until Life Flight landed in the street, afraid to look at his sister's face. Zaul paused here a long time. He said his mom and dad had bailed him out so many times that he couldn't face them again, so he fled to the only place he could think of. When he landed in Costa Rica, he called some guys he'd met the summer prior. Career surfers. Things soon spiraled out of control, and before he knew it, there were two hundred people trashing his folks' house. Again, trying to be like us, he thought he'd buy and sell and try and make good on all he'd lost, which took him to León. He actually had visions of walking back into his parents' home in Miami with enough money to repay all they'd spent to bail him out. Once in León, he heard about the poker game and flashed around enough money to get invited. He quickly lost, and when he tried to run, the foreman unleashed his bouncer on him. Low on funds and without a vehicle, he and his surfer "friends" began living in hostels and a few resorts, which they left in worse condition than when they arrived. Somewhere in there he got in a drunken fight with a man wielding a knife, which explained his stomach. When he ran out of money and wouldn't call his dad for more, his friends turned on him—which explained the cuts above his eyes and broken ribs. Like a pack of wolves, they'd attacked when he was wounded and literally kicked him when he was down. The result was what we saw before us. They took what little money he had left, left him in a ditch, and he crawled his way to the highway, hitchhiked south, and then walked once the truck entered Costa Rica. He said he knew I'd be looking for him, and sooner or later, I'd either find him or his body at the house.

When he finished, he was tired. He leaned back and closed his eyes. The telling had exhausted him. Leena pulled up a blanket, and I told him to get some sleep. We'd talk more later.

He was asleep before I left the room. Leena met me outside the door. "He's weak. Needs another day here." She held her hands behind her back and rocked back and forth on her tiptoes. "Don't you think a chocolate-filled croissant would be really good right now?"

I needed some time to process. "Be right back."

The day passed and Zaul slept through most all of it. Late in the evening, after all the priests had shut the huge doors of the cathedral and gone to bed, Leena found me napping on my pew. She shook my foot. "Got a second?"

I sat up. "Sure."

"Not to be overly pushy, but what's your plan?"

A shrug. "He doesn't want to go home. I can make him, but I'm not sure how long that'd stick or what it would accomplish. I can take him to the house in Costa Rica and let him recuperate, but that's a constant reminder of where he's messed up, of the ongoing tension with his folks, and there would be no one there but us. I think we'd get cabin fever once he got healthy. I can get a room at the hotel here, but once he got up and about, we'd run into the same problem. Not to mention that he'd be more likely to bump into some of his friends around here, which neither he nor we need. I can take him with me back to Bimini, but I think that would just reinforce the whole drug runner thing. Plus, I'm pretty sure I don't need that, either."

Leena sat next to me. "What about spending a

few weeks in Valle Cruces? With us? We could add a bed to the chicken coop. You and Paulo could fix it up a bit. I've seen what you can do with wood. Maybe you could make it less . . ." She laughed. "Barn-like."

"I paid you to help me find him. Not nurse him back to health."

"I'm not asking you to pay us."

"I know, I didn't mean—"

"Zaul's wounds are much deeper than his skin and bones. He's a scared kid who has no idea who he is."

She was right. I nodded. "You're really perceptive."

"I'm a woman."

I smiled. "That you are."

"When I was young, younger than Isabella, my father would walk me up in the mountains where he was tending to his coffee plants. Sometimes, he would come upon a plant that would not flourish. No matter what he did to it, it just produced no fruit. No coffee. So rather than just ripping it out by the root and throwing it off the mountain, he'd gingerly dig it up and transplant it to another place where the soil was different. Then, he'd stake it up with something stronger than itself, he'd water it, fertilize it, and give it a chance to put down roots someplace new. Sometimes a change of soil is all that's needed."

"With all deference to your father, a change in

geography does not necessarily mean an improvement in circumstances. In my experience, problems have a tendency to follow you whether you're in Boston, Miami, Bimini, or Nicaragua."

She laid a towel across her lap, pulled a mango the size of a small football from her bag, and began peeling it, while the juice dripped off the knife and onto the towel. She offered me a slice, which I accepted. She then cut herself a slice and placed it in her mouth. She spoke with her mouth full. "In my experience, I usually run into some trouble when I let my experience dictate another's." She turned to me. "I don't have the corner on the market, but I have known some pain in my life. And I see the same when I look in that kid's eyes. His body will heal, but it's his heart that's in question."

I smiled as she gave me another slice. I, too, spoke with my mouth full. "Did your father teach you all this?"

"Which part?" A sly smile. "The peeling part or the giving of unsolicited advice part?"

"The advice part."

A single shake of her head as mango juice trailed from her lip to her chin. "Mom."

"Smart woman."

She pointed the knife at me. "She'd have liked you."

"I highly doubt that."

She laughed and stood. "So, it's settled then?"

"I'm pretty sure you had it settled before we started talking, but just so I can feel like I had some say in this situation, I need to run it by Colin. I think he'll agree—and I imagine you've already thought about that."

"I have."

"I know what I'd do if he were my son but he's not, so in a very real sense, I'm stuck between Zaul on this end of the phone and Colin on the other."

"If Colin is smart, he'll see that you have more influence in Zaul's life right now."

"He's pretty smart."

"Evidently he's pretty dumb if he's the one that suckered you into the family business."

"Well, yeah. There's that." I sat back, crossed my legs, and folded my hands over my knees. "Can I ask you something?"

"Sure."

"Was it your mother who taught you this leading line of conversation, which not even the experts at Harvard ever mentioned to me?"

"You went to Harvard?"

"Graduated."

"No kidding?"

"No kidding."

"So you're smart?"

"I wouldn't say 'smart' as much as 'able to adapt.' "

"What's your degree?"

"Finance. Followed by an MBA."

Her jaw dropped. "You have that in your back pocket and you run drugs for a living?"

"Ran."

"Whatever."

"Yes."

She considered this and then returned to my question. "You asked whether it was my mother or father." She shook her head. "Neither one."

"Who then?"

"Wasn't a who. It was a what."

"Well, what was the what?"

A hard-earned belly laugh. "Life. After we lost the plantation, I had control over very little, so I had to learn how to protect Isabella and myself and later Paulo when his wife died—the three of us. You learn by talking, asking questions. It doesn't grant you control, but it does help eliminate and name the players who don't have control over you from those that do."

She walked toward the clinic and left me chewing on everything she said. I had two responses: First, I'd single-handedly created the circumstances that caused her to lose the plantation. As that realization settled in my gut, a pain rose beneath it unlike any I'd ever felt. Second, I liked watching her body language when she talked. There was a concert between what she said and how she said it. Maybe it was the way the Spanish language is spoken by those who are native to it, but it's beautiful and mesmerizing. And, okay, maybe there was a third. Maybe I was self-aware enough to know that she was trying to convince me to do something I already wanted to do anyway.

Chapter Twenty-Seven

The following morning, I helped Zaul out of the clinic, steadied him, and let him lean on me as we walked out into the sunlight. Paulo and Isabella sat in the front seat with the engine running. Incredulous, he stood staring at his dad's truck. "How'd you—"

"Won it in a poker game."

"You beat that guy?"

A shrug. "Don't feel bad. He had a thing going with the dealer. You got worked by a couple of pros."

"That explains a lot." He smiled, hobbled to the truck, and was gingerly climbing in when the sight of two flowing brown robes caught his eye. He stopped, backed out, and returned to the door of the cathedral, where two priests stood watching him with muted curiosity. Holding on to the door-frame with his left hand like a drunken sailor, he extended his right and said, "*Muchas gracias.*" Then he returned to the back-seat, where Leena sat next to him and hung the

IV bag—through which she was dripping anti-biotics and pain medicine—on the clothes hook above the seat. Maybe it didn't sink in how weak he was until he sat down, leaned his head back, and closed his eyes. By then, he had broken out in a sweat and had to work to catch his breath. If I had visions of a speedy recovery, I was mistaken. Zaul had lost more blood than we previously thought, and this was going to take time. I sat up front, chewing on what I'd just seen. I'd never seen Zaul thank anyone for anything.

We returned to Valle Cruces and moved Zaul into the chicken coop, which under the haze of medication, he found humorous. He turned to me. "When I need you, do I just cluck?"

He slept through the afternoon while Paulo and I made several trips to the hardware store for lumber, tin roofing, a door, and a bed. By evening, we'd patched the roof of the coop, plugged holes in the rafters, hung a real door, set up a new bed for me, and purchased a second fan. Evening found Paulo, Paulina, Isabella, and me sitting in plastic chairs beneath the mango tree, quietly listening to the sound of Zaul sleeping.

In my life, I'd known times of rest. Of peace. Of quiet. But rarely had I known all three at the same time. Sitting beneath that tree, I felt maybe for the first time the three come together. And the only way I know to describe the sum of those three was "contentment."

And while that described my life, I knew it would not describe Zaul's if I attempted to take him home. Colin and I needed to talk and waiting wasn't helping any. What I needed to say to him was in the end his call, but I needed to get it off my chest. I dialed, said "Billy," hung up, and he dialed me back. I picked up.

Colin said, "How's he doing?"

"Better." He waited, knowing the tone in my voice meant I had more to say. I cleared my throat. "I know you want me to bring him home—to you and Marguerite and Maria—but I don't think Zaul wants that. I can force him, and if you want, I'll put him on that plane but he'll just run. Yes, we found him, but we haven't done anything to fix the hurt. This will continue. And then one day we just won't find him."

"What are you saying?"

"I'm not saying as much as I'm asking."

"What are you asking?"

"I'm asking you to let me not put him on the plane. Let me nurse him back. Give me a few weeks. A month. Maybe two. I'm asking you to trust me with your son."

I heard the quick inhale. The breath he caught before it escaped. The long pause. The shuffle. The sniffle. "You think he'll stick around?"

"I don't know. But my guess is that he'll stick

around here longer than he will anywhere close to home."

As much as it hurt, he knew I was right. "Whatever you think best."

"You want me to talk with Marguerite?"

"No. I'll tell her."

The following morning, I woke early. It was still dark. I checked my watch: 4:27 a.m. I rose, checked on Zaul, and then walked next door to where Paulo lay sleeping. I shook him gently. He woke and stared at me as I made signs mimicking a man digging. "Dig? We dig?"

He swung his feet over. "*Sí. Sí.* We dig. Dig deep."

Paulo and I spent the morning at the well. Me on one end of the rope, he on the other. I surfaced for lunch and he and I ate a sandwich, and I played with the kids who had appeared to watch us dig. Then I descended again. When my arms were noodles, I pulled twice on the rope, and Paulo once again lifted me up as I scaled the inside of the well like Spider-Man.

This continued all week.

While Leena and Isabella cared for Zaul, Paulo and I dug. Standing at the bottom of a deep, deep hole in the earth, with thinning air and only the dim light of a headlamp, gave me a lot of time to think. Sometimes I thought about the rope—my sole tether to the surface world of light as I rummaged around below in a world of darkness. Several times, as I squatted in the hole or leaned against the side, waiting on Paulo to return the dirt bucket, I cut the headlamp and stood in the darkness, waiting for my eyes to adjust. But they never did. No matter how long I stood there, and no matter how many times I blinked or tried to adjust, my eyes never made sense of that black world until I turned that lamp back on or climbed up toward the pinhole of circular light above me. Until then I was just groping about in the dark. Credit the thin air, credit tired muscles, credit exhaustion, I stood down in that muddy hole amazed at the absolute absence of light. Call me simple, but it was tough to miss the lesson: If it's dark and you want light, you either need a source outside yourself or you need to get to one— because nothing resident in me lit that hole. And as quiet as it was, I was not able to silence the voice that questioned when I was going to tell Leena about my role in Cinco Padres' collapse. Every time I climbed down into that hole, that voice was waiting on me. The more I dug, the louder it got. And I had no answer for it.

By Friday night, I climbed out having spent the better part of the week down in the earth. Paulo pointed me to the rope coiled neatly at his feet and kicked it with his toe. With a satisfied smile, he patted me on the shoulder. "*Trescientos*."

I knew he was speaking of a measurement, but he said it so fast that I couldn't make it out.

I shook my head. "*No comprehende*."

He smiled and said, "Three hundred."

I understood that. In the last week, I'd dug almost a hundred feet.

In the evenings, I took walks with Zaul. First, we just walked from the backyard to the front. Then a few houses down the street. Then around the block. The sight of two gringos in a village where few seldom ventured off the hard road was akin to the circus being in town, so we were often followed by an audience. One of the things that amazed me was how the kids gravitated to Zaul. They tried to hang on him like a jungle gym until Isabella shooed them off. If they had a ball, they kicked it to him. If they had a Popsicle, they offered him part. If they had a toy, they shared it. I'd never seen someone attract children with such a magnetic draw. One afternoon, I came back from digging, covered in mud, and when I walked out of the shower, Zaul was sitting on top of a five-gallon bucket with another upside down in front of him holding two homemade drumsticks. The kids around him were sitting on the ground, with sticks in their hands and buckets or bowls or anything that worked or sounded like a drum, and he was giving them drum lessons. I didn't even

380

know he played the drums. And as I stood there listening with Leena, I watched as a kid began to shed a dark blanket that he'd wrapped himself in a long time ago. The more he played that bucket like a drum, the more those kids smiled. And the more they smiled, the brighter Zaul became. With the kids joining in as a chorus, he busted loose. His arms waving, his hands spinning the sticks, his face smiling. We were watching a kid bloom. Walking in a circle around him and his class, I took a short twenty-second video on my phone, which I sent to Colin. Moments later, he responded with a single word: "Tears."

I wrote him back. "Me, too."

Sunday afternoon, I found Paulo shoving wood into an outdoor oven that rose up out of the ground behind the chicken coop. It looked like one of those large brick ovens that pizza places use to cook their pizzas at a thousand degrees. In a few moments, he stoked a raging fire, and after shoving in more hardwood, we stepped back as the heat grew intense. The oven had two large holes about the size of a window, which he covered with pieces of tin roofing just slightly larger in size. He left a small "intake" opening that fed the fire with air while the chimney poured white smoke. While he prepared the fire, Leena and Isabella, both wearing aprons, appeared with several bowls and trays and oil and smiles. Leena waved me closer. "Come on. You need to get your hands dirty."

I washed my hands and stepped up to the table, where Leena tied an apron around my waist, which prompted a quick giggle out of Isabella. She looked up at me with a smile and one upturned shoulder. "I'm laughing with you. Not at you."

Leena walked me through the process of making and then kneading dough. Making it was easy, kneading it broke me out in a sweat. Evidently, the kind of bread we were making cannot have any bubbles in the dough, so I had to roll it and beat it and slam it until the bubbles had been worked out. By then, my forearms were cramping.

Then we sliced the dough into small doughnut-sized pieces, which we then flattened like tortillas and spread with a coarse, brownish-looking sugar; raw cinnamon chunks; and some sort of smelly, crumbling cheese, which curled my nose and convinced me I had no desire to taste it. Then we "folded" all of that inside the bread, leaving essentially a triangle pastry.

We lined the trays with about forty triangles, and then Paulo, using a long stick, removed the glowing red pieces of tin roof and pushed all of the fire out the main window onto the ground, where he rolled buckets of water underneath it. Having cleared out the fireplace, he then used a broom of sorts to "brush" out all the ash. When finished, he was left with a clean oven where the inside was hovering around between eight hundred and a thousand degrees—which it would do for the next hour.

Leena handed the four trays to Paulo who—using a different stick—slid them into the fire much like a man cooking pizzas. He leaned the tin against the windows again, covering the holes, and then stood there, tapping his foot. After ninety seconds, he threw off the pieces of tin and, using the reverse end of his stick, hooked the corners of the trays, removing them from the heat, and Leena, donning hot pads, set them on the table to cool. When finished, Leena placed a napkin in her hand, set a browned, puffy tart in the middle, and handed it to me with a raised eyebrow. I viewed it with suspicion and sat hesitantly until the smell wafted up, convincing me to sink my teeth into it.

In the next ten minutes, I ate seven pieces. When I was finished, I sat back—my stomach taut like a melon—and marveled. "Best bread ever. Hands down."

Leaning against the back of the house, soaring on a sugar high from which I was soon to descend like a rock, I was once again struck by the simplicity and matter-of-factness of life around here.

Leena chuckled at my heavy eyelids and motioned toward the hammock. "Best thing to do is sleep it off."

I fell into the hammock and don't remember

closing my eyes. Three hours later, when I woke and forced my head up, one eye half open, Leena was sitting next to me in a plastic chair sewing a patch onto a piece of clothing. I pulled myself up, sat upright, then decided that was too much too fast, so I lay back down and hung one foot out of the hammock, dragging my toes on the ground. She pointed her needle at me, smiled, and squinted one eye. "Nicaragua looks good on you."

The second week, Zaul felt strong enough to venture up the mountain where Leena held her medical clinic. Paulo held the rope, I held the dull remains of a shovel, and Isabella held every-one's attention. In between naps in the back of his dad's truck, Zaul assisted Leena, talked with Paulo, sent me funny notes attached to the bucket, and played his makeshift drum while Isabella danced with the other kids. Digging that hole was a constant process of moving in a tight circle while squatting and digging out the ground beneath my feet. It was maddening. My feet were constantly shuffling, never stood on anything even, and were always covered in dirt and mud. I seldom saw my toes. And to say my lower back ached would have been an understatement. The more I dug, the more I became convinced that this well had been plugged. Maybe intentionally. Based on the stories I'd heard about this well and the amount of water it used to put out, I kept thinking, if I could just break through the blockage, the spring would shoot up like a geyser and clear water would fill this nearly four-hundred-foot cylinder and carry me to the surface.

By Wednesday evening I was digging ankle-deep in mud and growing more and more convinced that I was standing on top of a water rocket that was poised to shoot me to the surface as soon as my shovel struck the trigger that held it cocked. I dug gently and moved slowly. As I was digging what I promised myself would be my last bucket of the day, my headlamp crossed my feet, and for one brief second I saw something shiny. When I poked around, I turned up nothing, and I'd grown so tired that I had not the patience to look. But as Paulo tightened the rope, pulling me earthward while I scaled the wall of the well, I knew that I'd seen something below my feet. My trouble was that while most would have been excited at finding something of possible value, I had a feeling that I didn't want to find whatever it was, and I was secretly hopeful that it would either be nothing—a figment of a tired imagination—or it would disappear by tomorrow morning.

When I crawled out of my hole, I found Zaul dancing—Isabella in one hand and Anna Julia in the other. Leena and an audience of forty or fifty people were clapping and singing a song whose words I'd not heard, but whose melody I'd known my entire life. Paulo lifted me out, dusted me off, and then pointed to the rope with a wide smile. Not much remained. We were close. I could barely lift my arms. He squeezed my biceps. Then squeezed it again. "You good dig. You good gringo."

That night as we sat quietly beneath the mango tree, Leena asked me, "You okay? You seem . . . distant."

"Sorry. Just tired."

She smirked. "You're lying to me."

I nodded. "Well, I'm also tired."

She let it go, but she was right. Something was bugging me, and I was pretty sure I knew what it was. Like it or not, I'd find out in a few hours. To be certain, I replaced the batteries in my head-lamp and stuck a small penlight in my pocket.

The next morning, as Paulo checked the rope and then steadied himself against the side of the well, I turned to Leena. "You be around?"

She looked at me strangely and sort of shook her head. "Need to go check on some kids up in the barns. Might need to treat them for parasites."

"You mind hanging around till I've been down there a few minutes?"

Her complexion changed from hope to concern. She placed the back of her hand gently on my cheek. "You okay?"

"Yeah, no, I'm good." I waved her off. "I'll come up for lunch. Forget it."

I dropped into the hole, but the look on her

face and the one raised eyebrow told me I'd not convinced her. Which was good.

When I got to the bottom, it didn't take long. It was right where I'd left it and it was exactly what I thought. A polished stone wrapped in a gold fitting connected to a gold chain—the match to the one Leena wore. I held the stone in my hand, digging gently to loosen the chain when my shovel hit something hard beneath the surface of the water. Digging with my fingers, I lifted the obstruction and held it before my eyes. It was a bone. Shining the light below me, I realized I was standing in bones.

I held the chain in my hand, making sure it matched Leena's. It did. I wasn't quite sure what it meant, but I had a feeling that I'd just found Leena's mom, and if I dug around enough, I'd probably find her dad, too. I squatted in the hole, leaned against the wall, and considered what to do. It wasn't like I could just mix everything in the bucket and send it to the top without her knowing. I had to climb up and tell her. I had to climb up and give her the stone.

I tugged on the rope and Paulo immediately began lifting me to the surface. Something was stuck in my throat and it would not budge. The closer it got, the more it threatened to cut off my air supply. I exited the hole and Leena was there waiting. The crowd hushed because this was unusual. Previously, I'd come out only at lunch and at evening, but this morning, I'd been down there only a few minutes. Everyone knew this meant something. They didn't know what it meant but they knew it was significant. They inched closer, prompting Paulo to spread his arms and force them back.

I motioned Paulo and Leena a few feet away. I tried to speak, but what could I say? What words could I offer that would not hurt her? Not knowing what else to do, I gently placed the stone in Leena's hand. At first, she just stared at it, not making sense of it. Then, when the image in her hand matched the memory in her mind, her mouth opened and she sucked in an uncontrolled breath. She touched the stone with her fingertips as the tears rolled down her cheeks.

Soon she was shaking uncontrollably and sobbing. The crowd around us, normally joyous at our presence and the possibility that the well might one day produce water, fell to silence. No one spoke. No one moved. No one made a sound. Everyone just watched Leena cry. And after almost a minute of no breath being inhaled or exhaled, the cry and wail that she'd stuffed and held for a decade exited her body and echoed down and across the mountain. And when it did, old and young alike began to cry as well—a testimony to how they carried her and wanted so badly to share in, even carry, her pain.

Leena, the necklace woven through her fingers

and the polished stone dangling beneath her hand, pressed it to her lips and kissed it, then clutched it to her chest. Finally, head bowed, she lifted it before the crowd. An offering that needed no explanation, and when she did, the older women untied the scarves from around their necks and began to cover their heads.

Paulo held Isabella, who clutched his neck, while Zaul and I stood helpless. After a moment, Leena fell on me and soaked my shoulder, clutching me. I wrapped my arms around her and offered what I could but I fear I was little consolation. The wound was deep and my friendship only reached so far. The wounds of the mudslide, the loss of so many friends and family, the loss of her parents, the loss of the plantation, the loss of her husband—all of it landed in her hand when I set that stone in it. She was inconsolable. When she collapsed, I caught her. We slid together down onto the ground and leaned against the well. Mango tree above us. Her parents entombed below us. Surrounded by a quiet and rapidly growing community, Leena cried.

After a few minutes, she stood and was stepping into my harness, speaking incoherently and instructing Paulo to lower her into the hole when I touched her hand. "Leena." No response. "Leena." Still nothing. "Paulina."

She turned to look at me. I said, "Please let me do that."

She shook her head. "No, my father—"

"Leena, if he's down there with your mother, you should be here to receive them. Not us."

That stopped her and she knew I was right.

I buckled in and descended. Once at the bottom, I tried not to disturb the manner in which the bones lay. Gently I picked my way around. Trying to delicately pry them loose. I knew I'd found her father when I uncovered a wedding ring. I looked at that ring and remembered the one and only time I'd ever seen Leena's father.

When Marshall had first sent me to make the offer to the Cinco Padres what seemed a lifetime ago, I took the offer to the attorney who was acting as our middleman, and I remember sitting at a café across the street, hiding behind my Costa Del Mars, wanting to see the owner's reaction. I watched him walk into the office, and then about three minutes later, he walked out. He walked down the steps wearing a frayed straw hat, a farmer's tan, and the weight of the world on his shoulders. I remember thinking how strong his hands appeared and how his broad shoulders were no stranger to hard work. How the crow's-feet beneath his temples made it appear as though his eyes were smiling. I remember him walking down those steps, and despite the look of pain on his face, he stopped to talk to an older woman. He took off his hat and smiled and bowed slightly. After that it was a man of about the same age.

Then an older couple. By the time he'd reached the sidewalk, he'd stopped to talk with seven different sets of people. Everyone wanted to say hello. Shake his hand. I remember thinking that despite worn boots, a tattered, dirty shirt, and fraying jeans, he had more distinction than Marshall. Than any of us. He had not bought the honor bestowed on him by those he passed in the street. He'd earned it. I also remember one more thing that came to mind—I didn't know him, never met him and never would, but one thing that afternoon on the street taught me . . . that man was beloved. The proof was in the faces of the people he met. He'd given them something, and each wanted a chance to thank him. As he walked away, I realized what it was. What he'd given them. It was something neither Marshall nor I could ever offer. Something we didn't know the first thing about.

He'd given them hope. In comparison to that coffee farmer, we were subsistence farmers and he the billionaire.

I sat here in the mud, tears rolling down my cheeks, remembering that time in my life when I'd worked for a man who pretended to be great, who thought his money made him significant, yet walking across the street in front of me had been a man whose boots Marshall wasn't qualified to polish. Marshall didn't hold a candle to Alejandro Santiago Martinez. The reaction of those he met spoke volumes about his greatness. I stared down in the mud, wishing I'd stood, taken off my hat, and shaken his hand.

Marshall had never had that effect on me. Ever.

At the bottom of that hole, tethered to the world via a wet, muddy rope, I took off my head-lamp, cleared my throat, and spoke to those bones. "I want to tell you both, and you especially, sir, that while I had nothing to do with this mud, I had a lot to do with what happened after this. Your family has suffered a lot, and it's safe to say that I'm the cause of that. If I were you, I'd be real mad at me. I'm sorry for what we did. For what I did. For not being a better man." I paused, not knowing what to say next. "You'd be real proud of Leena. She's . . . well, she doesn't know any of this about me and I've been living most my whole life with half-truths and no truths, and every time I'm around her I want to be around her a lot more but there are a few things she doesn't know about me—namely that I did all this." I glanced at myself, at the mud covering every inch of me. "I've been like this my whole life." I shook my head. "I want you to know that I'm sorry for the pain I've caused you and"—I glanced up toward the pinhole of light some three hundred–plus feet above me—"will cause."

Digging out that man and his wife broke some-thing loose in me. I loaded them through tears in ragged, bony chunks into the five-gallon bucket. I cannot tell you why, but as I did, I remembered something that happened to me as a kid. I was five. Maybe six. Coming off the beach. Surfboard tucked under my arm. The taste of salt on my lips. Sun-bleached hair draped across my face. I walked up through the dunes and began walking across the grass toward our house. My first three steps onto the grass were uneventful. My fourth stopped me and sent a bloodcurdling scream out of my mouth that brought my mom running out the front door. Sandspurs are a small weed that grow among the blades of grass, and they're tough to pick out if you're not looking. They produce small balls with fifteen or twenty spikes per ball. They can pierce hardened leather and stepping on them is like sliding across shards and splinters of glass. They are also known to grow quickly and without warning. I'd walked across that grass a thousand times and never stepped foot on a sand-spur, but for some reason on that day, they'd sprouted and I stepped into the center of them. I knew when my foot touched down that I had just driven about five hundred little spikes into the sole of my foot, and what's worse, I couldn't move. I had to stand there and take this until someone with shoes walked across the land mine and lifted me out of that patch of grass. Mom ran across the street, lifted me, and carried me inside, where she spent the next two hours plucking them out of the base of my foot with a pair of tweezers. She pulled out several hundred. With each one, she'd pluck it and then hold it to the light, making sure she got the whole thing.

Loading that man and his wife into that bucket and then tugging on the rope and watching it rise to the surface was a lot like that experience with my mom. It plucked the shards of glass from my heart, and as it lifted toward the light above me, I got to stand there and wonder if I'd gotten all of it or if a portion remained.

I filled and sent up five buckets with large pieces of volcanic mud turned rock, which held the skeletal remains of Leena's parents like ancient fossils telling a story of tenderness, of a final hug that had been a decade or better in the making, of love lived out. Once I was certain I'd unearthed them, I surfaced and found Leena staring at a piece of rock, which she'd just rinsed in a bucket of water. Protruding from the edges of the porous stone were the bones of a hand. As she picked away at it, chunks of mud fell off, revealing two intertwined hands. The larger holding the smaller. And on the larger, Leena found her father's wedding band.

The effect of that on Leena was more than any of us could hold. Some turned away. Others covered their mouths. I knelt next to her not knowing what to offer. Finally, she turned to me, holding the hands in both of hers. She didn't need to speak. Through painful tears, she cracked a broken smile. The image was clear—they had died together. The crowd around us formed a firemen's line from the creek sending bucket after bucket of water, allowing us to rinse the piles of rocks and bones clumped together. As we rinsed and then pieced together the rocks much as they had been in the hole, we were able to make sense of her parents' last moments. Or moment. Somehow, with the wall of mud approaching, they'd climbed into the well thinking it would provide protection. And it had until a wave of mud thirty feet high swallowed the hole, pressing them down. Leena's dad was only able to hold them so long. Judging from the protective halo of white bone encircling the smaller frail bones of her mother, he had cradled her mom as the caustic mud filled around them and then carried them to the bottom, where their last minute together had been forever entombed. I never knew them, so I cannot comment on how they lived, but I can comment on how they died. Her mom's head was resting on her father's shoulder. It was an undeniable picture. Their fingers were intertwined. Locked within each other's. When those around us saw it, they gasped and shook their heads. Old women cried. Young girls covered their mouths. Old men took off their hats and crossed themselves. My uneducated guess was that they'd died near the top, engulfed in a wall and pool of mud. Then, in the following moments, when the mud cooled and dried and hardened into rock, it pulled away from the sides of the well and shot toward the center of the earth. Given its weight, it descended the shaft of the well like a giant cylindrical bullet, lubricated by the water. The column of rock fell nearly four hundred feet, then it slammed into the cap rock of the spring below, stopping up the well like a stone cork, cutting off the water supply and burying her parents.

Word spread quickly. The gringo at the end of the rope had found the bodies of Alejandro Santiago Martinez and his wife. Soon the road up was cluttered with people coming from all over the mountain to pay their respects. Throughout the night, more and more people appeared on foot, in horse-drawn carts, and then by the busloads. Near midnight, we stared down the mountain and could see a stream of people walking up like ants. Leena gazed down on a sight that had never been seen in her lifetime, locked her arm in mine, and passed from sadness and heartache to smiles and deep, deep joy. To hugs offered and received. For hours, she stood at the top of the mountain thanking those who'd climbed up to pay their final respects.

When daylight came and she asked me to drive her up the mountain in Colin's truck, and she saw how many people still remembered her mother and father, how many people had camped along the road, how many were streaming in, something broke loose in Leena and her mourning turned to dancing. Finally, she asked me to let Paulo drive, and the two of us walked the last three miles up the mountain where more than five thousand people had gathered.

Seeing the mass, the horde of people, I turned to Paulo and handed him every penny I carried. Several thousand dollars cash. Offering it all to him. He smiled, patted me on the shoulder, and shook his head. "No need." He waved his hand across the sea of faces. "Nicaragua pay for this." And he was right. Campfires filled the early morning light, as did the smell of cooking tortillas, rice, and beans. Pigs were led up the mountain on leashes and then slaughtered by the dozens, and once butchered, sweaty men turned them slowly over white embers that they continued to feed and stoke throughout the day. In a nearby barn, several old women sat for hours grinding coffee beans to make enough of Alejandro's coffee for everyone to sip and remember. Groups of ladies, wearing aprons and scarves in their hair, cleaned and cut vegetables; others made loaf after loaf of bread, piling it high in huge baskets. Leena took me by the arm, and we walked through tents and hammocks and cook fires and checked on the preparations. She thanked hundreds of people who knew her father or her mother or had been impacted by his life. By their lives. Leena never tired. It was a solemn day, reverent sadness that would birth vibrant joy. Countless children, nursing mothers, and old men approached Leena and offered a hand or a hug. The honor bestowed on her was unlike any I'd ever witnessed.

Because of the number of people, and those rumored to be coming from well past Managua— eight hours by bus—the funeral was postponed until the following day. The problem, and it was a big one, was water. Somehow they had prepared food and somehow they had enough latrines, but clean water on the mountain was nonexistent. Leena came to me at noon, sweat mixed with concern. "How much water do you think your truck could carry?"

"Several hundred gallons. Why? What's up?"

"That wouldn't last the afternoon and probably wouldn't get to a quarter of these people." She shook her head, took off her scarf, and wiped down her neck and face. Defeat was setting in. "These people climbed up here and used most of their water to do that. It's hot and they'll be dehydrated by tomorrow and then they've got to get home. In their thirst, they'll start drinking from the stream that runs out of the pasture higher up, and many of these people will go home sick and in worse shape than when they came."

I turned to Paulo, who was equally concerned.

Zaul was standing next to him. "How strong are you two feeling?"

Paulo shrugged. *"Hermano?"*

Zaul shook his head. "Still pretty weak but I'll do whatever you need."

I began walking to the well. "I've got an idea. It's a bit of a long shot, but it might work." I turned to Paulo. "I need a piece of steel, couple of feet long, that I can use to drive with. Like a wedge if you were splitting wood. A root ax. A spear. Something long and sharp and strong."

He held up a finger and disappeared toward the tractor barn while I climbed into the harness. Leena's face did not exhibit faith in me. Paulo returned with a steel pry bar, five feet long, worn sharp on one end and mushroomed at the other from people hitting it with a sledgehammer. My problem was that I also needed a hammer, but it couldn't be very long 'cause I'd never be able to swing it. Paulo then handed me a sledgehammer about a foot long. Just enough room on the handle for my hand and then the twenty-pound steel head.

I tied both to my harness and lowered them into the hole so that they hung below me as I descended. Before I touched off and began my descent, I spoke to Paulo and Zaul. Leena listened intently. "I need you two to do me a favor. When I pull hard, I need you to pull me up as fast as you've ever pulled anyone."

Paulo took off his shirt, spit on his hands, and

ran the rope through the pulley wheel at the top, and then wrapped the rope twice around the tree and braced it against his hip.

After checking my headlamp, I kicked off the sides, hung briefly, and then let Paulo lower me into the hole on what I hoped was my last trip. As the light above me grew smaller and the darkness wrapped around me like a blanket, I thought about the incongruity of my life. So little made sense.

The rope above me was piano-wire taut. How precarious life was down here for me as I hung by a few fibers. If the rope broke, I might climb out, but if I were to slip, it'd be the last time I ever slipped.

Finally, the rod and hammer clanked rock below me and my feet touched down. I stood, ankle-deep in water, and began trying to make sense of my world. It was tough to tell whether the water in which I now stood had seeped down or leaked up. The area around me was wider—whereas the well shaft was maybe three to four feet in diameter, here it was wider than my outstretched fingertips. The walls were worn smooth where the pressure of the water through the years had hollowed out a cavity.

The water was cold, which was a change from the water I'd been standing in since I'd started digging. Previously, the water and mud were a slimy, warm mush, but this was different. This was like a mountain stream. It was cold, and when I cupped it in my hands, clear. I knelt and ran my fingertips along the rock beneath the surface of the water trying to sense any flow of water. Any place at all where I could feel a trickle. While I didn't sense water flow, it did get colder. There was a definite place below my feet where the rock and water were the coldest.

The steel pole and hammer were concerns. If I struck water and had to get out of here fast, I didn't want to leave them in the bottom of this well to forever fill it with rust and poison those above, so I made sure the tethers to each were tied. I didn't know what would happen when I broke through the rock, but I had a feeling it would not be gentle.

I steadied my footing and placed the point of the steel pole in the center. Getting a good grip on the hammer, I practiced raising it above my head and bringing it down onto the pole, making sure I had enough headroom to swing and then asking myself where the hammer would end up if I missed—which was both possible and likely.

I'd hesitated long enough. People were thirsty. I held the steel pole against the solid ground with my left hand and raised the hammer with my right. I'm not sure if it was my crouched position or what, but the reflection of the rock at eye level caught my eye. A smooth piece of rock had been carved and there were words in it. I couldn't make them out because they were packed with mud, but after a few minutes of tracing the letters and prying out the lines of rock, I smiled at that old man. He was obviously shorter than me, and while he hadn't signed his name, his signature was clear. I rinsed the wall several times. It read: "AGUA DE MI CORAZÓN."

I thought about trying to cut out that rock and give it to Leena, but it was part of the whole and Michelangelo himself couldn't have cut that piece out of the shaft. It was staying. If I'd had my phone I could have taken a picture, but cold, wet, damp holes in the ground are no place for electronics so I'd left it in the truck up top. This note would have to be between me and the old man.

I'd wasted enough time. I raised the hammer, steadied the pole, and slammed the head of the hammer as hard as I could down against the pole, driving it into the rock below my feet.

Nothing.

I waited, thinking whatever was about to happen might take a second.

Still nothing.

I hit it again. No response. Again. I was met by silence and no water. I struck it six or eight times. Then twenty more. But nothing changed down in that hole. Over the next hour, I chipped and bored and banged my way into that rock, making very little progress. My right arm had become a noodle, and my left hand and forearm were bruised and tender where the hammer had hit the pole and then slid or slipped off. I was growing increasingly frustrated because, standing in "new" water, I thought for sure I was close. Exhausted and not wanting to surface, I sat, soaking my hands in the water that had crept over my ankles and contacted my shins. I knew the water had not been that deep when I got down there. Water had to be coming from somewhere because there was more of it, but it was certainly not coming up. I'd have better success against the Rock of Gibraltar. I leaned back, staring up at the pinhole of light above me. Only then did I feel the drip.

Against my neck.

I turned, and just below the rock where Alejandro had carved his inscription was a small indention, or cavity, that oddly enough stood at heart level. Didn't take a genius to realize that the rock in the middle of the cavity was of a different feel than the rock that surrounded it. As I studied the old hammer and chisel marks made in the older rock around the edges, the newer rock stuck out. Smoother. More porous. No chisel marks. Took me a minute to realize that the power and pressure of the mudslide had stopped up the well. Without giving it much thought, I tapped it with the hammer and the drip increased. Another tap and the drip turned to a tiny, solid stream. Ready to be done with this, I reached back and slammed the hammer against the face of the rock.

Bad idea.

Evidently all my pounding had worked the plug loose, and all it needed was one more swing of persuasion. The bowling ball–sized rock shot past my face, followed by a fire hose stream of water that slammed me against the far wall and pressed me against it with such force that I couldn't budge. My head ricocheted off the rock and the whole world went black. My headlamp was gone, but I was also having trouble staying conscious. Water had filled the cavity and risen to my neck by the time I registered what was happening.

In the dark, I reached up and pulled down hard on the rope, which was followed by a slight delay. Then without warning, it snapped back hard and rocketed me from the water. I sucked in my first deep breath of air in half a minute and held fast to the rope above me. My feet had just cleared the water when something below me snagged and held me to the bottom. The rope tightened, and I was caught in the middle between a force pulling me up and a force that wouldn't budge below me. The water rose around me, bubbling up with massive force, quickly filling the shaft and rising past me. Within a matter of seconds, I was immersed and the water was shooting past me as I hung suspended in the shaft unable to free myself. It took a second to register that the line attached to the steel spear was taut and would not budge. That meant that the pole itself was lodged and preventing my exit. I groped in the dark, finally finding it braced horizontally across the shaft of the well where it was caught in the narrowing of the shaft. The only way to get it to release was to return down, which was exactly what my long single tug on the rope had told Paulo and Zaul that I did not want to do. They were topside pulling with all their might, thinking that's what I wanted.

The water had long since engulfed me as I twisted and writhed in the well shaft, caught between those pulling me up and the steel rod holding me down. Somewhere in there the thought occurred to me that I might very well die right there, drowned in that shaft, only to float to the surface days or weeks from now as whatever held me down set me free.

My reaction to that thought was strange. I wasn't afraid and fear was not my primary emotion. I mean, I'd rather be alive than not, but if I drowned in that dark hole, I can make a pretty sound and fast argument that I deserved it. Anyone with a cursory look across the effect of my life would agree. I was not a good man, had not been, and the effect of me on the rest of the world had not been positive. As the picture of my life played like a fast-forward video across my eyes, I saw more tears than smiles. More anger than laughter. The sin of my life had been and remained indifference, and in that instant, I was indifferent to my own death. Something deep inside me had to be dysfunctional.

The cold shock of the water slowed my movements, and my attempts to free myself were feeble at best. Growing weaker and beginning to need air in a desperate way, my overriding emotion can best be described as sadness, even grief, at how the pain of my death would affect Leena. In her life, I'd be the third person to die in this hole and one more among three thousand to die on this mountain. One more white cross driven into the earth to prick Leena's heart like a needle.

While I was indifferent to me, I was not to Leena, and if there had been a sleeping giant in me, that thought kicked him out of bed.

In desperation, I pushed my arms outward toward the slick walls of the well shaft and braced myself against the force of Paulo and Zaul. The force pulling me upward had increased, suggesting that more hands had joined in. For reasons I still cannot understand, there was a reprieve from up top, a momentary slackening of the rope. A ripple more than anything else. And in that millisecond, I kicked below me, trying to turn the steel bar like a clock hand. Anything to jar it loose from its midnight hold. As the rope tightened a final time on the tether of my harness with a force greater than I'd yet known, I kicked at the steel rod one more time. The rod loosened, turned vertically, and the opposing force of hands at the other end of the rope shot me toward the surface of the earth. Unable to help and watching a narrowing column of light in my mind, I pulled my arms in and tried to give as little resistance as possible.

My last thought was a memory of the fastest mile I'd ever run. It had been at night on a track all alone. I'd run four minutes, seven seconds in a meet twice but was having trouble with the four-minute barrier. Angry and frustrated, I tied on my spikes, lined up on the starting line, clicked "start" on the watch in my hand, and took off. The first three laps were painful, but nothing like the fourth. I remember coming around the last turn with a hundred and fifty meters to go as the world closed in and the light before my eyes narrowed. I think I ran the last twenty yards in a nearly unconscious state. I crossed the finish line, collapsed, rolled, and only then hit "stop." Moments later, when I caught my breath, I read the time: 3:58. I remember standing on the track, a bit wobbly, glancing one more time at the faceplate of the watch and then pressing "clear." I'd done it. That's all that mattered.

Stuck in the well shaft, as my lungs used the last bit of oxygen in my body, I remembered that moment and that feeling. It was a good memory. A good one to go out on. As the tunnel in my mind narrowed and the light closed in and out, I let go. I'd fought it long enough.

I don't know how long I was like that because I'm not sure I was there. In a strange shift of perspective, I remember staring down from the mango tree onto Paulo and Zaul and Leena and a dozen other people who were frantically pulling on the rope. Paulo's hands were bleeding and his face was frantic. Leena was screaming. Zaul was leaning into the rope with every ounce of muscle he had, and I remember thinking, *Wow, he's really strong*.

A strange sensation.

I don't know if I died or just passed out or if my spirit was leaving my body, but I felt a tightness and a compression on my body unlike anything I'd ever known, accompanied by a darkness that I could not explain. Then without warning and without explanation, the well spit me out of its mouth and threw me onto the ground surrounded by nearly four hundred feet of coiled rope and a lot of sweaty people breathing heavily. I remember somebody pressing their mouth to mine and forcing air into my lungs and then somebody standing on my chest. Finally, I remember vomiting and then sucking in the most glorious and sweet breath of air I'd ever known.

As the world came back to me and my senses sent messages to my brain, I heard screaming and laughing and crying, and I remember small hands clutching my neck. Then I remember another face, older, beautiful but similar, pressing against mine.

I remember coming back from that cold, dark, quiet, dirty world to this world of light and sound with Leena pressing her laughing and crying and tearstained and snotty face against mine.

It was a beautiful birth.

Having caught my breath and opened my eyes, Paulo stood me up and I worked feverishly to catch my balance and force my eyes to adjust. He stood in front of me, holding my arms in his powerful and bleeding hands. He brushed me off, nodded, and smeared the mud across his face. He tried to make words but few came. Finally, he waved his index finger in front of my face like a windshield wiper and just grabbed what few words he could. "You no more dig."

I remember laughing and chuckling and thinking to myself, *Agreed.*

The next hour or so around the well was a lot of fun. Even the old people don't remember the well ever having the force that it currently displayed. Water rolled out of the cap in an arc across the ground where we stood and created a shin-deep stream that filled the old, dried creek bed where it had once flowed.

Having created an instant water park, maybe a hundred kids appeared, held out both hands for me to hold and then to play and laugh. It was the most glorious fun I'd ever witnessed. Old-timers, those who remembered the well from its former days, approached me with smiles and hugs and handshakes. Leena stood by, translating. Paulo, along with several men from the plantation, worked to secure the well and build a makeshift wooden barrier to keep kids away and out until he could build something more permanent. And while I was grateful for the thanks and the attention, I liked one thing more. Throughout the afternoon, Leena stayed by my side and her hand never left mine.

Afternoon faded to evening as more and more people showed. A team of adults had been put in charge of the well by Paulo to help create an orderly ingress and egress to the water source and to help the elderly with their buckets. It worked. The mountain—both the people and the dirt—was hydrated. As was I. Matter of fact, I'd be okay if I didn't drink any water for the rest of the day.

Leena and I stood on the mountainside beneath the trees walking among the tents and hammocks and campfires of those who had come to attend her father's funeral. If we listened to one story about her father and how he'd helped someone or showed someone kindness, we must have listened to a hundred.

The attention I received as the gringo who

"stabbed the earth and brought forth the water" was akin to that given to a rock star. People wanted to touch me, hug me, shake my hand, or offer me theirs in tribute and honor. Around midnight, Paulo drove us down the mountain to the house. Leena asked me if I wanted to bathe, and I waved her off, saying, "I think I've had enough water for one day." Seconds later, I was asleep.

I woke at daylight to the smell of a campfire, coffee brewing, and the sound of a mango falling on the tin roof. Three of my favorite things. Zaul was asleep close by. He looked better. His color had returned, his hair was growing out, and his general complexion suggested he wasn't quite so angry at the world. Isabella had softened him. Maybe Nicaragua had, too.

I walked outside, shaky but upright, and found Leena waiting for me. A smile and a cup of coffee. Hidden in the seclusion of her backyard, she had done something she rarely did. She'd let her hair down. Prior to my waking, she'd showered, washed her hair, and now sat brushing out the tangles. It was an intimate window into her life. I knew enough about the culture to know that women here let only a select group into this moment and time, and it was mostly other women, a husband, or a child. It was a reveal shared only by a few. I sat, sipped, and soaked it in.

Leena had asked that her parents be buried in one coffin but with two crosses. So Paulo, Zaul, and I drove to town later that day, bought the lumber, and built both the coffin and the crosses. I was glad we'd had some practice on Roberto's coffin as we made a few improvements to this one. The edges were cleaner and the lid sealed better. I think that Hack would have been impressed. Both Paulo and Leena seemed happy and that was all that mattered. When we'd loaded it into the back of the truck, Zaul asked, "You teach me to do that?"

"Sure. You like working with wood?"

"Don't know. Never done it. But I'd like to try." For growing up with such privilege, there was a lot Zaul had not done. Evidence that money did not buy experience.

Somewhere, Leena had found time to buy both Zaul and I long-sleeved white dress shirts, which was the Nicaraguan national dress code for men. We showered, and then the five of us drove up the mountain in Colin's truck. Since we'd returned here with Zaul for his recovery, he and Paulo had become fast friends. Zaul knew a good bit more about mechanics or how things worked than I had originally thought. Paulo picked up on this and was constantly asking him to help fix something, as there was always something broken in Nicaragua. As a result, the two had become inseparable, and I think Zaul had grown in his appreciation of and affection for the old sugar-cane farmer. Driving up the mountain, I sat in the backseat with Leena and Isabella while Zaul sat up front and alternated from looking at the road in front to Paulo driving. His head was on a slow swivel and the slight smile on his face told me he was happy about what he saw. I could see his wheels spinning and I had an idea what he wanted, but I could also see an internal conflict rising. Zaul wanted to give Paulo the truck, but he knew he'd taken so much from his dad that he didn't have the right to ask or give. Somewhat deflated, he looked out the passenger's side window and chewed on his lip. I tapped him on the shoulder. "What are you thinking?"

He spoke without looking back. "I'm thinking how I made a pretty good mess."

"How so?"

"I've lost or wasted a lot of money, and now that I want to do something good with it I don't have any or don't have the right to ask."

I leaned forward, smiling as I spoke. I glanced at Paulo. "He looks good driving this truck, doesn't he?"

Paulo watched the road in front of him; since he spoke only a little English he was oblivious to the conversation about him. Zaul's nod was accompanied with a frown. "He does."

I motioned toward Paulo. "Go ahead."

He shook his head. "I've caused enough—"

"I'll clear it with your dad. Go ahead. Do something right for a change."

He glanced back at me, then at Paulo. He chewed on this several minutes, until we crested the top of the mountain where it appeared most of Nicaragua had shown up overnight for the funeral. We exited the truck and Paulo was handing the keys to Zaul when Zaul glanced at the truck. "Nice truck?"

Paulo nodded emphatically and wiped the sweat off his brow with a dirty white handkerchief.

Zaul prodded him. "You like?"

Paulo's hands were raw from yesterday and one palm was oozing from rope burn. "Nicest truck in Nicaragua." Another nod. "God drive that truck."

Zaul accepted the keys from Paulo, hefted them, and then tugged on Paulo's short sleeve as he turned to walk away. Paulo pivoted, Zaul took his hand and turned it over and laid the keys in his center of his palm. "Your truck."

Paulo's face told us he didn't understand. Zaul wrapped Paulo's fingers around the keys and slowly closed his hand.

"Yours now. You . . . you keep it."

Paulo looked at me, then back at Zaul. An uncomfortable smile. "I no—"

Zaul waved him off. "I—" He motioned to me. "We . . . want you to have it. It's yours now."

He sliced his hand through the air horizontal to the ground. "Forever."

Paulo eyed the keys, the truck, Leena, then me. I nodded in agreement. "You should take it."

Paulo let out a deep breath that seemed to accompany a masked hesitation and wiped his forehead—something he did both when it was sweaty and when he needed time to think. Folding the handkerchief, he placed it back in his pocket and then he put a hand on Zaul's shoulder. Paulo stared at Zaul several seconds. I could tell his mind was turning, but his lips were silent. Several times he tried to talk, but could not. Finally, he nodded, pulled hard on his frayed hat, slid the keys in his pocket, and walked off toward a crowd of people. Isabella slid her hand in mine as the four of us watched him walk away. Leena put her arm around Zaul's shoulder. "Don't take it person-ally. He doesn't know how to say thank you. No one's ever done anything like that, and it's more than he can comprehend."

Zaul was smiling, his teeth showing. It was the first time I'd seen him truly happy in almost a decade. He watched Paulo's broad shoulders widen as he walked away. "I like giving stuff away. It beats getting it. Plus, I'm pretty sure he'll take better care of it than I would."

Not even the old folks remembered seeing a funeral with as many people. The line of people strung out behind the coffin was more than a mile long. It took an hour to process from the viewing to the graveside, where Leena drove two more crosses into the mud of Valle Cruces. The church that served the plantation had set up a micro-phone and huge speakers, allowing her to speak to the crowd, which she did with a grace and composure I'd never witnessed.

At the conclusion of the service, Paulo and I lowered her parents into the hole and Leena—wanting those who had come so far to feel they had a role in her parents' burial—invited everyone to scatter dirt on the coffin. People waited on into night for that moment of closure. If a mountain can heal, Leena knew that, and as she stood receiving that endless line of mourners, helping them cover her parents in the same mud that killed them, she helped speed that recovery. If the soul of those people had been broken when her mother and father died, the hugs Leena gave sewed it back together. The fissure, the gaping wound, had been mended, and it was Leena who stitched it closed.

Until that moment, I could not articulate why I was drawn to Leena. Of course, she was beautiful. Mesmerizing even. But, that didn't scratch the surface. There was something else, and as I stood there feeling dark and dirty in the shadows watching one woman heal the soul of several thousand people, of a region, I realized that Leena shined a light everywhere she went. She was a walking headlight. A coming train. A rising sun. Unafraid, she walked into the darkness, and when she did, the darkness rolled back as a scroll.

It was dark when we finally made it to the picnic. The people pulled her away and Leena danced and laughed and ate and laughed some more. Isabella ran between her mom and me and Zaul and Paulo. She was covered in food, and at about ten o'clock I took her to the pool where parents were washing their kids and just washed her off. She loved it.

I watched Leena, spying from a distance. I was falling further and further from my resolve to tell her about my role in the collapse of this place. What did it matter? Her parents had been found, people were happy. There had been closure. She knew she was loved. Was it selfish of me to want to tell her? Get it off my chest and dump it on hers under the guise of being truthful when in reality I just wanted to make myself feel better? I couldn't answer that. All I knew was that I was carrying a weight and I wasn't sure where it would land when I unloaded it or what damage it would cause.

But I knew better. For the first time in my life, the truth was eating me. Like gasoline in a Styrofoam cup, it was eating me from the inside out. Even Zaul picked up on it. "You okay, Uncle Charlie?"

As I watched Leena, I remembered the first time I'd seen her. The memory flashed.

It was here. On this mountain, on the road just below us. When I'd rented a motorcycle and ridden up here as everyone was walking down after we'd foreclosed. A woman was walking down, pregnant and alone. The emptiness on her face caught me then and returned now. It was Leena. I had watched her walk right past me. An enormous unseen millstone driving her like a piling into the earth. The pain pierced me as I remembered the empty, lifeless look in her eyes as she glanced at me. Seconds later and seemingly unaffected, I'd cranked the motorcycle and left that mountain and its people in my dust. I boarded Marshall's plane and stared smugly down at this world from thirty-five thousand feet while that new-jet smell enveloped me, insulating me from the smoldering hell I'd just left, where Leena had just buried her husband. Buried everything.

Zaul nudged me, awaiting my response.

I brushed him off. "Yeah. I'm good."

He knew better. My face betrayed me. I was a long way from good. Even an inexperienced player like Zaul could read that bluff. I had to tell her. If I wanted any relationship with Leena, I needed to open the door on the closet in me that held this secret. Watching her dance and twirl and sweat and sing, I realized how completely I'd fallen for Leena. Evidence to the depth of my fall was my 180-degree gut reaction, which was *not* to keep my life a secret, but to tell her everything. Tell her now so there'd be no chance that I couldn't and wouldn't hurt her later.

I made up my mind that when the right chance presented itself, I'd open the door and turn on the light. Tell her everything. And save her from the truth of me.

Problem was, I never got the chance.

Chapter Twenty-Eight

I'd often heard the warning but never really understood: For every action, there's an equal and opposite reaction. Valle Cruces was holding a funeral for one of Nicaragua's most beloved farmers. Word spread. Carrying with it the news that two gringos—one young with tattoos, recovering from a beating—were on the mountain and had been instrumental in this. Evil men reacted to that news differently from the majority of the population. You'd think that after looking over my shoulder for more than a decade that I'd have thought about that, but I had not. It had never crossed my mind. And while the majority of Nicaraguans joined the party and filled themselves at the table and drank their fill and laughed and sang and danced, others were not quite so happy. And those select few hid beneath the mango trees.

I never saw them coming.

Paulo waved me toward the punch table, where they'd run out of punch. I grabbed two five-gallon buckets and headed to the well. Zaul followed a few steps behind. Just beyond the lights of the festivities, where the road narrowed and leveled out slightly, I heard a shuffling. I thought maybe Zaul had stumbled but he had not. When I turned around, he was smiling. Whistling even. Stepping from rock to rock in the moonlight. I thought it might be kids playing in the trees. It was not.

Three muscled bodies appeared in front of me, one on either side made five, each held something in his hands that looked like a stick of some sort. Maybe one carried a machete. Without so much as a sound, the guy in front of me—either the leader, the most brazen, or both—swung for the bleachers, threatening to send my head with it, but I ducked, turned, and told Zaul, "Run!" When I did, two more appeared behind me—their silhouettes suggested they were bigger. While the first guy had acted prematurely and mistimed his swing, they were patient and timed theirs perfectly. The next blow took me off my feet and I felt something break in my face. The pack quickly followed and pounced on me. I felt something slice the side of my head, then again on my face, followed by a third deeper cut above my eye. I tried to stand, to make an escape, but my eye had swollen shut so fast I couldn't see. Something hard smashed down across my collarbone, snap-ping it and dislocating my shoulder. I rolled, pushed myself up on my good arm, but I couldn't see out of either eye. They used my hesitation to their advantage, regrouped, and somebody struck me from behind.

You know all those movies where the out-numbered and overmatched underdog gets hit from behind and then manages some Herculean return to stand back up, fend off, and conquer the marauding horde? As if the head-splitting concussions and consequent beating only served to make him more mad, more dangerous, and finally release the superhuman character that's resided in his soul his entire life? Well, forget that. There's a reason Hollywood deals in make-believe and all the fight scenes are staged. I didn't know much about my present situation, but I did know that there were too many. They were too strong. And they'd gotten the jump on me. A quick inventory told me that I wanted no part of them. Further, following the skull-splitting pain from my shoulders up, all I wanted to do was crawl in bed and pull the covers over my eyes.

Then they hit me again, and I didn't have much choice.

• • •

When I woke, people were screaming and I had a sense that lights were shining on me, but when I tried to focus, to open my eyes, I could not. I could move my fingers and toes, but my head was splitting and I could not stay conscious. I kept fading in and out. Someone was cradling me, screaming incoherently, holding my head while someone else was putting pressure on my face. In the background, I heard a truck engine. Leena's voice sounded close in my ear. She was saying, "Stay with me," but I had no control over my ability to do so. My mind was a fog. Her voice was cracking, and I felt like someone was pouring warm water over my head. Finally, I heard Zaul. He was screaming. Crying.

I reached out a hand, and somewhere in the dark, he took it. He couldn't stop apologizing. I tried to quiet him but he was inconsolable. Finally, I pulled him to me, put my hand on his head, and pulled his hair, bringing his face inches from mine. "Zaul!"

"Uncle Charlie, look what they—"

Leena was whispering to someone over my shoulder. I think it was Paulo. She was in mid-sentence. ". . . die in Managua. They're not qualified to—" Some screaming drowned them out. ". . . bleed to death on the way there."

Chaos had set in all around us. "Zaul. . . . Call your dad. Send the jet." Blood puddled in my mouth, making it difficult to talk. "Land it"—I pointed west—"on the highway." I spat. I meant to say "Get me to Miami," but the only word that actually made it out of my mouth was "Miami."

Leena understood that I was actually making pretty good sense. If he made the call, I could be in Miami in three hours, and if we started driving now, we wouldn't be in Managua for almost four with no guarantee that they'd admit me or even be able to see me when I got there. Knowing what I was trying to do, she turned her attention to him.

"Zaul, call your dad."

I turned toward Leena's voice. Something was choking me so I again said one word, "Miami?"

She was crying now, too, and shaking her head, "Charlie, I don't—"

I heard a ruckus a few hundred yards off. It sounded like a lot of men hollering in very loud voices. In a few short minutes, I'd lost a lot of blood. I pressed her hand against my face. "Just keep me—"

"I don't—" She wasn't making much sense, either. No one was making sense.

I was growing dizzy, and it was getting more and more difficult to focus. I reached in my pocket, fumbled for my phone, and offered it to whomever. A hand took it from me. Leena's, I think. And I tried to recite Colin's number.

I passed out shortly thereafter.

Details are sketchy after that. I remember a

bumpy ride in a truck and something cold on my head and face. I remember Leena wrapping my head in something. I remember Isabella crying and I remember the sound of Paulo's voice, but I couldn't hear what he said. I remember bright lights, the feeling of being cradled in someone's arms, my head pressed to their chest, and the sound of their heart pounding real fast in my ear. I remember a voice whispering to me, but I couldn't understand what it said and I'm not sure I could make out who the voice belonged to— though it seemed familiar. Then I remember the feeling of being carried, lying down flat, and then the floor tilting up and my being pressed back hard against the floor. Leena was crying, pleading with anybody who would listen, and her voice was cracking. Urgency rippled through the air like electricity.

In a final moment of lucidity, aided by what was probably my last shot of adrenaline, I placed my finger on her lips to quiet her. Leena pressed her face close to mine and held both my cheeks in her hands. I felt her breath on my face. She was shaking and her hands were slippery. "Sometimes, we pay for our sins."

She was screaming when the world went silent.

Somewhere above forty thousand feet traveling close to Mach 1, beneath screams and radio traffic and requesting clearance for landing and something about "B positive on hand," the slide show played across my mind's eye. I've always liked movies so I enjoyed watching one about me. I wasn't expecting that. I saw my mom; caught a rare glimpse of my dad in his cab and for once he was smiling, saw myself surfing and delivering pizzas, watched a wrestling match in high school, hovered over the finish line in several track meets, visited classrooms in Boston, played poker with the big boys where I won a car, landing in London, meeting Amanda on a midnight run, dinner with her parents, Marshall, Brendan, watching through the window as Amanda opened the envelope and screamed at Marshall, watching her disappear in the rearview mirror, rebuilding my hurricane shack in Bimini, bumping into Hack in the hardware store, watching him chain-smoke while I nursed a cup of coffee, building a skiff, fishing the flats for bonefish, Colin giving me a tour of his boathouse and looking down on the world he'd created but had little interest in, Marguerite, Maria singing, Zaul driving the boat, tripping over a mound of cash in my shack and hiding it on the island, hearing Hack's cough, my first glimpse of Shelly, late night deliveries in Miami, fast boats, Agents Spangler and Beckwith, Shelly as she placed my watch in my hand, Maria's mummified face in the hospital, Colin hanging his head in his hands, skirting Cuba in the Bertram, the Panama Canal, the swimming pool in the living room of the house, Isabella pulling back my eyelid and saying *"borracho,"* Paulina, the chicken coop, mango juice dripping drown my chin, the oscillating lion breathing on my face, Paulo's forearms as he swung a machete and stacked sugarcane, pulling teeth and the smell of pus, *"el doctor,"* Leena's arms wrapped around me as we rode dirt roads on a motorcycle, the best coffee I'd ever had in my life, the biggest mango tree in Nicaragua, Isabella slipping her hand in mine, descending the well shaft, white bones sticking out of the rock, swinging a hammer in the dark, a trickle of water on my neck, cold water swallowing me, the sound of laughter, Paulo's bloody hands, a long-sleeved white dress shirt, the smell of campfires, and the way the light reflected off Leena's sweaty face as she danced and twirled, campfires across the mountainside showering sparks like fireflies.

The last image that played itself across my mind's eye was something that happened when I was young. Maybe seven. Possibly eight. I'd been surfing. Or trying to. Just getting the hang of it. My mom was sunbathing, and rubbing sun tan oil on a guy I didn't know and didn't like. Gorilla hair covered his chest and back. His toupee sat canted at an angle, making me want to tug on one side to straighten it. He wore several thick gold chains, and a Speedo two sizes too small. But my mom was broken and blind. Had been. She was looking for a Band-Aid. I was, too. Only problem was this poseur lying next to her. When she finished greasing him up, he returned the favor and made a real show of it. I'd taken a spill in the surf and was walking up the beach dragging the two halves of my board. My head hurt. Blood ran down my leg. Mom saw me coming and waved me off. Attention elsewhere. "Go wash it off." Standing there on the edge of that giant ocean, dizzy, the salt stinging my cut, holding two jagged pieces that would never again comprise a whole, an emotion pierced me. While the water around my shins turned red, and my broken board slipped from my fingers and drifted away, I whispered, "Charlie, you are alone and always will be." Right there, nothing but a kid bleeding on the beach, life stained my soul.

The lights of the plane dimmed and I felt someone's face close to mine. Tears dripped onto my cheeks. Lips pressed against mine. Breath forced into my lungs. Chest expanding. Somewhere in between this world and the next, I saw how the Loneliness had colored my DNA. Of all the days in my life, that day on the beach was the one day I wanted back. I wanted to grab that kid, wrap him in my arms, doctor his leg, wipe the tears and snot off his face, buy him a shiny new board, and cradle his very soul.

While the blood trickled out, staining the new carpet in that $7 million plane, the truth flooded in and laid bare the wound. The simplicity struck me. I'd spent my life medicating *that* wound. Since *that* moment, I'd bought into the idea that isolation would ease my pain and indifference was the remedy for rejection.

Clarity was quick in coming. Isolation is a prison and indifference is a lie. Neither work.

As the breath exited my lungs and the screams and cries faded above me like a passing siren, the video of my life ended with a sequence of sepia-colored slides. The first depicted me standing on the shore as that broken and bleeding kid, sun-bleached hair, bronzed skin, with the beginnings of hardened muscles in my back. I was climbing into the skiff Hack and I built and paddling out through the waves and onto open water. But as I tried to paddle out, all stoic and self-reliant, Leena held on to the stern, pulling back, digging her heels into the sand. She was shaking her head. "Don't . . ." But she was no match for the current of my life so I slipped from her fingers. Out beyond the breakers, I turned back. Her mouth was moving but the pounding waves between us garbled her words. When I reached the horizon where the ocean fell off the side of the earth, I turned and found her still standing there. A dot on the shoreline. Hand shading her eyes. Beneath me, the boat jolted, rocking side to side, balancing on the same knife's edge where I once so confidently and coldly held my life and those

I valued. Straining to see her, I teetered on the same precipice where I'd once been so willing to nudge others if circumstances arose contrary to my freedom. As if they didn't matter. She beckoned, "Charlie . . . Please—"

The bow dipped and the stern rose, blocking my view of the beach. The world had gone black but her breath washed my face. *Charlie, let me give you me.*

Two hands violently jerked my head toward Leena while powerful, stinging blows pounded my chest. I turned and readied myself for the frothy death by drowning on the rocks below when Hack appeared in my boat. Legs crossed. Not a care in the world. His hair had grown. Gone was the yellowed cigarette stain. Regal white had taken its place. His skin looked younger. No wrinkles. No crow's-feet. He dipped Alejandro's well bucket in the water and held it sloshing over my head. "Charlie, lonely washes off." He waved his hand across the sea. "It's why God made the water." He laughed deep and long as he turned that bucket upside down. I expected hot and salty. What I got was cold, sweet, and tasted like mango. At first, the water that ran out of me was India-ink black. Just what I expected. Undeterred, Hack kept pouring. Flushing out the stain. Soon, the color changed, and as it did, the pain eased. When the color turned red, the pain was gone altogether.

Finished, he handed me the bucket and patted me on the shoulder, chuckling. He glanced at Leena on the beach and raised an eyebrow just slightly. "We're made to walk 'with.' Not 'without.'" Glancing over the side of the boat and down into the precipice, he cocked his head at an angle and asked, "What's that in your hand?"

So I started paddling back.

Chapter Twenty-Nine

I'd always thought that when you died and came back that you were supposed to see people dressed in white and hear angels singing the "Hallelujah!" chorus. Not so. I couldn't see a thing and the only thing I heard was hospital bells and alarms and a blood pressure cuff on my right arm. I woke to complete and total darkness. Not a ray of light touched my eyes. Despite that, I knew that I was holding a hand in each of my right and left hands.

Over me, to my left, I heard the whisper, "He's awake." Then I heard a bunch of shuffling and talking and it seemed like the room filled with people.

In my right ear, I heard Leena's voice. "Charlie, can you hear me?" When she spoke, someone squeezed my right hand, causing me to think that she was holding my right hand. And in my left ear, I heard Shelly say again, "He's awake." When she said this, I felt someone both squeeze and pat my left hand. One minute I was paddling, rain on my face, and the next I was waking up with Shelly in one hand and Leena in the other.

Weird.

Somewhere beyond my feet, I heard the voices of Colin, Marguerite, Zaul, and then in my left ear, I heard the angelic whisper of Maria. "Uncle Charlie, Aunt Shelly says we're twins now."

I raised my hand, reaching for her, and she took my hand, kissing it.

All the world was right.

I couldn't talk as there was a tube down my throat. I made a signal like I wanted to write something. Someone placed a pen in my right hand and paper in the left. I wrote, "Tube out, please."

They laughed.

Throughout the day, I got bits and pieces of the story.

I was attacked by Zaul's friends, who had somehow crossed paths with and been hired by the foreman. A nasty combination. Unfortunately for them, after killing me, their escape was hindered by several hundred Nicaraguan farmers. In pretty bad shape themselves, they were turned over to my good friends the chief of police and the mayor of León. Their futures are not bright.

Zaul called his dad, who immediately dispatched the jet, which landed on the highway about seven miles from the plantation. Paulo drove us down the mountain, Leena grabbed her passport from the house, and we met the plane as it was landing. They loaded me up, turned around, and took off before Nicaraguan authorities ever knew they had a plane in their airspace. Given the speed of the G5, we landed in Miami a little over an hour later. I died twice on the plane; both times Leena brought me back. I died a third time in the ambulance, where the paramedics shocked me until they got me to the hospital. In the truck and on the plane, Leena had cradled me while also attempting to keep pressure on the bleeding, keeping my face elevated; she'd also packed me in as much ice as she could get to lower my pulse—which explained the cold. At the hospital, Colin had the best trauma surgeons he could find on standby, and they immediately went to work. Colin also went to work finding B-positive blood, which he said he found in a myriad of donors. He laughed as he told me. One unnamed pop diva, himself, Zaul, my new friend Liv-ed (aka William Alfred Butler), and Leena. I'd lost most of my blood, so it took a lot of donors to bring me back. Colin said if I started speaking in rhyme, that'd be the Mr. Butler part of me. Once I'd been stabilized, and my collarbone set and my shoulder put back in its socket and the cartilage in my knee repaired, Shelly was brought in to put my face back, as the guys who attacked me had done a pretty good job of carving it off—which explained the blood. Shelly had done what she could and chances were good that I'd smile again, but it'd take a while. They were afraid that I'd lose my right eye, but she thought she was able to save it. We wouldn't know that until they pulled the gauze off sometime in the next few days. Colin continued to say that Leena had not left my side since I'd been there and she had kept me alive—when she got off the plane, she was covered in me. And I'd been in a medically induced coma for a week in order to give my body a chance to heal.

I told him I felt rested enough.

He said Zaul had been living in the house. "No piercings. No friends. He's been hanging out with Maria, and the first night we were all home together, Marguerite made dinner. When we were finished, he got up, disappeared into the kitchen, and had most of the dishes cleaned by the time we got there. Strange. What did you do to my son? Oh, and did you know he plays the drums? Pretty good, too." He finished by telling me that every-one had been worried, and in an uncharacteristic show of emotion, he had teared up and said he, too, was worried I might not make it. I held up my left wrist and asked if anyone had seen my watch. He said Zaul had been wearing it, keeping it safe until I got well. I told him Zaul could keep it. I'd get another. Not sure that one was good for me. In the time that I'd had it, Maria had been hurt, I lost my fiancée, I nearly drowned in a well, and I had been attacked and nearly bled to death. I told him I'd find another or not wear one.

He also told me that once Zaul had explained the situation in Valle Cruces, he sent the jet back and Zaul returned with Paulo and Isabella. They'd been here ever since. Maria and Isabella had become fast friends. Colin explained that neither Paulo nor Isabella had passports, but that he had contacts in immigration who fast-tracked a visa. He shrugged. "It pays to have friends."

Three days later, they unwrapped my face, and thanks to Shelly and her gifted hands, I could still see out of my right eye. Things were foggy, as was expected, but I'd recover. The first image I saw when I lifted my lids was Maria's smiling face. She pressed her nose to mine. "In case you're wondering, you look a lot worse than me."

Later that afternoon, they had me up, walking the halls, and straining my muscles in therapy. After two weeks in the hospital, when I finally asked if I could go home, Shelly relented and said, "Yes—" She then looked at Leena. "Provided she goes with you."

Leena knew the story of Shelly and me, so when she sensed Shelly wanted a moment with me alone, she disappeared in search of bad hospital coffee. When Leena left, Shelly held my hand

and said that operating on me was one of the more difficult things she'd ever done. But she was glad she could do it. She laughed and said that putting my face back together helped patch up a few things in her. When she finished, I told her I was sorry for keeping the truth of me from her. That she deserved better. That if I had it to do over, I wouldn't do it that way. And that I hoped she found someone that made her happy.

She nodded toward the door and said, "You can be kind of thick when it comes to women and the signals they send, so I'm going to help you out a bit." I waited. "That woman—" She pointed in the direction that Leena had walked. "That gorgeous Nicaraguan goddess, who's got all of the rest of us looking in the mirror to see how we measure up, has fallen for you. She's crazy for you. You realize this, yes?"

"Well, actually—"

"Charlie—" She laughed. "You need a keeper." The laughter was healing. For both of us. "Have you told her what you do for a living? Your occupation?"

I held up a finger. "Previous occupation. With emphasis on 'did for a living.' "

She smiled. "Well?"

"Yes. She knows."

"You may as well know now . . . we may have patched you back together, but she's the reason you made it here alive. Somehow"—she shook her head—"she kept you alive on that plane. And she hasn't left your side since you arrived."

I turned the tables. "Thank you for what you did for me."

She kissed me. "My pleasure, but I'd rather not ever do it again. Now don't change the subject, you do understand why she's still here?"

"Well, I guess—"

"Charlie?"

"I don't know, I—"

"Let me put it in terms you can understand: She's 'all in.' "

That did make sense.

The hospital discharged me and Colin took us to his house where, in about fifteen minutes, I'd convinced him to take us in the helicopter to Bimini, that the saltwater and ocean air would do us some good. Leena helped persuade him, as she'd never ridden in a helicopter and never been to the islands. By sundown, fifteen days after the attack, unstable on my feet and trying to wean myself from pain medication, I was walking on the beach in Bimini, Paulo and Isabella plucking lobster from the rocks, and Leena's arm tucked in mine. And while her heart tugged on mine, so did the one thing I had yet to confess.

For the life of me, I just could not figure out how I was going to tell Leena.

Colin left us alone for three days, allowing me

to introduce them to the island. I showed them where Hack had lived and where we worked. Paulo was incredibly interested in his tools and how we used them. I showed him the unfinished skiff that lay in his shack collecting dust, and he just could not get over how smooth the edges were and how seamless the boards met one another. He wiped his fingers along one of the joints and said, "It's magic."

Morning and evening, the four of us spent hours walking the beach. I tried to get my strength back, which was slow in coming, and Paulo and Isabella sought to catch every lobster on Bimini, as they'd developed quite the taste for large crustaceans. I taught them how to drive my boat and discovered that not only was Leena good at it but she enjoyed going very fast. At one point, idling back into the dock, with her hair blown into a wild state of disarray in which she looked like she'd stuck her finger in an electrical socket, she turned and joked with Isabella, "You know, life just gets so much better at a hundred and ten."

Leena's love of speed was exceeded only by that of her daughter, who looked like someone had not only plugged her into an electrical outlet, but set her hair on fire and looped the sides of her smile around her ears.

Colin offered to return them in his jet, which they'd accepted. Leena was hesitant to be overly forward, but I could tell from her body language and from Isabella's outright requests that she was wanting to make plans for my return "visit."

The clock was ticking.

The night before they left, Paulo orchestrated circumstances in which Leena and I had time on the beach to ourselves. She could tell I was trying to get something out of my mouth so she walked quietly beside me—evidence of how comfortable she'd grown around me. There was no easy way to do this, so I finally just dove in. "Leena, do you remember, prior to Hurricane Carlos, when an American company made an offer to buy Mango Café from your father?"

She was surprised I knew the name. "Yes."

"You remember how much they offered?"

"Ten cents."

"You remember the second offer."

"Twelve."

"And do you remember when someone bought the competition and flooded the market with coffee so cheap that you couldn't sell your own?"

A surprised nod.

"You remember your father slaughtering his own animals to feed his workers?"

"I remember."

"You remember him working without sleep to harvest what would be his last crop, thinking by some miracle that he might salvage something and be able to feed his family and his workers?"

"Charlie, what are you getting at?"

If I hadn't hurt her yet, the last question certainly would. "Do you remember climbing down from a mango tree, placing a rain jacket across your father's shoulders, and crying in the mud next to him as the world he'd built crumbled around you both?"

Her eyes turned cold and welled up with tears. Her voice rose as she spoke. "Charlie?"

"Leena, I did that. I am that company."

We had walked knee-deep into a tidal pool rolling in gentle waves. Disbelief spread across her face as she shook her head. "How?"

I told her. I told her everything. Told her how I'd caused it, then hired people to spy on their misery and report back so we could strategize how to capitalize on that, turn the screws, and make it worse. Then do it again.

When I'd finished, Leena was staring at me. Remembering events and the pain that accompanied them. My voice fell to a whisper. "Do I scare you now?"

Somewhere in there, Paulina and I came face-to-face with the real me. No more smoke and mirrors. She took a step back, put her hands on her hips, and considered me. Her face told me she didn't like him any more than I did. But this is where her reaction to me and my reaction to me parted. This is where she did the unexpected.

Leena had a tenacity unlike any woman I'd ever met, and it was about to surface. While her emotions were very real and they gnawed at her with a raw sincerity, she was listening to something deeper. She was listening to her will, not letting what she felt dictate what she would do. Didn't let it dictate her life.

And given my experience—with both myself and other women—I wasn't expecting that.

She shook her head like she was shaking off a perception. Or swatting a gnat. As if something in her gut was having an argument with her eyes and ears. Her will was telling the rest of her what was about to happen.

Careful not to bump the screws in my collarbone or tug too hard on a shoulder that was still pretty loose in its socket, she pulled me toward her and kissed me. Gingerly. Tenderly. Purposefully. Holding it long enough for me to taste the salt in her tears. When she spoke, she was close and I felt her breath on my face. She shook her head ever so slightly. "You're right. You're touching some deep places in me. They're tender. They hurt. There is a part of me that wants to walk away from you so that you can't hurt me anymore. As if my turning away from you hurts you in return and you get what you got coming. What you deserve. And you're right, I don't like the man who did those things." She held my hand and wrapped her arms inside mine as we continued walking. "But can I tell you something you might not know?"

"Please."

"My father used to hire men with troubled pasts. Prison. Everything. Give them a second chance when no one else would. One of them—a murderer—asked him one time while they were picking beans shoulder to shoulder, 'How does a man wipe his life clean?' You know what my father said to that man?"

I shook my head.

"He said, 'With the one that you have.' "

She leaned her head on my shoulder and turned to look at me. We were walking along the northern end of the island—within a few feet of where Shelly had returned in the helicopter and given me my watch. Atlantis under our feet. She said, "Can you guess who that man was?"

"No."

"Paulo." She registered my reaction with a slight smile. "You look surprised."

"I didn't see that one coming."

She nodded. "My father would have liked you."

The amazing thing about Leena is that while I had pushed her away, she'd not recoiled. What I'd thought would push her away had brought her closer. I said, "I saw you one time." A single nod —gesturing toward my past. "Back then."

She looked surprised. "When?"

"After we foreclosed. You'd lost everything. Parents. Mango Café. Your husband. You were pregnant, walking down the mountain. I'd been

441

in León packing up my office at the hotel. Before I flew out, I rented a bike and rode up in the mountains. I was wrestling with what we—with what I—had done to these innocent, unsuspecting, hardworking, beautiful people. And when I saw them walking down the mountain, and you specifically, I knew I'd done the one thing that Hurricane Carlos and the loss of everything else could not do."

"What's that?"

"Broken your hope."

She weighed her head side to side, considering my words. "Bruised it? Yes." Then she cracked a smile and shook her head. "Never broke it."

How I love that woman.

The next day, before they climbed into Colin's jet, Paulo shook my hand and held it several seconds. "*Gracias, hermano.* You dig well." Isabella clung to my leg. I kissed her forehead and the two disappeared inside the plane. Leena touched my hand and then began climbing the steps. Reaching the door to the plane, she stopped and returned. She lifted my Costas off my face so she could see my eyes and placed her finger on my lips. "You don't scare me, Charlie. Never have."

The plane lifted off and quickly disappeared into a blue sky, carrying a part of my heart with it. Colin, Marguerite, and the kids had gone with them, as they planned to route through Costa Rica and spend a week or two at the house. That left me alone on my island. As my heart disappeared into the sky, one emotion bubbled up: Her forgiving me is one thing. Me forgiving me is another.

I spent the week roaming the beaches of Bimini. Getting my strength back. Then a second week during which I'd walk for miles at a time. Somewhere in the third week, I actually went for a jog and ended up running several hours, clearing my head. Standing barefoot on the beach, sweat pouring off me, I knew what needed to be done.

I bought a ticket to Boston. Time to see the old man.

Chapter Thirty

I didn't bother to make an appointment, as I was pretty sure I wouldn't get one. Besides, the only card I had left to play was surprise, and I would need it if I had any thought of winning this hand. Pickering and Sons had moved, so I gave the cabbie the address and he dropped me off on the curb. Modern, trendy, the building reflected Marshall's desire to remain relevant as well as Brendan's desire to wrest the company away from him. Fat chance. The conflict between the design and the artwork was thick enough to cut with a knife.

The receptionist's smile quickly turned to a frown as I walked past her toward the suite of extravagant offices. There were three. Amanda on the left. Brendan on the right, across the hall. Both doors were shut. Marshall's door stood open in the center. The receptionist offered a verbal protest, but when I ignored her and walked past her, she began quickly dialing. It was too late.

Marshall sat behind his desk staring at one of his three screens covered in numbers that measured the value of his world. He was smiling. He'd aged but he'd aged well. Still trim. Fit. His hair had turned completely white. He stood to meet me. "Charlie, you should have called."

Friendly as ever, he walked around the desk to shake my hand with his right and pat me on the shoulder with his left. His smile said one thing, the coldness in his eyes said another. He called past me, "Amanda. Brendan." I heard a noise behind me as both Amanda and Brendan walked in. Brendan had plumped up a bit. Amanda had not. She walked up and hugged me, kissed me on the cheek. Amanda was as beautiful as ever, but she, too, had aged and the years had not been kind. She looked older, less vibrant. She, like her father, looked cold. Pilates, yoga, personal trainer, whatever, she'd obviously done them all and it showed. As did the plastic surgery both above and below her neckline, which did not mask the sadness beneath her eyes or in her chest. I almost felt sorry for Brendan. A decade "in the family" and the whipped look on his face told the story. He'd been conquered and, like a dog pulled on his collar by his chain, had become Marshall's yes-man. His face was rounder. Belly, too. Bags beneath his eyes. I acknowledged him but did not offer to shake his hand. "Gunslinger. How's that moving target treating you?"

He laughed an embarrassed chuckle.

Marshall attempted to cut the air. "What brings you to Boston?" He waved his hands across the plush sofa behind me. "Please, sit."

I did not.

I'd played with this man enough to know that he was still and always better. I really had only one play, and it would be my first, as I wouldn't get a second. I needed to catch him a bit off guard, I needed to pick a fight, and I needed to go all in, all in the same move. "Cinco Padres Café Compañía."

One of the things that Colin had discovered for me was that during the foreclosure, the shell companies for Pickering and Sons had ended up with the deeds to Cinco Padres. I thought those deeds had been sold on the courthouse steps, but when the Cinco Padres companies were closed, all assets were not sold but transferred to Pickering. Aka, to Marshall. Where the deeds collected dust with more than a hundred other companies. Though I had not known this until Colin dug it up in his research, I'd be willing to bet it had been Marshall's plan all along.

Marshall attempted to look like he didn't know what I was talking about, but the old man had aged and his bluffs weren't quite as polished. Or maybe the time away had seasoned me as a player after all. He scratched his chin and nodded, attempting to act as if the cloud were clearing and the fog lifting. "Seems like I remember something about some coffee and Central America. Nicaragua maybe." He turned to Brendan. "What do we know about Cinco Padres?"

The two-word shortening of the name told me he knew exactly what I was talking about. A check and a raise. Brendan walked behind Marshall's desk, punched several keys, and the screens quickly changed. He scanned them and then began reciting values like a robot. He finished with his assessment, which Marshall neither wanted nor cared about. "Dead weight. No production. It's a total of five farms and the dirt is worth more than any possible coffee production as those ignorant people have never recovered from the mudslide that put them out of business in the first place—along with that stubborn old man who, I imagine, wishes he had sold now. Might find a possible buyer in a rum company looking for sugarcane soil."

Amanda sat across from me. Legs crossed. The beginnings of a slight smirk. She was enjoying herself. Marshall leaned on the front of his desk, one leg to the side, his foot off the ground. The total value of his suit, shoes, and watch was hovering around two hundred and fifty. He spoke to Brendan while never taking his eyes off me. He knew the answer without asking. "And what's the value of that dirt to the right buyer?"

Brendan checked his screens. "Five. Maybe six."

Marshall considered his cards. Then raised. "Seven." The smiled spread across his face as he expected me to fold. I paused and turned to Amanda, who shook her head ever so slightly. Marshall saw something he must not have liked in my eyes because he raised again. He tapped the table. "Closing in seventy-two hours."

I stepped toward Marshall into his personal space—which he did not like—and extended my hand, shaking his firmly. "Deal."

I walked to the door and turned to stare at two ashen white faces and one smiling. Guess I don't need to tell you who was smiling.

I returned to Miami and knocked on Colin's door. I had three days to find a lot of money. I had about half in the bank. I still owned my childhood home across from the beach in Jacksonville. My shack in Bimini. And I felt I could get a loan from Colin, but I needed to do some digging first. Zaul answered the door, shadowed by Colin. "Was wondering if you felt like flexing those muscles."

"Sure."

Two hours later, Colin, Zaul, and I walked into the San Angeles Catholic Chapel on the northern tip of Bimini. They'd ceased services here decades ago and now used the chapel only for weddings. It was tucked into the trees but backed up to the beach just a few yards away. Making sure we were alone, Zaul and I slid the stone altar out of the way and began hacking at the floor with an ax and a pick. The double layer of boards beneath the tile were solid, reminding me that when I'd buried this money, I'd buried it. Zaul swung with an apparent glee at the thought of tearing something up and finding money. He smashed through the floor and there beneath sat my duffel bag and my $250,000. He unzipped the bag. "Good thing I didn't know that was here until now."

I smiled.

He was stepping out of the hole when I pointed at the concrete below him. He shrugged. "More?"

"Let's just call it a hunch."

Zaul began breaking up the concrete while I sat on the front pew and remembered my friend Hack and how he loved cigarettes and a good cup of coffee. When Zaul's pick smashed through the floor into a cavity beneath him, he looked at me with wide eyes. I told him, "Be careful. I'm not real sure what's down there."

An hour later, Zaul had unearthed four large trunks. "Jamaican Rum" had been stamped on the top. We lined them up and pried off the top of the first. Zaul's jaw dropped. "That's a lot of money."

The other three were just like it. Colin smiled. "Always loved that old guy."

Zaul looked up at me. "What're you planning on doing with all this?"

I smiled at Colin, then Zaul. "How would you like to learn the coffee business?"

After seventy-one hours and fifty-three minutes, I pushed a cart carrying five duffel bags into Marshall's building and rode the elevator to the top. The receptionist didn't protest as I walked by. Marshall was standing at the window. Three men in suits I did not know sat busying themselves with a pile of papers at the conference table. I pushed in the cart prompting Marshall to acknowledge it and then me. Amanda and Brendan followed me in.

When Colin had heard my plan, he immediately offered to finance whatever I needed. Thanks to Hack, I didn't need much. To help me and help me quickly, Colin agreed to buy my house in Jacksonville Beach along with my shack in Bimini—where he told me I was welcome to stay anytime. Then I took out a gentleman's agreement loan with Colin for $500,000—using the land as collateral. Given that I was employing Zaul, he offered to give it to me, but I declined, stating that it might help for Zaul to play some role in paying it back. That gave me $5 million plus Hack's $2 million. Marshall would never see it coming.

I placed the transfer confirmations on top of the duffels. "Five million transferred this morning, plus . . . two million in cash." The attorneys raised their eyebrows. Marshall had never said "how" he'd like me to make payment and that was coming back to bite him at this moment. Which is what the awkward smile on his face told me.

His question was the first time I sensed a crack in his wall. "What do you expect me to do with that?"

"I'm sure you can launder it through a hundred different companies or pay your hired guns in cash, so through your ingenious bonus system, you can avoid any taxes or payments of penalties."

The attorneys looked up at me, wondering how I knew about the payment scale for bonuses. I walked to the table and checked the deeds to make sure they'd been designated per my instructions. Finding them in order, I ignored Marshall and looked at the lawyers. "Where do I sign?" They looked at Marshall, who reluctantly nodded, bringing a satisfied smile out of Amanda.

There was always the chance that Marshall could double-cross me after I'd left, but I still had one ace in the hole. She stopped me as I turned to walk out. She said, "I'll ride down with you." When we stepped onto the elevator, Brendan tried to ride with us, but I put my index finger on his chest and pushed him backward. The doors shut, Amanda stood at my side. We stared at each other in the reflection of the doors. She spoke first. "I'll make sure that goes through."

"Thank you."

The elevator signaled as we descended each floor.

She turned to me. "You look good."

"I am."

"Any regrets?"

I shook my head. "No."

She nodded once. "I have one."

The doors opened, and we walked out into the glass-walled foyer. She kissed my cheek and then gently wiped off the lipstick with her thumb. "Take care." Holding my hand, she kissed me again. "Send us some coffee."

Chapter Thirty~One

Colin offered to fly me, but I told him I was a child of the water. Always had been. As a thank-you for finding Zaul, and for giving him a job when he was quite certain no one else would, he handed me the title to *Storied Career*. When I tried to protest, he waved me off. "Charlie, shut up and take the boat."

I did.

I packed up my life in Bimini, including my

Costa collection, said good-bye, bought a couple cases of water, and charted a south-southwesterly course where the week on the water was food for my soul. I returned through the Caribbean, across the Panama Canal, and into the Pacific, where I motored up the coast, finally turning into the inlet that bordered the resort that Zaul and his friends had wrecked. I tossed the owner my bowline. He said, "How you been?"

"Good. Wondering if you wouldn't mind letting me dock this thing here?"

"Sure. I'll put her next to mine. How long?"

I looked around. "How 'bout forever?"

He chuckled. "Sounds good to me."

"You don't happen to have a bike I could rent, do you?"

"No, but—" He pointed. "A block that way. Guy has a shop next to the hardware store. He'll sell or rent."

I bought a KTM 600 similar to Colin's, made one additional purchase at an outdoor store that catered primarily to college kids trekking from hostel to hostel across Central America, and then headed toward Valle Cruces. It was hot, getting hotter, and the only thing missing were two hands wrapped around my stomach.

Over the last week I'd realized, really for the first time, that what Leena said was true. I'd been letting the pain of my past dictate the hope and promise of my future. As much as it surprised me,

I had become an adult and my single overriding characteristic was that I was afraid to hope and, even more, afraid to let others hope in me. If she was right and hope was the currency of love, then I'd been broke a long time.

That's a crummy way to live.

I pulled into Valle Cruces carrying only a backpack and a ring from a jewelry store in León. I stopped at the roadside builders' supply store—primarily a lumber and construction supplier—bought what I needed, and carefully slid it in my pocket. The house was empty when I arrived, and given that it was Wednesday, this did not surprise me. Everyone was up top. Wanting to stretch my legs, I left the bike and started walking. People came out of their houses as I walked by. They waved and were genuinely happy to see me. People hugged me and walked with me. One set of teenagers stopped me, laughing. "*El doctor*, you dig well," one said with a shake of his head followed by more laughter. "Fight not so good."

For the first time in my life, I was home. I glanced at the kid. "There were twelve of them. One of me."

He put his arm around me. A wide smile displaying a mouthful of large white teeth. "Not one anymore." He waved his hand across a street filling with people. "Now you are many."

I took my time walking on, letting the sweat pour off me. Soak me.

When the trees grew large, towering overhead, where the monkeys howled at me on all sides and the breeze fluttered through the leaves and the shade cooled my skin, I turned left and walked the narrow well-worn path around the side of the mountain to the twin white crosses.

The grave no longer looked fresh. Weeds had sprouted up through the dirt and covered the ground in a blanket of green. Someone had placed fresh-cut flowers against the crudely carved headstone as early as this morning.

I took off my hat and smeared my forearm across my brow. Several minutes passed as I stood there trying to find the words.

I couldn't. Above me a monkey was racing through the mango tree, plucking fruit and throwing it down where he anticipated eating it later. A mango rolled up next to me, so I sat, peeled it, and started carving slices.

As the juice smeared across my face and dripped down the right side of my mouth, I made myself say something. "Sir—it's Charlie. I'm . . . I'm back." Feeling foolish, I shook my head, put my hat on, then took it back off. "I wanted to stop by and tell you that, if you were here, I'd ask your permission for what I'm about to do. But since you're not and since I have no way of knowing how you'd respond, I'm . . . well . . . I want to tell you that if what I'm doing doesn't meet your approval that I'm sorry. That said, I'm doing it. If that's wrong, I'm sorry for that, too. Sir, I never really had a dad, and I can't tell you that I've been a good man. I have not. In fact, I've been a child of evil. Spreading more poison than anything else. I'm, or I have been, the exact opposite of you and your daughter and granddaughter—who, by the way, really favors her mom and she's really something. You'd be proud. But, back to me, if I could say one thing in my defense, it's that I know that what I'm doing—" I eyed my backpack sitting next to me. My hands were sticky and dripping. I sliced another piece and shoved it in my mouth. "What I'm carrying to the top of this mountain—well, I've never done anything like this before. This is real different. I'm not sure I can tell the difference right now between what's good and what's not, but if this is evil, then I'm at a loss as to what is good. To what could be. And I guess what I'm saying is—" Tears spilled out the corners of my eyes and dripped onto the dirt below. "I guess what my heart would really like to hear is that you approve and, just being gut-level honest, that you're proud of me, 'cause maybe for the first time in my life I am. Or I could be. I've got forty years of stuff I'm not proud of that I'd like to bury down there with you, but this right here, this I'd like to keep topside. Let it sprout. Grow up. This is the one thing in my life that has the potential to live beyond me. To make good on some of the bad or just take the sting out of it. To buy back some of what I sold a long time ago." Fingers sticky, I pulled the brass lensatic compass out of my pocket—my outdoor store purchase—and set it on the beam of the cross where the red tip of the needle waved from eleven o'clock to three o'clock, finally settling at one thirty, pointing north through the summit of Las Casitas. I wrapped the paracord around the hinge and secured it to the beam. "Sir, I've never lived by one of these. Checked no compass. No magnetic north. Until I stepped foot on this mountain, it was a foreign concept. Which would explain the splinters of my life. Then Leena trips over me on the sidewalk and that precocious and precious Isabella pries open my eyelid. I think maybe that's the moment. That right there might be my beginning." I brushed my hand across the face of the compass. "You've been this for a lot of people for a long time. And without really knowing it or trying to, you are this for me. I'm just telling you that, and I hope that's okay with you." A long pause. "If I'm wrong, if you're lying down there shaking your head and you don't think this is a good idea, well, I'm sorry for that, too. It won't be the first time I've drifted off course." I attempted an uncomfortable chuckle. "If I've proven one thing time and time again in my life, I'm good at making a mess." I turned to go, but stopped. Turned back. "I guess the idea that's got me walking up this mountain is Paulo

456

and the fact that you took a chance on him when nobody else would. That you saw past what was . . . to what could be. I'm standing here with my hat in my hand, hoping that the dirt and distance between us doesn't blind you to what might be possible. With me." Another mango lay several feet away. Despite a loud and howling verbal objection from the monkey who didn't like me stealing his mangoes, I picked it up, peeled it, and bathed myself in the taste of Nicaragua.

Thirty minutes later, I reached the top, walked past the well, and dunked my head under the pump spigot, washing my face as the cold water trickled down my back. Through the trees, I could see Paulo's truck and a line of people snaking away from it. Rubber-gloved Leena, blowing strands of hair out of her face with her mouth, was leaning over my friend Anna Julia and pulling a tooth while Isabella entertained the kids. Paulo stood just beyond in the tractor barn helping a man change a tractor tire.

Life had continued—and the pace had not changed.

I walked up next to her. She was holding a pair of needle-nose pliers inside the open mouth of Anna Julia, who was looking out of the corner of her eye at me. I looked over Leena's shoulder and said, "Better pull the right one. She doesn't have too many left."

She smiled but held her hands steady. Leena pulled the tooth and handed it to Anna Julia, who smiled at it and then slid it into her pocket. Leena pulled off her gloves and threw her arms around my neck. Followed by Isabella, Paulo, and then about fifty of the people standing in line. Gave a new meaning to the term "group hug."

When they'd finished, Leena looked at me, blushing, having totally lost her concentration on the group in front of her. I chuckled. "Miss me?"

She kissed me. Then kissed me again. "Just a little."

Isabella hung vacuum-wrapped around my leg. With no explanation, I opened my backpack and handed Leena the folder of documents. She eyed them. "What's this?"

I wasn't quite sure how to answer. I swallowed and offered what I could. "Love with legs." A shrug. "Water from my heart."

She opened the folder and the draining look of suspicion told me she never saw it coming. She began flipping more quickly through the documents. Reaching the end, she looked at Isabella, Paulo, and then me as the tears that she'd held a decade broke loose and rained down. Disbelief set in along with the it's-too-good-to-be-true look, so she turned back to the beginning and read the names again. Her voice cracked, then rose. "You did this?"

A nod.

"How?"

"Long story but it involved selling everything I owned and then digging up old drug money in an abandoned church."

"You bought Mango Café with drug money?"

"No, I bought Cinco Padres with drug money."

She looked confused and began flipping back through the documents. "What?"

"All five farms." I laughed. "I hope you like the coffee business 'cause you're neck deep in it now." Paulo was listening to me, but he was having a difficult time making out exactly what I was saying.

She shook her head in disbelief as she read back through the documents. Slowly the fog lifted. Paulo looked at me confused, and like him, the crowd milling around couldn't tell if she was happy or sad. Finally, she turned to me. Even with all her strength and tenacity, the absence of one name was too much. She looked at me. Eyes welling. She pointed. "But your name's not on here." A shake of her head. "Anywhere." She wiped her face with her shirtsleeve. "Are you . . . you leaving?"

This time I had enough presence of mind not to cheat the woman I loved out of the moment she desired and deserved. I knelt and extended my hand, uncurling my fingers to reveal the simple gold band cradled in my palm. "Not if you let me stay."

· · ·

Word spread. Quickly.

When people found out that Leena and Isabella owned all of Cinco Padres, they came out of the woodwork to congratulate her.

The next morning, I was awakened in the chicken coop by the sight of sleepy-eyed Leena holding a steaming mug beneath my nose. She'd let down her hair, which draped across her shoulders and rested on mine. It was the beginning of an intimate revelation. Leena was sharing herself with me—a sign of things to come. I sat up, sipped, and said, "I haven't been entirely honest with you."

"Oh, really."

"First, I told Zaul I'd give him a job. He'll be here in a few days."

"And?"

"You need to know that I have nothing. I am completely and totally broke. I don't have enough money to fill up the tank in my boat, which, if I'm honest, I should sell so we'll have something when it rains. I don't know where we will get money to do anything. When I tell you I am broke, I mean we are week-old-leg-stubble-with-a-rusty-razor-don't-have-enough-to-buy-a-new-one broke."

Leena stood and held my hand. "Let me show you something." She walked me to the door of the coop, leaned into me, wrapping her arms around my waist and chest. "We don't need money." She waved across the world spread before her. "This is Nicaragua."

Across the backyard, a dozen or so pigs, a few cows, and several goats had been tied to trees. Baskets of fruit and vegetables filled every inch of the yard. Melons had been stacked along one wall. Flowers had been laid out. It was as if someone had spilled a grocery truck on the back lawn. She laughed. "They've been coming all morning." I looked down the street, which was flooded with people carrying baskets and leading animals. Paulo stood smiling in the center of the yard, ghost white in awestruck amazement. Leena continued. "We have water, food, we have" —she placed her hand on my chest—"your mountain, and we have the best coffee . . . anywhere."

I nodded. "And we have a guy in the States who has promised to import every bean we grow. Even has some famous friends who he thinks will help market it."

She hung her arms around my neck. "I've always wanted to get married beneath my father's mango tree."

"If word gets out that you're getting married, you're liable to have five thousand people show up."

"My father would love nothing better."

Isabella wrapped her arm around my leg and stood hugging me. Pressing her cheek to my thigh. I picked her up and cradled her in my arms. "How about you?"

She smiled, pressed her forehead to mine, and cradled my cheeks in her palms.

I'd never felt so clean.

On Digging a Well

In 1998, Hurricane Mitch stalled over Nicaragua. With sustained winds of 155 knots and gusts reaching 200, the Category 5 monster hovered for several days. Mountain outposts recorded from 72 to 96 inches of rain. Others, where the instruments were washed out or ripped off their foundations, suggest amounts closer to 144 inches. That's right. Twelve feet. Nobody really knows. What they do know is that a lot of water filled up a lake atop a dormant volcano called Las Casitas. The resulting weight cracked the mantle and caused an eruption and mudslide. The thirty-foot-high wall of mud traveled down the mountain and toward the sea some thirty miles away. Satellite imagery records the mudslide traveling in excess of 100 miles per hour and cutting a swath a mile wide. Naval and Coast Guard vessels would later pick up survivors, clinging to floating debris, miles out in the Pacific.

During the deluge, Moises and twenty-seven members of his family huddled, cold, hungry, and wet, in his cement-block, tin-roof house where rushing floodwaters had cut them off from the rest of the world. After five days of soggy isolation, Moises—a dollar-a-day sugarcane farmer and volunteer pastor—heard something that sounded like helicopters. Thinking the UN or some relief agency had flown in to rescue them, the entire family rushed out of their house, eyes searching the sky. Expectant and hopeful. But there were no helicopters. Instead, they were met by an apocalyptic wall of mud wider than their field of view. Before them, giant, ancient trees were crumbling in its wake; houses were being ripped off their foundations. Giant boulders tumbled toward them. Death had come to Las Casitas. Moises had time to glance at his wife and his children and voice this: "*La sangre de Jesus! Vamos a estar con Jesus.*" Translated it means, "The blood of Jesus [cover us]! We are going to be with Jesus." The caustic, super-heated tsunami of mud reached his yard, towering. Only one thing stood between Moises and the mud.

A well.

A simple hole dug into the ground with a pump and enough pipe to lift the water out of the earth. The well had been drilled six months earlier by an NGO and provided enough water for Moises and his neighbors to cook, bathe, and live. In this part of the world, dirty water is both the source of sickness and the feeder for continued sickness, so the advent of available clean water had changed living conditions, shrunken swollen stomachs, and brought new life. Wells do that. Moises was the keeper of the well for reasons that will soon become apparent.

Moises watched the mud reach the well, but then a strange thing happened. The mud split. Parted. To their wide-eyed amazement, the mud rerouted around his house, sparing his family, only to come together again on the other side of his house and continue its death march to the sea. From mountaintop to sea, the Las Casitas mudslide would cover thirty-two square miles and kill more than three thousand people, but not Moises or his wife or their kids or the twenty-seven people who saw this happen.

I know. I talked to several of them. If you ask Moises, he shakes his head confidently. *"La mano de Dios detuvo el barro."* Or, "The hand of God stopped the mud."

Over the next seventy-two hours, Moises and other able-bodied men combed the mud, pulling both the living and the dead from treetop and barbed wire and muddy grave. To combat disease, they buried the bodies and burned decomposing livestock. For weeks the air smelled of smoke and death. As one of the lone standing structures, Moises' house became both triage and housing for some of the mudslide victims who lost everything. Moises exhausted himself responding to the cries of man, woman, child, and animal stuck in the mud. And because the mud started in the belly of the volcano it was hot, caustic, and burned much of the skin off his feet and shins. He still carries the scars. Surrounded by a sea of mud, Moises doctored the sick, prayed with the dying, and cried with the heartbroken. It would be days before anyone in the outside world knew they were alive and needed help.

In the aftermath of more than a billion dollars in damage and a decimated infrastructure, relief organizations from around the world poured millions into the local economy to help rebuild a landscape that looked more like the moon than earth. Seeing the devastation in Moises' village, a foreign NGO bought new land away from the mudslide area and offered to rebuild. To do so, they needed a trustworthy man to lead the effort on the ground. A supervisor of sorts. Someone with whom they could trust tens of thousands of dollars and who commanded the attention and respect of the community. When they asked around, every finger pointed to Moises. The NGO entrusted Moises—equipped with his third-grade education—with more than $200,000 with which to rebuild his community. At the end of eighteen months, he presented meticulous receipts and apologized for not being able to account for six bags of concrete—for which he offered to pay. Think about it: After having spent a couple hundred thousand dollars rebuilding an entire community, he was losing sleep over a few bags of concrete. Oh, and he had built twice as many homes as they had budgeted. Literally, twice as many.

In the months that followed, Moises grew in name and stature. He planted more churches, and because the carpet of mud didn't just scar the land, he worked to heal a deeper wound. If God has hands, they are muscled and calloused and muddy and bloody and tender—like Moises'.

A year later, I was brought in. A green writer asked to tell this story. My guide was a seasoned Mercy Ships volunteer named Pauline Rick. Pauline knew Moises and his family. Six months prior to the mudslide, she'd found him. She's the reason you're reading about Moises.

Without Pauline, this is a blank page and there is no story.

Over the next week, Pauline and Moises guided me back through the timeline. The installation of the well, the hurricane, the mudslide, the relief effort. To educate me, we hiked up Las Casitas, stood on the edge of the scar, and stared down at the Pacific; then we followed its path. It wasn't difficult. Our first stop was Javier's house. Javier was a coffee farmer who had also heard the helicopters. Javier was taller than most, had huge hands, and was physically very strong. Imposing for a Nicaraguan. He walked me out of their house, retracing their steps. He spoke in hushed tones. Pauline translated. He pointed at an invisible line along the ground. "We walked to here." He pointed again, just a few feet away. "My two daughters stood there." Tears appeared on Javier's face. Javier broke off. He gestured with his hand. "The wall of mud . . ." Javier quit talking.

He hasn't seen his girls since.

Halfway down the mountain, Javier's voice echoing in my ear, my own tears drying on my face, Moises stopped along the road and pulled fruit off an overhanging tree while a howler monkey screamed down on us. I think it was a howler monkey. It looked like a monkey and it was certainly howling. I didn't know the name of the fruit so I asked Pauline, who was peeling the greenish-orangeish thing while the juice seeped out between her fingers. She looked like a kid in a candy store. "It's a mango."

It didn't look like what I thought a mango looked like and, to be honest, mango had never been my thing. My wife, Christy, was always trying to get me to try it but I always thought it tasted a bit odd. I shook my head. "Not really a fan."

Pauline offered again with a knowing smile. "Just eat it."

I remember sitting there, the juice running off my chin, thinking to myself, *Where has this stuff been my whole life? This is the best fruit I've ever eaten. Christy would love this.* Staring up through the trees at Javier's rusted tin roof, I could not then and cannot now make sense of that place—of shattered souls, sadness untold, a mud scar *across* and *through* the heart of a people. And then there were the crosses. Too many to count. Every time I turned around, I saw two or three or seven more, rising up out of the dirt. And they weren't organized like at Arlington or on the beaches of Normandy. They buried these people where they had found them—where their arms and legs had stuck up out of the mud.

But that mango started me thinking. Amid all that grotesque horror and loss and pain, there was that fruit. Just hanging there. An offering for the taking. And as I looked around, I saw beauty in the blooms rising up through the mud, tasted sweetness dripping down my face, heard children's laughter bubbling up out of a dirt shack on our left, saw a lush, green San Cristóbal smoking behind us into a clear blue sky. While death had cut a wide swath, the place where I stood was teeming with life. Colorful birds danced in the trees, blooms painted the landscape, singing touched my ears. Right there, I stood in the midst of it. One of those rare self-aware moments where I sucked the marrow. Death had come. A murdering thief in the night. But then morning came and life—rich, thick, dense, beautiful, sweet, vibrant, laughter-charged life—had sprouted up through the very same mud.

I seldom taste a mango and don't think of that moment.

That afternoon, Moises introduced me to his

church, his wife, his children, and his new home in the community he built. That evening I ate dinner at Moises' house. A king's banquet of roasted chicken, soup, rice, and thick corn tortillas. His children sat wide-eyed and smiling at the table. I asked Pauline, "They always smile like that at dinner?"

She paused, considering whether to protect me from the truth. She said, "They've never eaten two chickens at one dinner."

That night I slept in a cot in what might be called their living room. My companion was an enormous, grunting pig that Moises brought in at night so no one would steal it. She was, how should I say, a little on the heavy side. Made for an interesting night.

Just before lights out, I passed by the door, or curtain, that led into Moises' room. His children were sleeping on rope-woven bunks to my left. No sheet. No blanket. Just a hemp rope. I found Moises kneeling next to his bed, Bible open before him, lips moving. Several hours later, when I rose to go to the bathroom, he was still there. Lips still moving.

Even now, when I think of Moises, that's my image. A man on his knees. Speaking face-to-face.

That night—now over fifteen years ago—God did something in me. DNA-deep. Something only God can do. He both broke and filled my heart at the same time. I still don't understand that.

Over the course of my career, I have witnessed poverty and war-torn landscapes firsthand. I've walked the bullet-riddled streets of Freetown, Sierra Leone, following their civil war. Men my age with no arms stood healthy and helpless with cups hanging around their necks, unable to go to the bathroom by themselves. I have been stranded —with raging amoebic dysentery—for five days in the Ivory Coast amid a riot and an airport strike. And no, I don't speak either French or any African dialect. I have walked through an overcrowded prison in Honduras and backed up against a wall when a fight broke out, and then ambled along the docks where families live in damp cardboard and the mosquitoes swarm by the tens of thousands and coughing children just cough night after night after night. Each of those experiences challenged my calloused indifference; they cut me deeply—especially Freetown. But it was Nicaragua and Moises that broke through the granite in me.

Let me say this directly: Indifference is the curse of this age. We need to hear that. Indifference is evil, and it could not be further from the heart of God. Don't think so? Let me point you to the Cross. Hanging there, Jesus was anything but indifferent. Don't think I've somehow got a handle on this. I don't. I am as guilty as anyone, my rags are filthy, but lying on a cot in Moises' house with a pig racing beneath me, with the smell of the outhouse floating on the breeze, the deep scar trailing down Las Casitas, the look on Javier's face burned on the backside of my eyelids, the long shadows thrown from so many white crosses, the absence of food in Moises' house, and the sound of his own whispering prayers rising up over the wall, I saw my own indifference maybe for the very first time. It shook me awake. Shattered me. It shatters me still.

And for the record, I am so very sorry.

Over the years, Moises and I have stayed in contact via e-mail. He drives forty-five minutes to an Internet cafe with a dial-up connection. I glance at my phone. I don't speak Spanish and he doesn't speak English, so Pauline faithfully translates. I keep promising to learn, but *no hablo*. I've been back several times. Taken friends. Taken Christy and my oldest son, Charlie. John T. and Rives are next on the list.

A year ago, I returned and rode in a truck back up Las Casitas. And yes, the tears returned as if they'd never left. They streaked down my face and, no, I didn't wipe them off. I cried for that place, for my friends, and for myself. It felt good to cry. That night I spoke in a church by candlelight; we handed out rice, beans, oil; we prayed for some folks; we hugged a lady with no teeth and a beautiful smile that has become tender to my heart; then we rode back down with a new pig that Moises bought on sale. Standing in the back of that truck, surrounded by fifteen sun-weathered Nicaraguan men and a rather unhappy pig, many things struck me: That landscape is dotted with fruit trees, cows, wood smoke, sugarcane, plastic-wrapped dwellings, and three thousand white crosses—many now covered in weeds and vines.

But what had me thinking then and has me thinking now is this: These people, these sweating men next to me, these Children of God—they live here. Those bones beneath the crosses are their wives and children and brothers and mothers and fathers. And they never leave that image behind. Never escape that this is the reality of their lives. Me? I fly home. I smile at the attendant, stow my bag, buckle up, adjust the AC above my head, order water or coffee, check my e-mail, and . . . fill my mind with anything but that reality. The luxury of leaving allows my mind to drown out the deafening pain in my heart. Put it behind me. And let's be honest, at times I have.

For Christy and me, Moises' community has become dear to us. To our hearts. It is the place on planet Earth where the Lord challenges our notions of pretty much everything. Moises has nothing. We have everything. He prays for enough money to buy rice and beans. To feed his grand-kids. I pray that the GPS in my truck gets me where I'm going in the shortest, most traffic-free way. He makes less than $2 a day. I spend that on a coffee. Without blinking. He prays for rain for his crops and cows when drought threatens his existence. I complain about our grocery bill. "Did that salmon taste fishy?" During the rainy season, his wife places buckets beneath the holes in her rusted tin roof and guards the pictures. I watch it fill the pool and frown at how it will affect the delicate balance between our chlorine and salt.

But what Moises lacks in stuff and comfort, he makes up for in faith. If God were writing Hebrews 11 today—adding names to the great Faith Hall of Fame—he'd include Moises. In a land where many have lost faith and have little hope, Moises is truly a Moses to his people.

Here's just one recent example: A woman in his church had been bleeding for weeks and in immense pain. The community raised enough money to take her to the hospital because her husband is crippled and lives in a wheelchair. She is both breadwinner and caretaker. The biopsy proved uterine cancer. Advanced. They sent her home to die. "Sorry, can't help you." As she lies in bed, waiting for disease to do what the mudslide did not, Moises asks the church to fast and pray. So they do. The entire church. No food. No water. After three days, the church comes together for a praise and worship service. From there, several of the elders travel to the dying lady's bedside, where they lay hands on her, anoint her with oil, and pray. When I ask Moises why, he points at his Bible and shrugs. As if to say, "I read it. James says do this. We do it." So they pray. She feels a bit better. Sits up. Again, they pitch in and return her to the hospital, and the hospital gives her two liters of blood and, reluctantly, a second biopsy. The looks on their faces say, "We already sent you home once. There's no hope for you. You're wasting our time." Moises and the family wait quietly for the results, which, when they return, inexplicably provide no evidence of cancer. The doctors scratch their heads. "We must have mis-diagnosed you." She's home now. Playing with her kids. Healthy as can be. Ask Moises and he will break open his Bible, point to Luke 8, and say, "God worked miracles then. He works miracles now. Period."

The Book of Acts says, "Signs and wonders followed those who believe." Well, signs and wonders follow Moises. With a budget of zero, Moises has planted seven or eight churches and invests his time, encouragement, and leadership in some thirty more. He gives when he has nothing—which is all the time. He is a magnificent practical joker, smiles constantly, loves to sing, is tender with his wife, children, and grandchildren, and calls me *"mi hermano."* That means "my brother." To say I'm honored is an understatement of mythic proportions.

The contrast between us has proven this: I'm a spoiled American. I have hot water at the flick of a dial, a smartphone, a truck with AC, two televisions with a couple hundred channels each, an ice maker, cough medicine, a Tempur-Pedic mattress, deodorant, the list goes on. Yet the Lord has used this map dot twelve hundred miles south to reveal another piece of His heart to me. And most of that He's done through the lives and words of both Moises and Pauline.

Pauline doesn't seek the spotlight. Never has. But everywhere I've been in Nicaragua, she's been there first. Checking it out. Making sure. Protecting me. She's the window through which I've perceived this beautiful country and these magnificent, towering, and tender people who've stolen my heart. And when I'm there in that country, and Moises asks me to speak in a church, which is most every night, she is my voice. She translates me to all of them. Without her, there really isn't a me in Nicaragua. And if you ask Moises, her name would be written in Hebrews 11 before his.

Water from My Heart bubbled up and out of this soup. This love, this laughter, these tears, this pig, these roaches in the outhouse, these mangoes, these whispers beyond the wall. I'd like to think I'm less indifferent but let's be honest: I'm typing this on a new iPad via a wireless keyboard in a car with a seat heater 'cause it's cold outside. David Crowder is singing on the Bose speakers next to me. He is singing, "We will never be the same."

Let me end with this: About two years ago, Moises needed a well dug on the land where he keeps his cows, so we paid a skinny local to dangle from a long rope for about three weeks. Today, that well is much like the one you've just read about. Moises and his sons use it every day to provide for their cows. Water their plants. You can tug on the rope. Raise the bucket. Soak your head. First time I saw Moises drink from it, he wiped his mouth and put his hand on my shoulder, nodding. He spoke slowly, knowing I couldn't follow him otherwise. *"Agua de mi corazón."*

I turned to Pauline. My face spoke a phrase I have asked ten thousand times. "What's he saying?"

Her eyes welled. "It translates, 'Water from my heart.' "

But translation and meaning are often two different things. So I said, "But . . . what's it mean?"

Moises, one hand still on my shoulder, put his other hand flat across my heart. His face close to mine, he spoke. Pauline made it so my heart could understand. "It means that every time he drinks here, he will remember that this water comes from your heart." I didn't know how to respond to Moises so I just hugged him and kissed his cheek. If I spoke Spanish, I'd tell him that his words washed my soul far more than my water washed his face.

More than fifteen years ago, God took my pen to Nicaragua. Once there, He led my crusty heart to a courageous, tenderhearted woman named Pauline and a humble friend of God named Moises. I've seldom felt so clean.

If there's something satisfying in this story that filled you up, washed over you, that something rose out of a deep place. The kind of spring only God can make—where the tears are clean and rinse the soul. To get there, He had to break through the stony bedrock of my indifference. It took some doing. There was a lot of junk in the way. No ordinary pick and shovel would do. He needed some special tools, which He placed in the hands of Pauline and Moises. Together, they dug a well in me.

I pray the water is sweet. Even more, I pray it tastes like mangoes.

Center Point Large Print
600 Brooks Road / PO Box 1
Thorndike, ME 04986-0001 USA

(207) 568-3717

**US & Canada:
1 800 929-9108**
www.centerpointlargeprint.com